THE COMFORT
OF GHOSTS

Books by

Jacqueline Winspear

Maisie Dobbs
Birds of a Feather
Pardonable Lies
Messenger of Truth
An Incomplete Revenge
Among the Mad
The Mapping of Love and Death
A Lesson in Secrets
Elegy for Eddie
Leaving Everything Most Loved
A Dangerous Place
Journey to Munich
In This Grave Hour
To Die But Once
The American Agent
The Consequences of Fear
A Sunlit Weapon

The Care and Management of Lies
The White Lady

Non-fiction
What Would Maisie Do?
This Time Next Year We'll Be Laughing: A Memoir

THE COMFORT OF GHOSTS

A Maisie Dobbs Novel

JACQUELINE WINSPEAR

Published by
Soho Press, Inc.
227 W 17th Street
New York, NY 10011

Library of Congress Cataloging-in-Publication Data

Names: Winspear, Jacqueline, author.
Title: The comfort of ghosts / Jacqueline Winspear.
Description: New York, NY : Soho Crime, 2024. | Series: A Maisie Dobbs novel ; 18
Identifiers: LCCN 2023056228

ISBN 978-1-64129-606-9
eISBN 978-1-64129-607-6

B&N Exclusive Edition: 978-1-64129-650-2
B&N Exclusive Signed Edition: 978-1-64129-631-1
BAM Edition: 978-1-64129-632-8

Subjects: LCSH: Dobbs, Maisie (Fictitious character)—Fiction. |
Orphans—Fiction. | World War, 1939-1945—England—Fiction. | Great
Britain—History—George VI, 1936-1952—Fiction. | LCGFT: Detective and
mystery fiction. | Historical fiction. | Novels.
Classification: LCC PR6123.I575 C655 2024 | DDC 823/.92—dc23/eng/20231211
LC record available at https://lccn.loc.gov/2023056228

Poppy image: Vecteezy.com

Printed in the United States of America

10 9 8 7 6 5 4 3 2 1

To the memory of my first editor, Laura Hruska (1935–2010).

Laura was a true publishing pro, having co-founded Soho Press in 1986. In her manner and with her insightful editing, together with our conversations regarding my very first novel, Laura educated this neophyte fiction writer in what to expect from the very best editor-author relationship.

With this final novel in the Maisie Dobbs series, and to honor Laura's memory, it was time to come home to Soho Press.

That's one more thing that I detest about war. It's not over when it ends . . . It still lives inside the living, doesn't it?

—*Birds of a Feather*, 2004

MY LETTER TO YOU, THE READER . . .

This is the final novel in the series featuring Maisie Dobbs and her companion characters, some of whom have stood alongside Maisie since the first book was published in 2003, and others who were friends and associates collected along the way. Life is like that—there are those we have known for many a year and others who are just as cherished, but arrived in our lives at a later point—and of course those who stay for just a while and depart, yet we remember them with hand on heart.

Some of you may be dismayed to learn that there will be no more additions to the series (though I suppose I should quote James Bond and add "never say never again"), but I have come to the end of the story, having taken a young woman called Maisie Dobbs from girlhood to middle age, and through two world wars with another conflict in between. Along the way I've endeavored to create a body of work that is in equal measure a family saga and mystery series. Now I must heed Maisie's counsel: "That's enough. You've told my story—it's time for us both to move on."

Whether you have been a follower of the series from the beginning, coming back every year through eighteen published novels, including this one, and the nonfiction *What Would Maisie Do?* or whether you have binge-read every book through the pandemic, I thank you all. Thank you for your enthusiasm, your loyalty and the wonderful letters and emails you've sent to me over the years. Often I have been so busy with research and writing, I've not had a moment to reply, but I am ever grateful to you for taking the time to share your family stories of wartime and heroes, and letting me know how much Maisie Dobbs has meant to you.

With much gratitude,
Jacqueline

PROLOGUE

LONDON
October 1945

The man caught a glimpse of his reflection in a shop window as he walked away from Victoria railway station. At first he did not recognize the face, nor the body below it. The shoulders were too narrow for the suit hanging about him like a shroud. "Demob suit," they called it. They had handed him some cash too—he remembered shoving it in a pocket. One of the pockets. He couldn't remember which one. Lingering for another second or two, he thought perhaps a shroud would have been a more appropriate fit. Might have hung a bit better on his body. He had avoided mirrors during the long journey home, not that he was home, not really. He couldn't face home. Not yet. Perhaps not ever. Couldn't face the wanting in the eyes of others, the wanting for him to be himself again, the man they had known so long ago. But that old self had perished, and now he was looking at the reflection of a wraith that turned out to be him. Alive. Against all odds.

Blimey, he was tired. Bone tired. Getting up from the seat, walking through the carriage to the door, stepping off the train and then the effort of making his way along the platform to the street—it had demanded too much of his legs, his wounded body. Perambulation had taken it out of him. He had to find somewhere to lie down, to rest his head because his bones couldn't bear the weight of it anymore. Heads were heavy old things, sitting there on top of your shoulders. He thought of his mates— they'd laughed, once, when he said they could all save themselves a lot of bother if they just lay down in a grave together like spoons in a cutlery drawer—all big heads and nothing much in the way of a body each, no more than very long spoon handles. Then the laughing hurt their caved-in chests and distended stomachs, so they stopped. He wanted to gentle the pictures in his mind, let the memories settle into the past, banish them, make them go away and the ghosts disappear.

Passing a street of four-story mansions—grand residences that should have been white, but London's soot, smog and war had rendered them grey and lifeless, though in truth it was a miracle they were still standing—he made his way to the narrow mews flanking the semicircular sweep behind those too-big houses where gentry lived. He remembered the number of the house he was looking for. Number fifteen, a house that, cross fingers, was still empty; mothballed for the duration and not yet opened up. He was sure he could gain entry via the mews. There was a means to do it, a way to get in.

He wasn't sure how he managed—perhaps luck had remained with him, because it was a blimmin' miracle he was alive at all— but soon he was at the top of steps leading down to the kitchen door. The servants' and tradesman's entrance. He remembered coming to the house with his dad when he was a boy, to see his dad's employer. This was the door his dad had knocked on.

No one was about today—lucky for him, it was a quiet area. Quiet for London, anyway. Taking a penknife from the pocket of his overcoat, he slipped the smaller of two blades into the lock and jiggled it around. He knew how to work a lock—he had mastered the craft as a nipper, until his dad caught him and gave him a clip round the ear for his trouble, telling him he wasn't having a criminal in his house, and if he found out his boy was carrying on like that again, he would take him to the police station himself. "See how being put away suits you, son." He never fiddled a lock again—until today.

Easy. The door could have done with some oil on the hinges, squealing as he closed it behind him, but who was around to hear? They were all away, safe in the country, settling back into being normal. He wouldn't ever be normal again—he knew that. He'd seen what war could do even when he was a child. He only had to look at his dad.

Back stairs. He knew there were back stairs. There were always back stairs in a gaff like this, for the servants to move silently in and out of rooms in those days before two wars, when the sort of people who lived upstairs had lots of servants. Bloody servants were likely all dead. Hitler bombed the workers first. That's what his mum had told him in a letter. It was a note received a long time ago, before his own terror began. She told him they had bombed the docks and all them back-to-back houses in the East End at the same time. Their old house had gone—lucky his mum and dad moved out of there when they had the chance, when he and his brother were still boys. Moved up in the world, his mum and dad. Out of the East End and into the suburbs.

He staggered up three flights, into a corridor of old servants' quarters. Cast-iron bed frames with the mattresses rolled up and blankets stacked with pillows on top. All blue ticking and no covers. It was a wonder the mice hadn't had them, or the moths. Mind you, too cold for moths. He stared at the bedding. *Soon*

3

sort that out, soon lay my bones down. He rolled out a mattress and pillow, all but fell onto the bed and pulled a blanket across his body. The sleep of the dead beckoned like a soft hand taking his, while a voice whispered in his now half-conscious mind, "Rest now. Put your head on the pillow. Sleep, my dear big brother, sleep."

She had always come to him, his sister. Every day when he buried another mate, another bag of bones to be laid to rest, or not, because he was sure even the dead didn't rest in that place. There was something coming for all of them. If it wasn't a bayonet in the gut, it was malaria. Dysentery. Beriberi. Cholera. But now he could settle. He was away from all that.

"*Tenko! Tenko! Tenko!*"
The man opened his eyes wide and screamed as the machete pressed into his back.

"Hold on, mister. Hold on. You alright?"

He turned and stared at the girl before him as he shimmied away, his back to the wall.

"Don't be scared, mister. I only poked you with my finger—thought it was time you woke up. You've been spark out for hours and hours. I've brought you a cuppa. Bit weak. We don't have much here."

"Who are you?" The man struggled to move again, to even breathe, the weight of blankets almost too much for his frame.

"Might ask you the same question." The girl held the cup of tea. "You was shivering, so we put more blankets on you. Looked like you were all in." She reached forward to lift his head, but stopped when he flinched. "Alright, just try to sit up on your own." Still the man struggled, so with care, making sure he could see her hand as she moved toward him and slipped it under his head, she put the cup to his lips. "Here, get this down you. We've made a fire downstairs, in the kitchen. Blimmin' big house, this, so we're keeping to the kitchen and a couple of other rooms; bedding down there to keep warm when it's really cold."

The man sipped the weak tea. "I asked you once—who are you?"

"Me and my mates, we found out the place was empty and we moved in—why not? The people what own it don't need it, do they? If they did, they'd be here, living in the house. A lot of the toffs left these big houses and got out of London, you know, when the bombs came. And if the place isn't in use and you can find your way in, there's laws to protect you. Squatter's rights and all that. If you can get through the door or a window what someone's left ajar, you might as well stay. Looks like you thought the same. It's cold in this place though, but not as nippy as some of them barracks the Yanks left behind—homeless people have moved into them too." She looked at him as if he didn't quite grasp the situation. "There's tons of homeless now, everywhere. They reckon there's a couple hundred thousand without a roof over their heads. Not just people like us, but whole families and children, and men and women with nowhere to go, on account of all the houses bombed."

He sipped more tea. "Don't you and your mates have family to take you in? You're a bit young to be dossing down here."

The girl shrugged. "Yeah, well, we sort of had people. Anyway, we were called up and now it's, you know, hard to go back."

"You were too young for the services—stop telling me porky pies."

The girl shook her head. "No I'm not, mister. It's not a lie. We was all called up, and it was for special work in case of the invasion. Besides, I've told you too much now. I can't talk about it anymore. There's four of us, all together—me, I'm Mary, then there's the others."

"All living here?"

She shrugged. "And now there's you. Five."

He took a deep breath and sat up. "I can manage." With shaking hands, he took the cup from the girl and sipped more tea.

"What's a tenko? You were shouting it out in your sleep."

The man flinched again. "A word I picked up in the army."

"Funny word, that. Where did you hear it?"

"A long way away, love. A very long way away."

She stared at him. "There's something else, mister whatever-your-name-is. We can't let you go now. You've got to stay in this house, because you know we're living here, and you know my name."

"Look, Mary, there's going to be plenty of people knowing you're here soon enough, and I'm not one for telling tales." He drained the cup. "Anyway, what've you been up to? You in trouble?"

"It's not what we've been up to, mister. It's what some people *think* we've been up to."

The man shook his head and lay back on the pillow, his eyes closing once again, as if he could fight sleep no longer. The girl caught the cup before it crashed to the floor. As she came to her feet, a boy, about the same age, no more than sixteen years old, opened the door.

"Do you know who he is?"

She shrugged. "He didn't say. Poor old sod looks like death though—I mean, none of us is carrying weight, but let's face it, none of us has seen anyone as thin as him. He's like a bag of bones wrapped in brown paper. He's a soldier though."

"Got a wallet on him? Identification card?"

"If he has, it's inside his jacket and it's wrapped tight under that overcoat. You can see he's wearing one of them cheap demob suits they hand out to soldiers when they get out of the army. We'll have to wait until he's slept a bit more, then I'll find out."

"Archie's gone out again to get some nosh."

"Hope he's careful."

The boy rolled his eyes. "Archie could get in and out of the market and no one would know he's been in there."

The girl named Mary laughed. "And lucky for us them posh people what own this place left a lot of tinned stuff in the pantry."

"It was probably the servants' food. The gentry eat well, don't they? But tinned is alright by me. Food is food."

"Come on, Jim, let's go back downstairs," said Mary. "And don't forget to turn off them lights again. We don't want the coppers coming."

"Never mind looking for us—they could be after him."

"Tenko! Tenko! Tenko!"

The boy named Jim jumped backwards. "Blimey, what's he screaming now?"

"He did that when I tried to wake him up. It's something from the army, he said. Not the British army and that's a fact. Come on, let's leave him to it. I reckon he'll have gone to meet his maker by the time we come back in here again, and then we'll have to work out what to do with his body—not that there's much of it to do anything with."

Another man, not fifteen miles away, worked in the large suburban garden of his new house at the edge of a well-to-do town in the county of Kent. Shrubs had been trimmed for the winter, and rose bushes were covered with cotton gauze to protect their fragile forms from the nighttime frosts that would surely come. A new black motor car was parked in what the estate agents had referred to as a "driveway." He suspected the neighbors would think him absurd if they witnessed his vain attempts to break cold, hard earth with a spade time and again. They might wonder why he had not left such a task to the gardener, for surely a man in his position would not soil his very clever hands on a job better suited to a laborer. In the new year he would be taking up the position of senior lecturer in the physics department of University College. He was too young for the role of esteemed professor, but with research credentials that would far outshine a number of his geriatric fellow academics. Yet he had no pride in his stellar curriculum vitae.

This man was digging for absolution. Yes, it was absolution he craved, having decided that backbreaking physical exertion was the antidote to what ailed him. He wanted to exhaust himself, to push every muscle, bone, nerve and fiber in his body to its limit. Physical struggle was the only means by which he might begin to pour oil on the troubled waters of his soul. He had to wear himself to the bone, perhaps halt the torment in his mind and stop himself asking how an opportunity—a very golden opportunity that brought him an enviable status with remuneration to match—had betrayed him. No, it had not been pure ambition or a desire for laurels, though he thought in years to come some might brand it so. Indeed, there were those who were doubtless already coming to such a conclusion, not that they knew what he had done, because his part of the crime—and yes, it was a crime, no two ways about it—had been committed behind very heavy closed doors. He had not done it for the money or the opportunity to cross an ocean and work alongside others just like him, scientists who were the best in their field. In truth, it was pure curiosity, the same sense of wonder he had displayed since boyhood, conducting experiments with test tubes and Bunsen burners, pressing forward while asking those very big questions: Why does that added to this make steam? What will happen if I shake the two together? And what will be the outcome when I add more flame, or more sulphur? Will it work as I think it might? He knew even in childhood that an ability to take a simple scientific inquiry then dig and dig and dig until he found the answer would become his lifelong quest—and he would do it time and time again. He often wondered why his calculating mind would spin in expanding and contracting circles until he came to the point where a new truth was revealed. What was it his mother called him, years ago? "You're my little 'why' boy. Always why this and why that." She had ruffled his hair, smiling, as if she were reading the title of a children's book. "My Little Why Boy."

The role for which only the finest minds were recruited promised a depth of human inquiry that would push against the laws of the universe, and he could not resist joining the quest to see if it could be done, to answer so many what-ifs and whys. He had stood alongside the most accomplished men—and women—scientists of the same stripe, "why" people who wanted to break through the boundaries of exploration, pressing on to find out if they might achieve the impossible. And they had done it. They had taken the tiniest, most minuscule element, an almost invisible measure of energy, a mere speck—and created hell on earth with it. They had blended elements to create a power the planet had never known before, and with it rent a chasm in the soul of mankind. *Man. Kind.* He shook his head. He was a man with not a bone of kindness in him, perhaps not even a soul—he understood that now. And he knew he would never forgive himself for the small part he had played in a very serious game. "Why?" had become the dangerous question, rewarding him with nothing but despair.

Each time he looked at his wife—the woman would bear their first child in a matter of months—he understood that he might as well have signed their death warrants. The lid on Pandora's box had been pried open, was hanging on shattered hinges and could never be shut tight again. The devils he had conspired to release would one day slaughter everyone he loved. Of that he had no doubt.

He was thirty-six years of age, born five years before an Austrian archduke named Franz Ferdinand and his wife, Sophie, were assassinated in a country most Britons might never have found on a map. Now, in the silence of his English wintered garden, as he struggled with all that had come to pass through his childhood and this second terrible world war, he remembered a poem written by a man named Wilfred Owen, a soldier of the Great War. The words had come to him time and again over the past several months: "Oh what made fatuous sunbeams toil to break earth's sleep at all?"

The man lifted his spade high and bounced it against the cold solid earth as he fell to his knees and wept. His clever, curious mind and limitless imagination had swept him into the future, and it terrified him. No god worth his salt would ever forgive him for what he had done.

CHAPTER 1

M aisie Dobbs glanced around, taking account of the congregation gathered in Chelstone's ancient parish church. She was sure not one more person could be squeezed into the edifice. Every single pew was packed with villagers and visitors who had traveled from far and wide to pay their respects to the deceased. She sighed, drawing her gaze beyond those gathered to the rounded entrance, a hallmark of the church's early Norman architecture, and then up toward the wooden buttresses holding the roof fast, as if to catch the prayers of those below. She had met a woman, once, who told her she could see the prayers from distressed souls littering the ceiling of every church she had ever entered, as if those heartfelt messages had been inscribed on fine tissue paper and cast up so God could reach down to collect each one.

Maisie had always been intrigued by the names bestowed upon the different parts of a church: the nave, the chancel, the transept, altar and apse. The sanctuary. *Sanctuary.* The word echoed in her soul. The church's vintage attested to the hundreds of years local folk had come to mark baptisms, marriages and the burials of loved ones; to celebrate Christmas, Easter and her favorite, the Harvest Festival. Today marked the laying to rest of Lord Julian Compton.

For a moment Maisie stared at plaques dedicated to "The Glorious Dead" of two world wars, then cast her eyes toward the carpenter's tools left on a bench set against the cold stone walls. She was wondering how many more names would be added, when she felt a light squeeze against her fingers as Lady Rowan Compton took her hand. She pressed the liver-marked hand in return, and Lady Rowan leaned into her, a gesture revealing the older woman's need to be grounded in her presence, for though Maisie had remarried, she was still the widow of Rowan's only son. In her much shorter life, Maisie had worn the black of mourning twice to mark the loss of a man she adored, and during that time, Rowan had come to appreciate her daughter-in-law's strength even more, grateful for her fortitude at the worst of times. Maisie knew all this, not least because the motherly love bestowed upon her was returned.

Seated in the square, paneled section of the church designated for generations of the Compton family, who had once owned the entire village and still presided over some four thousand acres of the surrounding land, Maisie whispered to the matriarch.

"Rowan—"

"Don't worry—I'm bearing up, Maisie." She squeezed Maisie's hand again. "I won't let down my wonderful Julian with tears."

"I'm here, Rowan."

"I know."

The vicar gave an almost imperceptible nod in their direction, and as Rowan released her grasp, Maisie came to her feet, walked toward the grand brass lectern and stepped up to the Bible, already open to the page from which she would read. It was a tome so heavy, only the pages were ever moved. She felt the urge to cough mounting, and cleared her throat.

"Our first lesson is from Matthew Five . . ." She began to read, her eyes meeting those of Lady Rowan as she reached the words "'Blessed are those who mourn, for they will be comforted.'"

Maisie felt her voice catch. *There has been too much mourning. Too great a need for comfort.* Stepping down from the lectern after speaking the words "Here endeth the lesson," she saw her husband of almost four years give a half-smile and nod. Mark Scott was seated on the other side of Lady Rowan, holding her right hand as the funeral service for Lord Julian continued. Maisie knew that if asked later, she might not be able to remember anything but approaching and leaving the lectern. Her heart was filled with missing the man who had assisted her so many times in her work, who had once been her father-in-law and, as age had softened his demeanor, had become a much-loved friend.

Later, the service over, Maisie stood alongside Lady Rowan, who insisted upon acknowledging each parishioner as they left the church.

"So kind of you to come . . ."

"Yes, he will indeed be missed."

"Do join us at the manor for a cup of tea . . ."

"You were so kind—His Lordship would have been delighted."

"Ah, Mr. Jones, every year he maintained your hot cross buns were the very best!"

And so it went on; the mourners, wrapped in heavy coats and woolen scarves, were now waiting to pay their respects in the low sunlight of a chilly autumn morning. As the crowd thinned, Maisie noticed one man who had waited until all had left the church, and stepped away toward him.

"Edwin, I take it you've come in place of your father today, and are here to read the will."

"Yes, I'm afraid he's not been at all well, Miss Dobbs—oh dear, sorry, I should have said 'Mrs. Scott.'"

"Please, do not apologize—I still use my maiden name for any assignments I choose to undertake. It makes things easier, though perhaps more difficult for some." She smiled to put the young man at ease. "Your father has been our trusted solicitor for many a year, and I am sure as his son you are more than up to the task."

Edwin Klein, who was some six feet and four inches tall, appeared to have become used to leaning down to speak sotto voce in situations where he had no desire to reveal his words to anyone but the person with whom he was in conversation. His shoulders became rounded as he bent forward, his voice low.

"Indeed, we should of course gather to discuss the last will and testament and aspects of the Trust, but I have been observing Lady Rowan and I would suggest we wait—after all, as an executor, you know the details, as does Lady Rowan, so no surprises there. However, there are a couple of somewhat urgent issues of some concern."

"Oh dear—I don't like the sound of that."

"We have discovered that there are squatters at the Ebury Place mansion. As you know, last week I sent a clerk over to take a complete inventory of everything in the house, yet he was unable to gain entry due to interior bolts being drawn across. There were no signs of forced ingress, so the interlopers must have found a window open—and I'm afraid due to laws protecting squatters in such circumstances, there's nothing much that can be done. Of course, the police have been alerted, but their hands are full. If it's any consolation, I've spoken to one of our land lawyers, and he predicts the problem will only escalate across the country, and that by next year, given the sheer numbers of homeless left by six years of bombing, the Ebury Place mansion will be regarded as just the first of many vacant properties to be inhabited by goodness knows who!"

Maisie nodded. "Perhaps there's something I can do, but I really don't want to concern Lady Rowan with the problem, not at the moment—you're right, she's very tired."

"Granted, but Mrs. Scott, she has to be informed soonest. Our firm will take your instructions, though at the moment our hands are rather tied."

"Was your clerk able to see inside? Is there damage?"

Klein shook his head. "All appears to be in order inside, though there's a broken window or two on the second floor—likely caused by land vibration from a bombing at some point. Minor issue. I would imagine the squatters are using only the smaller upper rooms and the kitchen—it's easier to heat, and of course there was a goodly amount of fuel left in the coal bunker adjacent to the scullery."

"Well, at least they won't go cold."

"I beg your pardon?" Edwin Klein registered alarm. "Mrs. Scott, squatting is an offence, albeit a protected one in certain circumstances. Lord Julian gave instructions for the property to be made available for sale, and we would like to proceed as we understand there are interested parties, with at least one inquiry from an overseas government seeking suitable accommodation in London for a consular official of high standing. As you know, we were able to construct robust plans to limit death duties, but certain monies will remain due to the government, and a sale of the Ebury Place mansion could well solve the problem."

Maisie reached forward and touched the younger Klein's arm. "Mr. Klein—Edwin—Lord Julian was very particular about the order of service for his funeral, and he personally chose Matthew Twenty-Two for one of the readings. 'Thou shalt love thy neighbor as thyself.'" She held his gaze. "We have all had rather a lot of the opposite, haven't we? Let me see if I can solve this problem without much ado, while at the same time respecting poorer souls who have been made homeless during this terrible war."

The solicitor tilted his head and stood to his full height. "Right you are. I'll let my father know where we stand, and I will wait to hear the outcome of your efforts, along with your instructions." He paused. "In the meantime, are arrangements in hand for Lady Rowan's removal from Chelstone Manor, or has she decided to remain in the older garden wing while the rest of the property is made ready for transfer?"

Maisie sighed, brushed lint from the sleeve of her black velvet coat and shook her head. "Edwin, the war has barely ended. We have recently offered rooms to young refugees from a German concentration camp, and they are expected to join us within weeks, plus everyone in that church is mourning the loss of a much-loved, deeply respected man, a hero held in high esteem within the village and—indeed—across an ocean. Let us rest for a little while—as you kindly suggested. I will deal with the squatters and I will let you know the situation regarding Lady Rowan's choice of residence." She placed a hand on his arm. "If you will excuse me, Mr. Klein, my place is with her, at her side, but know we are most grateful for your assistance and will be in touch."

She turned away just as Mark Scott approached.

"Everything okay, honey? From a distance that seemed a bit tense."

"Well, all I can say is, he's not his father!"

"Poor Rowan is all in, so George has taken her home—where there's a whole mass of people waiting to talk to her," said Mark. "I think you should take over as soon as we get there so she can go upstairs to rest. She's a determined lady, but this has been

THE COMFORT OF GHOSTS

a long haul for her. Your dad and Brenda are helping out, and as always, Priscilla is doing her bit—as you might say. She can hold a conversation with ten people at once and still have room for more."

"You're right, we should be on our way now. I hope Anna and Margaret Rose have minded their p's and q's at home."

Maisie's adopted daughter, Anna, was now ten years of age and had become close to Margaret Rose, the daughter of her business partner, Billy Beale, and his wife, Doreen, after the family moved into the bungalow owned by Maisie's father and stepmother. It had been a temporary tenancy engineered by Maisie after the area around Billy and Doreen's home in the London suburb of Eltham was bombed. For their part, Maisie's father and stepmother came to live with her at the Dower House, a large property situated just within the boundary of the Chelstone Manor estate.

"Don't worry, hon," said Mark. "I predict those girls have their heads in books while snuggled up to Little Em. Our daughter is way more sensible than I was at that age. Anyway, Billy told me that they'll go straight over to the house and wait until we're back before they head on home with Margaret Rose."

Maisie rested her hand on his arm as they walked toward a waiting motor car. "Mark, I'll be coming into London with you on Monday after all. I'll stay for a couple of nights at the flat—I know you'll be busy at the embassy preparing to leave for Washington, but we'll have some time together until you leave. I daresay Lady Rowan will be resting for most of my absence anyway. It appears there are squatters at the Ebury Place house, so I'm going to try to sort it all out."

"Squatters? Can't you just send in a few hefty young men—Priscilla's three boys look like they would be up for the job."

"Mark, over here squatter's rights go back to the Middle Ages, so it's not quite that straightforward."

"I would rather have your problem than the one I've got on my hands."

"I can't believe you're flying off again so soon," said Maisie. "I wish you could stay."

"I wish I could too, but there's work to be done and I'm one of the poor diplomatic souls lined up to do it. Ambassador Winant thinks that because I'm married to a lovely English woman, I know more about your people than the rest of the department, so my title 'political attaché' now encompasses getting my fingers in more pies than I would like." He smiled. "Anyway, I shouldn't be more than a week or so this time, and at least we don't have to worry about the Luftwaffe anymore. Just all those stops in a shaky Douglas DC-4—Bournemouth to Shannon, Shannon to Lisbon, Lisbon to Gander, then Gander to Washington."

Maisie nudged her husband. "And at the end of it all, Britain will be in even more debt to you lot."

"My lot? If it all works out, at least America will be giving you guys a big old wad of money in the new year, a loan to get you over the hump."

"Ah, but think of how that wad will help us—we'll be able to put a roof over the head of every homeless family."

Maisie looked up at the grand Belgravia mansion she had first entered as a thirteen-year-old girl in 1910, when she reported for work at the kitchen entrance of the Compton family's London home, where she was to take up the post of under-parlor maid. Some nineteen years later, having set up her own business, Maisie was asked by Lady Rowan to accept the offer of rooms at the mansion, as she and Lord Julian were spending more time at Chelstone Manor, the family seat in Kent. Though the request was put to Maisie as the necessary task of keeping an eye on the property and its London staff during the Comptons' absence, Maisie knew very well that Rowan wanted her to live in more comfortable surroundings than the rented bedsit situated next to her office in a less than salubrious area.

Later still, following Maisie's marriage to James Compton, the couple lived at the Belgravia property together, becoming master and mistress of the home where on hands and knees she had once scrubbed floors; where she had fluffed cushions, washed skirting boards, dusted even the tops of door frames and where, in time, she enjoyed one half-day off every fortnight. In girlhood Maisie's working day had started at five in the morning and did not end until after eleven at night. And it was the house where she had been discovered studying in the library at two in the morning by Lady Rowan, an event destined to change the trajectory of her future, though at the time she believed she had forfeited her job in a secret quest to further her education. Rowan enlisted the help of her friend Dr. Maurice Blanche—a forensic scientist, psychologist and something of a philosopher—to advise on how best to help a young working-class girl who showed such intellectual promise. Maurice became Maisie's mentor, and in time she would learn the craft of forensic investigation when she accepted the offer to become his assistant, joining him in his work as an investigator.

Maisie thought of all these things as she stared at the house, wondering how she could find a way to gain entry, a means to talk to whoever had claimed shelter in one of the finest mansions in the most elite part of London. She set off across the street and made her way up the steps to the front entrance. Taking hold of the heavy door knocker, she rapped it against the small protruding brass plate a jaunty seven times, as if she were beating out a tune. It wasn't a rhythm the police would have used.

There was no answer.

She bent forward, lifted the letter box flap and called inside. "Hello! Anyone at home? I know you're there, so may I have a quick word?" She paused. "You're not in trouble—I believe I can help you. Hello!"

Leaving the flap open, she listened. There was no sound, so she tried again.

"You won't be reported. Come to the door—you don't have to open it. Just come here and talk to me."

Maisie moved the side of her head to the open letter box and strained to hear. Yes, there was whispering—she was sure she could hear voices. She called out again.

"Look, I know you're there. I'm not with the police. I'm not with any government authority. And I'm not trying to kick you out—I know you need a roof over your head, and I know you're probably frightened." She took a deep breath. "I promise I can help you." She waited another second. "You can trust me. I know . . . I know this is your . . . your sanctuary, the only place you could find. Trust me."

A few seconds passed, and as Maisie leaned forward to have one final try, she heard someone walking toward the door, light of step as if on tiptoe. She held the letter box flap open.

"Who are you?" It was the voice of a girl. From her tone, Maisie estimated her to be fifteen or sixteen years of age, but it was difficult to tell. Even younger children sounded older having endured a war.

"My name is Mrs. Scott. I used to live here—upstairs, where I think you must be bedding down. It's a cold house, isn't it? But the servants' quarters are smaller, so you can keep the rooms warm. Did you find the coal cellar?"

"We're alright. And warm enough."

"Are you getting enough to eat?"

"None of us is going hungry."

"How many of you are there? I just need to know, for . . . for insurance purposes. Are you with your family?"

The girl seemed to falter.

"Hello—did you hear me?" Maisie paused, then added, "I promise it's alright to tell me."

"There was four. But now . . . but now there's five. And we're not related, but I suppose the four of us are sort of family."

"You don't sound quite sure, my dear. Do you need help?"

No answer.

"Are you there?"

Maisie heard the girl sniff.

"Oh, sweetheart, are you sure you're alright? Do let me help you."

"Yes, we're managing, but . . . but there's a man here and he's very ill. Every day I think he'll be dead by morning. He's everso poorly."

"What man? Do you know him?"

At once a pair of eyes appeared on the other side of the letter box, as the girl bent down to look at Maisie.

"What's your name, my dear?"

"Mary. Just Mary."

"Mary, tell me about the man. Has he given you reason to fear him?"

Mary shook her head. "No. Poor sod can hardly stand, let

alone hurt anyone. I reckon he's the one who's in pain and I'm not much of a nurse. He turned up about six days ago, and us lot had already been here a couple of weeks. Never seen him before. He came in the back way."

The girl sniffed again. Maisie reached into her shoulder bag and pulled out a fresh linen handkerchief.

"There you are." She pushed the handkerchief through the letter box. "Take this, wipe your eyes and have a good blow. You'll feel better."

Mary took the handkerchief, turned away to blow her nose, then came back to peer at Maisie.

"Thank you."

"Now tell me about the man—it sounds as if he's suffering."

"Every day I wonder whether he'll be dead when we go in there, and what we'll do with him when he's gone. And he's wearing one of them demob suits—he said he'd been in the army. He scares me—he screams when he sleeps, and he sleeps a lot. We've brought him some soup every day, but we've almost run out of the tins in the pantry."

"How are you all feeling? Do you think he's had something that's catching? An illness?"

"No, but we're . . . we're all scared, and . . . and we've got to stay here so we can work out what to do next." She turned away.

"Mary! Mary—are you still there?"

There was a hiatus, as if the girl were indeed wondering what to do next.

"I'm here."

"Mary, is there something else you're afraid of?"

"No. No, but . . . Nothing."

Maisie was silent, concentrating on the young person on the other side of the door. *Please don't close down, stay with me.*

"Mary, listen to me. I'm going to leave now—and don't worry, as I said, I'm not with the police or the council or the bailiffs. But I will come back with some supplies for you and your friends, and I'll make some nice broth for the man. I've some tinned food at home, so I'll bring it in for you. I'll leave a box by the back door, the one leading into the kitchen."

"That's how the man got in."

"Through the kitchen?"

"Yes. He knew how to unlock the door, you know, without a key."

"And you found him upstairs?"

"Like Goldilocks, he was, falling asleep in someone else's bed. But I suppose that's what we've all done, though none of us can sleep properly, in case they come for us."

"In case who comes for you?"

Another pause.

"Mary? In case who comes for you?"

"Doesn't matter. Anyway, I'll look out for the things you said you'd leave for us. But don't try to trick us."

"No, no tricks."

The girl began to move, but Maisie called after her.

"Has he said anything, this man?"

"Mumbles most of the time."

"Has he made any sense?"

"Doesn't say much. But like I said, he screams in his sleep. Tenko—tenko—tenko. Like that, only louder."

"Tenko?"

"He doesn't make sense."

"Hmmm, no, he doesn't."

"And I reckon he's got a wife somewhere, or a girl, because he calls out for her."

"That could be a start."

"I doubt it—there's a lot of women called Lily, aren't there?"

"Lily?"

"Well, it could be something else, though it's definitely an *L* name—you know, Letty, or Lizzie. We can hardly understand him. He gets all white and frothy around his mouth when he's asleep and mumbling. Rotten sad, it is. Anyway, thank you for trying to help. When do you think you can fetch some food for us? One of my mates here is bound to get caught if he keeps going out trying to get more."

"Tell him to stay here. And . . . and keep yourselves occupied. If you go into the library, the big room with the books next to the drawing room, you'll see a cupboard in there with all sorts of games and puzzles. And you can read the books. Don't let yourselves get bored."

"Oh that's alright. We practice what we was taught."

"Practice? What do you mean?"

"Mary! Don't say any more." The voice came from behind the girl.

"Nothing. Sorry. Got to go. Bye. Thank you, Mrs. Scott."

Maisie continued to watch as the girl named Mary walked away, stopping once to reach down and pull up long grey socks that had slipped down to her ankles. A boy of about the same age stepped into her line of vision. Now she could see that Mary was tall for her age and slender, with long legs that reminded Maisie of a young racehorse. She wore a pleated schoolgirl skirt, two cardigans and a blue blouse, and her shoes were ill-fitting.

"You couldn't keep your mouth buttoned, could you?" said the boy, who was the same height as the girl, though his clothing would have been better suited to a shorter lad, and it appeared the most recent cutting of his ragged brown hair had not been executed by a barber.

"She was trying to help us—I could see that."

"See it could you?" said the boy. "Just with them eyes of yours."

"Give it a rest, Jim."

"I'll give you this."

The boy raised his hand, yet as Maisie continued to watch, in an instant the girl had swept him off his feet with a swift move, her leg shoved forward to hook around his right ankle as she pushed up his chin with the heel of her right hand, then brought her other hand down on his neck.

"Don't ever do that again, Jim. What's the matter with you? You losing whatever's left in that brain on top of your shoulders? We've got to stick together, us lot, so just you get a grip of yourself. And if it crosses your mind to swing for me ever again, remember, I was always faster than you. I'll kill you, truly I will."

Maisie let the letterbox flap close without a sound, as the girl who called herself Mary approached the staircase. Turning away toward the square, she lifted her collar against a sharp breeze and looked up at cobalt clouds merging overhead as if to reflect her quandary. She walked on, determined to busy herself gathering a collection of foodstuffs, a task made more difficult by the limitations of her ration book. Mark would help—courtesy of the American embassy, he was able to obtain foods that were otherwise unavailable to the British people. The youngsters would be very grateful for a bar or two of American chocolate tucked inside a box of comestibles. And she needed to think, needed to consider her next move, because she had to cradle the information revealed by Mary with a light hand. For if she were not mistaken, the unknown man was calling out for a girl named Lizzie—and Lizzie died a long time ago. Then there was the other matter—it was clear a girl in her teens had been trained in unarmed combat. Therefore it would be fair to assume her friends were equally adept at taking care of themselves.

CHAPTER 2

As a rule, whether Maisie was expected at the Fitzroy Square office or not, if she were in London, she would take the opportunity to drop in to see Billy Beale, but following the visit to Ebury Place, she decided against the stop. Billy, once her long-time assistant and now a partner in the business, was responsible for his own cases, for the most part involving security appraisals for property owners. He had surprised Maisie, forging valuable alliances with insurance agents and building firms—and if there was one element of life predicted to boom as Britain found its feet in the post-war years, it was in the construction of new homes. Indeed, whole new towns at strategic locations across the United Kingdom were in the midst of being planned. Rows and rows of houses with indoor bathrooms and flushing toilets, accommodation for a bombed-out and distressed population of homeless, from Crawley and Harlow in the south of England, to East Kilbride and Livingston in Scotland. Now, however, given Billy's excitement about the revenue he was bringing in and his enjoyment in his work, Maisie knew she had to protect him—she understood only too well that those lingering wounds from the Great War could rise to the surface in an instant.

Stopping at Victoria Station, she approached a telephone kiosk, stepped in and drew the concertina doors. Lifting the receiver, she placed the requisite coins in the slot and dialed a number she knew by heart, one that would have never been listed in a London telephone directory.

"MacFarlane!"

Maisie pressed button A to release the coins, and the call connected. "Robbie—it's Maisie."

"Might have guessed. And I do hope this isn't trouble—you know I've only a couple of months to go before my desk is cleared and my life will be free of Scotland Yard, the Special Operations Executive, the Secret bloody Service and any other department standing between me, a fishing rod and a flask of single malt by my side. All I've got to do is give a bit of evidence at Nuremberg, and I'm off to find a quiet loch as far north in my bonnie Scotland as I can venture and still land a fish for my supper."

"In the freezing cold of a Scottish winter? Even on my most grey days, Robbie, you never fail to amuse me."

"Glad to be of service, hen. Now then, spill the beans while I still have a few brain cells left. Is this about Beale the younger again?"

"Yes, it is, and—"

"Before you go on, the news is exactly the same as it was a week ago. He's back on home soil and has been for some time. He turned up for his army pay and his demob suit. Then he left the face of the earth."

Maisie heard paper rustle and an expletive from the man she had first crossed paths with when he was a senior detective with Scotland Yard's Special Branch. Later, even before the war, Robert MacFarlane was assigned to an elite role, becoming the vital linchpin between the Yard and the Secret Service. He was yet another high-ranking official with a "finger in a lot of pies."

And though there was often banter amid the odd row between Maisie and MacFarlane when they worked together, there was also a deep respect and affection.

"I assigned someone to search for him, Maisie, but to all intents and purposes, Will Beale has vanished into thin air— and remember, it was a few years ago that one of his mates attested to the fact he wanted to be known as 'Will' and not 'Billy' because he was fed up with being seen as a chip off the old block." MacFarlane paused, and Maisie heard more rustling of paper. "Now, the medics who examined him upon his release from Japanese captivity and again when he landed here wrote in their reports that he was suffering from extreme malnutrition and would need a slow introduction of solid foods. Apparently, a good number of those lads got stuck into the first big nosh that was put in front of them and lost the whole lot in short order. The poor buggers working on that bloody Burma railway were given only half a cupful of rice per day, and little water. Will's kidneys were all but packing up due to dehydration, and he's had every bloody Asian illness in the book. It's a miracle he survived and—hate to say this, Maisie—he might not be now. He wouldn't be the first returning soldier who has gone through hell and decided to throw in the towel on life in the hope of finding something akin to heaven."

The line was silent.

"Maisie?"

"Robbie—Robbie, I know where he is. At least I think I do. And I'm not sure quite what to do next, because I—I must protect Billy and Doreen. They are aching to see him, just beside themselves, but I don't think he wants to go home."

"Just as well I'm talking to a lady, because the air would be blue if I wasn't. Those stinking, bloody . . . I'd better stop now. But you should have seen the state those boys have come home in. Some of them went out and got themselves drunk at every port of call on the return to Southampton, and the strain was more than they could manage—you can't pour beer into a bag of bones and expect a shrunken, ulcerated gut to absorb it. And the stories, Maisie—I mean, there's war and there's the sort of brutality we've never seen before, as if we've not enough on our hands with the bloody Nazi camps and the poor bastards we found inside. And right now that's another problem—we expected thousands of displaced persons, but we didn't expect genocide. New word on me, that, but I was sent over to Germany and Poland to bring back a report after V-E Day. I've seen what that word means, and on a sickening scale . . . It's . . . it's . . . ."

As MacFarlane issued a deep sigh, Maisie felt as if a cold breeze had found its way along the telephone line.

"Maisie." MacFarlane was calmer, his tone matter-of-fact, as if he had galvanized himself and by force dragged his mind into the present. "There are a few different choices here. First, you can see if he'll speak to you. I think you're better at all that business of getting people to talk when they don't want to. Second, we can go together—he knows me, but not well. I remember him as a nipper when he came with his dad to your office and we had a bit of a laugh together. Good lad, he was. I was a soldier in the last war, so I've an idea how it's been for him—though look where he's seen a fair few horrors: Dunkirk, Singapore, Changi and then Burma. He's no one's 'boy' anymore. Third, you can either send his dad round, or you can both go, or—"

"Or what, Robbie?"

"Or you can send his mum."

Maisie was silent.

"Yes, his mum. If the man wants to cry—and I would bet he

wants to weep for every mate lost and for the life he's frightened to live—my best guess is he'll hold it back with his dad."

"But he knows his father loves him beyond measure—you should have seen Billy when his son came off that boat from Dunkirk."

"Yes, I understand all that, Maisie, but the lad also knows that his dad's shell-shock—and let's call it what it is—has never been far from the surface. I am not in your league when it comes to knowing what goes on in the human mind, Maisie, but after all these years, I've cottoned on to a little bit of knowledge about the spirit. I reckon that lad saw some things when he was growing up—and what with his mother being in an asylum for a while, then everything that happened when they lost their little girl, well, say no more."

Maisie was thoughtful for a moment. "You're right, Robbie. But here's another spanner in the works. He's among company. There's about four others, all about fifteen or sixteen years of age I would imagine, and they're trying to look after him. Every day they're scared he'll be dead when they go in with a cup of tea." She sighed. "But I can say this for them—because I witnessed it—those youngsters can take care of themselves." She described watching Mary dispatch the lad named Jim to the ground.

MacFarlane did not respond, though Maisie thought she could hear a pencil being tap-tap-tapped on the desk. Another second or two passed.

"Robbie? Are you still there?"

"Oh just distracted by some papers. Anyway, more bloody squatters—it's not getting any better, is it? In that case, why don't you have a word with his mum and see what you both think might be best."

"Thank you, Robbie. I just had to talk to you about this one."

"One more thing—over the past three weeks, your Billy has telephoned me almost every day or so to ask if I can pull strings to find out anything about his son. I've conveniently been 'out of the office' a lot lately—usually just down the corridor—because I don't know what to say to the poor man anymore. But I want to remind you about something you probably don't need reminding about."

"Yes?"

"There should be no secrets between man and wife."

"I know, Robbie. Billy will be in the office today. I'll telephone Doreen to talk about it. She's been remarkably strong, you know—you'd never believe she'd had that horrible time after Lizzie died."

"I would believe it, Maisie. And I'll tell you this—in two wars I've seen more backbone in women than in a lot of our bloody politicians, and that's a fact." He laughed. "But don't tell anyone I said that. And let me know what happens."

"Of course, Robbie."

"Don't forget to drop in for a wee dram before I officially retire. We can have a chat about something that isn't war, eh?"

Maisie smiled. "I remember what happened the last time you offered me a dram or two."

"My mistake, wasn't it? You went off sloshed and said 'yes' to the Yank!"

They both laughed, before MacFarlane spoke again.

"Just a minute, Maisie—you didn't give me the address, you know, where those lads and lasses are holed up . . . the squatters."

Maisie hesitated. "Robbie? Robbie, are you there? Oh

dear—that's the pips and I've no more change. Sorry, Robbie . . . I'm being cut off."

"Maisie . . ."

She set the black Bakelite receiver down on the cradle, and remained in the telephone kiosk, her hand still on the telephone for a moment before opening the concertina doors and making her way through the busy station, now filled with as many returning soldiers as civilians. She wanted to think, to consider her own actions. She had placed sufficient coins in the slot for a lengthy call and there were more in her purse, yet in an instant she avoided giving MacFarlane the address of the property occupied by the squatters. Might he guess? MacFarlane was no fool and would know soon enough—but would he suspect that a change of tone in his voice had alerted in Maisie a feeling she could not yet put her finger on?

She needed fresh air. Maurice had taught her: "If you move the body, you move the mind." So she walked and soon admitted that it was a matter of trust. MacFarlane's query was not an idle afterthought on his part. It was a question presented as a simple passing curiosity, but Maisie recognized it for what it was: an investigative technique she had used many a time. The second the person being interrogated saw her turn, they began relinquishing vigilance, letting go of attention to every word spoken in response to her questioning. MacFarlane had just tried the same trick on her as she was coming to the end of the call. She was sure he wanted to know where the young people were located because he was interested in them. Recounting the conversation in her mind, she knew his curiosity had been sparked when she described those skills in the art of self-defense demonstrated by a girl who called herself Mary—if indeed Mary was her name. In that moment, Maisie concluded that for the time being, protecting four young squatters might be just as important as doing all she could to make sure Billy Beale's son had not survived the extreme cruelty of his Japanese captors only to die in London.

By the time Maisie reached her flat in Holland Park, she had decided to return to Ebury Place alone. MacFarlane was right. If she was correct and the ailing man was indeed Will Beale, telling Doreen her firstborn was in trouble and expecting her not to tell her husband was futile. The Beales loved their children, though she also knew "young Billy"—a name conferred on him from the time he could walk—might not want to see his father. She also understood that the reticence was in all likelihood borne of a desire to protect his family, as well as wanting to keep a distance from Billy in particular, because he feared the reunion would reignite his father's shell-shock.

Later, while Maisie packed a box with foodstuffs to take to Ebury Place the following day, she spoke of her concern for the man she believed to be Will Beale.

"This is none of my business, Maisie," said Mark Scott, as he poured two glasses of wine. "I only know the Beales from the lunches and dinners we've had at the Dower House, and a few conversations at your office."

"But?" She turned around to look at her husband. "I can hear a 'but' coming."

"But what if he dies without seeing them, or more to the point, without Billy and Doreen being with their son one last time? You can't take that responsibility." He passed a glass of wine to Maisie. "I think this is a case of protecting one person yet, at the same time, not respecting the others involved. And those kids—Maisie, those squatters can't stay there at Ebury Place. They told you they weren't real family, so where are their parents?"

"Mark, if they're over fourteen, they are all of working age. They're considered adults, though without the right to vote or marry."

"That's all very well, but I'm interested in what's happened to them—or what they've done to make them want to stick together and not go home. They're a little gang, and like horses in a field, it sounds as if they've become herd-bound."

Maisie was thoughtful.

"Maisie? I know that face."

She looked up at her husband. "Or something has pushed them to become like family."

"I'd concentrate on the soldier first, if I were you," said Mark. "He needs help and I don't think these kids, however well intentioned—or not—can look after him, and they certainly can't bring him back to health." He took a sip of his wine. "Do you want me to come over there with you? I have some time."

"I think I should go alone, not least because you've a lot to do before you leave. But I'll let you know if I need your help."

"You come first, my love. You and Anna. You should get back to her as soon as you can, because I'm going away."

"You're right, of course. I'll sort all this out and try to get down to Chelstone later tomorrow morning. And you're planning to leave tomorrow night."

Mark set down his glass and put his arms around his wife. "I never thought I'd get married and I never thought I'd have a child," he said. "I wasn't settled in myself enough—but here I am, besotted with my womenfolk."

"Womenfolk? You sound like my father." Maisie laughed.

"I'll take sounding like Frankie Dobbs to be a compliment."

Mark released his hold and opened a cupboard. "Here, three bars of our best American chocolate."

"To go with the tinned food—excellent. That might be the thing that gets me in the door, along with this very important loaf of bread I brought back from Chelstone."

"You're giving them our one good loaf of home-baked bread?"

"'Fraid so, Mark. We're both leaving soon anyway."

"You might as well take the rest of the butter."

"I've already packed it."

The following morning, Maisie stood at the top of the flight of steps leading down to the kitchens at Fifteen Ebury Place, but before descending, she took account of her surroundings. Although she had hailed a taxi to bring her to Ebury Place, there was one point when she suspected the vehicle was being followed, so she instructed the taxi-cab driver to take evasive action. "I've been bothered by a man knocking on my front door at all hours, and I think that might be him behind us."

"Don't worry, madam—I delivered my fares to safety during the Blitz. I can get you to Belgravia."

"Thank you—but just the nearest Underground station, please."

"Right you are, madam."

The driver was as good as his word, in short order losing the motor car that appeared to be following the taxi before Maisie asked him to pull over to the curb. She stepped out, but instead of descending into the Underground station, she caught two buses, then walked a short distance to Ebury Place. She made one stop at a telephone kiosk, where she placed a call to her friend Priscilla, who agreed to her request without a second's hesitation. She placed one more call, to a man who had become a dear

36

friend. Though they had once been lovers, Andrew Dene was now married with three children. Maisie had met Dene when he was working at a specialist hospital for soldiers suffering physical wounds and the lingering effects of shell-shock from the Great War. He, too, had once been mentored by Maurice Blanche, and later treated both Billy Beale and Frankie Dobbs, the latter after a fall. He was the first person Maisie had called when Priscilla's son returned wounded from his quest to join the flotilla of "little ships" in a bid to save soldiers desperate to evacuate the beaches of Dunkirk. Without hesitation, Dene agreed to meet her at Priscilla's house in just over an hour.

Maisie stepped out of the kiosk, and as she cast her gaze along the road around the square, she realized she was looking for Mac-Farlane's motor car.

M aisie rapped on the kitchen door.
"Hello—I'm here! I've brought some food for you!"

She knocked again and was about to knock once more, when she was aware of a face at the window set into the door.

"You on your own?" It was Mary.

"Yes. There's only me, and I've a box of food for you—and a few bars of chocolate too. Please open up, because I've been carrying this for quite a while."

Seconds passed, the girl continuing to stare at Maisie before she moved and began drawing back iron bolts securing the door.

"I'll take the box, and you can go."

Maisie put her foot across the threshold. "I want to see the man."

"Don't think that foot of yours will stop me shutting this door—I could cripple you if I wanted."

"But you won't, Mary, because I believe you need my help with that man—I'm a trained nurse. And I think you need help to get out of this situation where you have no real home to go to."

Maisie saw tears well in the girl's eyes, which she wiped away with the back of her hand.

"Don't you go thinking I'm soft, Mrs. Scott—and is that your real name?"

"Yes, it is." Maisie paused, then added, "But I sometimes go by another name."

"What's that then?"

"Maisie Dobbs. I worked here a long time ago. I was a maid."

The girl laughed, looking her up and down. "Yeah, I bet you were."

"Let me in to examine the man. I want to see if anything can be done for him."

Mary twitched her lips from side to side. Maisie pushed her foot farther across the threshold.

"Alright. But just so you know, I will knock you down if you try anything—you won't get the better of me."

"No, I don't think I could," said Maisie, entering the kitchen. "Though I've had a few lessons in the martial arts myself, when I was about your age." She set the box of groceries onto the kitchen table. "I'll leave everything in the box, because I doubt you'll be here much longer."

"Why wouldn't we be?"

"I'm going to stick my neck out here—I think you are on the run, and if I'm right, you can't afford to stay in one place for long." She allowed her words to hang in the air. "Now then, let's go up to see the man." She reached for the door leading to the back stairs.

"If you know about that door, I reckon you're telling the truth about working in this gaff."

"No one would lie about being a maid in a house like this," said Maisie. "You go first."

Maisie could have identified the exact room where the very ill man was bedded down, for the stench of sickness had wafted along the narrow corridor.

"We've helped him along to the toilet, but he's been sick a lot. Can't keep down his soup. We had to leave a bucket in there." Mary stopped at the door, while Maisie entered. She did not put a hand across her nose and mouth—she wanted the man to see her. When she was little older than Mary, having lied about her age to serve as a nurse on the Western Front, she had been trained never to look away from a wounded man and never to let her emotions show. In an instant, she knew the man was indeed Billy's eldest son, the one who never wanted to be called "Young Billy" and who had rechristened himself "Will." She turned to Mary.

"Mary, I want you to go downstairs, make up the fire in the stove and bring a couple of kettles of water to boil. I felt the warmth when I walked into the kitchen, so I know you've managed to get the fire going. Put some more fuel on, and it shouldn't take long to heat up the water. There's salt in the pantry, so pour the water into two sturdy enamel bowls—you'll find a couple in the cupboards next to the sink—and add a goodly measure of salt, a couple of handfuls to each bowl. Go to the laundry cupboard—along the corridor on the right, past the kitchen—and bring me four towels and some face flannels. Where are your friends? Get them to help you. And, Mary—for heaven's sake don't linger to natter."

Mary left without speaking, her eyes wide. Maisie heard her run along the upper corridor, knocking on a door as she went. A brief argument ensued, but Mary could be heard telling her companions to shut up and help her. The footsteps of four young people clattered down the back stairs.

Maisie moved the bucket and knelt down alongside an emaciated Will Beale.

"Will—Will, wake up. Can you hear me?"

Maisie began to rub her hands together, and closed her eyes until she felt heat in her palms. When she was even younger than the group in the kitchen who were now trying to make up a fire to boil water, a man named Khan had taught Maisie that her hands could be used to heal, that human touch could cure many ills. All she wanted now was Will Beale's attention, and not in a half-stupor. She laid her left palm on his shoulder, and with care brought her right hand to rest across his forehead.

"Lizzie, are you there—have you come to take me with you, Lizzie?"

"Wake up, Will. You're safe now. Open your eyes."

Maisie could see the man's eyes moving behind swollen eyelids, as if he were struggling to lift them.

"Just a bit more effort, Will, and you'll be able to see me."

His eyes opened, and Maisie lifted her left hand from his shoulder and took Will's right hand in hers.

"Is that you . . . Miss Dobbs? Is that you?"

Maisie recognized the moment of panic as Will glared around the room. She knew he expected his father to be with her.

"I'm alone, Will. I know what happened to you, but you can't stay here. I'm taking you with me. Alright? You can come with me."

"I can't see them. I can't see my mum and dad. It'll destroy them—they'll die."

"You don't have to yet, but we must get you to a place where you can be cared for." She took a deep breath. "And when you're ready to see them, then they will come."

Will began to shake his head, then winced as if the effort had caused a bolt of pain. "You don't know what happened to me, Miss Dobbs. You don't know what happened to our boys, to my mates."

"I know a little, Will—enough to believe that you have the strength to survive."

"What if I don't want to, what if I'm like my dad and keep remembering the terrible things?"

"Your father's demons have softened over the years, Will," said Maisie, her voice little more than a whisper as she spoke. "They may have tormented him throughout your childhood, but those dragons rarely come for him anymore."

Will moved as if to shake his head but, remembering the discomfort, became still. "Oh, I bet they do. I bet they still come."

A sound in the corridor marked the return of Mary, who gave a light knock at the door before she and the boy Maisie had seen dispatched to the floor during her earlier visit entered with two large bowls of piping hot water. Another girl brought towels and a second boy brought a jug of cold water and a glass.

"Right, set the bowls on the marble-topped dresser there, and let's get started." She slipped her hands away from Will, removed her jacket and rolled up her sleeves. "Mary, you and your friend—sorry, my dear, I don't know your name—"

The girl, not as tall as Mary and with short dark-blond hair growing in a mass of curls, was dressed in the same ill-fitting schoolgirl uniform. She hesitated before speaking. "I'm Grace."

"Right you are, Grace." Maisie gave a brief smile before issuing an instruction. "Mary and Grace, you should leave now. Jim—I take it you're Jim—you can stay and assist me. This is Mr. Beale and we must do all we can for him." She looked at the other boy. "You must be Archie."

"That's me, miss." Archie stepped forward, causing Maisie to stifle her amusement. He reminded her of an engraving of the Artful Dodger she had once seen in an old copy of *Oliver Twist*.

"I will need your help in a little while, Archie, so wait outside." Turning, she called to Mary as the girl reached the door. "Mary, go down to the floor below where there are four large bedrooms. In one you will find a row of men's suits and other items of clothing. Look for a nice pair of trousers and a tweed jacket, and in a chest of drawers you'll find men's shirts and underwear. Oh, and a pullover—it's chilly outside. And bring me a pair of shoes—I think they'll fit Mr. Beale. Don't forget socks."

"Miss Dobbs, you can't—"

"Just close your eyes again, Will—forget I'm a woman you know and just think of me as your army nurse."

Maisie scrubbed her hands and began to remove the soiled and sweat-soaked clothing from Will Beale's wounded body. She passed each item to Jim, along with bloodstained dressings lifted from festering wounds, while signaling for assistance as needed. The appearance of infection was a cause for concern, bolstering her desire to remove both the squatters and Will Beale from the house. Only once did she look up at the lad, and could see tears in his eyes as he stared at Will's prominent ribs and the many lacerations across his almost transparent flesh. The boy's emotional reaction made her heart ache; for whatever they had endured, as Mark said, they were just kids. While she knew little of their circumstances, they, too, had seen more than enough of war.

Some forty-five minutes later, after Will had been washed from head to toe, after he had been towel-dried and dressed in good clothing, a shirt that smelled of lavender and clean socks, she helped him to stand.

"I've asked Mary to heat some soup I made last night—can you manage a little? There's bread from Chelstone."

"I'll try."

"Jim and Archie—help me now."

Descending the stairs was not without a worrisome moment or two, but in time Will Beale was seated at the kitchen table with Jim and Archie on either side, solid beams making sure he did not fall.

"Right, now I just have to sort out our transportation. I'll be a little while, as I've to make a few telephone calls."

"Where are you taking me?" asked Will. "I can't go back to Mum and Dad."

"For now you're going to the home of Mr. and Mrs. Partridge. They already know you're coming and they have a room ready for you. There's a doctor meeting us there—an old friend of mine, Dr. Andrew Dene. He's one of the best, Will. He treated your father, years ago."

Will Beale looked down at his soup, pushing the spoon back and forth. "I'm scared, Miss Dobbs. I'm a soldier, and I don't mind saying that."

"I know you are, Will." She looked at each of the young people in the kitchen, all of whom were staring at Will Beale. "You're not the only one—there's four others in this kitchen who have reason to fear."

"We're not scared," said Jim, his manner haughty as he pressed his shoulders back.

Recalling how she had felt compelled to end the telephone conversation with MacFarlane, cutting off the call with a lie, she added, "Then you should be, Jim, and not only because you have moved into someone else's property and are squatting here, but because I have a feeling you might be in the crosshairs of something bigger than you understand. To be clear, I don't understand it either. But give me time, and I will."

Mary stepped toward Maisie. "Where else can we go?"

Maisie looked up at the kitchen clock. "Oh don't worry, I have plans for you. As I said, I just have to place a call or two from the telephone here—I know it's still connected. If I manage to reach the people who can help us, and all goes to plan, within an hour or so, an American man will arrive at this door. He'll take you to a motor car and you'll go with him."

Maisie studied Will, made sure he was steady, and left the kitchen to walk toward the telephone situated on an ornate sideboard in the main entrance hall. As she ended each call, she sighed and took a deep breath before dialing the next. Having made arrangements for Will and the four young people, Maisie returned to the kitchen, just a little lighter for having each request met with the words "Of course—I'll get everything ready now," followed by "Yes, I'll be there" and "You can count on me, honey."

"How do we know we can trust you?" said Mary, as soon as Maisie entered the kitchen.

Maisie was about to answer, when Will Beale spoke up, his voice stronger than she had heard since entering the room where he had lingered for so many days and—she thought from the faces of those gathered around her—more resolute than they expected from the man they envisioned finding dead when they checked on him every morning.

"You can trust Miss Dobbs with your life. You could ask my dad, if he was standing in this room. And my mum. There's a lot of people she's helped. And the Yank is her husband, and he even knows the president of America."

Maisie smiled. "Let's not over-egg the pudding, Will. Now, come on, we should be getting a move on. I'm going to walk to the end of the street to hail a taxi."

"I'll go." Archie moved toward the door.

"No you won't." She looked around the room. "Not one of you is to leave this house until Mr. Scott gets here. Is that understood?" She waited. "Good. Keep quiet and the door closed to anyone else, no matter who they claim to be and even if they say they know me. Is that clear? I'll be talking to you later."

"But where are we going—where will your husband take us?"

"Pimlico, to a flat. It's recently been vacated and is just waiting for some good tenants. For now."

"What will we do there?"

"For a start, when I get there in a few hours, you're going to tell me what the hell you've been up to. In the meantime, settle in. There's two bedrooms, so boys in one, girls in the other. You can take the groceries with you, and keep the flat tidy—Mary, you're in charge."

"She always is," said Jim.

CHAPTER 3

As the taxi-cab drew up outside Priscilla's house in Holland Park, Andrew Dene and Douglas Partridge, Priscilla's husband, rushed down the steps to help Will Beale from the motor car.

"Careful, son, just lean on us," said Dene.

"We've got you," added Douglas, wrapping his one arm around the young man. Douglas had suffered an amputation after his wounding on the Western Front during the Great War.

Maisie could see Will trying to speak, but as he looked from one man to the other, it was clear he was overwhelmed.

Priscilla stood at the top of the steps, with the housekeeper—who went by the name of Mrs. R.—beside her, holding the door open.

"Come on in, Will—we've made up the best room in the house for you," said Priscilla.

"I'm sorry to bother you, Mrs. Partridge," said Will, stuttering his words. "I—I won't stay long, I p-promise."

"Young man, you will remain in this house until I'm ready to allow you to cross my threshold again, so let that be the end of it," said Priscilla. "Now then, let's get you settled."

Maisie waited in the high-ceilinged drawing room until Priscilla and Douglas joined her, seating themselves on the sofa.

"Mrs. R. has made one of her egg custards," said Priscilla. "She maintains it would be best for a poor digestive system, and who is anyone to argue with Mrs. R.? Fortunately, I brought some fresh eggs home from Kent. She told me you can only buy them one at a time in the shops now, and that's if you're lucky. We almost had to put an armed guard alongside the chicken run. Brilliant idea though, keeping hens at the cottage."

"Thank you both very much for your help. Will needs to recuperate, and I think the worry of his parents in close proximity would have been too much at this point."

"Maisie, they should be told soon," said Douglas. He rested his arm along the back of the sofa; his wife moved toward him. "I cannot imagine one of our boys being in that same situation and us not knowing where they were."

"I know and I will speak to Billy and Doreen as soon as Will is a little more at ease with the thought of seeing them. It'll only be a day or two, I'm sure. But if he's adamant, I know if I'm to respect his parents, it will mean breaking a promise to Will—and then just hoping it all comes right."

"It'll come right," said Priscilla. "In fact, perhaps you should have a word with Will now he's settled. We've had our ups and downs with the boys—our men, as we keep reminding ourselves—so we know how tricky it is. It hasn't been easy with Tim, not since his exploits at Dunkirk and losing an arm—'like father like son,' as the saying goes. Thank goodness you were able to get hold of Andrew when we saw the state Tim came home in. Andrew Dene really is a most wonderful physician."

"Do I hear you talking about me?" Andrew Dene entered the drawing room.

Maisie came to her feet, and the two old friends greeted each other with a kiss to the cheek before taking their seats in armchairs set on either side of the cold fireplace.

"I can't thank you enough, Andrew," said Maisie.

"I was working at our London clinic today, so it was easy to come over—but let's sit down and talk about Will. By the way, when did he become Will instead of Billy?"

"Before he went out to Singapore," said Maisie. "Apparently he decided he didn't want to be a chip off the old block anymore."

Andrew Dene gave a half-smile. "He's a chip off the old block whether he likes it or not. I remember his father—" He looked at Douglas and Priscilla. "Did Maisie tell you? I treated Billy at All Saints' Convalescent Home in Hastings, after he returned from the last war. Shell-shock, leg wounds and gas inhalation. Nasty triad of symptoms. Poor man kept saying that everything was alright, when it clearly wasn't. Now, Will's condition is miserable—Maisie, you will have seen the external scars on his body—but the first thing he said to me was 'I'll be right as rain soon, I don't want to be a burden.'"

"I hope you told him he is staying exactly where he is until he's as fit as a fiddle."

"You might have to put a lock on the door, Priscilla." Dene turned to Maisie. "Maisie, I would like him to talk about what has come to pass. There's no rush, but perhaps at a later date he would do well to literally dump out all the terrors and then dump them again—a prescription of talking was shown to be somewhat successful with neurasthenia patients during the last war, and this man must get those memories out of his head and into a . . . into a confession, is one way to look at it. He will never forget what happened to him, but he has the burden of guilt that attends a survivor when so many of his fellow soldiers perished." The doctor rubbed his chin. "You know, I've seen a few other men, prisoners of the Japanese who have now been repatriated, and all are having similar problems with assimilation—yes, they are happy to be home, often very jokey and 'hail fellow, well met' with everyone they encounter, but then the deep veil of terror descends. They're trying not to let their families have a window into the hell they left behind, but the wives, mothers, fathers—and children—aren't stupid. Will's experiences are compounded by growing up in a household with a father who suffered shell-shock."

"I know Billy and Doreen did their best to protect their children," said Maisie. "I am sure he heard his father's night terrors, and of course, there was little Lizzie dying and Doreen's breakdown."

"So all of that is now on Will's shoulders?" asked Priscilla, reaching for her silver cigarette case. She took out a cigarette and tapped it on the engraved case. "It's a wonder the country got through anything since the last war, let alone the bloody Blitz, the bombing and the doodlebug rockets."

"But that's the thing, Pris—we haven't come through it, not really," said Douglas. "I know Andrew sees a lot in the hospitals, but in my line working for the press, I've been talking to a good number of people—let's just say in 'high places.' We all know what's going on, that housewives are still queueing in the streets for food rations, and even those have tightened up because supplies are being sent to liberated countries. Imports are either slow or stuck at the docks half the time because we don't have the manpower to unload them, or the dockers are on strike because they can't earn overtime by working on a Sunday. We've a generation of children who are behind at school, many of them leaving even earlier than fourteen so they can try to earn a living to help out the family. And look at the housing disaster. Thousands of homes with a big hole where a roof used to be, and that's before you even look at the mounds of rubble on every street and the enormous number of homeless. I spoke to a soldier the other day who said he had been looking forward to coming home until he got here. He said, 'Britain is like a battlefield.'"

There was silence for a few moments, broken by Priscilla, who blew a smoke circle before speaking. "Well, we've just all got to bloody get on with it—or we'll sink—and do what we can for those who, unlike us, *don't* have a roof over their heads."

Andrew looked at Maisie and raised an eyebrow.

"Regarding Will," said Maisie, knowing that Dene found Priscilla's forthright manner difficult. "I'll have a word with him, and I'll think of what to do about getting him to talk to someone in due course. I know this seems strange, given all you've said, Andrew, but I've started to wonder if the person most qualified might be his father. The conversation could help both of them, and might have a positive effect on the way they look upon each other and what the future holds for them as father and son."

"You could be right," said Dene. "But in the meantime, he has to be built up physically—that will help." He smiled at Maisie, then turned to Priscilla and Douglas. "We were both students of the Dr. Maurice Blanche way of thinking, weren't we, Maisie? We were taught that healing the body is a huge element in healing the mind, and vice versa, unfashionable as his teaching was at the time. Can you imagine how my professors in medical school reacted when I quoted something Maurice had taught me? Especially with me being the poor scholarship boy from Bermondsey!" He shook his head. "Anyway, Will should keep to a good, simple diet, which is thankfully just as well considering the food-supply question. It should be as nourishing as possible. Not too much raw food—for example, if you bring apples back from Kent, get Mrs. R. to stew them. Steamed greens, carrots and other vegetables, if you can get them. His constitution needs soft foods, but not mashed to oblivion. I will write a prescription for something to help him sleep so he can get sufficient rest without nightmares, but on no account is the medicine to be left where he can find it." He turned to Priscilla. "Let your Mrs. R. know to administer once a day at night in a hot drink of some sort." He came to his feet. "I'll visit again in a couple of days. Maisie, I take it you're going back to Chelstone."

"Yes, a bit later on."

"Good, I'll telephone tomorrow. And do apprise Will's parents of the situation—I don't want two more patients from the same family suffering mental anguish because they don't know where their son is."

Following Dene's departure, Maisie went to Will Beale's bedroom, knocked on the door and entered. Though it had been painted in a cool yellow shade in recent years, Maisie knew it had once been Tom's room. She remembered Priscilla complaining that it was never worth painting her sons' bedrooms, because the bouncing of a football against the wall seemed to create a distinct pattern of chaos. Will was lying in bed, staring out of the window, his arms tucked under the thick eiderdown. For a second or two Maisie said nothing, an image in her mind of the first time she had seen Billy's children. The two boys—"young Billy" and Bobby flanked their mother and little sister Lizzie in her pushchair. Doreen had come to the office knowing Billy would be out that morning. She wanted to talk to his employer because she was worried about her husband and the lingering shell-shock from the Great War that seemed to be pulling him into a darkness where she could not reach him. Maisie remembered the boy staring at his mother, moving closer and linking his arm through hers as if to protect her. Both boys had their father's unruly fair hair, with fringes that were cut at a slant as if Doreen had taken the scissors and started at one side, then snipped away from the eyes toward the hairline. It seemed that once she had embarked upon the task, she became fearful her hand might slip and blind them with the pointed scissors. And Maisie remembered their sweet young sister, Lizzie, with her blond curls and easy smile. Her sudden death from diphtheria had devastated her family.

"Feeling a little more settled, Will?" said Maisie, as she pulled a chair next to the bed and took his hand.

He turned his head. "Thank you, Miss Dobbs. If I had enough strength, I'd leave—I don't want to put out your friends, sleeping in their house, eating their food."

"I found your ration book, so they have it and that will help— but to be honest, there's no inconvenience."

He turned toward the window again, as if looking out at the sky soothed him. "You know, Miss Dobbs, up here, staring out of that window and seeing the birds and that treetop there, still standing, you'd never think there had been a war." He paused, taking a breath. "When you're on the street, all you can hear is the flapping of tarpaulins on the top of houses with no roofs and no windows, no nothing—and people are living there because there's nowhere else to go, and compensation means another government office to deal with, but there's not enough people to . . . to look after the people. And no one can leave a broken-down house because the looters will take everything."

"The peace seems harder than the war, doesn't it?"

"It does, Miss Dobbs. When I was a prisoner, I made myself keep on going, you know, when I wanted to survive, just to show the Japs they couldn't get the better of me, even if they did their best to almost kill me. And I mean 'almost.' Sometimes they'd beat you and stop before you were dead. Coming near to being finished off is terrible, a stinking no-man's-land of not knowing what will happen and being in pain so terrible it starts not to hurt anymore." He sighed. "But I don't know if I can keep going now."

"You can, Will—I've known you a long time, and I know you can keep going."

Maisie allowed silence to descend.

"I watched them hack my best mate with a machete until he died," he whispered.

"It's a terrible picture to carry with you, Will."

Another silence before Maisie spoke again.

"Will, I want to ask you a question or two about the youngsters at the mansion."

"It's a wonder that place wasn't requisitioned—and it still had coal in the cellar! Who has any coal now? They kept that on the q.t., your friends, didn't they?"

"To be honest, I don't think it occurred to anyone that it was there, and it is a miracle no one took it."

"Some people are lucky like that, aren't they? You know, to not have things occur to them on account of being rich." He shook his head. "When I went for my demob suit, they told me what to expect in London because they didn't want soldiers too shocked when they got home. Right chatty they were, about everything going on, so by the time I put on that suit, it felt as if it had bricks sewn into the shoulders and in the pockets, all filled with these miserable heavy things that had happened, and they were laughing about it, saying we just all had to carry on."

"I know, Will—but Mary, Jim, Archie and—"

"That quiet girl. What's her name? Grace? Gracie? I heard them saying something about her not talking much because she was trained to be like that, on account of being a message carrier and knowing where dead letterboxes were."

"Really?"

"When they first let it slip about 'serving' in the war, I thought they were having me on, telling tales and all that. But now I don't think they were."

"Did they say anything else about their past?"

"Not much, really, though they talked in the room when they thought I was sleeping—you see, I had my eyes closed a lot of the time because it felt like my eyelids had a weight on them. I could hardly keep them open. It was strange though, because I heard them say they had to use every bit of what they were trained to do to keep themselves safe. And they're definitely afraid of the police—I just knew that."

"Did they say why?" She took his hand. "Will, I'm sorry to press you when you're so tired, but I want to do what I can for them—I think they're in trouble, and any information is useful."

"That's alright. They tried to get me going again, bless 'em, but I reckon they need all the help they can get."

"Will—"

"It was something I heard that one called Archie say—it made me wonder if someone, somewhere, thinks they killed someone. They seem tough, like little villains, but I reckon they're really scared."

Maisie took a deep breath. "Will, there's one more thing—"

He turned to her, pulling away his hand to wipe the tears streaming across his temples. "Miss Dobbs, I know what you want to say, so I'll start the ball rolling. Can you tell my mum and dad where I am? Tell them I'm safe, and could you try to explain to them . . . explain that . . . explain—"

"Don't worry, Will—I'll let them know you're safe, in good hands, and that you'll be ready to see them soon. Perhaps in a day or two—how does that sound?"

"Thank you, Miss Dobbs."

"You rest now, Will."

Maisie stepped away toward the door. Looking back at Will Beale, tucked into a bed with fresh linen sheets and the low autumn sun shining through the window, she watched as he turned his head to stare at the sky above, his eyes slowly closing as he listed into sleep.

On her way to Pimlico, to the flat she had purchased so many years ago, but which had been empty since the most recent tenant had moved on, Maisie considered a recent conversation at the bedside of another ailing man. Unlike Will Beale, there was nothing Maisie could have done to save the confidant she had come to regard as a much-loved uncle, even though in earlier days she suspected he did not approve of her or his wife's enthusiasm for her education, which amounted to the support of a young woman of lower class, a maid no less. Yet Maisie had consulted him regarding a number of her cases, and his deep connections in the more shadowed realms of government had helped her on many an occasion. In short, Lord Julian Compton had softened over the years, embracing her as his daughter-in-law when he saw how much his son, James, loved her, and later, after James was killed, Julian became a stalwart figure in her life and a beloved grandfather to her adopted daughter, Anna. He welcomed her new American husband into the family, to the point where she thought Mark had filled some of the ache in Julian's heart, lifting the sadness at losing his son.

A week or so before Lord Julian died, Lady Rowan had decreed that only a "good rest" would see off the bad cold he was unable to shake, though it was a rest that would soon become a slide into his final hours as the onset of pneumonia undermined his grip on life. Julian had asked to see Maisie during those troubling days, and upon receiving the telephone call from Lady Rowan, without delay she ran from her Dower House home, across the lawns to the manor house.

"Maisie, so kind of you to come." Julian pressed his hand to his chest as a racking cough punctuated his words.

Maisie reached for the pot of warm honey and ginger tisane set on a side table and poured a glass, holding it to his lips.

Julian lifted his head. "Thank you, my dear."

Maisie waited, watching as Julian once more placed a loose-skinned hand on his chest. How many wars had he fought? She knew he had once been an army officer, long before the Boer War, and had served with the War Office from the grim days in August 1914, when no one quite believed there would be all out war, yet young men rushed to enlist for king and country, under the impression that they would experience the glory of seeing off the Hun from poor little Belgium and then be home by Christmas.

"Maisie, there are elements of the government's work that have become a burden to me."

"Julian?" Maisie frowned, unsure of her place. Was this well-connected man about to confess something untoward? Might he be searching for words of solace from her? There was something about his tone that unsettled Maisie—and she realized it was because he had always been so strong, so resolute, even as he grew to old age.

He coughed again, but seemed determined. "People do things in a time of war that they would never even consider when the world is at peace. Men in power make decisions in the moment, and they are not always for the best."

Maisie felt even more uneasy. Should she ask if Julian would like to speak to a man of the cloth? Was he searching for atonement in his final days?

Julian smiled. "Don't panic, Maisie. I'm not going quite yet—but I wanted to talk to someone who might understand, so I thought of you because I am completely aware of your exploits in Gibraltar, in Spain, and indeed, when you least wanted to be involved, in Munich. I kept abreast of your assignments even when you had no idea I was watching through the eyes of my informers—and I have never been less than very impressed. You asked for my assistance on a few of your cases—you might not have guessed, but you helped me to keep my hand in the game."

"You were always more than helpful, for which I am ever grateful."

"But this is something else. It's to do with the children."

"Anna? Margaret Rose? Which children, Julian?"

"No, others—the children we pulled in to work with the civilian army."

"Civ—?"

"It was to fight the Germans after the invasion."

"But Hitler didn't invade, Julian." Maisie wondered if Julian had become confused, if sickness had altered his recollections of the war. But there was something in his eyes, the old sparkle had not yet faltered, and his mind was as sharp as ever.

"Maisie, he came so close. The French had one of the best armies in the world and it took only six weeks for France to fall. Look at Poland, the Netherlands, Belgium—his next stop was us. We had to prepare for the most devastating outcome, so we trained a civilian army."

"And your part?"

"Kent was considered to be the front-line county. Hitler's army would have landed here first, so the powers that be thought—"

He began coughing again, so once more Maisie held the cup of tisane for him to sip. He took another shallow breath, and continued. "It was thought civilian units could be trained in what they call 'guerrilla warfare,' and many of those civilians were twelve, thirteen, fourteen, though at the time, we didn't think of them as children—they were all potential soldiers. And you know Churchill was all for underground armies—he learned that in Africa." He coughed again, but waved away the offer of more tea. As he continued, she leaned forward, straining to hear. "The civilian army comprised housewives, the postman, the butcher, baker, the local vicar—even nuns! They were trained in all manner of tasks, from the very worst—though the men and women of God drew the line at killing—to gathering intelligence, delivering messages and, yes, even the young were trained to defend themselves. And in time it wasn't limited to Kent—these local units were suitably educated across the country and deployed to do their bit when action was called for, though of course there was an emphasis on the vulnerable coastal areas."

"Lord Julian." Maisie stared at the man she knew was dying. "Why are you telling me this? I don't doubt this is the truth—but why are you telling me?"

Julian attempted a wry smile. "You've signed the Official Secrets Act, haven't you? Mind you, it wouldn't matter if you hadn't—every British subject is bound by it anyway."

"But—"

"But you should know. You must know, Maisie, because . . . because . . ."

Julian had started coughing again, but this time could not stop. Maisie reached for the bell-pull at the side of the bed, and the nurse rushed into the room to help her raise Julian and rub his back. Rowan came soon after.

"I'll do that, Maisie. Julian wouldn't want you to see him like this—go on, we can manage. The doctor will be here soon."

Maisie knew she had been dismissed, that Rowan was protecting her husband's dignity as his passing approached.

S ince that day at Lord Julian's bedside, Maisie had considered the conversation time and again. Though it came as no surprise that he had been at the forefront of any decision regarding the protection of the county given that he was a prominent landowner in Kent and his standing in the corridors of government power, she was taken aback by his confession. It was clear he had given his support to the plan for an army of civilians around the country: ordinary men, women and children who would be tasked with making the invading Nazis regret they had ever thought to cross the English Channel—yet it was the children about whom Lord Julian harbored regret.

As the taxi-cab arrived at the flat in Pimlico, Maisie acknowledged that when she discovered the four "squatters" living at Ebury Place, she knew straightaway why Julian had revealed information about a civilian army, though the lion's share of her concern became focused on Will Beale and his suffering. She considered her instinctive action to end the call with MacFarlane, stalling his attempt to discover the whereabouts of the youngsters. Maisie felt herself take deeper breaths as she faced a truth she at last understood when she witnessed Mary dispatch her friend Jim to the floor without so much as breaking her stride. Of course, Lord Julian *knew* they were at the house because *he* had arranged it, of that she had no doubt. He had, by hook or by crook, at some point facilitated a communication with four young people, that in a grand house on a well-to-do street in the middle of London's most exclusive area, they would find a place to hide in plain sight. Julian would not have informed them in person, so he would have given the task to a go-between, and knowing her former father-in-law, he would have chosen someone discreet, above all suspicion. At the same time, perhaps she was missing something obvious because, as she knew only too well, there was an element of surprise in every case. *A case.* Yes, against her better judgment—at a juncture when she wanted to spend more time with her husband and now ten-year-old daughter, when she wanted to be a support to her elderly father and stepmother, and to Lady Rowan, who needed her to help navigate a move away from Chelstone Manor—this was a case. She was at work. Julian knew it would be so, yet he went to his grave unable to give her more information, though she understood enough—the rest she would find out. She had a feeling that the lives of four young people depended upon what they would be willing to reveal to her over the next few hours.

"Just drop me here," said Maisie.

"That's a very nice motor parked outside your gaff, madam, and with a chauffeur waiting. Looks like a Yank 'automobile,' doesn't it? Mind you, they're a bit big for our little roads."

"Oh, I think you can just about squeeze by," said Maisie, handing him a little more than necessary to pay for the journey. "Thank you—and keep the change."

"Much obliged, madam. True lady, you are," said the taxi-cab driver, who was still looking at the motor car as he pulled away from the curb.

"Hi, honey," said Mark, as he emerged from a door-shaped gap in the mound of sandbags stacked to protect the glass entrance. "I heard that—does he know you really are a lady?"

"I'm not anymore, Mark—marrying you put an end to that! Have you been here long?"

"No—we just brought the kids in with their belongings, nothing more than a paper bag each. And those groceries. I managed to get my hands on some more candies from the embassy, so they think they've just died and gone to heaven."

"Good, I want them nice and sweet for me."

"You going to tell me what this moving around is all about?"

Maisie reached up to kiss her husband. "Later—give me a telephone call from the airport this evening, when I'm back at Chelstone. I'm going to see Billy, then straight home as soon as I've finished my work today."

Mark Scott took Maisie in his arms and kissed her. "I don't care what the neighbors think, honey, but this is because I'll miss you."

"I wish you didn't have to leave so soon."

They kissed again, their arms around each other for another moment.

"I'd better be on my way."

Maisie smiled. "Oh, and the neighbors—you know what they really think?"

"What's that?"

"That I'm taking my chances with one of those Yanks over here on the make."

"And long may it continue, Mrs. Scott—long may it continue."

She watched her husband step into the embassy motor car, and waved once more as the chauffeur drove away. She turned toward the archway of sandbags that were now, following years of war, beginning to leak fine sand across the path. She made a mental note to talk to the caretaker about moving them. After all, they were safe now, she thought, as she began to walk toward her next task—asking questions of four young people who were not only trained to kill, but could well have been schooled in the subtle art of deflecting an interrogation.

CHAPTER 4

"We're still wondering if we can trust you," said Mary. The tall adolescent girl folded her arms across her chest and tapped her foot as she spoke to Maisie. "I mean, we've been thinking about it, and you've been very helpful and all that, but people like you are nice for a reason."

Maisie rested her elbows on the arms of the Windsor chair set alongside the fireplace, and felt the well-trained sense of calm envelop her, a settling of her breathing employed to put not only herself at ease, but the person from whom she was endeavoring to extract information.

"A valid question, Mary—and you all have a right to an answer from me. But let's just reflect on a couple of things, shall we?"

Archie nudged Jim, who stared at Mary, the three seated on the sofa, while Gracie sat on the floor, at their feet. *Interesting*, thought Maisie, wondering if the position was a mark of established rank. Or was it reflective of family order, and Grace happened to be the younger of the four? She suspected that not one of them had family connections, so the relationship to one another had become their closest bond.

"You came to London from—where? I assume you made your way up here from Kent. You were looking for somewhere safe to stay while you made a plan and worked out how you could extract yourself from a situation. Am I right so far?"

"Yeah, that's about it," said Jim.

"Oi, I'm doing the talking, not you," said Mary, elbowing the boy to her right.

"I don't care who answers the questions because I just want to get to the bottom of what's gone on. It's clear to me you need some protection, and I'm prepared to look out for you—but you've got to help me too." She took a deep breath. "I've gleaned enough to know you were recruited to be part of action against the Germans if they invaded. I'm also aware that you were trained to undertake all manner of work—that's why you can fight a good fight if necessary."

Maisie regarded the widened eyes now focused upon her, and felt as if she were caught in a Beatrix Potter story with a clutch of young rabbits staring at her in shock. She was at once touched by the youth of the group and how unformed they must have been when caught up in the very adult world of wartime resistance. She pressed her lips together for a second as she fought the urge to look away.

"I think I know who was ultimately responsible for arranging for you to stay at the Ebury Place house, and—"

"It was a rich bloke somewhere, one of them who could pull strings."

"You just can't stop yourself, can you, Jim?" Mary glared at her co-conspirator.

"Mary, let's all be honest—I know more about you than you might imagine, so let's just get to the most important point here. Someone was the middleman—or woman—and while I will want to know who it is so I can continue to help you, I must know why you are all as scared as . . . as little rabbits with the fox sniffing around your burrow."

Grace had begun to shed tears.

"Oh, Gracie," said Mary, but instead of admonishing the other girl as she had the boy next to her, she slipped down to the floor to sit alongside Grace, her arm around her shoulders.

"Come on," said Maisie. "Let's get it all out, then I can consider how best to guide you."

"I don't reckon you can, missus, because we're in really big trouble, and we didn't do nothing—not what anyone might have thought we'd done anyway," said Archie.

Maisie sighed. "One thing at a time then. Who are 'they'?"

There was silence, then Mary began. "The police and—"

"And who else?"

"We don't know who they are, but they're some of these secret people."

"Now we're getting somewhere." Maisie paused for a few seconds to give everyone time to catch their breath and recollect. "When you say 'secret people,' do you mean people you've met or seen before, or who you are aware of in connection to the job you were expected to do if we were invaded?"

"Yes," said Mary. "There were people who came to our training to watch us. We weren't told who they were—we weren't told much at all about anything other than what our jobs were. But we knew those bods were important."

"I'm going to come back to the question of the 'bods,' but I want to get to the bottom of what the police, or whomever you believe to be in pursuit, think you might have done."

Mary and Grace looked around at the boys, then all four turned to stare at Maisie. Mary spoke up.

"They think we murdered a man," said Mary, staring at Maisie. "You don't look surprised."

"Very little shocks or surprises me, and I half expected the story to run in that direction. This might sound like a silly question—but *did* you murder a man?"

"No!" Four voices spoke in unison. Grace began to weep again, leaning into Mary, who, Maisie thought, had taken on the role of big sister. Or a mother soothing her child.

"Thank goodness we've cleared that one up. Now then, tell me the story of what happened on the day a man was murdered and you were—all of you—put in a position to be under suspicion."

Once again the four looked at one another. Archie cleared his throat.

"It was my fault."

"Go on," said Maisie.

"I was doing my paper round, you know, on my bike and off I went. It was raining, so I was being quick about it."

"You're always quick about it—"

"Jim, please let him speak. I want to get this all straight in my mind," cautioned Maisie. "Let's go back a bit. Where were you doing the paper round, Archie?"

"Where we were living, in a place called Hallarden," said Archie, running fingers through his wayward fringe to reveal a hairline in need of soap and water. "Anyway, I was pushing the newspapers through the letterboxes as fast as I could, you know, so they wouldn't get wet from the rain. If papers get wet, Mr. Rhodes at the newsagents will hear all about it from the customers, and he'll dock my pay. He's a tight old sod. There's this big house— well, they're all big houses on Sandstone Avenue. Lots of trees and really big gardens with fancy plants and all that. They have walls around them so no one can see the grounds and the house, and tall gates I have to give a good shove to get in. I went up to the door of the really big house at the end, and I could see into the windows, you know, them ones that open so you can walk out."

"French doors, stupid," said Mary.

"Alright, French blimmin' doors, miss know-it-all."

"Mary, do us all a favor and let Archie finish," said Maisie. "I'm sure you have your own story, and I'm anxious to hear it, but at the moment, this is Archie's turn."

Archie sighed, shrugged and went on. "I looked through the big French windows because I could see there was a party going on. I was careful because I didn't want them inside to see me, but . . . but I couldn't stop staring." Archie wiped the back of his hand across his lips.

"Why?"

"They must've all been Germans! And there was a great big flag hanging down from the ceiling, you know, with one of them swastikas. And there were some of the men in uniforms that looked German, and the war was supposed to be over. Then one of them saw me, so I ran, then I got on my bike and I was off. I looked back once and saw the curtains being drawn, but I could hear dogs, so I really got myself going."

"Was someone killed? Did you see someone die?"

"No. I just got on my bike and pedaled as fast as my legs could go and even missed the next house."

"Then what?"

"He told us," said Jim.

Maisie nodded, signaling her understanding, her attention drawn to the young fighters one at a time.

"Did you report what Archie had seen?"

"No." Again, the reply came in unison.

"But we decided to go back to have a look, you know, because—" said Jim.

"They didn't believe me," said Archie.

"We wanted to find out more so we could go to . . . to Sergeant Kirby with solid information," added Jim.

"Solid information?"

"That's what we were always told we had to get when the Germans invaded," said Jim. "If we was gathering information, it had to be solid with no mistakes, which meant that nobody would get hurt if it was acted upon."

"They used words like that," said Archie. "You know, 'solid' and 'acted upon.'"

"And what happened then?"

Mary picked up the story. "We went to the house a couple of days later. We decided it was best in the late afternoon, just as it was getting dark. It was a good time because we couldn't be out late anyway, and if they've got glims, they don't work very well in that light, so it's easier to hide if the people inside went after us. Anyway, we had a good look around and though we couldn't see any Germans—or dogs—we thought we'd investigate a couple of big sheds, and another building that was posher than a shed and not that old, but it was locked."

"And you picked the lock?"

Mary began to twist a wisp of blond hair around her fingers. "We were really quiet, creeping in to look. That's where we saw all the Nazi stuff. So we buttoned it up again fast, because we knew we had the right information to give to Sergeant Kirby."

"Sergeant Kirby? Right. Then what happened?"

"That's when we saw the man killed," said Jim. "Shot with a gun."

"By whom?"

"We don't know," said Mary. "It was someone—looked like

a man—all dressed in black with a black balaclava covering his head and most of his face. So, we ran. But we thought someone in a motor car saw us coming out of the gardens—they tried to follow us along the road, but we ran through the woods. We knew the police would be after us in no time and if they caught us we wouldn't stand a chance. No one would believe us, because we would have been the first they fingered for it."

"Why?"

"Because we're all from the children's home." Grace almost whispered, adding to the account. She glanced around at her friends as if seeking their approval, then stared at Maisie, raising her voice. "I'm the youngest here, but we're all older than everybody else in the home and Matron was about to turn us four out in any case, on account of not being little children anymore, and the war being over."

Maisie rubbed her forehead and looked down, not wanting to reveal emotion. *That explains everything. Training the dispensable. Accusing the easiest of suspects.* She looked up, directing her gaze to Archie.

"Who was the victim—do you know?"

"The man who lived in the house—Mr. Hawkin-Price. He is—was—an 'honorable.' You know—the Honorable Jonathan Hawkin-Price," said Archie. "I know everyone's name in the houses I go to. Well, the houses I used to go to anyway."

"I've heard that name associated with Hallarden. In Kent. So that's where the children's home is—you were there? Didn't it used to be the old orphanage?"

"That's right," said Jim. "It's a big scary building. It's even got bats in the roof."

"How did you know the man who was killed was Mr. Hawkin-Price? Couldn't it have been someone else?"

"He lives in that house alone," said Archie. "Except when he's having his German parties."

"He came out and we just knew it was him," said Jim. He seemed to shiver and tugged at his shirt sleeves as if he wanted to make them longer.

"And how did you know he was dead?"

"We saw him go down," said Mary. "The man with the gun was close, then he walked up to him and put another bullet in him."

"And you witnessed all this?"

"We had a quick look back—Mary and me," said Jim. "So we saw the man on the ground and ran a lot faster in case the one with the gun came after us, but he didn't."

Maisie closed her eyes, imagining the scene. The four adolescents scared, running, but curiosity pushing them to look back in the dusky fading light.

"And there's something else, and it got us worried," said Mary.

"Yes?"

"It was everso quiet after that—which was what really frightened us. We've kept an eye on the newspapers and we listened to the wireless at the big mansion where you found us, and no one said anything about it on the news. We're not stupid—we know there are people who want it kept quiet about us, or about him, or about all of us."

"Good point," Maisie agreed. "Look, I can see you're all tired, and I must leave very soon, but I want you to know I am on your side. This is my flat—we're lucky because the last tenants left a while ago and it's been empty. I'm amazed there have been no squatters. I know you have plenty of food, and I also know there are distractions here—a number of books, puzzles. If you need some exercise, then . . . then run around the rooms. Don't keep late hours, and catch up on your sleep. I'm going to burden you with my trust—is that clear?"

The four exchanged looks, turned to Maisie and nodded to signal their understanding.

"Good. And I know the man who arranged for you to have shelter at Ebury Place. He was one of my dearest friends, and he helped you for good reason."

"What was that?"

"I am sure it was because he knew you to be innocent and understood you were at risk. Someone told him your story. He believed it and wanted to help. I have more questions, and I want to start with Sergeant Kirby, so we've got to make this very quick and no arguing or snapping at one another—is that clear?"

Again, the four heads nodded accord.

"Mrs. Scott," said Archie. "What are you going to do, about all we've told you, and when we answer these questions you're going to ask us?"

"I'm going to find out who killed Mr. Hawkin-Price, so you'll be off the hook."

"Then what will happen to us?"

"The worst thing you could imagine."

"What's that?"

"A settled place to live comes first. Then we'll see what suits you best—which is either education or an apprenticeship. But for now, let's get on. I have an important appointment later." Maisie looked at her watch. "First things first—who was your initial contact, the person who told you about the Ebury Place house being empty?"

Yet again the four glanced at one another, but were silent.

"Your heads will fall off if you keep looking back and forth like that."

Jim, Archie and Grace stared at Mary.

"We didn't know where to go, so we went to a hideout."

"What's a hideout?"

"A 'hideout' is a place where people in the unit could go if the Germans invaded and we were on the run after a . . . after causing some trouble for them. There's food there, that sort of thing." She looked down at her hands. "We shouldn't be telling you any of this. We could be hung for it."

"Anyway, they're starting to get rid of them," said Jim. "We was told to forget all about them, because the army blokes are going in, taking out everything and then filling them in, because the war's over."

"Filling them in?"

"They're underground. Sort of like tunnels with places to sleep," said Jim. "They're all over the place—down to Cornwall, up to Scotland, though we're not supposed to know that. And there's a lot in Kent, because it wouldn't have taken long for Hitler's mob to get across the English Channel."

"I see," said Maisie, though she was having trouble "seeing" the scenario described. "You went along to the 'hideout' and what happened then?"

"A man we hadn't seen before came and told us where to go," continued Jim. "We didn't really need to break in to that house, because he gave us a key."

"This man gave you a key?"

"Yes," said Grace. "And we *had* seen him once before, because he was the one who taught us how to get into a motor car engine and then how to disable it. That was his word. 'Disable.' No one told us his name and he didn't let on."

"And he taught us where to cut brakes too," added Archie. "So the Germans crashed their motor cars."

Maisie frowned. *Oh, the penny's beginning to drop.* "Were all your . . . your fellow . . . fellow operatives and instructors local?"

"I suppose so," said Mary. "Some we'd never seen before, but if we know the person, we're not supposed to say anything if we see one another on the street. Mind you, we're not really in town much anyway and I've never seen anyone else."

"Don't you like going into town?"

"We're only allowed to go if we're supervised, because all the shopkeepers think we're light-fingered. It's not worth the trouble if you ask me, and the local children aren't very nice to us anyway, so we keep to ourselves. I reckoned I saw Sergeant Kirby once, but then I thought twice about it."

"Yes, let's discuss Sergeant Kirby."

One hour later, Maisie checked her watch as she left the flat, and shook her head. It was later than she anticipated, but Billy was waiting for her. She had placed a call to him after instructing the four guests not to make telephone calls from the flat. Instead she issued them with directions on answering a call from her. The telephone would ring three times, then stop—that was a signal the next call should be answered a few seconds later. The greetings would be coded. Her only fear was that her charges would become bored, so she anticipated a test of their ability to follow her instructions would come soon.

Crossing the quiet street, she stood in the shadow of a neighboring building, and waited. Soon a shabby figure emerged from the tunnel of sandbags and began to walk away, looking over his shoulder and pushing his hands into the pockets of an almost threadbare navy blue school blazer that would have been small on a younger child. Amid fear for the safety of her young charges,

Maisie realized she had been slow to do something about fresh clothing for them. Archie wore trousers in need of a wash, along with a stained check shirt underneath a moth-eaten Fair Isle pullover. His shoes, like the shoes of his friends, were scuffed and worn.

"Archie!" Maisie called after the boy, ready to discipline him for his own safety. "Archie, don't let me ever catch you ignoring my warnings again. Go back inside—now!"

The boy turned, his head low. "I was only—"

"Only nothing," said Maisie, approaching him. "Do you know how at risk you are, Archie? I didn't want to put the frighteners on you, but this is the situation. You could walk down this street and someone might be waiting to kill you. You won't see them coming. Go back indoors and tell your friends that if they leave the flat, they endanger not only their own lives, but it could lead to you all ending up very much like Mr. Hawkin-Price—and being 'honorable' didn't save his life, did it?" Maisie saw the boy's chin wobble, and put an arm around his shoulder. *He's just a boy trying so hard to be a man.* "You're such a brave lad, Archie, and I admire you for it, but I've seen grown men and brave men make silly mistakes that cost them their lives—don't you do it. Promise?"

"Yes, I promise."

"And you'll make sure the others follow the rules?"

"Yes, Mrs. Scott."

"Good. I'll watch you go inside. Lock the main door and the door to the flat. Alright?"

"Alright."

"Go on now."

Maisie watched the boy scuff his way toward the sandbagged entrance on down-at-heel boots with no laces. She waited until the door closed, and she heard the loud click of the dead bolt, before turning in the direction of the bus stop.

"Oh, Julian, I wish you had told me more."

Maisie observed Billy as he sat in the chair opposite her at the Fitzroy Square office. She had drawn two armchairs toward the gas fire and set one on either side. At first she had considered positioning them in front of the floor-to-ceiling windows over-looking the square. Maurice Blanche had taught her that a difficult conversation could be made less fraught if the person to whom bad news was being imparted had a place to which they could direct their line of vision. So would it be into the hot gas jets, or across the wintery square, where sunshine belied the fact that people walking across the flagstones were hunched over, pulling coats even tighter and hats down toward their ears? She had decided against the cold square and settled on the location offering warmth. Given the fact that all forms of energy were rationed, the area near the window remained chilly whether the fire was lit or not.

Billy frowned as he stared at the flames, clutching the arms of the chair until his fingertips were white. He looked up.

"Let me get this right. My son Billy—sorry—Will. I'd better remember his preferred name." He blew out his cheeks and exhaled, shaking his head. "Will has been home in this country for quite a while and didn't get in touch because he was . . . he was scared? Of me? His dad? And scared of his mum?"

"Billy, he is not scared *of* you, but *for* you. I'm not going to beat around the bush; he has been tortured, and it shows. His external scars are . . . horrific. The wounds inside are beyond anything either of us could imagine, and we went through the war they said would end all wars."

"But he couldn't come home, to us, his family?"

Maisie took a breath. "He held you with him, Billy—that's what brought him home. The love of his family is what sustained him through a terror I cannot even imagine. And . . . and he talked to Lizzie. He says his little sister came to him and kept him going."

Billy looked away. "I blame myself. We all grieved when we lost Lizzie, but I was worried about Doreen, wondering if she would get through it all. I thought the boys were alright, you know, that their heads were above water. Then Margaret Rose came along, and I reckoned, 'We're all going to be steady now. We've got a new little girl, and the boys have a sister again.'"

"And your heads *were* above water. Your family came through hard times, but Will's the eldest and he took more of the brunt than anyone could imagine. Calling himself Will has been his attempt to be different, to break away. He has been so brave, Billy."

"And he's with Mrs. Partridge now?"

"Yes, and Douglas. They have a nurse who comes in, and Dr. Dene is attending."

"Dr. Dene. That's one good thing. He helped me to sort myself out." He stared into the flames. "Pity I couldn't have spent a bit more time in convalescence after I came home from the last war. Might've helped me, you know, in the early days."

"Yes, it might."

"When do you think we can see our son, miss?" Billy stared at Maisie, his forehead lines gathered in a concertina of concern. "I mean, it doesn't feel right being kept from him, even though he's a bit . . . a bit fragile and all that. And believe me, it'll be all I can do to stop Doreen from marching over there and breaking their door down to see her boy."

"I understand, truly I do. But I have to go on Will's state of mind and Dr. Dene's advice. But how about Saturday afternoon? Give him a few days to get some strength back and feel better in himself. He's been wandering since coming home, so Priscilla's housekeeper is feeding him up, but it has to be done with care, or he can't keep it down. I'll have a word with him on Friday morning—I am seeing Dr. Dene at Priscilla's house, but I think after lunch on Saturday would be a good idea."

"Do you reckon he'll come home? Doreen will want to look after him."

"I think as soon as you have a good chat and he feels better, he'll want to stay with you. I can arrange for a motor car to bring him to your house in Eltham when you're ready to leave."

Billy sighed. "I wouldn't feel so blimmin' upset about all this, but I wish he'd gone to someone else's house."

Maisie inclined her head. "Why? I asked Priscilla because she and Douglas have sons too—one who was wounded at Dunkirk and another who risked his life flying Hurricanes during the Battle of Britain. They know what it is to be fearful for your son's life."

"Yeah, I know that, but remember, our Bobby had all them plans to have his own garage, working on motor cars and doing well, then big mouth Tom Partridge, her blimmin' Brylcreem Boy eldest, mentioned to Bobby at one of your lunches that he should train to be an aeroplane mechanic. He told him that if he was going to be called up anyway, he might as well do something he's good at. Then look where that took him—flight engineer on a Lancaster bomber, in and out of Germany every blimmin' night. And the thing crashed coming in to land again with half the engines gone and the tail-end Charlie dead!"

"He survived though, Billy—and now you would never think he'd been hurt. We both know it could have been worse, and whatever happened, he was going to get called up. To be fair, Tom thought Bobby would remain as ground crew and not have to go into any sort of combat. He was trying to help him."

"I know, I know—but what you don't know is what's happened since then."

"What do you mean?" asked Maisie.

"Turns out our Bobby and Tom bumped into each other at an aerodrome somewhere, so they went off for a pint. Bobby asked Tom about his fiancée, that American nurse—you knew her father, from the last war."

"Charles Hayden. Yes. And Patty is a lovely girl. Her parents were very happy to know she came to Chelstone on her days off."

"That's all very well, but Tom Partridge is going to America soon to get married, and he told our Bobby that what with the war being over, American commercial aviation is going to take off." He laughed. "Yeah, I thought that was a bit of a giggle, at first—you know, aviation taking off. Anyway, then Tom informs Bobby he's hoping to work for an American airline, and—I tell you, I wish he kept his big posh trap shut—he says, 'Bob, you should come over there too. They'll be crying out for top-notch aircraft engineers like you. I've got some good contacts, so you could even get into design.' So, that's our Bobby with his head in the clouds. One minute he was saying he wanted to stay in the RAF so he could have the chance of being stationed all over the world, and the next thing you know, he's got it into his noddle that he's going off to America to find his fortune. That's all very well for these Partridge boys because their mum and dad can just sail out there when they like or the boys can afford to come home to see their people. Not the same for the likes of Doreen and me, plus we've got Margaret Rose to think of and our Billy—I mean Will."

Maisie exhaled, blowing out her cheeks. "I see." She rubbed

her forehead. "But, Billy, one step at a time. Bobby is still in the RAF, so cross that bridge when you come to it." She stared at the man who had been at her side during some of her most testing assignments.

"What?" Billy looked at Maisie. "I know that face, miss—something else is up."

"I'd like your help with a new case."

"I thought you said you weren't taking on anything big anymore, just occasionally if it was small, to keep your hand in if something came up of interest."

"You're right. I wasn't."

"Must be important then."

"It is. It concerns four adolescents who witnessed a murder."

"And because whoever reports finding a body is usually the first suspect, they're in trouble because someone, somewhere, thinks they did it—that it?"

"Part of it."

"What's the other part? And I bet it gets nasty here."

"It does—but this is highly classified information."

Billy rolled his eyes. "We always seem to be dealing with highly classified information, don't we? You've no need to tell me that, miss—I've never spoken about what we do for a living to anyone but you. Not even Doreen."

"The four youngsters have been part of a secret civilian network of resistance operatives recruited to thwart the Germans in the case of an invasion."

"Blimey. Who did they see get himself murdered?"

"A Nazi—or at least someone in favor of Hitler."

"Whoever topped the bloke deserves a medal."

"Be that as it may, Billy—but we have to ensure the safety of four young people. Let me explain."

CHAPTER 5

The following day, having returned home to the Dower House the night before, just in time to read Anna a bedtime story, Maisie was seated alongside Lady Rowan Compton in the drawing room at Chelstone Manor. She held the older woman's hand.

"You have been my strength, Maisie," said Rowan, patting Maisie's hand. "Such a strength, a godsend."

"Lord Julian was not feeling well for a long time, though he surprised us all with his determination to—to not be a burden. But you're tired, Rowan—it will be a while before you feel like your old self again."

"I thought he would go on and on, you know, with the odd setback, the occasional week of worry about his chest. He always seemed to come through, didn't he?"

Maisie smiled. "He was a man of valor, of that there is no doubt. They could write a book about him from that wonderful obituary in the *Times*."

Rowan sighed, touching fingers to a lock of silver hair that had escaped the chignon at her neck. "We lost two children, Maisie . . ."

"Yes, I know, Rowan. I understand. It's the ache that remains."

Rowan reached across with her other hand. "If anyone knows,

it's you. When James was killed . . ." She shook her head, continuing even as her voice broke. "We were grief stricken, but I wondered if you could go on. It was an utter tragedy—there's no other word for it, for you to have seen your husband killed and then have the shock cause you to endure the loss of your child, your future."

Maisie bit her lip, remembering James, so excited, laughing, slapping an engineer on the back as he walked toward the brand-new aircraft undergoing tests for flightworthiness. "Don't worry, darling," he had told her. "Don't fret—it's only for about fifteen minutes up in the clouds, putting her through her paces, and I'll be down again. If you get someone to put the kettle on, I'll be back before it comes to the boil." And as she watched him step onto the wing and climb into the cockpit, she whispered, "You promised. You promised me never again—never would you fly again." But now she must offer solace to Rowan, whose daughter, her adventure-loving firstborn, had perished in girlhood, drowning in a local river despite Rowan and Julian diving into the rushing water time and again to save their child. Young James witnessed their attempts, and Maisie knew it had haunted him, boy and man.

"My children and grandchildren, lost to me."

"Rowan—?"

Before Maisie could ask a question, Rowan put her hand to her chest and smiled, as if anxious to deflect dark memories. "Anna has been balm for my aching heart—and Julian loved her, adored that child as if she were indeed his blood granddaughter."

"And she loved him, Rowan—look at how she would often run over here for tea after school and burst straight into his study. Anyone else would have been treated to the sharp edge of his tongue." Maisie looked up at the grandfather clock. "In fact, any minute now we'll hear the kitchen door banging and Mrs. Horsley yelling at her to take off her shoes."

"Yes, but she'll also be smiling and pretending to be upset when one of those gingersnaps goes missing." Rowan was thoughtful. "Gingersnaps—isn't it funny that Anna loves gingersnaps and they were James's favorite too? Do you remember how he used to get his hands slapped for filching them straight out of the oven? Mind you, I don't think our new cook is quite up to Mrs. Crawford's standards."

"New? Mrs. Horsley has been with you for well over ten years now."

"Oh dear, time does fly, doesn't it? And I'm not getting any younger."

Maisie smiled, bracing herself for the conversation she knew she must initiate.

"Rowan—"

"Maisie, I have known you since you were just thirteen years old—do you think I am not aware that you are doing your duty and must broach a troubling subject? I'm ready to discuss the move. It was what Julian wanted, so it is incumbent upon me to do his bidding. After all, this is a Compton family house and we are on Compton family land. With no heirs, he made the very best decision."

"Yes, without doubt he thought of all possible outcomes and took the necessary steps." With a gentle movement, Maisie extracted her hands from Lady Rowan's grasp and lifted a buff-colored folder from the document case at her feet. "Now then, I've had another letter from Mr. Klein—who, thankfully, is well on the mend."

"Not sure if I'm in favor of the son."

"Neither am I, but as long as he's a competent solicitor, we should be in good hands. Mr. Klein has said that while there is not the urgency to put into action the necessary arrangements for you to move from your home, we should look toward the near future. He acknowledges that such plans were rather difficult during Lord Julian's final illness."

"Understatement."

"Indeed." Maisie leafed through more papers and laid out a map of the Chelstone estate. Chelstone Manor was situated at the center of a shallow valley surrounded by farmland managed by the estate's tenant farmers. A long carriage sweep extended past the entrance and the rose-clad Dower House at the top of the hill to the left, followed by the Groom's Cottage—where Frankie Dobbs had once lived—secluded among trees farther down into the valley. Visitors would pass lawns and acres of landscaped gardens before reaching the manor house. "The National Trust would like to take possession before next summer, which they think might be a good year for visitors," she explained.

"Oh dear—that will come around at speed."

"Yes, but remember the refugees? I've instructed Mr. Klein to put it to the Trust that, as we have been approached by the Central British Fund to assist, and have agreed to take in a number of the Jewish refugees from . . . from . . ." Maisie looked at the papers. "It's in Czechoslovakia, yes, here it is—Theresienstadt—then we should be accorded more time until they take over the property per Lord Julian's will. The children will be arriving after they have completed their recovery and immersion into Britain. They are in the Lake District at the moment, mainly boys, but there are a number of girls. As a charitable concern, the Trust should be sensitive to their plight and not press us on time to honor the bequest." Maisie leafed through the documents once more, then looked at Lady Rowan. "I think the children will require at least a year, and I've said I will do my best to arrange education and training, and also place them with families."

"Gosh, how will you do that? Not everyone has the resources to take in another mouth to feed."

"It will be my work for however long it takes." Maisie closed the folder and took Rowan's hand again. "You could live in the garden wing of the house, and the children the newer wing—after all, it has a lot of rooms."

"You mean I'm in the fifteen hundreds and they're in the seventeen hundreds!"

"If we have a few boisterous youngsters, any damage will cost more to repair in the fifteen hundreds, Rowan—though I've been told they are extremely well behaved and could be trusted in the older part of the house if necessary. I think the biggest leap has been in rendering them unafraid of their very shadows, and to go on despite having lost so much. They have been living in a state of terror."

"We all understand that, don't we, Maisie? We've heard such horrific things about what has happened in the occupied countries—it beggars belief. And the weight that so many people have to lift every single day to endure life here in Britain has been devastating enough—really, I know I am so very fortunate, because while bombs fell in the village, none came through this roof."

Maisie looked down at the folder, and pushed it back into the document case.

"We'll take it one step at a time, Rowan, but I will ensure that when the Trust takes over, you will move into a wonderful house with a resplendent garden, and you will be given leave to return to Chelstone Manor whenever you wish."

"And watch people tramping all over our lawns?"

"I'll put up 'keep off the grass' signs."

Rowan smiled. "As long as you're not far away, my dear."

"Don't worry—"

"Oh, my goodness—"

The women were startled by the loud crash of a heavy outer door slamming, followed by the cook shouting, "Those ginger-snaps are straight out of the oven and still hot! Young lady, it will serve you right if you get indigestion!"

"Oh dear—" said Maisie.

"I love it!" said Rowan. "Just like my James when he was a boy. Please don't reprimand her."

"Mummy, Mummy, Mummy! Grandma Rowan! I'm here!"

Maisie's adopted daughter, Anna, rushed into the drawing room clutching three gingersnaps in her hand while holding on to her school satchel with the other. Though she was now ten years of age, she still ran into the arms of those she loved as if she were a much younger child. Anna had first come to Chelstone as an orphaned evacuee, and soon won Maisie's heart. In time Maisie took steps to formally adopt Anna, and immersed her-self in motherhood. Following Maisie's marriage—which took place on the day before the Japanese attacked Pearl Harbor in December 1941—she asked the family solicitor to initiate the necessary steps for Mark to become Anna's legal father. The child was thrilled with her new name, Anna Scott, and along with Maisie's father and stepmother, and her former in-laws, they had become a devoted family.

Having been instructed by Maisie to return to Mrs. Horsley and apologize for taking the gingersnaps, Anna sat next to her mother to tell Lady Rowan about her day, about the new school she loved so much, and the friends she wanted to invite to stay. When Maisie observed that Rowan had absorbed enough of Anna's abundant energy, they said their goodbyes, Maisie taking her daughter's hand for the amble home to the Dower House.

Maisie's father and stepmother, Frankie and Brenda, were once more living at their own local bungalow, though they looked forward to a steady stroll along to the Dower House every day to see their granddaughter. Together with Anna's beloved giant Alsatian dog, Little Emma, they would be waiting to welcome daughter and granddaughter home, for they, too, considered the exuberance Anna brought into their daily round a blessing. As she walked, with Anna swinging their clasped hands back and forth, Maisie harbored a strange sense that in the exchange with Rowan something had tilted out of kilter in her world at the very moment Rowan cut her off as she was about to query what appeared to be an error of speech or memory on the part of the elderly woman. She persuaded herself that it was probably due to talk of Rowan's beloved James, the man whose death Maisie once feared she might never recover. Yes, without doubt, that must have been the moment that unsettled Rowan. The poor woman was in the throes of grief, her mind filled with sadness, so the fact that she might experience a brief error in recollection was understandable. That was it. The past could do that to you—it could upend your day so everything felt as if it were not quite right, as if you had almost completed a difficult jigsaw puzzle, only to realize you were holding a single remaining piece and it did not fit. It was not surprising that Rowan seemed older than her years of late, her mind suffering the shock of losing a beloved husband of many decades; her heart broken anew as she lingered upon the deaths of her two children. And if Maisie were to be honest with herself, what with the war and now an uncomfortable peace, it would be something of a miracle if even a slender slice of life felt as if it were back on an even keel. With these thoughts, she banished her unease.

"Mummy, what time will you be home today?"

"I think I'll be home before you, but if not, it will be shortly afterwards. I'm picking up Uncle Billy from Paddock Wood station at half past nine, and then we've some work to do."

"Will Margaret Rose be coming to stay soon? I've missed her since she moved back to Eltham and started her new school."

Maisie reached for her daughter, understanding the bond that had grown between Anna and young Margaret Rose Beale during the time the Beales lived in the village. "I know you have, sweetheart. I'll speak to Uncle Billy and see what Auntie Doreen says. Margaret Rose is older than you, so she has a lot more homework to do if she wants to pass her school leaving certificate—and if she wants to go on to be a librarian when she leaves school, then she must work hard."

Anna reached for the hairbrush on the dressing table in front of her, and handed it to Maisie, along with a navy blue ribbon. "I don't want to be a librarian."

Maisie plaited her daughter's hair. "I know—and she may change her mind. There's plenty of time."

"I want to be a vet," said Anna. "Then I can look after horses and dogs."

"What about the poor cats?" said Maisie, securing her daughter's hair with the blue ribbon.

"I'll doctor them if they're brought in, but Grandma Brenda says cats can take care of themselves."

"She's got a point there, Anna. Now then, your hair is at last under some control, so we've just enough time to have a quick breakfast and then we must get down to the bus stop."

"When will Daddy be home?"

"Another week, darling. Only six nights and he'll be home."

"He told me I could always learn to be a vet in America if I wanted, because I have two nationalities now. He says they have some very good veterinary colleges there."

Maisie turned her daughter around. "Oh he did, did he? Let's wait and see what happens in a few years. You might change your mind too."

She shook her head. "No, I won't. If I was a vet, I could have saved Lady when she had colic."

Maisie took a deep breath. Although the little white pony had been laid to rest over a year earlier, she could not forget her daughter's racking sobs as she held her close. The child's grief came to a sudden halt one morning, when Anna declared she had dreamed about Lady being all better, running around in a field of rich green grass. Now talk of Lady led to either fond recollection or a determination on Anna's part to save every horse she encountered.

"She was getting on, darling—and Mr. Fuller did everything he could," said Maisie. "Now, chin up—Daddy said that next spring we can think about a new horse for you. Until then, if you want to be a vet, we'd better get you to the bus, because you don't want to miss school and fall behind. Come on, hurry up and eat your breakfast."

Having leashed Little Emma for the walk down the lane to the bus stop, Maisie waved Anna off to school, and was about to leave Little Emma at home, when she changed her mind. "You can come with me today, Em," said Maisie. She locked the house, and opened the rear door of her Alvis motor car, whereupon Little Emma—who she knew very well had the look of a fierce guardian, but the heart of a soft toy—jumped in and curled into her nose-to-tail sleeping position. "I should have found a cat to bring with me," said Maisie, though she also thought that if push came to shove, Emma would protect her family with her life.

Government restrictions on the daily ration of precious petrol meant that Maisie had to plan with care if she wanted to retain the convenience of a motor car during an investigation, hence the plan to meet Billy at Paddock Wood station. From there they would drive to the village of Hallarden.

"Brought the old cherry-hog with you today then, miss."

"I haven't heard you use rhyming slang for a long time, Billy."

He smiled. "My daughter told me straight that it wasn't very funny anymore, so I thought I'd better not embarrass her in front of her friends."

"That'll pass. She's just going through a phase, you know."

"One of many. But she's a good girl." He turned around to look at Emma. "That dog snores a lot."

"So would you if you were rushed off your feet by a ten-year-old with too much energy."

"Talking of kids with too much energy—"

"Apparently they were from the orphanage—it's now called Hallarden Children's Home."

"Bit old for that, aren't they?"

"Yes and no. They told me they thought they would be asked to leave soon, given they are old enough to go out to work, but I know any children's home has a duty of care toward their charges due to the fact that they are all orphans. I managed to take each of them aside and found out that Jim and Grace had families who were killed in the Blitz on London while they were evacuated.

One was born out of wedlock—that's Archie—and given up. I'm not sure about Mary—she's a bit secretive."

"Sounds like they were all worn out with keeping their secrets, and for a start, they shouldn't have gone telling you about what they did in the war—or what they were trained to do."

"You're right on both counts. They can be a bit mouthy, but I think that's to bolster their resolve—in my estimation, they're really exhausted and very scared. But to be fair, I put some pressure on them."

"Are we going to the children's home first?"

Maisie shook her head, then pulled over into a lay-by.

"What's up, miss?"

"I want to know more about them, but I don't want to alert anyone to the fact that I am looking into the lives of those four specifically."

"Is that because someone else might be waiting for you to inquire, and you think the person in charge might run the flag up the pole and let them know you've been to see them?"

"That's the measure of it, Billy."

"Who is it?"

"MacFarlane."

"Blimey." Billy took a deep breath and whistled as he exhaled. "Why do you reckon that?"

Maisie was thoughtful, staring out of the window for a moment.

"I think he wants to ensure that nothing gets out about the deceased, which is one thing, but he also wants to find out how much the four youngsters know. I would say he wants to get to them before anyone else, which suggests there's another person or department looking for them. There's also the man's killer—was it a hired assassin, or someone closer? Plus, of course they know a fair amount about our secret wartime defenses, and from what they've said, it's clear the government is in the process of destroying evidence of their existence. I knew a lot about what went on overseas, Billy—but I knew nothing about what I suppose you could term 'domestic resistance.'"

"But what if the government is mothballing these secret places just in case?"

"Of another war?"

"Of any pushing and shoving that goes on between countries before they go to war, miss." Billy regarded Maisie as he turned and ruffled Emma's ears; the dog was now awake, nose forward, looking from Maisie to Billy as they spoke. "Or MacFarlane might be trying to protect someone else."

Maisie sighed. "Billy, you know your friend, the reporter? Do you think he could wangle his way in, perhaps think up a story? An angle, or whatever they call it."

"It's an idea. I reckon I could talk to him. Tricky though, because he'll know there's something bigger in it if I ask him to go to the children's home to talk to the superintendent. And he can't mention names, or she'll know—because let's face it, they've gone missing, though he could say he had word of that from someone he knows." He shook his head. "No, on second thoughts, I reckon it's too risky."

They were quiet for a few moments, both considering what might come next.

"I didn't want it to come to this."

"I know."

"Billy—"

"We're going to have to break into the home or something like that, aren't we?"

"I think this is going to be one of those cases where we change our minds about the best way forward every now and again. Let's keep all possible paths open. We'll have more information later. I'm sure something will come up after we've been to the Sandstone Avenue estate—where the Nazi lived."

Maisie parked the motor car some distance along the avenue, a broad boulevard with trees on either side of the road. She imagined that in summer, driving along the avenue would be like making your way through a verdant tunnel with shafts of dappled sunlight piercing the canopy above. She suspected the people who lived in such a place might have felt safer than most during the war, though anyone living in Kent, whether rich or poor, would have heard the bombers flying above at night to target London, the docks and the capital's grand buildings that were beloved the world over. And on the return journey to their bases in occupied France, the Luftwaffe released any remaining bombs to fall across the market towns, small villages, rural farms and isolated hamlets peppered across the Garden of England, earning Kent the nickname "Bomb Alley." In truth, nowhere in Britain had been safe. Even the home of a man whom the squatters had tagged a Nazi could have been bombed. She reminded herself that it worked both ways—as anyone living in Berlin, Hamburg or Dresden knew only too well. When she had pointed out the devastation in Germany to her stepmother, Brenda's retort, hands on hips, was a curt "They started the war and got behind their Mr. Hitler, Maisie, so it wasn't our fault we had to fight back, was it?"

Having arrived at the property, Maisie walked toward the gate with Emma, while Billy used a pair of binoculars to scan the perimeter of lawns and shrubbery visible from the land boundary.

"This gate isn't padlocked, Billy."

"Someone slipped up, didn't they? So, we're going in, are we?"

"Might as well—I don't want to drive all the way home with nothing to show for my day."

"Got an excuse, you know, if we're apprehended?"

"I'm an interested buyer and I heard this property was for sale. Did you see the sign outside the adjacent house? Easy mistake to make."

"Right you are. That's as good as any I could come up with. And no one's going to argue with you, not with Emma by your side."

"As long as they don't see her tail wagging."

Opening the gate, Maisie proceeded along what would have once been termed the "carriage sweep" toward the house. Lady Rowan had sighed when a representative of the National Trust visited Chelstone Manor soon after Lord Julian decided that offering the manor as a bequest would be an admirable solution to the death duties problem. "Lovely view coming up the driveway, Your Ladyship. And not a bad walk from the station or bus stop."

"He called it a driveway!" Lady Rowan had complained. "I was about to put him right and tell him that when I came to the manor as a young bride, it was in a carriage and four, but Julian raised his eyebrow to shut me up!"

Reaching the front of the house, Billy and Maisie turned and took account of their surroundings.

"Quiet, eh, miss?"

"If the owner lived here alone, you would expect it. But look— the grass has been cut in the past day or two."

"Looks like a cricket pitch, what with the way it's been mowed with them stripes." Billy looked up at the sky. "Anyway, I'm glad we chose a fine day—wouldn't want to be sloshing around here in the rain."

"Come on, let's walk to the back of the house."

Maisie suspected that the Georgian house had been subject to some modernization inside. The exterior was in good order. The drains were clear and working, gutters were new and the window frames appeared to have been painted in recent years, which surprised her, because builders, painters and decorators had been called up into the army. Older men in the construction trade were required to report for duty to help with the recovery of wounded during the bombings. If a house had been half destroyed, it was a builder who would know the best way to reach the dead, dying and injured without causing the other half of the property to come down or the dwellings on either side to become even more unstable. Now those same builders were either engaged in demolition, or recruited for the construction of new homes. It wasn't hard for an able-bodied returning soldier to find work.

"Lucky old him, being able to get the place painted," said Billy. "He must have had some pull in high places."

"My thoughts exactly," replied Maisie.

They continued walking around the mansion, stopping to comment on this or that aspect, or the fact that they had not yet been intercepted. Having reached the rear of the property, Maisie and Billy came to an abrupt standstill.

"Oh my, look at that."

"What was he, a cousin of the king or something?" asked Billy.

"Look over there—the estate extends far into the woodland and then around the back of the other houses. It was probably the original mansion on the estate, and then land was sold off at some point to build other houses along the avenue."

"Probably to pay off debts."

"The properties along the avenue are all quite large, but they look as if they were built about twenty years ago." Maisie was thoughtful. "I bet the heir was killed in the last war, and when his parents died, someone had to sell off the land to pay death duties."

"And that's one reason I'm glad I don't come from money—there's nothing in the Beale coffers for the government to take when I die," said Billy. "Look over there—I feel sorry for the poor bloke who has to go up and down that there back lawn with his mower and roller. You could put a herd of cattle in there and the grass still wouldn't be kept down."

The rear of the house comprised a wide stone terrace with statuary, steps leading down to what appeared to be a labyrinth created by the planting of low rosemary hedges, interspersed with rose bushes, and a fountain in the middle. Maisie turned and began to walk up steps toward the bank of French windows giving access to the terrace. She leaned against the window, cupping a hand around her eyes to see into a reception room. Until this point, Emma had been quiet as she padded alongside her mistress, but now she whimpered.

"Getting fed up, is she, miss?"

"Dogs are sensitive creatures—and Alsatians more so than most. I would imagine she knows something untoward happened here." Maisie reached down to stroke Emma's head. "You know, Billy, I think Archie told me a lie. He said that he was delivering the newspaper to the front door of the house, and he could see what was happening inside due to the French windows. But there aren't any at the front of the house—they're here at the back."

"He was having a snoop around."

"But was it an innocent curiosity? Or was he looking for something?"

Billy rubbed his chin. "If people had been here, there would have been motors parked at the front of the house, so perhaps he thought he'd have a gander to see who it was, especially if the cars were big and posh—you know how boys are with motor cars."

"And newspapers are usually delivered first thing in the morning, not in the evening when a party is in progress."

"We should have a special word with Archie, I think."

"A very special word. Anyway, Billy, let's continue on round. I'm not finished here. And I want to find that other building they described."

Leaving the terrace, Maisie and Billy proceeded to the eastern flank of the house and along a gravel path giving access to a side entrance.

"Look at that, miss—through those rhododendron bushes. You can see from here—I think it's a garage and a couple of sheds. Miss—"

Maisie was concentrating on the side door to the house, but looked up. "The squatters mentioned picking a lock on one of the sheds—but look here, Billy, this door is unlocked. It probably leads to the kitchens."

"Blimey. What d'you think?"

"You hold Emma and keep watch. She might whimper a bit, but just stroke her on the head and she'll be alright. I'll go in."

"What shall I say if someone comes around?"

"Explain that you and your friend were walking past the house and happened to see the 'For Sale' sign, so you thought you'd take a quick look. There was no answer at the door, so you decided the owner had moved pending the property being . . . being available for prospective owners to look at."

"Miss, one word out of my mouth with my dyed-in-the-wool Cockney accent and they'll know that no one I'm friends with could afford this gaff."

"If they question it, tell them they obviously didn't see your most recent moving picture, and it's been a very lucrative time for the British in—what's that place called? Hollywood? Tell them that, and add that our money is as good as anyone else's."

"Yours might be, miss, but I'm not sure the story will fly."

Maisie passed Emma's leash to Billy. "If push comes to shove, give it a try. I'll be about fifteen minutes."

"More like half an hour or more, the size of this place."

CHAPTER 6

Having made her way through the kitchen, Maisie walked toward the entrance hall with its extravagant black-and-white Art Deco tiles, and stopped for a moment to get her bearings before entering each of the downstairs reception rooms, where she lingered for a few moments before deciding there was nothing of interest. She did not want to waste time, so her priority was locating the owner's bedroom, his dressing room, his study and the library.

As she suspected, the interior had indeed been modernized. Good money had been spent on maintaining a balance between respect for the past and a nod to the future, though she found some of the decoration to be austere, with none of the comfort a woman's touch might provide. She went from room to room in a quest to get the measure of the owner, a man who was—if Archie, the Artful Dodger among the group of young squatters, was to be believed—a follower of one of the most brutal leaders ever to have walked the earth.

Maisie came upon a door where she had not expected a room to be situated. It was set between two floors, so it was neither on the ground floor nor the first, but accessed through a door at the top of the initial half-flight of stairs. She was not surprised to discover the door was locked, so she reached into her shoulder bag and brought out a small velvet drawstring pouch that was now a little threadbare from many years of use. She pulled out a set of tools, selected one and knelt down to inspect the lock. It took a moment or two of working the pointed tool before she smiled, maneuvered it one more time and heard the tell-tale click she was hoping for. Coming to her feet, she opened the door and entered the owner's large study.

At first she found nothing of note. A few old newspapers had been set on the desk, along with a book about famous Italian gardens. The drawers were unlocked, but again there was nothing of significance to be discovered. The desk had been set at an angle, so Maisie sat down on the oak captain's chair, and as she looked around, she realized the position gave a view of both the front of the house and part of the side. A seated man could just about view the sheds and garage, but tires would be heard crunching along the gravel, so with a turn of the head he could see a motor car approaching the front of the house. Anyone visiting on foot could not do so in silence, unless they chose to walk across the lawns.

There was a bookcase behind the chair, two more before her on the other side of the window and a smaller one to the right of the door, which left enough space for a round table and two leather armchairs. A few feet beyond the armchairs, a selection of photographs had been framed and mounted on the wall, so Maisie pushed back the desk chair and walked across to look at the images. Throughout her work as an investigator, if she were in a house at the scene of a crime, she had always been drawn to photographs, for they held the story of a person's closest associations. Family members, professional colleagues, lovers, locations, smiles and frowns; all were caught in the moment, revealing something about those gathered, whether there was joy, adoration, discomfort, despair, ease or even hatred.

"Well, well, well—what a nice crowd the honorable man mixed with. Hmmm."

Though she could not have named each of the friends standing alongside the owner of the house in one of the larger photographs, she recognized four as members of the aristocracy; two lords, a sir and, yes, that woman was a countess. Herr Adolf Hitler was at the center of the group, and if she were not mistaken, the photograph had been taken at the Berlin Olympic Games, in 1936.

"Oh dear," said Maisie, as she stared at another photograph. Hawkin-Price was standing alongside the Duke and Duchess of Windsor, with another man on the other side of the newly married couple. Maisie recognized the face, but it took a minute or two to put a name to the smiling man—yes, it was a royal cousin, the German Duke of Coburg. The British royal surname had been changed from the Germanic Saxe-Coburg-Gotha to Windsor during the Great War, when the King decided it would be a good idea to remove any reminder of the monarchy's German ancestry, given the carnage at the Western Front and the great numbers of British youth perishing at the hands of the Kaiser's army. Queen Victoria had died in the arms of her grandson, the Kaiser.

There were other photographs taken on excursions, at elegant soirees and during what seemed to be hunting parties, before Maisie alighted on another photograph that could confirm her suspicion regarding the reason for sale of land to a building concern. A much younger Hawkin-Price was standing next to a man who was perhaps a few years older, with the duo bearing enough similarities for Maisie to conclude that they were either brothers or cousins. Whereas the older man's rank badges revealed him to be an army major, Jonathan Hawkin-Price was a junior officer. She would have to discover the truth of the matter, but it seemed her initial impression regarding the more recent history of the property was correct, that the house and land around it had once been part of a grander estate, but following the passing of the wealthy parents and older son—the immediate heir—a substantial acreage had to be sold off to meet crushing death duties due to the exchequer.

Having studied each photograph—and not finding anything endearing about the Honorable Mr. Hawkin-Price—Maisie turned to the first bookcase, where she concluded the owner was a widely read man on a broad range of historical subjects.

Maisie moved to another bookcase, where a line of tomes caught her attention.

"Ah, what have we here?" said Maisie, tapping three books shelved together.

She took out *The Communist Manifesto* by Karl Marx and leafed through the heavily underlined book. The next two were also annotated—both *The Principles of Communism* by Friedrich Engels and *The State and Revolution* by Vladimir Lenin were filled with the honorable reader's penciled thoughts about the content—and it was clear he was not impressed and at times the reading even rendered him angry.

Maisie ensured the books were replaced in order and searched for another book she suspected would be in close proximity, but was taken by surprise when she found not one, but several copies—one in German, one in English and the third in Italian. It was the German edition that caused Maisie to gasp. Even as she held the book in her hand, she felt as if her fingers might burst into flames. *Mein Kampf* had been personally inscribed by the author as a gift to the owner of the grand house in which she was committing the crime of trespass. She was handling a book that had once been touched by Adolf Hitler, and she felt as if every last cell in her body had been sullied by the experience. She dropped the book as if it were hot coal from the fire, but picked it up and set it back on the shelf before leaving the study, not even bothering to lock the door as she departed.

I must cleanse myself, she thought, as she ran down the stairs, across the entrance hall with the black-and-white Art Deco tiles so bold they seemed to be shouting at her. She had been caught out, a pawn on the board of a very ugly game. "I knew there was evil here as soon as I walked into that room," Maisie admonished herself aloud. "Shame on me for pressing on. Shame on me. I knew better. Much better." She continued the personal reprimand as she hurried along the corridor to the kitchen and her exit—straight into the back of Billy Beale.

"Oh, there you are—oops, mind how you step. Miss Dobbs, this is Mr. Chalmers, the head gardener here," said Billy, turning to face her again. "I told him you were interested in the property because you were thinking of moving out this way, but apparently we've got it all wrong—it's the house next door that's for sale." Unseen by the gardener, Billy winked as he spoke to her.

Maisie put her hand on her chest to still her breathing and felt Emma's pointed nose nudging her. She knelt down, not wanting the gardener to notice any anxiety on her part. Emma licked her face, something she would do to Anna if the child ever showed a sign of being out of sorts.

"I'm so very sorry, Mr. Chalmers," said Maisie, coming to her feet. "It was quite the exit, tripping over the step there. And I suppose it was rather a cheek, going in when we saw the door was left ajar—but you know, my late father-in-law, Lord Julian Compton, always said one has to strike while the iron is hot, and I thought this was too good a chance to let it pass."

"Lord Julian, eh?" said Chalmers, rubbing his stubbled chin.

He nodded toward Billy. "Mr. Beale here said you had to stop the motor car anyway to let the dog out, so you walked along the avenue."

Maisie smiled, making an obvious point of looking around. "It's lovely here. I must say, it's very quiet, so peaceful. Beautiful gardens. And please don't tell me you have to keep up this entire property on your own. The lawns are perfect, even given the weather we've had."

The gardener touched the peak of his flat cap by way of acknowledging the compliment. "The master's away at the moment. Gives the indoors staff a chance to have a bit of a rest. The other two gardeners—only three of us now, all told—are at the bottom of those lawns, next to the woods where you can't see them. They're mending the fencing where some youngsters took it down. There's the chauffeur, but he went off to get some special oil for the motor cars. Him and his wife live above the garages— she's the housekeeper, but she's away too, visiting her mother."

Maisie knew it was a common arrangement, having the chauffeur live above the garage. George, the Comptons' chauffeur, lived above the garages at Chelstone Manor.

"Do you live on the estate too?" she asked.

"Tied cottage, on one of the farms owned by Mr. Hawkin-Price. Very handy—I only have to walk across those fields and I'm at work." He pointed into the distance, as if to indicate the bucolic surroundings of his daily walk to and from the estate. "Anyway, I reckon I should lock up this kitchen door—we don't want squatters, do we?"

"Quite right, sir. If a door or even a window is left open, anyone entering can claim squatter's rights, so it's just as well I'm not a squatter, isn't it?" added Maisie.

The gardener raised an eyebrow. "I daresay you two and your

dog should get on your way. I'll walk down to the gates with you—blimmin' local nippers, having a go at them again. I'll have to get the police back here to keep an eye on the place."

"The police?"

Maisie noticed the gardener begin to run his teeth along the side of his lower lip, and understood it was an involuntary movement made the second he revealed something she guessed he would rather have kept quiet about.

"Nothing special," said the gardener, regaining his composure. "Local bobby comes around and has a gander at the place when the owner is away, on account of children thinking it's a big adventure to break in."

"Really—you've mentioned the local children a couple of times. Are they that mischievous?"

"Not the locals, but there's the old orphanage. They might have changed the name, but they can't change the likes of the nippers they've got in there. And then we had the evacuees."

If Maisie were a dog, she knew her hackles would have gone up, and as if intuiting her feelings, Emma gave a low growl and her thick coat was indeed proud across her withers.

"Or it could be local children taking advantage of the outsiders' presence—passing blame around," said Maisie, as they reached the gate. "Anyway, thank you, Mr. Chalmers. You've been most kind. And again, my apologies for the trespass—I assumed the house was for sale because someone had died." She looked back at the house, then at the gardener. "It has that sort of look about it, doesn't it?"

"Not for long, madam. Not for long. There will be someone home soon enough."

Maisie and Billy bid the gardener farewell and went on their way, walking along the road, toward the motor car. As before,

Emma leaped into the back seat and curled up as soon as Maisie unlocked and opened the vehicle.

"Now what?" said Billy, taking the passenger seat next to Maisie.

"The chauffeur. I want to have a word or two with the chauffeur and his wife, and I'd dearly love to see inside those sheds."

"But the thing is, how do we know those squatting saucepan lids—sorry—I mean how do we know the squatting *kids* are telling the truth? This place doesn't look as if someone was murdered here, does it? And people around these parts would have known if a bloke like Hawkin-Price had gone to meet his maker, wouldn't they?"

"I wonder . . ." Maisie tapped the steering wheel as she stared ahead. "Billy, I think I'm going to give Caldwell a telephone call."

"Not him. I mean, he's alright, as a bloke, but—Detective Chief Superintendent Caldwell? There's usually more egg on his tie than I've seen on anyone's plate for the last six years."

"You've got a point, but I've discovered he's good at his job, and we get on well now."

"Rather you than me. Anyway, did you find anything inside the gaff?"

Maisie started the motor car. "Did I find anything inside? Wait until I tell you about the photographs—if nothing else, they persuaded me that the party witnessed by our little friend Archie really did happen, and that leads me to believe there was also a death."

"Yeah, but where's the honorable bloke, and who did it?"

Maisie pulled out onto the empty road, and turned the motor car. "Could have been one of the hoity-toity Nazi friends with a weapon in his hand. Or a hired assassin. Or someone else entirely."

"Hired assassin? Blimey, I don't know if we should get involved then."

Maisie looked at Billy. "I haven't told you about the hoity-toity friends yet, if you think an assassin is something to worry about." Maisie shook her head. "You will be shocked. But let's get on—and in the meantime, I think you should plan a visit to the children's home, so you have it up your sleeve, should it become necessary. I haven't quite decided yet."

"If it comes to that, I'll need a good story."

Maisie stopped the motor car as they entered Hallarden, pulling onto a grass verge. "There's a telephone kiosk over there—I'll place a call to Caldwell now, and with a bit of luck I'll catch him. Dependent upon what he says, we'll decide whether I should drop you at the children's home, where you could present yourself as a reporter for the *Sunday Pictorial*. Your guise is that you want to know how the children are faring, now the war is over and the evacuees have gone home. You could ask what they think about the future of children's homes, especially given the housing shortage. You could quote the fact that tens of thousands of pre-fabricated dwellings are being imported from America and—"

"Are they?"

"Yes."

"Anything else you know that I don't?"

Maisie tapped the side of her nose. "Have a think about your questions. There's a notebook and pencil in my document case. And could you open a rear window for Emma? I'll be back in a minute or two."

Maisie nudged open the door to the telephone kiosk while she waited for her call to be put through to Detective Chief

Superintendent Caldwell of Scotland Yard's Murder Squad. The kiosk was musty, and a cold condensation seemed to mist every window as soon as she began to dial.

"Miss Dobbs—or is it Mrs. Scott? Can't for the life of me keep up with anything these days. I've not seen you since our little V-J Day party here at the Yard."

"Good afternoon, Detective Chief Superintendent. That was a nice get-together, wasn't it? Thank you for inviting me to join you."

"What with everyone being pally around the world again, we might as well have raised a glass together. Pity it doesn't feel like we've won anything though, that's all I can say."

"You're not the first to say that."

"Right then, you're not calling me out of the blue to be jawing about how nice it would be to get your hands on a decent loaf of bread without it falling apart because they're making up the flour with chalk. What's on your mind?"

Maisie could not help but smile. Caldwell never missed a beat. Niceties for about a minute, then down to business—and she respected him for it.

"Hallarden, Kent, about five miles from Paddock Wood. Local manor house and grounds, probably used to be a more extensive estate. Owner—the Honorable Mr. Hawkin-Price. Have you been asked to look into a murder at the estate? The victim would be named as Hawkin-Price."

The line was silent.

"Caldwell?"

"I'm here, I'm here."

"I can't hear papers rustling, so you're not having to look him up. What's going on?"

Silence again.

"Cald—"

"Alright, alright, Miss Dobbs. I'm just thinking."

"And?"

"Trying to make all the dots join up."

"And? I know you have your secrets, but could you just do a little sharing of intelligence?"

"I could ask you the same question."

"I asked first."

"If you come back as a dog, you'll be a terrier."

"If I come back as a dog, I might bite."

"Very funny. Right, here's why I was having a think. A few weeks ago I received a telephone call from the local police down there. They'd had a call or two come in from the supervisor at a local children's home, who said four of their inmates—"

"It's an orphanage, not a prison, Superintendent. They're not inmates."

"Well, whatever they call them. Orphans. Four of the older ones had run off. The chief copper was worried because a night or two earlier, a couple of the locals said they'd heard shots coming from the home of your Hawkin-Price chappie. Apparently it was reported because people were a bit upset with Hawkin-Price and the fact that he'd had some parties during the war and it was a bit noisy, what with motor cars leaving in the early hours of the morning and people not supposed to go anywhere in a motor car—they complained that it was one rule for the rich and another for everyone else."

"It's a well-to-do neighborhood."

"Yes, yet you and I both know there's a big difference between the landowner and the aspiring bank manager and it's the bank manager who gets huffy because he wants to be a toff but isn't."

"Be that as it may. But what happened after the complaints were made?"

"Couple of local bobbies went over and asked to look around. No Hawkin-Price in residence, and only a chauffeur and gardener about. They said it was all quiet, though some youngsters had been seen running from the property one evening and had broken a fence near the woods—the gardener thought they were just having a snoop, you know, wanting to see how the other very big half lives. Hawkin-Price is hardly seen in the village, so from what I've heard, most people don't care about him. But here's the thing—when the coppers arrived, the gardener was hosing down part of the path, cleaning it up. Now, I reckon that was part of his job, keeping the paths clean, and to be fair, they said he was cleaning right around to the veranda."

"Did you do anything?"

"Nearly there, Miss Dobbs—let me get to the point. I didn't like the sound of it. If I had that radar-scanning thing in my brain, it would have been going beep-beep-beep. You know what it's like when you get a feeling about these things. So I thought I'd take a run down and see for myself, ask a few questions. I'd called for the motor car to come round and was just about to leave, when I had someone on the blower, a higher-up telling me that it was nothing to be concerned about and that the honorable man should not be investigated. It was a question of security." He paused. Maisie did not interrupt. "But he asked me if I would set up a search for the absconding orphans, because it wouldn't do anyone any good if the press found out about children going missing, what with the fact that they're having enough trouble with children anyway on account of the war, and so many of them missing school and whatnot, you know, not being able to settle down." Another pause. "I wouldn't mind, but I'm a Murder

Squad detective with years behind me on the job, not a nannying service."

"Who made the call to you—do you know?"

The line was silent.

"I promise I will not tell a soul, Caldwell—but given what I've discovered here, I think it would be wise to let me know. If there's no murder, I am sure the press will be very interested in what I've discovered about our Honorable Jonathan Hawkin-Price, and indeed that four young people are now being pursued by a senior detective with the murder squad, who we know has much better things to do."

"Now then, don't be like that. I was just having a think. We've done well, you and me, since we decided to share and share alike." Another pause. "You have got to keep this to yourself, alright?"

"Promise."

"It was your friend and mine, Robbie MacFarlane."

"I thought it might be."

"So I reckon this is where we both have to throw in the towel on this one and leave well enough alone—and I can't be looking out for errant youngsters anyway. I've got enough going on with a couple of nasty murders here in London—and since they've started clearing the bombsites, certain deceased have come to light with injuries suggesting they were knocked off by someone closer to home than the Luftwaffe over their heads. War gave a few people a golden opportunity to get rid of a fellow man or woman who was getting on their nerves."

"I'm sorry to hear that."

"Oh, you knew, Miss Dobbs. Now then, I've got to get on here. Mum's the word on what I've just told you—alright? You promised."

"Don't worry, I'll keep my word."

"Right you are. I wish you'd keep your word about spending more time at home with your family."

"You won't hear from me ever again after December the thirty-first—those family commitments, you see."

"Promise?"

"I promise."

The call was disconnected. Maisie set the receiver on its cradle, and left the telephone kiosk, thankful that Caldwell had not pursued the question of what she might know about Hawkin-Price. She did not hurry back to the motor car, though she knew Billy was watching her as she left the kiosk.

"I reckon the way you strolled back here to the motor car, that chat with Caldwell gave you food for thought, miss," said Billy, as Maisie took her place in the driver's seat.

"It did. Yes, indeed it gave me food for thought."

"Are we still going to the children's home?"

"No—and I had a feeling I might change my mind on that one. I believe any knocking on that particular door will go straight back to someone else and I'm not sure how he's connected yet."

"Go on—who is it?"

"As I suspected—Robbie MacFarlane." She recounted the conversation with Caldwell.

"Blimey," said Billy. "So, we've got one of MacFarlane's secret departments involved, as well as a possible assassin, Scotland Yard being told to let go, a load of Nazi toffs and four orphans still wet behind the ears are on the run. There's a recipe for trouble if ever I heard it. What shall we do next?"

"We look after the most vulnerable."

"That's what I was hoping you'd say. Where will you take them?"

"I'll put them with someone who can keep them in line and occupied."

Billy laughed. "If I'm right about who you mean, those poor nippers won't know what's hit them."

Maisie started the motor car. "Neither will MacFarlane if he tries to cross Priscilla's threshold." She looked at Billy and smiled. "Priscilla can be very protective. She loves mothering people. Meeting Douglas and having Tom, Timothy and Tarquin was the making of her. It brought her back from the abyss after losing her brothers in the last war, then her parents in the flu epidemic. Now her sons are grown, she snaps up any opportunity to take on the mantle of caring again. She knows what it is to fall down, and I think she's become very good at picking people up again, especially the younger ones. Anyway, all being well, the current guest will be returning to his family soon."

"I hope so, miss. I really hope so," said Billy. "I'm a bit nervous, to be honest with you. I don't know what to say to him. Doreen will be much better—I reckon I'll leave it to her. I mean, I don't know how to say anything without him thinking I'm telling him what to do. I was in the army and I went through a war, but I never had what he had. I saw terrible things, but I—I dunno, was it the same? Was it worse? I can't even begin to think about what he went through, what was done to him. Not without getting angry and wanting to scream 'Look what you did to my boy! Call yourselves human beings?'"

"I don't think it's a question of what was harder or whether his war was worse than your war—the outcome is along the same lines. And as we both know, there's no perfect solution, though there are a few things that come to mind."

"And what are they? I need all the help I can get or I know I'll lose my son forever. I've got another chance, and I don't want to mess it up."

Maisie was aware that Billy was looking away, staring at the view from the passenger window. He wiped a broad hand across his damp cheeks.

"Time. Time and love, Billy. Add a bit of stability and a routine, some fresh air, giving him a chance to talk about what happened, but only if he wants to. And patience. A very good measure of patience. Andrew Dene will take care of his body—but those other elements form the prescription for his mind and heart. That's the way to keep the dragon mollified."

"The dragon?"

"That's how Priscilla described it once. We all have our dragons, we who have seen war, and though the dragon doesn't die, we can stop his tail thrashing around inside us. We can live a good life."

"I'd like to kill the bloody thing."

"Me too, Billy. Me too."

They said nothing for a while, until Billy began winding down the window next to the passenger seat.

"Another dragon I'd like to kill is the one giving your dog's insides a nasty dose of wind."

Maisie laughed, though she kept her thoughts to herself. *Oh, Billy, you always find some humor at the darkest of times, and bless you for it.*

CHAPTER 7

"My teacher says that next year we'll all be taking our eleven-plus exams. She said they were the exams to . . . to *assess* us, then they would know where to stream everyone in the class so we could move on and move up." Anna sipped a cup of tea, one hand holding the cup, the other on Emma's head. "Did you have to take the eleven-plus, Mummy?"

Maisie set down her cup. "No, we had a different sort of test called the 'School Certificate,' which was awarded at the age of sixteen, but a lot of my schoolfriends were leaving school by the time they were twelve. I left at thirteen, but I took my exams later, when I was working. The test you're going to take is brand new. When it's done and you get your results, we will see where you might go to school next." Maisie smiled. "Anna, I know you're feeding Emma crumbs from the table, but please hold your cup with both hands or you'll spill the tea. And Emma won't starve— in fact, she's getting a bit round."

"She likes treats," said Anna, now clasping her cup with both hands and staring at Maisie. "Mummy, which school do you think I will I go to after my exam?"

"Well, we have some very good choices. Daddy was right about the international school, wasn't he? You like it there, so you could stay with the friends you've made until you're sixteen, if you like."

"Hmmm—it is nice to have two friends who catch the same bus, and I like everyone at the school—though I was a bit sad when Alexandra and Beatrice had to move when their fathers left London to work in another country. The teachers are really nice though."

Maisie picked up her cup and sipped the tea. "We can talk about it when you get your results. If you pass, you might decide to transfer to a girls' grammar school, either in Tonbridge or Tunbridge Wells. At any of those schools you could work hard and aim for university."

Anna tapped the table with both hands, decisive about her future. "I'll do that, because Daddy said I will need to go to a university to be a veterinary surgeon."

"And there go Anna Scott's brain cells—I can see them moving around inside your head," said Maisie, smiling as she watched her child.

"Would I still have to take the eleven-plus if I want to be a vet in America?"

"You have to take a lot more than the eleven-plus to go to university anywhere, my darling." She pushed back her chair. "So, one step at a time—just one step at a time. And there are very good places to study to be a veterinary surgeon here, you know—there's the Royal College in London, and I believe that in Bristol they established a school of veterinary science even before they had a medical school. Anyway, let's not get too ahead of ourselves. How about getting on with your homework?"

Distracted by the telephone ring echoing along the hallway, Anna leaped from her chair. "That might be Daddy! I'll answer it!"

Maisie called out as her daughter left the kitchen and sprinted toward the study. "Anna, it's not Daddy, please, don't—"

Before Maisie could intervene, Anna had answered the

telephone in the library and could be heard greeting the caller, "Oh hello, Uncle Robbie. Yes, Mummy's here—just a minute, I'll get her."

Maisie closed her eyes, whispering under her breath. "Blast!"

"It's Uncle Robbie, Mummy. Not Daddy."

"I know, Darling. Daddy probably hasn't even arrived in Washington yet." Maisie took the receiver from her daughter. "Anna, run upstairs and change out of your school uniform." She took a deep breath.

"Robbie, lovely to hear from you. To what do I owe the pleasure?"

"That daughter of yours will be sixteen before you know it, Maisie. Almost time to double the locks on the doors."

"Or circle the wagons, as Mark says."

There was a beat of silence. Maisie waited.

"Right, enough of that. You're avoiding me."

"Avoiding you? Not me, I wouldn't do that."

"Oh yes you would! You're avoiding me because you know I want some information."

"Robbie, if my memory serves me well, the last time we spoke, it was me coming to you on a mission for information. Is this about Will Beale?" she offered, in an effort to deflect the direction of MacFarlane's inquiry. She heard an audible sigh echo in the receiver.

"Robbie?"

"You also mentioned some squatters."

"Squatters? I—oh yes, I remember now. All moved on, I think. Storm in a teacup. And as far as I know, it's the same everywhere with the many homeless people—they move on until they find somewhere a little more permanent. A decommissioned army barracks, for example."

"Maisie?"

"Yes?"

"Do you know where those four children have disappeared to?"

"I have more pressing things to consider—reuniting Billy and Doreen with Will is high on my list."

"You wouldn't—"

"If any information comes my way, I'll let you know."

"One thing."

"Yes?"

"I only want to help them, hen. I don't want to get them into more trouble, but there are bigger people than me involved."

Maisie was quiet. Could she trust MacFarlane? Every cell in her body seemed to be screaming at her to proceed with caution. No, she would wait. Gather more information, that's what Maurice would have said. Leave no stone unturned. Make no pre-emptive moves unless your back is against the wall. Press forward with care.

"I know, Robbie. There are always bigger people involved."

Maisie returned to London the following day, stopping first at the Pimlico flat, where she was not at all surprised to see Mary had remained very much in charge, her three friends well under her thumb. Maisie had telephoned first, using the special code of three rings before ending the call and dialing again, placing the call to let her new tenants know she was on her way.

"You've kept the flat nice and tidy—thank you."

"She had me cleaning the toilet this morning," said Archie.

"Didn't do you any harm, did it, Arch?" said Mary.

"I swept the floors and under the chairs and Gracie went around with the duster," said Jim.

"And when we pulled down them blinds, we noticed the people what was here before hadn't cleaned them, so we did it," added Mary.

"Very nice it is too, thank you very much. Right, let's sit down and have a chat," said Maisie.

"I can make a pot of tea," said Mary. "But we've got no milk."

"It's just as well I brought a bottle with me and some home-made bread along with a few other comestibles." Maisie tapped the shopping bag she had brought with her.

"Any more of that chocolate?" said Jim. "It's not as good as British chocolate, but it's still nice to have a bite."

"Not many people are connoisseurs like you, Jim." Maisie raised an eyebrow and smiled at the young man. "If you're not too choosy, I may have some next week, but let's press on, shall we? And thank you, Mary—a cup of tea would be lovely."

Mary tapped Gracie on the shoulder. The younger girl stood up, took the bag from Maisie and went into the kitchen.

"I've been to the house—the one where you said you saw the owner killed, and I've some questions, especially for you, Archie." She waited, taking note of the boy's heightened color, and the fact that he did not look up at her. "Archie, you said that when you went to the house, you were about to push the newspaper through the letterbox and that's when you saw the party full of Nazis through the French doors. Is that right?"

The boy blushed even deeper, giving a half-nod. Jim looked away, while Mary came to her feet, announcing that she would give Gracie a hand in the kitchen.

"Sit down, Mary," said Maisie. "Here's Gracie now."

The youngest member of the group handed her the cup of tea, and was about to return to the kitchen, when Maisie instructed her to join her friends.

"Archie." Maisie took a sip of her tea, extending the boy's discomfort with a pause as she set the cup in the saucer and rested it on a table beside her chair. Taking an audible deep breath, she went on. "Could you explain something to me? What made you tell me a lie? Because not only are the French doors at the back of the house, but there is no letterbox on the door. Plus you don't deliver newspapers at night, do you? I believe the postman leaves the accrued mail in a metal container attached to the trunk of that large oak tree just inside the gate. Oh, and as you probably know, there is a sign on the gate clearly stating 'No Hawkers, No Circulars. No solicitors'—which means the owner does not want anyone calling at the house to sell, to bring unwanted advertising mail or to solicit business. You said you were delivering newspapers ordered by the owner of the property—but as a rule you would leave the papers in the metal box. True?"

Archie looked away.

"I'll take that as a 'yes.'" She allowed an uncomfortable silence to go on for a few seconds before she spoke again. "I'd love to know what made you lie."

Maisie had been careful with the framing of her question. So many years before, during her apprenticeship, Maurice had counseled her to take care with "why" questions: The person you are questioning might be able to use a 'why' to lead you into a long tunnel of reflection, personal stories and conjecture. 'What' is simple. It ends the tunnel before the person you are questioning can run away with words. It demands a clear answer, though of course a clever suspect will always endeavor to wriggle free of a verbal noose.

"Archie? I trusted you and you lied, so I'd appreciate an explanation."

All four faces before her were now blushing.

"What he said was—" offered Jim.

"Let Archie speak, if you don't mind."

"I lied because I didn't want to tell you why I went in the first place. Mind you, I am the paperboy for that street—and about ten other streets in the town—so I keep an eye on things. Well, I *was* the paperboy. I won't get my job back now."

"What took you to the house at that point?"

"Sergeant Kirby wanted the information. He wanted me to go to the house on that day at that time."

"What made him choose you?"

"He's a sneaky little whatsit, that's why," said Mary.

"So, Sergeant Kirby chose you because you're good at hiding in the shadows and can get in and get out."

"I reckon so."

"Then what inspired you all to return—in fact, did you all return?"

"He asked us," said Mary. "Sergeant Kirby. And we was all to go together, so one of us was to wait near the gate to give a warning of anyone coming. That was Gracie—she was supposed to stay and keep her eyes peeled. I'm the leader, and Jim was there to pick the locks."

"Pick the locks?"

"Sergeant Kirby wanted to find out about the shed with the paraphernalia in it."

"And how did you know there was even a shed with 'parapher-nalia' in it?"

Archie said nothing, but looked at each of his friends in turn.

"Just tell her everything," said Mary. "Our goose is cooked anyway, for talking about all of this to anyone. We might as well let her know, seeing as we're all going to end up in the clink."

Archie stared at the older girl and rolled his eyes, before turning his head as he sighed and looked at Maisie. "Alright then. I'd had a look around before, one time when there was no one about. It was easy to see into that big garage and the gardener's shed. This other shed had no windows, but I had a feeling light was getting in somehow, 'cause light was all I could see in a crack where the doors met. So, I climbed a tree and got onto the roof and there were a couple of them skylight things. So, I stared down and I could see some of them swastika flags. I heard someone coming, so I had to get out of there sharpish—slid off the roof, went through them rhododendron bushes, over the wall and I was away, legging it down the road. I told Sergeant Kirby, and he said he wanted more details, so off we all went again to try to get in there. And you already know the rest, about when we broke in."

"One thing I still don't know though—who is this Sergeant Kirby?"

Maisie waited as the quartet exchanged glances, with a nudge between Mary and Jim. Once again she wondered how she could have failed to take account of their clothing—yes, she would have been able to compile a list of what each of the four was wearing, but now she noted the poor state of repair and age of the garments. The girls had been wearing faded coats over pleated uniform skirts of summer-weight cloth frayed at the hem. Their socks fell down for want of fresh elastic, and their scuffed footwear was doubtless donated to the children's home in years past. The shoes worn by the girls had once been heeled footwear for women, but someone had sheared off an inch or two from the heels. Jim was dressed no better than Archie; however, at least Archie, who was smaller, had clothing that made it seem as if he had simply experienced a growth spurt. The lanky Jim wore a man's trousers that were far too big for him and cinched at the waist with string, and he had rolled up each long trouser leg to a point where his ankles were visible. His jacket, again too large, was threadbare at the elbows, which he wore over a pullover atop a grey shirt. She had already noticed that his shoes were too big, causing him to shuffle as he walked.

"Come on, who is Sergeant Kirby?"

Mary shrugged. "We don't really know. He was just the man who came to the home to recruit us—that's what he said, that we were being 'recruited' to serve our country when the Germans invaded, to save us all from the Hun. And he was one of the ones who trained us."

"He used the word 'Hun'?" asked Maisie. "Then would you say he was about fifty or sixty years of age?"

"He was old, definitely old," Gracie piped up, as she removed a hairgrip and repositioned it to one side in an effort to keep a wayward fringe out of her eyes. Maisie was reminded that each of the four would benefit from a visit to a hairdresser, or for the boys a good barber.

"And he was something to do with a place called 'the Garth,'" said Jim. "It's a place where the people who trained us go to, in Kent. What they called the 'HQ.'"

"Hmmm, interesting," said Maisie, aware that the youngsters seemed as if they were not quite so braced against the world around them. They had settled into telling their story as if they were shedding worn skin, though she knew there was still fear—and a deep discomfort—attached to their situation.

"You won't tell anyone we told you all this. They said to us that we'd be goners if we even whispered a word to anyone else," said Jim, again seeking reassurance from Maisie. "And we wanted to do a good job. We thought that if we did well, we'd be set up, you know, that someone would take us in. Blimmin' rotten, being grown up and in that home."

"I'm sure it is, Jim." Maisie gave a knowing smile, holding Jim's fierce gaze for just a second longer until he softened. Returning the cup and saucer to the side table, she steepled her hands, resting her lips against her fingertips. She had to think. She had been given more information yet nothing much in the way of threads to attach one loose detail to the other. Were these orphans really in trouble? Might a crime have been covered up, perhaps allowing time for the perpetrator to get away before the police apprehended him? And did they really see a man killed? Could the dusky end-of-day light have altered their perception? No, there were four of them and all agreed upon what they had seen and the shots heard, though she conceded that it could be a case of one believing they had witnessed something and the others viewing the event through their eyes and ears, as if they had observed the same thing. Maisie knew such phenomena had been investigated in the past, and often among people who were close and joined by a shared life-altering experience. She sighed and sat back.

Whatever the situation, MacFarlane wanted to know where they were, and indicated he wasn't the only one. Would Robbie be a danger to the youthful resistance unit? She had to decide, and soon. In the interim, she knew it was only a matter of time before he discovered their whereabouts.

"What are we going to do?" asked Mary.

"You're going to be moving, but not today. Tomorrow is Saturday, and I will come for you later in the afternoon, around four, so you will have to behave yourselves and remain very quiet until then. Can you do that?"

"Yes, we can," said Mary. "But where will we go?"

"To the home of a dear friend of mine." Maisie smiled. "She's very forthright and a bit bossy, but has a heart of gold and you'll like her. The man you looked after at Ebury Place is staying with her and her husband at the moment, but he's leaving to go home tomorrow."

"Will we have things to do?" asked Gracie.

"Oh, of that I have no doubt. Don't imagine you will be sitting still for a moment. In the meantime—Mary, have you ever done any needlework?"

"That's one of the things they taught us girls—how to sew, so we could be good maids or seamstresses. No one ever asked us what we wanted to be when we grew up."

"I want to race motor cars," said Archie.

"Yeah, getaway driver, knowing you," said Jim, nudging his friend.

"There's something you can all think about—what you want to be when you grow up, seeing as you're almost there. Now, getting back to business, if you don't mind. Mary, I'll find a tape measure—there's one in the kitchen, I think—because I want you and your friends measured so I can get you fresh clothing to wear, something more suited to the season."

"We've kept ourselves clean, you know," said Mary.

"I know, but your clothing needs some . . . let's say a little 'freshening up.' I should check on the food supplies in the kitchen and I'll help Mary with the measuring, then I must leave you until tomorrow."

"There's been a development," said Priscilla, as she greeted Maisie upon her arrival at the Partridges' Holland Park mansion, which was only a short distance from Maisie's flat on the same street, though she would not remain overnight at her London home.

"Oh dear, that sounds ominous. What's going on?" asked Maisie as Priscilla led her to the small sitting room overlooking the garden at the back of the house. Maisie knew it was her friend's preferred place to linger later in the day, often with a book and without fail a pre-dinner gin and tonic. Before conversion to three flats, Maisie's neighboring London bolt-hole had once been the ground-floor rooms of a house of similar vintage and architecture, so Priscilla's sitting room felt familiar to her. There was another reason Maisie loved Priscilla's house. It was once the home where her first love, Simon, had grown up. Priscilla and Simon were old family friends, so Priscilla had introduced Simon at a party she insisted Maisie attend. All too soon the three friends were at war—Priscilla and Maisie having given up their studies at Girton College, Cambridge to serve in France; Priscilla as an ambulance driver with the First Aid Nursing Yeomanry, and Maisie as a nurse. Fate brought Maisie and Simon—an army doctor—together at the casualty clearing station where they were stationed, and both were wounded during enemy shelling. While Maisie's wounds healed and the scars began to fade in time, Simon was plunged into the world of those whose minds had been ravaged by injury. He died years later, having never recovered from a vegetative state. Maisie thought of these things as she sat down at one end of the sofa, and Priscilla took the other.

"We were all so young, weren't we?" said Maisie.

"I could see what you were thinking the minute you stepped into this room." Priscilla came to her feet and walked toward the drinks trolley set in the corner of the room. "The sun must be over the yardarm somewhere in the world, so I'm having a mild G and T. Shall I wave the bottle over the top of a glass of tonic for you, so just a few fumes get in there? You look like you could do with it."

"I'd prefer a cup of tea, Pris, if you don't mind."

"I'll ring for Mrs. R. to bring us a pot. I'm having the real drink."

"What's the development?"

"Will has a visitor."

"Billy?"

Priscilla sat down, raised her glass and sipped. "No, his brother."

"Bobby? How did he know Will was here?"

"Through Tom, of course. Tarquin came home from the agricultural college yesterday—completely unexpected visit, he trudged half the Cotswolds into the drawing room on the bottom of his Wellington-booted feet. Tom telephoned the house, Tarquin spoke to him, mentioned that Will was here, and lo and behold, it transpires Tom is now based at the same aerodrome as Bobby Beale, and the next thing you know, Bobby applied for immediate twenty-four-hour compassionate leave and made straight for London." She took another sip. "I think they're both being demobilized from the RAF at the same time."

"I should tell you, Billy isn't best pleased about Tom impressing Bobby with tales of the wonderful life he could enjoy in America, extolling the virtues of aviation opportunities over there."

"Works both ways—I love my future daughter-in-law, but I cannot forget who introduced my firstborn to a gorgeous American nurse."

Maisie looked around the familiar room and smiled. "Funny, isn't it? How it all comes around. If I hadn't been introduced to Simon at the party you dragged me off to, I would never have met his American surgeon friend in Le Havre, and if I hadn't known the American surgeon friend, his daughter would never have been in contact years later when she came to London with the American Army Nurse Corps. And if I had not invited her to lunch, she would never have met—"

"Don't they call that the 'web of life,' or something like that?" said Priscilla. "Or there was always Shakespeare, you know, that speech in *As You Like It*. 'All the world's a stage and all the men and women merely players.'" She shook her head. "As you like it? I think sometimes it's a case of 'as we just make the best of it.' Anyway, the two brothers are upstairs, having not seen one another for five years. I've walked past the door, and all I hear is the low rumble of male voices dancing around the elephant in the room."

"Their father?"

Priscilla nodded, and sipped again, looking up when there was a knock at the door and the housekeeper entered with a tea tray.

"Oh, Mrs. R., thank you. Mrs. Scott is gasping for a cup of tea, and I think I will have one too now."

Maisie smiled as the housekeeper raised an eyebrow and set the tray on the low table in front of the sofa.

"The young men are still talking upstairs. I took them tea about twenty minutes ago, and happened to hear the airman tell his brother that he had to be leaving soon."

"I'll have a sip of my tea and go up," said Maisie.

M aisie gave a light two knocks on the door of Will's room, which was answered by Bobby.

"Hello, Miss Dobbs—oh dear, sorry—Mrs. Scott. Bet I'm not the only one to keep making that mistake!" He held out his hand. "I hope you don't mind, but as soon as I heard Will was here, I had to come. He's my big brother."

"Not so big at the moment, Bobby," said Will, who was seated in an armchair, a blanket across his knees. A fire was lit in the grate, warming the room.

"Of course I don't mind, Bobby." Maisie stepped into the room. "And, Will, it won't be long before you are back to your fighting weight. You look so much better already—and I could swear you've put on a pound or two."

Will Beale smiled. "It's that Mrs. R. She scares me more than the Japs, the way she looks at me if I can't manage all her custard, or another one of her soups. 'Long-simmer bone broth, that's the ticket, young man.' She says it every time."

Maisie smiled, glad to see Billy's son in better spirits.

"Here, you'll never guess what," said Will. "My little brother is an officer now. What do they call you, Bob? Second officer or something like that. I bet Mum and Dad will be made up when they hear the news. A Beale becoming an officer!"

Bobby Beale shrugged. "Nah, nothing to get excited about, it's just because of me being a flight engineer. They said I was good enough for the job but as a rule it's an officer sort of level, so they ended up making me an officer. I don't reckon it means much, not when I'll be leaving at the end of the year anyway."

"I wouldn't tell Dad you're leaving, not if I were you," said Will.

"He already knows, mate." Bobby Beale walked toward his brother, leaned down and put his arms around him. "Sod the shaking hands lark—we ain't too big for this, are we, Will?" He turned to Maisie, pushing his peaked cap under his arm to carry it downstairs. "Lovely to see you, Mrs. Scott. Thank you for looking after our Will."

As the newly minted RAF officer left the room, Maisie

pulled a chair to sit next to Will Beale, who wiped the back of his hand across his eyes, a mannerism that seemed inherited from his father.

"Not right, is it? Me being the eldest and not getting anywhere. But our Bobby—he's back on his feet and he's on his way. And he had some terrible things go on too. Didn't say anything, but he doesn't have to. I can tell. He's my brother."

"Will, as soon as you're on your feet, you watch, you'll be blazing a trail too. You come from a family of fighters—you'll be a winner, mark my words."

"You know what I'd like . . ." said Will, sighing as if it were an unachievable dream. "I'd like to run a little ironmonger's, the sort of shop people come into and say, 'I'd like the thingummy that you put on top of the whatsit that goes under the sink and . . . I can't remember what you call it.' And straightaway, I'd lead them to a big stack of drawers, pick the right one, take out a little screw and say, 'Is this what you were looking for, sir?' That's what I'd like, being in a place where I could help people all day."

"If you keep imagining the details, Will, I'm sure you will make that dream come true." Maisie reached for his hand. "But what about your mum and dad? Ready to see them tomorrow afternoon? Ready to go home?"

"I feel safe here."

"I know you do. No rush, absolutely no rush. But give it a chance."

"I didn't always feel safe at home, growing up. I thought about it a lot on the boat, trying to remember how I felt, what I wanted to say but never could. I always pretended to feel as if everything was alright, you know, for Bobby and Lizzie. Dad did his best, but I . . . Well, better not speak out of turn."

"You can tell me, Will. I won't tell your parents."

Will Beale shrugged. "I just never knew when he would crumble. I mean, he always picked himself up, but it was as if this big grey cloud was coming for him and he'd go off, you know, to get himself out of the house and I knew it was so he didn't upset us." He shook his head. "I'd be in bed and I'd hear him, leaving the house and going for a walk in the dark of night. He'd be out for hours, and I'd lie there, eyes wide open, trying not to wake Bobby, but I couldn't sleep until I heard his footsteps coming down the street again—and I'd always hear him, what with his limp. 'Dot and carry one,' he used to say. 'That's me, dot and carry one, dragging that dodgy leg behind me.' And the next morning, there he was, ready for work as if nothing was going on, but I could see his eyes were red, swollen, like he'd been weeping." He shook his head again. "I think I understand now, and I've been thinking about it a lot since I came here. I don't know how he was the good dad that he was, how he made us laugh and how he played with us. Truth be told, I don't want to bring him down with what I am now."

Maisie held on to his hand. "You're a very brave man. You've got your father's fortitude, and his love for your family. And I swear you have your father's sense of right and wrong, and if you're really lucky, his sense of humor. You have your mother's grit too, and that will take you a long way."

"I'm looking forward to seeing them—you know, scared, but looking forward." He sat up straighter in the chair. "Yes, I reckon I can do what he did and just get on with it." He smiled. "I heard that a lot when I was on the ship coming back here—and in that place where they gave me my demob suit. Seems everyone's got it in their heads that the only thing we can do is get on with it, and it's what people say to keep themselves going. 'Just get on with it.' Trouble is, I reckon 'it' covers a lot of things that are wearing people down."

"Time, Will. Time is the great healer—I've said that before." She sat back and regarded the young man before her. Was he ready to talk more? Too tired? She would take a chance.

"Will, do you feel up to answering a few questions, now that you've had a little rest?"

"About the war?"

Maisie shook her head. "No, about the squatters who took care of you at Ebury Place."

"Little tykes, though you can't help but admire them. What about them?"

"I know you were sleeping a lot, but you said there were times you were just lying there with your eyes closed. Did you ever hear them talking about someone called Sergeant Kirby?"

Will frowned, looking at Maisie. "I don't remember that exactly, but I remember 'the sarge' and 'old Kirby.' I don't remember what they said, not to the letter, but I will say this—I reckon they were scared of him. I know that voice, because I heard men scared when I was in the camp. People laugh a lot, crack jokes, or they cry alone but you can hear them. Yes, I think they were frightened—or, what's the word? There's a word for it . . . you know, when someone has a sort of power over you."

"Intimidated?"

"That's the one. And I remember wondering about it when I heard them talk about him, about how he helped them get away, and how this other bloke helped them."

"His name?"

"Well, there was two. A Mr. Blacker, and a Mr. Compton." He laughed. "Funny that, the second bloke having the same name as old Lord Julian, and . . . Blimey, do you think—"

Maisie was silent for a moment. "Will, keep that to yourself, if you don't mind. Just for now. I'm trying to help them, but there's a few lines of inquiry to follow."

"I'm good at keeping secrets. How do you think I managed to get home? Didn't always keep my head down, but I was good at keeping secrets, even when the Japs tried to beat them out of me."

Maisie came to her feet. "Eat your egg custard, Will. Get some good rest. Your mum and dad will be here early tomorrow afternoon." She took his hand again. "Truly, they cannot wait to see you."

Will squeezed her hand in return.

"Everything tickety-boo?" said Priscilla, waiting at the foot of the winding staircase.

"I think seeing Bobby did Will the power of good."

"Time for a drink before you go?"

Maisie shook her head. "I must get home. Brenda is holding the fort with Anna until I'm there."

"You're having to go back and forth a lot, aren't you? Why not stay overnight at the flat?"

"Not while Mark is away. And anyway, there are people who commute every single day, and this won't be for long."

"Right you are. Anything else I should know before my next four young guests arrive?"

"They've not endured anything on a scale of Will's experiences, but all the same—they're scared. Very scared."

"I can deal with 'scared' any day of the week," said Priscilla. "I've had practice."

Maisie kissed Priscilla on the cheek and felt the arms of her dearest friend around her. "I know you have, Pris."

There was much to consider as Maisie traveled by taxi to Charing Cross station for the train back to Chelstone. The fact that a Mr. Compton was named did not come as a surprise, but Mr. Blacker was something of a shock, for George Blacker was the Comptons' chauffeur, a mild-mannered man she had known for many a year.

CHAPTER 8

As Maisie made ready to leave the house the following morning, she settled her agenda for the day, which included meeting Billy and Doreen at one o'clock at her London flat. They would walk to Priscilla's house together, where Andrew Dene would be waiting to discuss Will's care with his parents. Maisie would summon a taxi-cab to take the Beale family home when they were ready to leave. Until then, she had another plan to put into action while Frankie and Brenda looked after their granddaughter during her absence.

"Are you sure taking the motor is a good idea, love?" Frankie had commented, while carrying Maisie's bag to the door. "I mean, you read such things, don't you? About vandalism, what with London not what it was before the war."

"I need the motor, Dad, not only to do some work today, but I've errands to run, plus I'll have it with me just in case the Beales prefer me to drive them home rather than go in the taxi. I just have to make sure I keep my petrol use down, but it should be alright."

"I'll take your word for it," said Frankie, placing the bag in the boot. "Funny, wasn't it? That old George didn't stop for a natter. I mean, I know he likes tinkering with the motors and keeping them in tip top condition, but he's always been one to linger for a bit and pass the time of day, or remind you not to do this or that with your motor car."

"Oh, I think he's just been a bit busy, helping Lady Rowan with other things."

"Yes, he's very good to her, always loyal. Anyway, I might wander over and say hello to him later on. I promised the littl'un I'd walk across the fields with her to the stables where they said she could ride the horses."

Maisie was about to get into the motor car, but turned to her father. "Just a minute—they said she could ride? Those horses at that riding school are all huge."

"They've got one or two no more than sixteen hands."

"That's one or two that are far too big for her."

"She's growing like a weed, Maisie. Take it from me as *your* father—if a daughter has set her mind to something, you're not going to stop her."

"Oh, very funny! But, Dad, don't let her onto one of those big horses. I'll deal with this when I get home. Perhaps we can look for a suitable pony as soon as Mark arrives back from Washington—after all, he'll want to be there when she rides. And we agreed that all our big decisions would be family decisions."

"Alright. I'll keep her away from the hunters. Now, where is it you're off to first?" asked Frankie, closing the door as Maisie started the engine.

"Hallarden—you know, not far from Paddock Wood. See you tomorrow, Dad—and remember, no big hunters for Anna."

Frankie tapped the roof of the Alvis as Maisie began to maneuver the motor car away from the house.

"Sixteen hands," whispered Maisie as she drove away from Chelstone Manor. "Not yet, young lady. Not by a long chalk!"

The equestrian exploits of her daughter were not the only matter Maisie mulled over on the way to Hallarden. Any kind of travel had always presented her with time for considering a problem or something that was otherwise nagging at her. The side-to-side motion of the train or the route taken across countryside when driving offered time to think. Her desire to become more of a support for her extended family in the years ahead meant she was often mulling over something that was not quite right in her world.

Maisie enjoyed her home on the Chelstone estate. At first, inheriting the Dower House had been a shock, an intimidating experience. It was a property of some size, part of a substantial bequest from her former mentor, Dr. Maurice Blanche, who had in turn purchased the property from his friends Lord Julian and Lady Rowan. Maisie suspected the Comptons had sold the Dower House to keep Maurice close as he grew older, and at a time when for the privileged couple a level of retirement was considered, but death was something further afield. It had become clear, though, that Julian had thought long and hard about *his* last will and testament.

For Maisie, the terms of Maurice's will had been a gift that changed the course of her life. As a girl she had first lived at the Dower House when she was moved up from being a housemaid at the Belgravia mansion to assume the role of servant-companion to Lord Julian's elderly mother. The promotion had been the idea of Lady Rowan, rendering it easier for Maisie to study with a view to gaining entry to a prestigious women's college— yet without losing the respect of her fellow "below stairs" staff, who could see that she was still working hard.

Maisie had come to love the Dower House. As the bombing of London intensified in the early years of the war, Maisie arranged

137

for Frankie and Brenda to live with her, while Billy and his wife took over the bungalow the new Mr. and Mrs. Dobbs had purchased in Chelstone village in 1935, at a point when it was time for Frankie to retire and give up the Groom's Cottage, a tied dwelling that was part of the Chelstone estate.

Soon the family expanded when they welcomed evacuees, among them the orphaned child who became a beloved adopted daughter and granddaughter. Another change came with Maisie's marriage to Mark Scott, who—much to everyone's surprise—had settled into English country life with greater ease than might have been expected, though his working week was spent at the American embassy in London. There had been much joshing in the village about "the American squire" up at the manor, though after he made a good account of himself with the cricket team, and was not backward in coming forward when it came to getting in the first round at the pub afterwards, word went around that he was a "good'un" after all.

Yet with the passing of Lord Julian Compton, Maisie was reminded that the Dower House belonging to a large estate was traditionally the home of the dowager, the widow of a lord of the manor.

Now Maisie felt she had a duty of care toward Rowan, not least given her place as the closest family member, albeit by marriage. She was still thinking of her daughter and Lady Rowan as she drove into the village of Hallarden. Saturday was early closing day, but she had time to visit the local shop and perhaps the garage; after all, the mechanic might be friendly with the Hawkin-Price's chauffeur—though she had to tread with care because small-town loyalties ran deep. As did local societal ruptures. Following her information-gathering efforts in the town, she planned another visit to the home of the Honorable Jonathan

Hawkin-Price. From the time she had first visited the house, she knew something was staring her in the face, a vital clue illuminating whatever had come to pass at the property. It would settle matters one way or the other, and her investigation would reveal the four squatters to be accomplished liars, idle fantasists or young people with a genuine reason to be afraid. The fact that they quoted both Lord Julian's surname and that of George suggested it was the latter, though untruths and fantasies could also have been woven into the fabric of their story.

The bell above the shopkeeper's door rang as soon as Maisie entered, summoning a woman from the back of the premises. She came out wiping her hands on her pinafore.

"Good morning, madam—I was just having a quick slice of toast. It's been a busy couple of hours, and not a spare minute for a bite to eat. Mind you, it's Saturday, and people like to get a few things in before early closing at one."

"Not to worry—would you like me to come back in ten minutes?" Maisie wanted to begin on the right foot, showing generosity of spirit, a helpfulness toward the shopkeeper.

The woman waved her hand. "Not at all, not at all. You go on, dear—how can I help you?"

"I'd like a box of matches, please. The long ones, for the fireplace. And do you have anything . . . anything for my sweet tooth?"

"Right you are," replied the woman, reaching behind the counter to take a box of long matches from a shelf, then placing them in front of Maisie. She smiled at her customer while opening a drawer underneath the counter, whereupon she lifted out a chocolate bar, setting it alongside the matches. "One of my favorites—I'm lucky to get a box of them in. I had an airman in here one day—he told me the RAF handed out those particular bars to the bomber crews during the war. Fry's Chocolate Cream kept our boys going. I make sure they're put away as a rule, otherwise some of the nimble little fingers around here will grab a bar while my back is turned."

Putting her hand to her chest, Maisie added a little drama to her response. "Oh my goodness—Fry's Chocolate Cream!"

"Only if you want it, my dear."

"I'm not going to turn down my favorite chocolate. Thank you! I'll have to save some for my daughter—either that or dispose of the wrapper before I get home."

The women laughed together, talked about the fact that the war would have saved a generation of children from tooth decay, what with the sugar rationing, but that didn't work because half the children were going hungry anyway, so their teeth were falling out due to malnutrition. Maisie used the conversation to warm the shopkeeper toward her, as if she were priming an engine with good-quality motor oil. She was soon ready to add a question or two to garner information that someone at the heart of a community—a shopkeeper—would have in her pocket before anyone else.

"It's so lovely here, isn't it? Nice and quiet—you would never have thought we've been through a war. I was hoping to find a house in the village for my family."

"There's a few coming up for sale, mainly by the better-offs not happy with the fact that the council has given planning permission for some two hundred homes to be built on the edge of town."

"Oh dear."

"It'll be more business for the likes of me, but I can see why people might be worried, what with housing for homeless Londoners going in—I mean, you don't know what sort of people they are, do you?"

Maisie was quick to maneuver the conversation in the direction she wanted. "I was walking along Sandstone Avenue yesterday, but made a bit of an error when I saw a house that I thought was for sale, but it wasn't—it was the house next door. I ended up in the grounds of a very large house with lots of land at the back."

"Oh, yes, that would be the Hawkin-Price house."

"It looks empty."

The woman leaned toward Maisie, as if bringing her into an exclusive circle of local secrecy. "Hardly there, that one. Never see him much in the town. Mind you, we're more like a village really. Only called a town on account of the size of the church."

Before the woman could divert into an explanation of the size of the church and the designation of city, town, village or hamlet, Maisie forged on with her line of questioning.

"One wonders why he doesn't sell. Is he in London most of the time?"

"No one really knows—well, I reckon Mr. King, the chauffeur, would know, because he takes him wherever he wants, but I've heard it's mostly to the railway station, sometimes Paddock Wood or Tonbridge, occasionally Sevenoaks. I reckon he only keeps on the few staff he has up there because the house would fall into rack and ruin if it were abandoned, and I can't see it changing hands until he's dead—though he sold off a fair few acres years ago."

"I would have thought that most men in his position would have relinquished responsibility for a house of that size—it's a lot, especially if he's not there."

"You would have thought so, wouldn't you? But here in town there's a good number of us remember his father and mother, and how they went a bit off after their eldest boy was killed at Passchendaele. He was the favored one, you know."

"Does Mr. Hawkin-Price have heirs?"

"Never married, though there was talk—" The shopkeeper leaned in toward Maisie. "He was spending a lot of time over there in Germany after the war—the first war, that is—and I heard talk about there being a German woman. But he wouldn't have brought her home to live here, not to England. And I know he was over there for the Olympics, before the war."

"Is that so?" said Maisie.

"Now, I shouldn't say he never brought her over here, his fancy woman, because Mrs. King—she's the chauffeur's wife and the housekeeper—she told me there was a German woman there a few times, but she kept to herself, and was never seen out and about in Hallarden."

"Is that so?" said Maisie, the repetition emphasizing her interest. "Someone—one of the neighbors I had a chat with when I was walking along the avenue with my dog—told me there used to be big parties there."

"Oh yes, that's true enough, and the German was probably there because that's the only reason I can think of for him being so quiet about it. I mean, let's face it, in the Great War you couldn't walk down the street with your dog if it was a Dachshund, could you?"

"I have an Alsatian. They used to be called 'German Shepherds,' but they had to be renamed due to anti-German attitudes."

"Can't blame people, can you? I lost my sweetheart in 1917, and then my brother a week after him."

"I'm very sorry to hear that," said Maisie. "My fiancé succumbed to his wounds after the war." She allowed a beat before continuing in a low voice. "About the parties—apart from his German lady friend, how did he keep the identity of guests quiet?"

"Sent all the workers off the estate for a start, gave them a couple of days holiday, and with pay. The chauffeur and his wife went off to the coast to see her sister, and the gardeners don't live at the property, so they just stayed at home. He never had a cook—Mrs. King used to put something out for him and she's very good in the kitchen—but apparently, to cater the parties, a van came down from London with the food. Perhaps they had a buffet and served themselves. All very private. Then before you knew it, whoever the guests were had gone—but they were definitely all very posh with big motor cars. Well-connected is Mr. Hawkin-Price. He's an 'Honorable,' you know, and they say he was a friend of the Duke of Windsor."

"Hmmm, yes, I knew he was an 'Honorable.'" Maisie shrugged. "Anyway, I was just curious. I was hoping he might decide to sell, but then I saw the extent of the property—we couldn't run to something like that."

"I doubt he'd sell, all things considered. I've heard he was angry enough when he had to siphon off a fair bit of his land to pay death duties. Went on and on about the government, and with some very ripe language by all accounts. He was in the local pub—not that he was a regular, and it might even have been only once or twice he was seen in there—but he told the landlord that Britain might as well have been the losers after the last war, not the winners. Then he went on about how Germany climbed out of the pit of despair. It was a pit of despair their kaiser dug in the first place, if you ask me." The shopkeeper looked around at the clock on the wall behind her, then turned back to Maisie. "Mind you, there's many folk saying the same thing about Britain after this war, aren't there? That we're in the pit of despair, like losers—not winners."

"I've heard that too," said Maisie. "But chin up—we've proved to the world how resilient we are, haven't we?" She extended her hand. At first the shopkeeper seemed taken aback, then accepted the gesture and held Maisie's hand as if grateful for the gift of human touch. "Lovely to pass the time of day with you," said Maisie. "I'm sorry, I should have asked your name. Miss—?"

"Rowe. Miss Rowe." She sighed, released Maisie's hand and reached into her pinafore pocket to pull out a well-fingered photograph, turning it so Maisie could see. The photograph had been taken in a studio, with a young man in uniform, cap under his left arm, standing next to a woman of about the same age, her hand resting on his right arm. They were smiling at the camera. "He was with the Queen's Own Royal West Kents. We'd just become engaged in that photograph." She laughed. "He said he was more scared on the day he asked my father for my hand in marriage than when he was over there fighting for his country."

Maisie put her hand to her heart as she studied the photograph.

"Wonderful boy, my Alfie Brissenden," continued Miss Rowe. "A good young man. We'd grown up here together. He died at Arras, otherwise I would have been Mrs. Brissenden. Mrs. Alfie Brissenden. That would have been lovely."

Maisie took her leave, thanking Miss Rowe for her time and the Fry's Chocolate Cream. She would proceed to the house belonging to Jonathan Hawkin-Price, but not before she pulled over in a quiet place, just to think, to shake off the image in her mind of another woman who had lost her love to war, a woman now in her fifties who continued to carry the photograph of a "boy" long dead. And it appeared to be even more of an irony to Maisie, that as she passed the town war memorial on her way to Sandstone Avenue, a stonemason was at work, adding names to the list of the town's fallen in yet another world war. On a whim, she turned the motor car and parked at the foot of the small garden surrounding the memorial.

"Good morning!" Maisie called out as she approached the stonemason. "I was just passing and noticed you at work."

The man turned and touched his flat cap with the forefinger of his left hand—in his right he held a stone-engraving tool.

"I hope you don't mind my having a look at your work. I served in the first war, so I always stop to pay my respects when I'm in a new place and see the memorial."

"Nurse?"

Maisie nodded.

"I was with the Buffs—the East Kents," said the stonemason.

"Do you live here in the town?"

The man shook his head. "No, I won't work where I knew the lads whose names I'm adding to the list. Everyone's got their limits—that's mine. I turn down a lot of good work, but I can't chisel out the names of boys I saw grow up and become men."

"I don't think I could either." She stepped forward. "May I?"

The man moved so she could study the names of those listed underneath the words "Lest We Forget."

"Graham Chalmers? Might he have been the son of Mr. Chalmers—the gardener over at the big mansion on Sandstone Avenue?"

The stonemason shrugged. "Could well be, I didn't ask his father how he earned his money, but from the look of his hands, he was a man who worked hard."

"His father came?"

"They do, you know." The man was silent for a few seconds, as if gauging whether to continue. He cleared his throat. "I've watched them sometimes, as I'm packing up my tools and putting them away in the back of the van. You see them coming up, the families. They usually wear their Sunday best when they visit. You see the mums shed a tear and the fathers comfort them. Young widows come with their parents and some bring the nippers along too. And the strangest thing—though, I dunno, perhaps it's not so strange—they go up and touch the name. They run their fingers over every letter, as if they could feel the one they've lost." He gave a deep exhale. "But the father of this one seemed to want to talk, so we had a chat—he was with another man, said they worked together. I reckon the other bloke must have been a chauffeur, the size of the motor they drove up in. Both lost their sons and at the same time—Tunisian campaign, I think it was. Their sons were with the East Kents, same as me in the last war. Mind you, once a soldier's name is up there, it doesn't matter where they died, does it? It's all war."

Maisie nodded. She had no more questions to ask of the man. He had given her enough to think about.

"I'd better let you get on. You're doing a lovely job there. Each name is perfect."

"Can't let our boys down, can I? Least I can do is make sure that in a hundred years' time people will know the names of the lads who gave their lives for their country. Just wish I could add all the names of the ones who came back but left half of themselves over there."

It now transpired the chauffeur and gardener had visited the war memorial together and their sons could well have been playmates, good friends as they grew to manhood. The owner of the house had a German woman friend. He spent a fair amount of time in Germany and gave parties for associates, and he didn't want locals to know much about either the gatherings or those invited. And he was an angry man when it came to consideration of his government. Yes, people could get very upset about money or what they thought was owed them, whether by society or the powers that be.

A sign outside the town garage indicated that it was closed until Monday, but she no longer needed to ask questions of the mechanic—Miss Rowe had given her worthwhile information, though a good deal was hidden between her words. Maisie was now in two minds whether to return to the mansion, the place she was beginning to think of as the Nazi house. Did she need to know more? Was there anything else to see? Yes, perhaps one quick visit, but not today. After all, the estate owner was a man who was, to all intents and purposes, a Nazi sympathizer, and two men who worked for him had lost sons fighting against the Germans in North Africa. It would be easy to draw a conclusion, but as Maisie knew only too well—indeed, as experience had taught her—it was far too simple to fall into the trap of accepting the first scenario that came to mind, not least because there might not even have been a crime committed. Or there could have been many.

Maisie offered Billy and Doreen tea when they arrived at her Holland Park flat, but they declined.

"We just want to see our Billy, if you don't mind," said Doreen. "Oh dear, I'm putting my foot in it already. I mean, 'our Will.'"

"Of course you want to see him. Let's walk along to Priscilla's house straightaway. Dr. Dene will be there, as you know. He'll have a quick word with you about Will's care and the limitations of his diet. Your son has done well in just a few days—and I know he's looking forward to seeing you."

Billy and his wife exchanged glances.

"Billy?" queried Maisie.

"I'm just a bit, well, nervous, miss. I don't want to say the wrong thing, you know, get him going."

Doreen reached for her husband's hand. "I'm his mum, Billy—I always say the wrong thing! Come on, one step at a time to see our son."

Maisie pulled on her gloves. "Right, let's be on our way. And if you're nervous, remember, breathe in for a count of four, and out for a count of six. Helps to settle you."

"If you say so, miss," said Billy. "Mind you, it might kill me, breathing like that."

The trio did not hurry along to the home of Priscilla and Douglas Partridge, though neither did they proceed at a strolling pace. At one point Billy stopped.

"What is it, Billy?" asked Maisie.

He pointed to a sign on the other side of the street. "Look at that. They're popping up everywhere, aren't they? These signs letting us know that when we're ill we won't have to pay for the doctor, on account of this new health service coming in a few years. But look at that one." He read out the message flanking the image of a small child. "'Diphtheria Costs Lives—Immunisation Costs Nothing.'"

"Not now," said Doreen, reaching for her husband's arm.

"But you can't help looking, can you? If they'd had that years ago, our Lizzie wouldn't have died, would she?"

"William Beale!" said Doreen, her voice raised. "Our son is just one minute away from us. I will not stare back at the past and fret about a . . . a needle in a child's bum that we couldn't get all those years ago. In a year's time you can bet there will be another immunization invented and it will save children from something else that's killing them today—and even more couples like us will wish it had come sooner. It's what they call 'progress' and I for one am all for it. I'm fed up with the past. Fed up to the back teeth with it! It's too much when you add it to the present, and I'm not going to be like Lot's wife."

Maisie's eyes widened. Doreen was known to be a woman of few words—Maisie had never before heard Billy's wife declare her feelings in such a tone.

Billy nodded, his tempered reply revealing equal surprise and an effort to placate his wife. "You're right, love. Let's get along the street and see our boy."

As Doreen Beale marched ahead, Billy leaned down and whispered to Maisie, "Who's Lot when he's at home?"

Maisie, Priscilla and Douglas waited in the drawing room while Andrew Dene spent a little time with Billy and Doreen in the study. They heard all three emerge and go upstairs to the room where Will Beale had been staying for a few days.

"I hope all's well," said Priscilla. "Douglas managed to persuade Will to come down to have breakfast with us this morning, and I must say, though he's still painfully thin, at least he has color in his cheeks and is a bit more . . . a bit more—"

"Conversational," offered Douglas. He looked at Maisie. "I've had practice—we both have. Tim was either up or down after Dunkirk. One minute optimism was the order of the day, and the next he was in the Doldrums and listing to starboard. And I think it did Will some good when Tim and Tarquin popped in yesterday, because of course Will was evacuated from Dunkirk, and Tim lost his best friend—and his arm—when they took out his friend's father's yacht and joined other vessels bound for France in a bid to rescue our men from those beaches." Douglas stopped speaking, as if the memory of holding his wounded son in his arms were too much to bear. He took a deep breath and went on. "I think the common ground helped. When Tim came downstairs after talking with Will, he told us he'd confided in Will about bringing home his pal's body, seeing him shot and knowing he was dead—I know there were details he had never talked about with us. And Will told Tim he had been tied to a tree with a knife hanging over his head, then made to watch while Japanese soldiers hacked a couple of his best mates to death. They did it because the men had killed rats to cook and eat in an effort to get some more food inside them."

"That family has a long road to navigate," said Priscilla, standing up and walking toward the drinks trolley.

"Priscilla—"

"Just a small one, Douglas my love, just a small one."

"Anyway, they have us to turn to, if they wish," said Maisie. "And Andrew's experience to draw upon. Billy trusts him implicitly."

Soon enough, Billy and Doreen came downstairs with Will, now clad in clothing offered by Tim when it was discovered he and Will were the same height, though it was clear Will required a belt to hold up the grey corduroy trousers. Shoe size was identical, and shirts would fit better when Will had more weight on his bones. As Maisie expected, there was not much conversation, just thanks extended and a shaking of hands all around—though Priscilla could not resist reaching out to hold Will, Doreen and Billy for a few seconds each, while distributing air kisses on either side of their faces. Will laughed.

"That's a good sign," said Dene.

"It's my dad's dial. That look on his face when Mrs. Partridge kissed him was worth a guinea a minute."

Maisie, Douglas, Priscilla and Andrew Dene waved to the Beales as they departed in a taxi.

"I'd better be off," said Dene.

"Could I have a quick word before you go, Andrew?"

"Of course."

"Priscilla?"

"The study is all yours," offered Priscilla.

"What's on your mind, Maisie—because I can see this is not about Billy Beale."

"No, it isn't—though I cannot thank you enough for your help."

"I've got a soft spot for that family—but I must get back to mine now, or my children will start to wonder if they have a father at all."

"I'll be quick. I know you have connections with various medical examiners, especially in West Kent. Could you find out if they have recently performed a post-mortem on a deceased male from Hallarden, age around fifty? I don't know what sort of story you can come up with to ask—perhaps you were treating him for an orthopedic condition and you hadn't heard from him, but you know he had a heart problem. Something like that?"

"Not an idle off-the-cuff suggestion—you've been giving this some thought."

"I have. I'll get to the point—and this is in confidence. I want to know if the body of a man named Jonathan Hawkin-Price was brought in for examination a few weeks ago. I believe it would have been on the q.t.—the examiner might have been told to keep quiet about it."

"Alrighty, I can do that." He looked at Maisie. "Anything for you, as always."

A moment's silence seemed to hang in the air, broken by Maisie.

"I knew I could count on you, Andrew. Give my very best to your lovely wife—and thank you, again, for everything you've done for Will."

Dene smiled. "As I said, for you, Maisie—anything. Now, I'm off home. I'll be in touch."

Maisie reached for the door handle, stepping out into the hall before any more could be said. She opened the front door, and Andrew Dene left, tipping his hat as he proceeded down the steps and toward his motor car. She sighed and turned back into the house.

"Everything alright?" asked Priscilla, as Maisie entered the drawing room.

Maisie nodded.

"I'm going to leave you two, if you don't mind," said Douglas. "I've to write something for the *Telegraph* before tomorrow morning, so I'd better get down to work."

Priscilla watched her husband leave, and turned to Maisie. "You're looking thoughtful."

"Just wondering how I had the cheek to ask you to take in the four young people so soon after Will—I was just stumped when it came to deciding upon a safe place for them."

"It'll keep me occupied. I'll be like a Border Collie with a small herd—I'll round them up and make a list of things for them to do around the house. And woe betide them if they get on the wrong side of Mrs. R." Priscilla took a sip of her gin and tonic. "Don't mind my saying this, but I think Dr. Dene burns a bit of a torch for you."

Maisie shook her head. "No, it's just the Maurice Blanche connection. Maurice helped him get into medical school and then assisted with money—scholarships don't cover everything. Maurice saw such promise in a boy from a poor background who had no chance unless someone lifted him."

"Your Maurice supported a lot of people, didn't he?"

"Yes. Without him . . . without him I sometimes wonder where I might have ended up."

"Well, you wouldn't have met me at Girton, for a start." Priscilla raised her glass. "That's one big thing we can both be thankful for!"

"Indeed it is, Pris. Indeed it is."

CHAPTER 9

Maisie returned to her flat along the street, tired from the highs and lows of a day not yet finished. As she walked, she cast her gaze across the road to the new poster that had attracted Billy's attention. Diphtheria. A new vaccine to save the life of a child who would have died only years before from the killer disease. Lizzie Beale had been the apple of her father's eye, cherished by her mother and beloved by her older brothers. She had cherub-red cheeks and the same fair hair as her father, though war and worry had taken the blonde from Billy and replaced it with grey. Maisie remembered watching Billy and Doreen carrying the small white coffin between them, burying their daughter after she succumbed to the sickness that claimed not only her life, but the spirit of her family for years to come. Yet they had endured, and as Maisie walked on, she held her hand to her heart, hoping the family could navigate Will's recovery, a return to health that would demand Billy and his son put their wounds aside.

Unlocking the door, she slipped her keys into a bowl on the tallboy, and looked in the mirror as she unpinned and removed her hat, setting it on a hook. She unbuttoned her jacket, and stepped into the kitchen to put the kettle on. A cup of tea would set her up before she left to collect the four homeless youngsters from the flat in Pimlico. She changed her mind, turned off the gas ring under the kettle and instead went into the sitting room, pulled a cushion from an armchair and sat down on the floor, arranging her skirt so she could sit cross-legged for just a few moments.

Whilst Maisie was still in her teen years, Maurice Blanche had introduced her to Khan, an elderly Ceylonese man who had been blind from birth. He had also been Maurice's own revered teacher. Khan had taught Maisie how to still her mind, how to maintain focus on the invisible eye at the center of her forehead, a practice that would allow her to return to conscious thought with renewed energy and insight, supporting her as she made decisions that could—and often did—involve life and death. In recent years, as her world became busier with family and professional commit-ments, she had all but abandoned the practice, though she had taught her daughter to find peace in silence during those days when Anna struggled at school due to bullying on account of her olive complexion. Though the child was not of Italian heritage, some classmates assumed she was allied to the wartime enemy, and treated her as such.

Now Maisie wanted to reclaim the peace stripped away by war, though she had only just settled into the deep breathing that would calm body, mind and spirit, when the telephone began ringing.

"If you're up there, Khan and Maurice, I hope there is good reason for the interruption," said Maisie, looking toward the ceiling as she came to her feet and answered the telephone.

She had just lifted the receiver when the caller began.

"Miss Dobbs! Caldwell here. Good—I've found you. Got a minute of your time for me?"

"For you, Detective Chief Superintendent? Of course."

"There's some funny business going on."

"Isn't there always? What's happened?"

"Miss Dobbs, I'm like one of them dogs who, when they're told to put down the bone, they can't resist sneaking back and picking it up again."

"Tell me about the bone you don't want to put down."

"I had the coroner from Tunbridge Wells on the blower. Let's just say we've crossed paths before on some big cases and we've a good—what do they call it these days? Working relationship? One of them new-fangled phrases—you know, like Churchill said in '44, about us and the Yanks. Special relationship and all that." He chuckled. "Bit like you and that Yank of yours."

"Caldwell—"

"It turns out my special friend received a word in his shell from on high, that there was not to be a public inquest on the body of an honorable man from Hallarden, and—"

"Jonathan Hawkin-Price?"

"The very one. As you know, when a death isn't straightforward—natural causes, old age and so on—the coroner asks for a post-mortem and then there's an inquest based upon the examiner's findings and the coroner's conclusions."

"No need for the lesson in procedure—I know that."

"Well, of course you do. Anyway, it transpires the death was far from ordinary and 'death by misadventure' has been recorded without a mention in the press or an inquest. And as we both know, this wasn't an accident or something unintentional. A bullet to the heart and another to the head isn't an accident or any kind of adventure. It's—"

"An assassination." Maisie took a breath. "But you're not involved in any way, because there's nothing to investigate."

"That's about the long and the short of it."

"Yet you're curious."

"Wouldn't be in my line of work if I wasn't."

"Why are you telling me this?"

"Because you're curious too, Miss Dobbs, and you've already been stomping around the outskirts of the case. And while I can't do anything because I'd be tripping over red tape—smoke and mirrors as far up the line as I can stumble—you don't have to be chained to protocols." Caldwell cleared his throat. "Plus, I think you've got another reason for wanting to find out what happened—which I am sure you'll let me in on in time."

"Thank you. I appreciate your letting me know about this. But did your coroner contact indicate where on high the instruction to drop the inquest came from?"

"He did indeed."

"And?"

"Your friend and my sort-of-friend, Robert MacFarlane. It wasn't done by telephone either. Car draws up outside, ATS driver in the front—wonder how he kept her on, what with all the demobilizations—and out steps MacFarlane with a government order to relinquish the examiner's report and any other records. Got a finger in a lot of pies, old MacFarlane."

Maisie wondered if she should tot up how many times she'd heard about fingers being in so many pies in recent weeks.

"I'll keep you informed—how does that sound?" she offered.

"Satisfactory to my ears. I'm up to my eyes in all sorts of cases at the moment, what with bombsite clearance going on, and bodies and parts of same turning up all over the place, and like I said before, not all of them from the actual bomb. But this business in Hallarden interests me."

"I should have something soon."

"Getting warmer, are you?"

Maisie hesitated. "Yes. Yes, I believe so."

"Cagey as always, Miss Dobbs. Right, I'm off. I expect to hear from you in a day or two."

Maisie settled the receiver on the black Bakelite telephone, and stood for a moment staring out of the window. MacFarlane was standing in the way of an inquest on a man no one admitted was dead. She sighed, turned and went to the bedroom to pack her bag again. With not a moment to spare she left the house to collect Mary, Archie, Jim and Grace—and it was Grace she would take aside for a little conversation when they arrived at Priscilla's house. Priscilla was not the only one who could be a Border Collie. Maisie planned to remove the quiet one from the herd, and with luck and the right questions, she would garner more information than the others seemed willing to divulge. She also felt that while Grace was not the black sheep of the group, she could be something of a dark horse.

"So, what's this friend of your'n like then, Miss Dobbs—I suppose that's what I should call you, seeing as you're sort of working so you're not Mrs. Scott," said Mary, seated next to her in the passenger seat. Jim, Archie and Grace were in the back, quiet, though with the odd nudge and an "Ouch!" if they thought one was trying to take up more room than the others.

Maisie smiled. *Your'n. Pure London talk*, she thought as she answered.

"You'll like her, and though she gives the impression of being terribly posh and perhaps a bit haughty, she has a heart of gold and a wicked sense of humor." Maisie paused and gave a sideways glance at Mary, who was staring at her, as if already weighing up how to get around the woman in whose house she would be ensconced for a few days. "She drove an ambulance on the Western Front during the Great War, and again during the Blitz—in fact, we were both volunteer ambulance drivers, but stopped after Mrs. Partridge was injured while saving children from a burning house." Maisie ran her fingers from her right temple to her cheekbone, close to the hairline. "You'll see some scarring from the severe burns here, but please don't stare at her. She's had several operations already."

"Blimey," said Mary, pulling a face.

"Anyway, we're almost there."

"Big houses, ain't they?" said Archie, winding down a window to look out.

"You watch him," said Jim. "The little cat burglar here will be in and out of these gaffs, knocking off their jewels."

Maisie looked in the mirror to stare at Archie. "I wouldn't if I were you or you will have me to reckon with, and thus far you've only seen my good side."

"That's you told," said Mary, turning to Archie.

Priscilla was once more at the steps, waiting for her visitors to arrive, along with Mrs. R., who was scowling in anticipation of having to knock young heads together for any misbehavior.

"See what I mean?" said Maisie. "One wrong step and I don't fancy your chances, any of you."

When the new guests were left to settle in, boys in one bedroom and girls in the other, Maisie and Priscilla were once again seated on the small sofa in the sitting room overlooking the garden.

"Priscilla, I cannot thank you enough—I think they are still wandering around with mouths open and eyes wide at the shock of a warm, welcoming house and bedrooms made up and waiting. And leaving a pile of fresh clothing on each bed—you've gone above and beyond the call of duty."

Priscilla shrugged. "Still got a debt to pay off, haven't I?"

"What debt?"

Priscilla came to her feet and walked to the drinks trolley.

"Pris?"

"Just a small one."

"But—"

"Maisie, you saved my life." Priscilla turned to face Maisie. "I—I would do anything to help you now, because it's clear you want to aid the four tykes upstairs, plus we all wanted to see Will and his family reunited."

"Priscilla, this is not the way to do it, but—" Maisie stood up, took the glass from her friend's hand, walked to the French doors, opened one and threw the liquid out. Closing the door, she placed the empty glass on a side table and stared at her dearest friend. "The dragon's back, isn't he?"

Priscilla patted a few strands of her dark hair to cover the mottled burn scar along the side of her face. "I see them all the time now. The dead. I have nightmares, and if it isn't about the last war, it's this one."

"I know. I know and so does Douglas—I can see it on his face."

"He saved me the first time, didn't he?" Priscilla shook her head as she sat down again and folded her arms, as if to protect her heart. "But I was lucky, wasn't I?" She paused as Maisie took a seat close to her. "After the war, with my brothers all dead and then losing my parents to that bloody influenza, I went off to Biarritz to drink myself to death—you know that. Then I met my wonderful Douglas, fell in love, and before I knew it, I was a married woman bringing up my three toads, and while I liked a nice light G and T at the end of the day, and not any old time or even every day, I had so much to do I never actually craved a drink. I loved being a mother. Every minute of it, even when they were screaming and yelling at each other. Now they've grown up. Tom will be across an ocean, Tim probably remaining in Oxford, and Tarquin is now talking about farming in bloody Australia! It's all falling apart, and the dragon rose up through the cracks in the road ahead of me."

Maisie opened her arms and embraced Priscilla.

"Help me, Maisie. Help me slay that dragon."

Maisie felt her eyes well with tears and the beast of her own nightmares stir.

"Pris, I have an idea," said Maisie, now holding her friend by the shoulders. "A good idea, I think. But give me time—do your best to drink more tea instead, and just give me time."

Priscilla pulled back, pressing her fingertips to her eyes. "I'm sorry. Not good enough, is it? Whining away when there are four orphans upstairs."

"I've never heard you whine, Pris, so don't whip yourself— that won't do any good. Keep an eye on those boys and girls; occupy them and help me get through this, then we'll make plans."

"I'll throw the gin bottle away. Douglas will be happy about that."

"He will indeed."

"I suppose we'd both better get on, eh? Things to do—keep my good self occupied!"

"And on that note, Pris—may I use your study again? I must have a little chat with one of the young ladies."

"Be my guest—my home is your home."

"One thing first—I want to watch you throw away *all* the gin."

"Please sit down, Grace," said Maisie, noting the way the girl had entered the study, keeping close to the wall as if she were afraid of space. Maisie suspected it might be a habit learned at the children's home. If Grace rendered herself invisible, she would not be picked on by teachers or other children.

Grace opened and closed her fingers as Maisie invited her to be seated, and stepped across the floor as if in fear it might open up and swallow her. She sat down in one of the armchairs situated alongside a bookcase. Maisie took the chair next to her and leaned back, her demeanor calm to settle the adolescent. *Adolescent*, thought Maisie. She realized there was no adequate word for the young people she had gathered together in her charge. Mark might have called them "kids," but they were not children, nothing about them was akin to the offspring of goats gamboling in the pasture. They were not adults, and the word "youngsters" only seemed to verge on accuracy. *Adolescere*. The time when a child was growing into maturity. While Maisie had only a passing knowledge of Latin, self-taught when she herself was a youngster, a kid, a person little more than a child, but one with an adult job of work, *adolescere* was a word she remembered. At the age of thirteen, in the early hours of the morning, she had crept from the servants' quarters high up on the fourth floor of the house, down to the Compton library, anxious to continue her education. Yes, the word would have suited her. *Adolescere*: the process of growing into maturity. Yet as Grace began to relax, running her hands across the brand-new skirt so it covered her knees, and rocking forward as if ready to run a race, Maisie could see only the child.

"Grace, thank you for coming down to have a word with me—I understand you're reading a good book."

Grace blushed.

"Grace?"

"I like books. I like being on my own, reading. So when I saw that library with lots of books at that big house, I read anything that interested me." The girl's eyes widened. "And I put them back—well, almost all of them."

"I was just the same when I was your age," said Maisie. "Always had my head in a book. Which one did you keep?"

Grace pressed her lips together, rolling them as if to make ready to express her thoughts about the book. "It's called *The Great Gatsby*. By an American."

"Are you enjoying it?"

Grace nodded. "It's different. Not like Charles Dickens. Or Jane Austen. It's modern. And I like it because America's different, but it's a sad story too."

"Sad?"

Grace nodded. "Sad rich people."

"I'll have to read it. I've not had time to dip into a good book for a while. And don't worry about the fact that you kept hold of the book—when you've finished, you can give it back to me."

Maisie regarded the girl for a second or two before continuing, understanding that this particular adolescent might be further along on the path to adulthood than she might have imagined. But wasn't that true of all children who had seen war?

"Grace, I want to ask you a few questions about the night you went to the big house in Hallarden, when you witnessed a man being shot."

Grace was quick with her response. "Are you asking all of us these questions?"

"I'll get to the others in time, but I wanted to start with you."

"Why?"

"Because I think you are more observant." Maisie watched as

Grace seemed to inhale the meaning of her words. "I think you see more than you let on."

"The matron at the children's home always told me to keep my thoughts to myself."

"Perhaps not forever—sometimes there's the opportune moment to let someone else in on what you're thinking." Maisie paused, allowing her words to gain weight. "But I was once told by a very wise man to do pretty much the same, because keeping the thought close gives you an opportunity to consider it a bit more, like looking at all the different facets of a diamond. When you've done that, turned the stone around a few times, you have more to offer by way of an observation."

Maisie watched as Grace gave the slightest grin, extending to a broad smile. The youngest member of the quartet was indeed something of a dark horse.

"Grace, you and your friends have described what you witnessed that night, though you spoke mainly through one person—Mary. Could you tell me in your own words what *you* saw?"

Grace stared at Maisie for a moment. "Mary does the talking, so the boys saw what she says they saw."

"And I take it you believe you observed something different."

"I read a book once and all the people—the characters—witnessed the same thing, but every one of them told it differently. It's been on my mind a lot, 'specially when we were in that big house where you found us. I was on my own for hours in that library room, and I sort of thought about it, and I reckon it's to do with sound."

Maisie inclined her head by way of encouraging the girl. "Sound?"

Grace fidgeted in the chair. "You know—sound can make a difference to how we see things, like when a motor goes by and there's a big pop from the engine, and some people run because they think it's a gun. That sort of making a difference."

"Ah, I see," said Maisie. "So, what did you see and hear?"

"Like Mary told you, I was supposed to stay near the gate, but I didn't. It was a bit creepy there, with the trees and the wind coming up, so I thought I'd just walk up to where the others were standing. I didn't run, because that gravelly stuff makes a noise, and we were supposed to be really quiet." The girl frowned, and closed her eyes, as if watching a moving picture in her mind. She opened them, staring at Maisie. "I was right next to Archie when I saw the tall man wearing black clothes and a balaclava on his head—only about, well, twenty feet away. But I'm not very good with distances. He was standing, watching that door to the right of the house. It looked as if he was waiting. Then the man in the suit came out, and the man all in black—he just shot him and he dropped down. That was what the others saw too. Well, Jim and Archie turned around, and Mary waited another second and did the same, but I—I was sort of stuck, staring at that man with his gun." She stopped speaking and looked away.

"What happened next?" asked Maisie, leaning forward. She could see tension in the girl's shoulders and neck.

Grace began to pick at a hangnail. "I was trying to think of how to explain the sound and the time to you—you see, it all happened really fast, but in my head it was happening slowly. I saw another man—a third—standing next to the man with the gun. I reckon he must have been there all the time. Then the man with the gun passed it to him, and he pointed downwards and shot the man who had come from the house. I reckon he was already dead from the first bullet. From what I saw, he copped one in his chest, right where his heart is, and then one in his head—his brain. Where he did his thinking. Heart and head. I thought about that."

"That's a very detailed memory, Grace."

"I reckon what happened to Mary was that she heard the gun go off, and because she had seen the man with the gun, she didn't actually watch the second shot, only heard it. But—but I don't think she deliberately lied or anything like that. She just thought she saw something she didn't." She took a deep breath, and at once seemed fearful. "Please don't tell her I told you a different story—I don't want to get into trouble with her."

"Not to worry—I won't say a word about our conversation to Mary," Maisie assured her. "I think you've done very well, Grace. But I do believe there's more."

"I remember things, Miss Dobbs. I remember what happened because it was strange, as if the man did the first one, the first bullet, and then handed it over so the other one could have a go, you know, as if they both had to do away with the first man." The girl shrugged. "If it was in a book, it would probably have been one of those old Westerns, you know, where the cowboys always have to settle up with someone—I read a few by a bloke called Zane Grey because the boys said girls don't like Westerns."

"Hmmm." Maisie let the sound hang in the air, an expression that registered neither a belief in truth nor a lie. She waited until the girl fidgeted—brushing down her skirt again—and continued with another question. "Grace, what else did you see? Or thought you might have seen?"

"The others were already running, so I went after them sharpish. I didn't want to be left behind and caught by the bloke with his gun. I looked back and I really thought he'd be coming after us to shoot us, but he wasn't. He was just standing there." She gave a long sigh. "I never said anything before, because there were a lot of shadows, what with the shrubs and trees, and it was dusk—that sort of fuzzy light outside, when it's not pitch black either."

"Would you say the second man you think you saw shoot the man was taller or shorter than the . . . the first killer?"

"He was shorter." She paused, thoughtful. "And bent a bit."

"Bent a bit?"

"You know, like someone when they've just lifted something heavy and they stand up, but not straight, as if they've got a bad back."

"Of course, yes, I see." Maisie was silent, taking time to look out of the window before turning back to Grace. "Grace, do you think you were really in any danger?"

Grace shrugged again. *Adolescere*, thought Maisie, as she watched Grace's expression change.

"At first I was sort of scared—I mean, that man had just been shot, and the one with the gun could have come after us. Then I wasn't scared." Grace paused, staring at Maisie. "And later I started thinking about all the things we had been taught, you know, when we were trained to set about the Germans after they invaded—which never happened, did it? Fat lot of good that did us! Anyway, I thought about all the secrets people we knew were keeping, and about the government, and it crossed my mind that the bloke with the gun didn't have to come after us, because someone else would do it for him."

"That was pretty clever thinking, Grace."

"We were told, in training, that we had to use our brains differently. That we had to always consider the enemy and take the path the enemy doesn't think we'll take, and that goes for what we do with our minds as well as our feet."

Maisie allowed another hiatus in the conversation.

"If you had read about the murder in a book, a story with four people of your age witnessing a crime in the way you've described, how do you think the story would proceed?"

Grace smiled again. Maisie was struck by the juxtaposition of innocence and worldly understanding in the face of the young woman before her.

"I'd say it was to do with spies." She leaned forward. "I've read spy books, and what happens is that someone comes looking for the witnesses, and then knocks them off one by one, but in the end there's a hero who puts a stop to it, and finds out that the killer wasn't who we thought it was all along, that it was someone . . . someone close to the crime. They always do that, crime books— you get to see the . . . the perpetrator right at the beginning." She giggled. "Unless of course you don't."

"I think I know your calling, Grace."

Grace gave a wry smile. "I think I know your'n too."

"You do?"

"I went off on my own and had a good look around that big house in Belgravia, and I found the room where I reckon you used to live. The one with the big roses on the curtains, and that nice bathroom right there next to the bedroom. And I went into the drawers and the wardrobe and I found a card." She reached into the small pocket at the front of her cardigan and passed Maisie her calling card. "I didn't tell the others who you are, but I know you're an investigator. And a psychologist."

"Do you know what a psychologist is?"

"You get inside people's minds."

Maisie smiled. "Well, I try to, Grace."

"You don't do a bad job."

"Much obliged, I'm sure."

"Do you have any more questions to ask me?"

169

"No. But I do have a request."

"What's that?"

"Remember I told you about that very wise man I knew? He was my teacher—he taught me how to do my job. Anyway, he once told me that the power of a question is not in the answer given, but in the question itself. It asks us to think, to ponder, to recollect and to reconsider our thoughts and observations. If any of the questions I've asked begin to nag at you—and you'll know if they do—think about it, and if there's more you believe would be helpful to me, just tell Mrs. Partridge you'd like to speak to me."

"Why do you want to know all this?"

"Because I want to rule out anyone being after you and your pals."

Grace came to her feet at the same time as Maisie.

"There was one thing," said Grace. "I've been thinking about it, and it wasn't something I actually saw. But it was just a feeling, so it's probably not important."

"Feelings should never be dismissed, Grace. Go on."

"I sort of thought they all knew each other, you know, the man in the suit and the one who shot him first—because I reckon he knew before he even came out of that house that there would be someone waiting for him. It was as if there was some sort of electricity going between them. I mean, I could almost see it— this thin line buzzing away from one to the other—but p'raps that always happens when one person wants to kill the other. Do you think it does? That there's a second when they're sort of together in their minds because they know what's going to happen? I didn't say anything to the others because they'd laugh at me. Because they're always telling me I'm different."

"You are who you are, Grace. Everyone's different—I daresay they would laugh because they've underestimated you. So thank you—that's information I believe in. And that's an interesting point, about the connection between a victim and his or her killer. I've thought the same thing myself. Now then, I've to be on my way. You've given me a lot to go on, Grace, and I'm much obliged to you."

Grace lingered. "You really mustn't think the others weren't being honest with you, Miss Dobbs. I mean, I might be wrong and they're right. But I know what I thought I saw and it's just a bit different from what they thought they'd seen. Please, please don't tell them."

"Grace, I made my promise. And as I said, you are a very observant young woman. I think in a few years I might tell my partner to take you on as an assistant." Maisie reached for the door handle and opened the door. "But before you go, Grace, what did you like best about the book—*The Great Gatsby*?"

"The ending." Grace smiled, as if pleased to be asked a question about a book. "I finished it just before I came down, because I was that close when you asked if I had a moment. Yes, I liked the ending best because it struck me as a message. I like books like that, what have a message. But I think it was the wrong one."

"Why?"

"Because it was all about looking back, and only a right twit does that."

Maisie watched as the adolescent Grace ran up the stairs two at a time, doubtless to squirrel herself away with another book.

"Everything alright, Maisie?"

Maisie closed the drawing room door, and walked toward Priscilla. "Thanks so much, Pris. Your new guests have settled in very well, I think. Grace seems to be quite the reader."

"She's already asked me about the library. In my opinion, she should continue her education as soon as possible—and that Mary, well, she has a future."

"Oh dear, I've missed something important, haven't I?"

"I don't think it's something you of all people would have noticed, Maisie, my dear," said Priscilla. "But if I'm not mistaken—and I'm not in these matters—if she were dressed in different clothing and learned to present herself with a little more care, she has it in her to become a top mannequin for a famous couturier. They say that hemlines will come down as soon as clothing rationing ends, and given her height and frame she could definitely carry it off. I think I'll put a book on her head and sort out her deportment."

"She'll run away—I know I would."

"No, she won't—not when I tell her how much she could earn! I bet she'll be following me around like a puppy, wanting to know more. Her nails need some attention though, and her hair and . . . well, everything else if she's to have a successful audition. Yes, we need to work on personal presentation."

"Granted, doing something physical might take her mind off things—she's wound up like a clock. In fact they all are, and I can't say I blame them."

"Don't worry, I will soon calm them down, and they will be loath to leave my house—you just wait and see. I'm a winner with children of that age."

"Priscilla, they've seen too much to be children."

Maisie watched as her friend looked away for a moment, then returned to the subject, ready to skim over the surface of their conversation.

"I know. That's the problem, isn't it? They're going to have to think up another word for young people approaching the age of consent, aren't they?"

"Well, until then, dear friend, I must be on my way. Thank you very much for . . . for everything. I believe this will only be for a few days."

"Plenty of time for me to make a start at bringing a little innocence back into their lives. I think they could do with it."

"Couldn't we all, Pris. Couldn't we all."

Maisie turned toward the door, but was stopped by Grace running down the stairs toward her, holding up a book.

"Here's the book, Miss Dobbs. I didn't want to pinch it—just borrow it."

Maisie took the copy of *The Great Gatsby*. "I'll put it back in the library for you—though I think I'll read it first."

"It's a good book, but I thought that Daisy was a bit, you know, soft."

"Can't wait to find out." Maisie smiled, and turned to the door, Priscilla's voice echoing as she closed it behind her.

"Young lady, I know you're confined to quarters, so to speak, but I think I might ask my hairdresser to come to the house—I do believe it's about time you and Mary had something more . . . more up to the minute for young women of your generation."

CHAPTER 10

During the hour-long drive from London down to Chelstone, Maisie took the opportunity to consider what had come to pass in recent weeks, and in the early night-time darkness with little traffic on the road, she asked herself question after question, though the most obvious—the identity of Jonathan Hawkin-Price's killer—was one she skirted around, as if it were the final stepping stone across a rushing river, the largest in a line of landing places extending from one side to the other, a rock from which she might slip and tumble if she hurried or looked down.

The telephone conversation with Caldwell was a relief, because she now knew there was indeed a body, and it was that of Hawkin-Price. Until then, there was only the word of four adolescents—four tired, unsettled young people suffering from their own kind of war fatigue. Each one alternated in mood between confusion and determination, and had a strong will to bring order to their lives because, it seemed, so much had fallen away that might otherwise have sustained them. And if their story about the stability and security—such as it was—of the children's home coming to an end was correct, what might happen next presented a terrifying prospect. But now Maisie had the proof that they had indeed witnessed a murder—which meant they had fair reason to believe they would be sought out and silenced.

But inconsistencies troubled her.

Who found the body? Who alerted the authorities to enable the deceased to be removed to the medical examiner for post-mortem? And how had word traveled to those who would ensure the death would remain under wraps until they were ready to reveal the demise of an important local man? With Lord Julian's passing, Maisie understood only too well the almost medi-eval attachment local people in a small community had to the "squire." Ah yes, Lord Julian—that was another link for which she could not find a chain, though there was George. And there was another name for whom she had no fit—Sergeant Kirby. If she had more detail, she might not need to approach either of these men. She had known George for years and wanted to protect him, and she had a feeling that any attempt to reach the mysterious Kirby would get her nowhere. But she would like to have a more detailed picture in mind of the chain of com-munication.

"It's like a wall with half the bricks missing in odd places," she said aloud, as she slowed the motor car while driving down Riv-erhill on the outskirts of Sevenoaks. She had once been driving on this same stretch of road when her brakes failed—they had been tampered with by a murderer, a woman she had been close to bringing to justice, so she never allowed her attention to wane for even a second when descending the incline.

The following day was Sunday. Her ability to move along with the investigation—which she knew very well was propelled by her curiosity as much as a desire to free the four young people from their fears—was therefore limited. She hoped Mark would tele-phone at some point either late that evening or on the morrow.

Though his position at the embassy was described as "political attaché," Maisie knew his reach extended into various areas of sensitive interest, and often involved his presence at meetings with the president.

"What my job title basically means, Maisie, is that I wear a lot of hats, and every single one might as well have 'dunce' written on the front, because I was stupid enough to take on the job when I was asked to serve my country," Mark had told her before leaving. "Sometimes I want to throw it all against a wall and run out of the building."

"Nonsense," she had replied. "You thrive on it."

"Hmmm, not as much as I used to. My priorities have changed."

When she pulled the Alvis into the gravel driveway alongside the Dower House, Maisie smiled as the back door opened and Anna rushed to the driver's side of the motor car. Soon she was being clutched around the waist by her child, while the tail-wagging from Little Emma seemed bound to leave a mark against her knees.

"Come along, Anna, let your mother get into the house," Brenda called from the kitchen door. "You can tell her your news later."

"News?" asked Maisie as her father joined them.

"I'll carry that bag for you, love," said Frankie, emerging from the kitchen. He kissed his daughter and went straight to the boot to take Maisie's carpet bag. "Don't you think it's about time you retired this old thing? It's frayed everywhere."

"That bag came to France with me, Dad—it's sentimental."

"Sentimental? Never mind that, it'll be weeping soon if you don't let it rest!"

"Very funny," said Maisie, holding her daughter's hand. "Now what's all this—?"

"Grandpa and I have something very exciting to tell you," said Anna, jumping up and down. Once again she reminded Maisie of a much younger child, though at other times, her maturity took everyone around her by surprise.

Brenda rolled her eyes. "What did I say about bothering your mother with that now—let's get in and have our supper, then you and your grandpa can have a word."

"Oh dear," said Maisie. "I fear four legs, a mane and a tail."

"And before you sit down and get comfortable, Maisie, that nice Dr. Dene telephoned—he asked if you would give him a bell at home as soon as you can." Brenda reached into her pocket. "Here's the number in case you don't have it—but take a cup of tea with you along to the library. You look all in."

Maisie kissed her stepmother and instructed Anna to wash her hands and set the table.

"Andrew? It's me." Maisie stood at the library desk, twirling the telephone cord around her fingers.

"Oh good. Brenda said you were expected at the house around seven, so you're bang on time."

"And if I'm calling you at home, then there's something important in the offing. Is it to do with the medical examiner? I heard from a detective contact that the coroner was prevented from going any further with the medical examiner's report, and that a public inquest was stopped from 'on high.'"

"That's indeed part of it, but there's more."

"Go on."

"Where to start? Right, both the examiner and the coroner are

THE COMFORT OF GHOSTS

friends. We've known one another a long time and are part of a medics cricket team."

"So we're on a sticky wicket, are we?"

"Very droll, Maisie! Anyway, it seems the deceased was shot at close range, and apparently in those cases there are often wounds to the hands, because the reflex action is to put up your hands to protect yourself. We know that won't do any good with a gun, but it's just how it is."

"So, no wounds on the hands. What else?"

"The second shot wasn't needed. It was pure . . . pure malice, I suppose. The first one to the heart pretty much finished him off instantly, then the next one was for show."

"Yes, I understand," said Maisie. "As if it stood for something. Is there more?"

"There is, and we have to take a step backwards—I'll explain. Not only was the coroner instructed not to proceed with an inquest, but did your friendly copper tell you that the order was delivered personally from a . . . let me see, from a man named—"

"Robert MacFarlane."

"MacFarlane. Yes. That's him. Anyway, he also took away the report. He instructed the coroner that death by suicide be recorded, and he presented him with a new report to sign and record, stating that the deceased took his own life—suicide due to a deterioration of his mental state. His body was found at the side of the house, not inside, so there is an additional note to the effect that he likely wanted his remains to be found, and given the fact that he lived alone, discovery of the body might not otherwise have happened in a timely manner. News that the poor man took his own life will find its way around the town by Monday morning—and it will be announced in such a way as to make it seem as if it were a recent occurrence, not an event of some weeks past."

"Yet your medical examiner friend's original report stated it was death by someone else's hand. It's a conclusion that mirrors the accounts I've received from witnesses who believe—and I emphasize 'believe'—they saw the man shot."

"Right—indeed, but that's what I meant by taking a step backwards and, just to be clear, looking at the event again. I know you engage in a good deal of reflection in this sort of case—even though you will probably reach the same conclusion. The first shot was to the heart—though the two bullets came in quick succession, so it's hard to know with one hundred percent certainty. There are ways to direct the shot toward your own heart with the Luger, but it's a bit awkward on the hands, dependent upon how you decide to get to the organ. You can go in the side, or the front, or up through the ribs."

"So to make MacFarlane's replacement report make sense, Hawkin-Price would have had to turn his hand so the weapon was firing directly into his heart from the front."

"Yes. Ditto the entry point of the bullet to his brain. Now think about it—if you've just shot yourself through the heart, you're likely to fall, and then you have to lift and turn your hand to score a direct hit into your forehead. If you're bleeding to death from the first wound, it's much easier to lift and position the pistol for side entry into the temple, or through the roof of the mouth. But why bother if you know you're on your last because you've just shot yourself in the heart?"

"Unless . . . unless he was so full of self-disgust that he was determined to shatter both his wounded heart and his equally sour mind."

"Maisie? What do you mean, 'sour mind'?"

"The man had Nazi connections."

"Hmmm. Then I'd say someone definitely did the deed."

"Who removed the body?"

"A gardener found him and an ambulance was called. My pal told me local police and the men who collected the body were instructed to hold the information in absolute confidence until given leave to make it known in the town."

"Tricky, I would think—gossip travels."

"Unless the person laying down the law is high enough up there to send shivers down the spine of the local constabulary. Mind you, like so many other public services, they've got their hands full. Apparently squatters are moving into a decommissioned airfield a mile outside the town, plus the locals are getting upset about new houses supposedly being built. Everyone's up in arms about something."

"Yes, I know—I've been to the town and heard all about it. But what about the staff at the Hawkin-Price house?"

"What about them? Apparently they had been dismissed by Hawkin-Price in advance of a party at his house on the evening prior to his demise, so no one else was on the premises, as the guests had all departed by late in the evening. The gardener lives in a tied cottage locally and came back early the following morning to check on the rose garden—he wanted to cover the bushes with some sort of gauze material to protect from the frost that came in." Dene laughed. "Completely lost on me—I can't keep anything alive in the plant world. Fortunately, I've been known to have success with human beings."

Maisie was silent, running the telephone cord through her fingers.

"Maisie? Still there?"

"Sorry, Andrew—just thinking. Nicely wrapped parcel of lies, isn't it?"

"One more snippet—both the coroner and the medical

examiner were required to sign a document to the effect that they are bound by the Official Secrets Act. As you may have gathered, the game of cricket trumps secrecy to a point, but my team pals are quite happy to wash their hands of the situation. They've also got quite enough to do without having to worry about this one, and as of now, so have I."

"You've been incredibly helpful, Andrew. I appreciate it—and I'm grateful for all you've done for Will."

Maisie heard Andrew Dene sigh.

"I've given strict instructions regarding his diet—that's most important. Small portions, working up to 'little and often' in the way of meals, and then when his constitution is up to it and he's put on some more weight, he'll be able to go to a more normal diet—which is a bit of a stretch, because I don't think anyone has been on a normal diet for a while. I've recommended lots of bone broth, and I don't care which bones, so I'm sure the butcher will help them out and not need to have their ration books to give them a bone or two. Mind you, Maisie, I doubt if the poor man will ever be able to face rice again at any point in his life, even if it's dished up in a pudding with a dollop of jam in the middle."

"As long as he's on the road to recovery, that's what matters."

"Physically, yes, he's doing well now he's been in better quarters for a few days, and the fact that he survived at all is testament to his strength of spirit. But his mind? That's where there's cause for concern. Based upon my work with men who came through the last war, even if he seems perfectly well on the outside, he'll still be suffering nightmares decades from now."

"I know."

"Yes, you do, Maisie. More than most." Dene paused for a moment. "On that subject, about your friend Priscilla—I couldn't help but notice—"

"I know what you're going to say," said Maisie. "She's had a lot of worry, what with Tim now minus an arm and Tarquin, the youngest, being pulled up for declaring himself a conscientious objector, which worried Priscilla no end. Thank goodness Tim has discovered he has his father's talent with words, and all the authorities did with Tarq was put him to work in a forest—if he had opened his mouth in such a cavalier fashion in the Great War, he might well have been shot! Priscilla was convinced he would be thrown in prison. And of course there was Tom flying and her own wounds to overcome." Maisie sighed. "Pris has always enjoyed a drink, but the operations and skin grafts, plus seeing those men at the hospital—it's all mounted up. I think I know what will help her, so I've a plan for something I believe will get her through this setback."

"Good. Let me know if I can lend a hand."

"I will. Thank you, Andrew. As always—thank you."

Maisie returned the receiver to the telephone cradle. She had been standing while speaking to Dene, so took the cup of now lukewarm tea and moved to one of the chairs positioned on either side of the fireplace. It was where she would have been seated so many years ago, while talking with her mentor, Dr. Maurice Blanche. She had never removed the carved wooden rack with a row of his pipes and a tobacco pouch resting on top. It was still within reach, to the left of the mantlepiece; there was a comfort in knowing they were there. The empty armchair before her was the one she considered to be "Maurice's chair." She would take the wingback chair opposite whenever she had a problem to mull, a detail to chew over, a case to consider, or even when weighing up the options for her daughter's education. She had become used to the quiet calm the library offered, along with an atmosphere that seemed to facilitate contemplation—and she had a certain faith that there was a lingering power in the room, a legacy from Maurice that would give her insight when she dearly needed advice.

"This whole case had nothing to do with me, I'll admit it," said Maisie. "I opened this bag of worms because I wanted to save four young squatters from ruin. I found Will—that's one good thing. But now this—and I still don't know if my four charges are safe or not." She stared at the chair as if Maurice were seated there, listening. "So, yes, I have to err on the side of due care and attention, assuming they are not yet out of the woods."

She sipped the tea, more to slake a thirst rather than for any soothing power lingering in the brew. What to do next? That was the question.

"Alright," she said, deciding upon her next move. "On Monday I'll drive over to Hallarden. I'll find out what rumors have been planted in the village, and I will go to the house." She came to her feet and looked at the empty chair, continuing to give voice to her intentions. "I believe I have the chain of events leading to the death of Hawkin-Price settled in my mind's eye. I just have to confirm them—and as usual, Maurice, it's the 'why' that might well lead me to the 'who.' There's also the question of George and this man named Sergeant Kirby. Anyway, it'll soon be time to see Robbie—unless he finds me first. After all, he's only doing his job." She shook her head. "The trouble is—I don't know which one."

Maisie helped Brenda dish up the evening meal, which they called "supper," as it was after six in the evening. If the meal was before six, it was referred to as "tea."

"Sausages and mash! My favorite," said Anna, reaching for her plate.

"I'll say this for you, my girl—you are a good eater," said Brenda, as Maisie set a plate in front of Anna, reminding her it was hot. "Mr. Barton kept back some sausages for me, for which I was very grateful indeed," added Brenda, who often kept a running commentary on what was available in the shops and what she was lucky to get her hands on because she had an "in" with the butcher.

"I wonder how long this rationing business will go on," said Frankie, winking at Anna, teasing her with his fork, as if to steal a sausage.

"Grandpa!"

"Oops, caught that time," said Frankie.

"It'll go on until there's enough of everything again," said Brenda. "In the meantime, we've just got to get on with it. Anyway, now we have sausages, so savor them!"

Maisie felt a familial warmth envelop her. This was what she loved—those she cherished most in the world gathered around her, together, the worries of the day set aside. It was the opportunity she never thought she would have during those dark times when she struggled with widowhood after the death of James Compton, and when she grieved the loss of her tiny son. But now she had a daughter, a loving husband, her parents and Lady Rowan, and they were all close—with the exception of Mark until he returned.

As they were about to begin eating, Maisie noticed a silence descend when Frankie and Anna exchanged glances, and Anna raised her eyebrows in response to her grandfather's nod.

"Alright," said Maisie, setting down her knife and fork. "Let's get it over and done with, shall we? What's the big news, because I would bet it's why you two have for some strange reason ceased to make a noise."

"I thought the quiet was very nice, Maisie—makes a change." Brenda looked at Anna over her spectacles. "And if I see even one bite of sausage make its way to that dog's lips, I will be very, very annoyed."

Maisie noticed her father look away, stifling a grin.

"Come on—out with it," said Maisie.

Anna set down her cutlery. "Mummy," she began. "Grandpa and I went over to see the horses."

"I know—the ones too big for you."

"But there was one smaller one," said Anna.

"Just under fifteen hands," added Frankie.

"Not the sort of just under fifteen hands that's actually almost sixteen hands then?" inquired Maisie.

"He's perfect, Mummy. Just perfect. And he's for sale."

"That's a lot of washing up for you to do, and dusting, sweeping and polishing, young lady. Horses don't come cheap," said Brenda. "You would have to earn the keep."

"Grandma's right." Maisie tried to keep a straight face as she responded to her daughter's plea. "Tomorrow we'll go over with Grandpa to have a look at this perfect horse. But no decisions until your father gets home from America. He knows horses from when he was a boy living on a farm in America, and not only that, he knows how to—"

"Do a deal," said Anna.

"Did he say that?" asked Maisie.

Anna nodded. "He said that when it comes to buying another horse, he'd do the neg . . . the neg . . ."

"Negotiating?" suggested Maisie.

"Yes, he said he'd do it because he's better at doing a deal and you'd pay whatever they asked because you'd feel sorry for the owner selling the horse." Anna began to giggle.

Frankie raised his eyebrows. "He's got a point, love."

"Right, let's get on with supper. No more horses until tomorrow."

Though she would have loved to receive a telephone call from Mark, Maisie was not surprised, knowing that along with others of equal standing, her husband would be in discussions with economists in the United States regarding Britain's request for financial support. The talks were between delegates Mark described as the "higher-ups" but Maisie knew his reports were of interest, given his unique perspective as a senior member of the embassy staff who not only had been stationed in London throughout the war, but was married to a British citizen and now had family in the country. Though the couple made a pact never to discuss their respective jobs—both were engaged in highly confidential work at times, and Mark had once been a decorated field agent involved in the security of his country—she knew her husband was feeling torn between responsibilities.

"They like the fact that my feet are in two camps, Maisie," he had explained before leaving for Washington. "But Americans think the United States has done more than enough for Britain, lost too many men and made a big enough investment in winning the war. There are 'Bring Back Daddy' clubs sprouting up across the country—the people want their boys home, and they want them home now. Yes, we know Britain held back the Nazis for two long years, and probably stopped them mounting a bigger invasion on the east coast—but the war's done and America is eager to motor ahead into the good times, plus we're in a position to do just that."

Maisie knew the preparations for economic negotiations had wearied Mark—but hadn't the war wearied everyone? People the length and breadth of the country were exhausted, no matter their station in life or their circumstances, and so many were bitter, knowing they faced a fast-approaching winter with no roof over their heads and little access to sustenance. It was clear, though, that Mark needed to voice his frustrations.

"The trouble is, your new PM has all these big plans for his 'New Jerusalem'—we've all read about them. A nice national health service, cradle-to-grave care, welfare, housing, new towns, everything to rebuild a broken country. And I know how broken it is, because I see it every single day. You Brits gave everything to keep the Nazis at bay and anyone who walks around with their eyes open can see the aftermath. Same in Germany, Poland, the Netherlands . . . the roll goes on. But Britain has not a dime—sorry, a couple of bob—for everything on its list, because the country is over two billion pounds in the red. Britain is bankrupt and America won't keep on being the bank of endless grants." Mark shook his head, sighed and went on. "When the British government's economist, that guy Keynes, first came to Washington, cap in hand, he talked about justice and honor, about what Britain had done for America. I guess your government boys hadn't grasped that we believed we'd done more than enough in return. Britain asked for money— but any US response to the appeal for help doesn't have a darn thing to do with loyalty or honor. To America it's just business. Big business. Plain and simple dollars going out, then coming right back to us over time and with a mountain of interest on top. I'll cross my fingers that Britain gets the loan, but the terms will be brutal."

Yet Mark Scott had left for Washington with a thread of

optimism that negotiations would result in assistance for Britain, even at great financial cost. Maisie was sure he would telephone as soon as possible, and even though the details would not be divulged, she would know from his voice if the talks were going in the right direction.

On Monday morning, after dropping Anna at the bus stop, where she ran to join her schoolfriends with only a flap of the hand as she looked back, Maisie set off again. However, as she was driving through Chelstone, she saw Sandra—her secretary who now came to the office in Fitzroy Square only once a week to catch up with administration. When the Luftwaffe bombing of Britain's cities began, Maisie had helped Sandra and her husband, Lawrence, secure a cottage in the village, part of her quest to make sure all those she loved were safer than they might be in London. Early in their marriage, Sandra and Lawrence had rented Maisie's Pimlico flat.

"Sandra!" Maisie wound down the window and called out as she drew to a halt alongside the woman who, like herself, had once worked as a maid at the Ebury Place mansion, though Sandra, too, had pulled away from the outcome her station in life predicted.

"Hello!" said Sandra, leaning down to speak to Maisie. "I've just taken Martin to school. Lawrence is in London today, so I've some time to myself. I mean, I've a bit of typing to do for him, and I'll be reading through a few submissions to his magazine, but otherwise—I'm a free woman!"

"Sandra, I've just had an idea—would you like to give me a hand today?"

"You're working on a case?"

"If you've a few hours, I could use your help—you'll be back in time to collect Martin from school and get your work done." Maisie smiled. "Usual rates apply."

Sandra laughed and walked around the motor car to settle into the passenger seat.

"So, where are we going?"

"Hallarden—you know, not far from Paddock Wood."

"Anything interesting?"

"A murder—possibly a planned assassination."

"What do you want me to do?"

"I'll tell you about it on the way. It's something you're good at—talking to people in the town. Finding out a few things."

"Oh yes, I'm good at that." She took a notepad from her shoulder bag. "See, I come prepared for any eventuality! Right, fire away."

Having dropped Sandra close to the village shop and given her directions to the garage and the small office that was home to the *Hallarden Inquirer* newspaper—a monthly roundup of local news and events—Maisie went on her way toward Sandstone Avenue. Once again she drove along the road under a canopy of trees. Only a week or so ago, she had noticed the leaves were hanging on as if they feared falling—a sure sign of a hard winter ahead. Now the tenacious brown, gold and red foliage was heaped up along the avenue and the street sweeper was hard at work, wielding his broom and shoveling leaves into the cart he would push down one side of the street, and then the other, back and forth before he set off to walk to the town compost heap, where he would empty the load before making his way toward another street filled with autumn's fallen colors. Maisie decided the man might have seen a few things in his time, so she dusted off her original story for being in the area.

She pulled up alongside the sweeper and wound down the window. "Good morning. My goodness, you've got your work cut out for you today."

He touched his cap and nodded. "Them leaves took their time letting go, and then all fell at once—that wind we had a couple of nights ago brought them down. It'll be a bitter winter ahead, mark my words."

"Exactly what my father said." She paused. "Anyway, I'm interested in a house along here—you might be able to help me. It's the big house at the end—I understood it was for sale."

The man leaned on his broom and pushed back his cap. "News spread fast and you're not even from around here."

"I'm not sure I understand. I thought I saw a 'For Sale' sign."

"Oh yes, you did. Sorry, madam. Yes, that's the house next door to the big one."

"I see—but am I to understand the larger house is indeed for sale? Your comment made it seem so—has it only just come on the market?"

The street sweeper looked both ways, as if there were someone lurking nearby who might hear him. "Word went around that the owner of the big house has gone—passed on. Found dead by one of the staff, right outside the kitchen door." He looked down the street and back toward Maisie. "I've heard talk that there's a cousin who'll inherit the lot. Apparently he's a relative who went out to Australia years ago, and hadn't been able to get over here for a long time on account of wounds from Gallipoli in the first war, and then this war stopped him sailing over."

"Oh, how terrible—and what a shock."

The man shrugged. "I daresay you'll see the manor up for sale soon enough. I thought you'd heard something about it and wanted to get a foot in the door before anyone else."

"It's too big and I am sure it will be too pricey for me, but I'm interested in houses and I was looking on behalf of a friend."

"The gardener and the chauffeur are down there now, so you could have a word with them."

"They must be very upset, if their employer has died."

"I don't know about that," replied the street sweeper. "There wasn't much love lost there."

"Really?"

"Anyway, none of my business, is it? I'd better get on," said the man, at once reminding Maisie of a snail gathering himself back inside his shell. "This street won't sweep itself and the sort of people here get a bit nasty if they think I'm slacking. They'll see one leaf left behind and the next thing you know, they're on to the council. It's a wonder they don't have me up in the trees picking off the dead ones before they fall."

"I know the sort." Maisie smiled. "Thank you, sir."

The man touched his cap once more as Maisie waved and set off toward the home of the deceased Jonathan Hawkin-Price. *There wasn't much love lost there.*

Maisie did not proceed along the drive toward the Hawkin-Price mansion, but instead parked under a tree on the avenue in an area where the sweeper had already been through—she did not want to incur his wrath by getting in the way of his cart. The small side gate was unlocked, so she entered, and as she began walking toward the property, she saw the chauffeur and gardener in discussion at the side of the house—the very place where she had tumbled out of the kitchen, and where the body of Jonathan Hawkin-Price had been discovered.

"Good morning to you!" Maisie waved to the two men as she

approached, glad she had worn her stout walking shoes, along with a woolen skirt with kick pleats for ease of movement.

Both men looked up, then at each other.

"Morning," they replied in unison.

"We met before—when I made a mistake about which house on the avenue was for sale."

"I remember," said the gardener.

"It's Mr. Chalmers and Mr. King, isn't it?"

The men nodded.

Maisie knew she had to tread with care, so she lowered her head just a little, almost as if she were preparing to say a prayer. "I was in the village when I heard the terrible news. I was so sorry to learn about the passing of your employer—you must be so deeply affected by his death."

There was no immediate response, though Maisie thought she saw the merest shrug from the gardener, Chalmers, as he exchanged glances with the chauffeur.

"Rotten way to go," said King. "Terrible. It was Mr. Chalmers here who found him."

"So I heard. What a shock for you."

"It certainly was," said Chalmers.

"And I seem to remember you had been away for a few days beforehand—what an unfortunate situation. I understand the poor man took his own life."

There was no response, though the chauffeur stepped toward Maisie.

"Can we help you, madam? Funny, you coming back again, seeing as you said the house would be too much for your pocket, and we don't even know when it will go up for sale."

Maisie nodded, quick with her response. "I'm inquiring on behalf of a friend—someone very well heeled, I must say. The family would like to remain . . . would like their interest to remain confidential at the present time, so I'm on a mission to find out who might be representing a sale of the property."

The men exchanged glances again. "Probably old Masters in the town, unless it's a big firm up there in London," said King. "Nothing's been said to us about it, though we've been told we're to stay on for the time being, you know, keep the place in order. There's apparently a relative in Australia, but it all depends on the will."

Maisie did not want to ask who had informed them of their continued employment, so took another tack. "Of course. And you say Mr. Masters in the town is handling the sale of the property, when the time comes?"

"Like he said, solicitor named Mr. Masters looks after estate matters, so it's likely him, unless it turns out to be a London firm," said Chalmers. "We don't know. Anyway, Masters and Kirby, the firm's called. Solicitors. Along the High Street, on the other side of Hallarden. Tricky to find—it's above the Westminster Bank, entrance at the side. You wouldn't know it was there unless you already had an appointment, and by all accounts you won't get past their secretary without one, so I doubt you'll be able to just swan in to show them the color of your money. Or your friend's money. But like we said, it's nothing to do with the likes of us."

"Yes, I understand. Thank you, you've been most generous with your time." Maisie smiled, knowing "generous" was something of an exaggeration, but mention of a Mr. Kirby had rendered the visit all the more valuable.

Both men touched their caps by way of acknowledging her departure, yet as she was about to turn, she looked at one then the other, making sure her eyes met theirs. "I'm sorry—there is one more thing, if you don't mind." She registered the seconds of fear betrayed in the way they regarded her. "I was passing by the war memorial the other day and stopped to talk to the stone-mason who is working on adding names to the memorial . . . lest we forget." She looked down, showing a mark of respect for the dead, then back to the unblinking stares of the two men. "I was a nurse, you see, in the last war—I served in France, so I . . . I like to pay my respects. I had a chat with the mason. Lovely man, isn't he? That's how I know you both lost a son. I wanted to say I am so sorry for your loss, both of you."

"They were mates," said King. "From the time they were littl'uns."

"Our boys looked out for one another," added Chalmers, looking up at the taller man and leaning toward him, almost as if there was a comfort in their shared loss.

"So I was told," said Maisie. "The mason said he'd had a chat when you came to visit."

There was no reply, so Maisie sighed. "Mr. King. Mr. Chalmers." She looked from one to the other. "I know I shouldn't have jumped at the opportunity to walk around the house when I came upon the unlocked door, but I went upstairs to see how many rooms were there—and I ventured into the study to find out what the view would be like from that room. That's when I saw the photographs, and I confess I was rather shocked to note the kind of people your employer counted among his friends." She took a deep breath. "All I will say is—it must have been troubling for you, knowing the sort of men Jonathan Hawkin-Price consorted with."

Chalmers seemed ready to anger, but King touched him on the arm. A few seconds passed, during which Maisie did not turn from the men.

"You're right, madam, you weren't supposed to be in there—you were trespassing, and that door was meant to be locked anyway." Maisie felt King's stare intensify, but did not step back. "Looks can be deceiving," he went on. "Mr. Hawkin-Price was a good guv'nor. He paid us well and on time. And we've both got roofs over our heads—for now, anyway, and it wouldn't surprise me if we're provided for in his will. All that matters to us and our families now is getting through every single day. We lost our boys and our grief will last until they put us in the soil. Nothing can bring them back. That's what it amounts to."

"You're right, of course—and as I said, I am so sorry your families have had to endure such loss." She paused, once again looking from one man to the other. "I'll go into the town now. I'd like to talk to Messrs. Masters and Kirby about the house. Thank you."

"Probably should have told you—the office is closed for a week. Happen to know that," said the chauffeur.

Maisie smiled. "You've saved me the trouble—thank you. I'll return next week. Good day to you."

She began walking away but looked back once, in time to see Chalmers proceed toward a series of flower beds and the chauffeur depart in the direction of the garages. Like many a gardener before him, the years of bending over plants, pressing a shovel into hard earth, pushing lawn mowers and rollers and stretching up and leaning down for the pruning of difficult-to-reach shrubs had all taken a toll upon Mr. Chalmers's spine. Or perhaps sorrow had weighed upon him, so he walked with a stoop as he ministered to the gardens he tended for his now dead Nazi-sympathizer employer.

CHAPTER 11

Maisie kept her speed low as she drove back toward the center of Hallarden. Despite the fact that she had come to a conclusion about the chain of events leading to the death of Jonathan Hawkin-Price, the question of whether Mary, Jim, Archie and Grace were out of the woods remained worrisome. They had witnessed a murder—yet it was a killing that came with a question mark, and the man she suspected would have all the answers was indeed Robert MacFarlane.

Driving through the town, resplendent on an autumnal sunny day, Maisie took account of the medieval buildings set among later Georgian and Victorian houses, some converted into shops on the ground floor with flats or an office above. Trees lined the high street, which was not as busy as it would have been on a Saturday morning, though there was a smattering of people going about their business, mainly shopping, and shopping still amounted to a good deal of standing and shuffling along, ration book in hand, after joining a queue for the butcher or the bakery.

As planned, Sandra was waiting alongside the telephone kiosk on the other side of town, so Maisie pulled the motor car into a lay-by and turned off the engine, reaching across to open the passenger door.

"Well, that was interesting," said Sandra, settling into the seat next to Maisie.

"I'm sure it was—what did you find out?"

"The news of 'the man at the big house' taking his own life is making the rounds, and of course it seems people are speculating about what will happen to the estate, especially as it was halved to pay death duties when the owner's father died. I didn't even have to ask many questions—I just sort of lingered in the little shop you told me about and kept my ears sharp. That woman behind the counter really is the holder of town gossip, isn't she?" Sandra shook her head. "I reckon there's one like her in every small town or village—the disseminator of all local news. Anyway, I don't think people had too many opinions about Hawkin-Price either way—he wasn't loved, nor was he treated with scorn—and it seems whenever someone mentioned 'that German woman' he had taken up with, another person reminded the gathered tattletales that the poor man fought in the last war, and only inherited because his brother perished."

"It's the sort of talk I would have expected. Go on—what else did you hear?"

"They can't wait to find out what is going to happen to the mansion, and people are worried that it will be used to provide shelter for the homeless, and there's a belief it will be broken up into flats—or worse, the land will be sold for even more houses to be built."

"Anything else about the fact that death by suicide has been recorded?"

"As I said, lots of 'poor man' and a couple of 'I always thought that might happen.' But the interesting thing is that one person said, 'He did it because we won the war and he was a blimmin' Nazi!' And there were a number of heads nodding in agreement, though that's when it went quiet and people started saying, 'I'd better be getting along' and 'I can't stand here jawing all day,' so off they went. I grabbed a toy motor car to put away for Martin's Christmas stocking, and paid Miss Rowe, but I didn't want to ask any questions, because I thought I had quite a lot of information to be going on with, and after all, I am a stranger to her—mind you, I think she would have liked to chat a bit more. She seemed quite lonely when I left and there was no one remaining in the shop to talk to." Sandra shook her head, and sighed. "Anyway, I went along to the police station. I pretended I was a reporter with the *Daily Mail*—I thought I might as well go for a big London paper, because I reckoned they knew all the local press bods."

"Good idea."

"To warm up the desk sergeant, I asked about the proposed house-building on the edge of town—I said I was writing about the government plans for new towns across the country, you know, to take in overspills after the war. Opinion is definitely against that. I received an earful about how the government is in league with the builders and everyone is profiteering, taking backhanders—so I moved the chat toward the Hawkin-Price mansion, and whether he thought it would be converted for homeless, now that the owner was dead. He went a bit quiet, then asked how I knew about it, and I said, 'Seems to be common knowledge in the town.' I asked whether there was any doubt about suicide, and he was a bit slow to answer, but then he said, 'It's what the coroner reported, so who am I to doubt him?'"

"Interesting," said Maisie.

"I dived in on that one and asked if he had any thoughts about the coroner's conclusion. He shrugged his shoulders and said, 'You're a reporter, you know there's always a few questions where a gun is concerned—he shouldn't have had a pistol like that anyway. Owning a hunting rifle is alright, but not a Luger.' And you know, it was the way he stared at me—I knew he had his suspicions, then he looked around and said, 'We're all a bit surprised around here. He wasn't the sort to commit suicide—too bloody-minded and cocky by half.' I wanted to dig a bit deeper, but another copper came along—plain clothes man; you can always tell them—and so the desk sergeant told me that was all he had to say about the new estate on the edge of town, and that I should go to the council offices for more information."

"Good work," said Maisie. "Everything you've said provides more for me to go on—you've done well, Sandra. We should form an inquiry team more often."

"Oh, there was one more thing. He told me there was some talk about the house being left to the children's home, so they could expand their services to include older children. But he didn't like that."

"Did he say why?"

"He said the older ones were trouble, and that after a certain age, the supervisors there just gave up on them, so all they learned in that home was how to get up to mischief in the town. But all the same, he felt sorry for them. 'Direction,' he said. 'They need direction or they'll all turn out to be villains.' But then he sort of went soft, and told me about one of the boys—by the name of Archie—who was always getting up to no good, but who he had sympathy for because when he was caught scrumping apples from a local farm, the lad just burst into tears." Sandra looked down at her notebook. "The sergeant said, 'At that age, if no one cares and they don't have a purpose, they're like half-formed vines left to grow wild without a trellis to steer them up straight.'"

"He's got a point," said Maisie, as she started the engine.

"Where are we going next?" asked Sandra, pushing the note-book into her shoulder bag.

"You know, I think we'll just go home now. I wanted to pop into a firm of solicitors; however, not only are they closed, but I believe I have enough information to be going on with so I can decide upon my next move. And to be honest, I want to get back to Chelstone to place a call or two and meet Anna from school. I've promised to go with her to look at a horse."

"Such a shame Lady had to be put down—Anna took it hard, didn't she?"

"Yes, she did. And she was always very responsible—she would get up early to do the feed and went down there as soon as she could after school to muck out again and bring round the evening hay. And that little pony was brushed within an inch of her life." Maisie changed gear as they passed through the town. "Anna's schoolwork will increase soon enough, so we have to be careful and ensure she can still make a contribution to the welfare of her horse and not have it all handed to her—it's not healthy for a child."

"She deserved some spoiling though, didn't she? Poor little mite was bereft when she came to you. She wouldn't even talk."

"Oh, Sandra, she deserved everything I could possibly give her—she's such a lovely child. We managed to get her past that bullying upset at Chelstone Primary, and she's flourishing at the international school. Now we want to do all we can to ensure she grows into a wonderful young woman. I've seen too many who have been spoiled by indulgence, and it's not attractive. The police sergeant got it right, about vines growing without a trellis." Maisie felt her eyes moisten. "I want her to dream, Sandra. I want to give her wings, so she can go far and continue to be a good, compassionate and considerate young person at the same time."

As they passed Sandstone Avenue, Maisie noticed another motor car emerging to join the main road into the town. She continued on for a short distance, and after checking in her rearview mirror, without warning, she swung the Alvis around and retraced their route, once again stopping close to the Hawkin-Price mansion—but not too close.

"Changed your mind about something, eh?" asked Sandra, raising her eyebrows.

"I've had enough of this—I want to make one more call to speak to the staff—specifically the chauffeur's wife, as I think he's just left the estate. If he's there, I'll just have to put it to him. I have but one question."

"I think you'll end up asking more than one," said Sandra.

"You could well be right, Sandra—you've known me too long!"

Leaving Sandra in the motor car, once again Maisie walked a short distance along the avenue and entered the estate via the unlocked entrance adjacent to the grand padlocked iron gates that, when drawn back, allowed vehicular entry and exit. There was no sign of either the gardener or anyone else in the distance, so she proceeded to the side of the house. She could not help turning the handle on the kitchen door, but it was locked. Directing her gaze through the rhododendron bushes, she could see the garage, which she estimated could house four motor cars with ease, and she was able to note that the upstairs flat could be accessed from the outside. She suspected there was an interior door and flight of stairs within the garage. She proceeded walking toward the smaller door to the garage, and rapped on the windowpane set into wood—just to make sure she had indeed seen the chauffeur driving and was not mistaken. There was no answer. Walking around to the front of the garage, she discovered the double doors open and one motor car was missing—she was right, it was the chauffeur she had seen driving a motor car and merging onto the main road from Sandstone Avenue.

Taking a deep breath, she made her way up the outer staircase leading to the flat and lifted the door knocker, but before she could summon whoever was at home, the door opened.

"I thought I could hear someone. Who are you? We don't allow hawkers on the estate, you know."

Maisie offered a broad smile and extended her hand. "My name is Maisie Dobbs—your husband may have mentioned that I visited earlier, when I came to inquire about the house and whether it was for sale."

The woman waved as if swatting a fly, a dismissive gesture instead of taking Maisie's hand. "That poor man isn't cold in his grave, and you're asking about the house?"

"To be honest, I didn't know about the exact circumstances of his passing—I've only just found out while in the town. And Mr. King may have mentioned to you that I confused the house for sale next door with this one—the sign is on the property line."

"I suppose it's an easy enough mistake, but here you are again."

"Yes, here I am. And before I ask a very quick question, may I say how sorry I am to hear about your son? He gave his life for his country, and I think for the entire world, because he fought the terror of Fascism." Maisie did not withdraw her focus on the woman as she stared back. "In case you wondered, I saw his name on the memorial. As I explained to your husband and Mr. Chalmers, I always stop at a memorial. I was a nurse, you see, in the last war, and I drove an ambulance in London, during the Blitz. I know what it is to lose someone."

The woman looked at Maisie as if she were reconsidering her initial poor impression, then folded her arms as if dismissing the thought. "Yes, thank you. But be that as it may—what do you want with me and my husband?"

"Very simple. You see, I live in Chelstone and the Compton family—you probably know the name—are very dear to me. I am the widow of their son, James. I believe you may have heard he was killed testing a new fighter aeroplane before the war—it was mentioned in all the county newspapers when it happened. Anyway, I really wanted to know if your husband was acquainted with George, the chauffeur there." Maisie smiled. "I don't know what I would do if George wasn't on the estate to keep my motor car in tip-top condition. I thought that, if he's known to you, I could pass on your regards, because I would hate to mention I'd visited the house only to have him say, 'I wish I'd known you were there.'"

"We know George," Mrs. King replied, showing no change in demeanor. "The men met years ago in London, both of them starting out working in them big houses at a time when the masters were giving up their horses and taking up with motor cars. The engines weren't as reliable as they are now, so there was a lot to learn, I suppose. They've kept in touch—and Ted who runs the garage in town is another one they knew when they were up in London. So, there you have it."

"Thank you, Mrs. King," said Maisie, smiling despite the lack of warmth emanating from the woman. "Do you have a message for George? I'll be seeing him as soon as I'm home." She consulted her watch. "In about three-quarters of an hour, if I have a good journey."

She noticed the woman's attitude change, her stern stoicism replaced by a fluster as she rubbed her hands together, and then across her neck, as if she were suffering a muscle strain. "Well, I don't know. I've not talked to him much personally since he lost his wife, but . . . well, you could tell him we send our regards and I daresay Mr. King looks forward to seeing him again soon."

"I'll tell him." Maisie thanked the woman and, as she turned as if to leave, added one more comment. "At least you'll now be able to talk about more than just the invasion if it comes, won't you?"

Maisie looked back once. The chauffeur's wife had not moved from the top of the steps and was staring at Maisie as she continued on toward the iron gates, watching her departure from the house belonging to a man who, she now believed, might have had many guises.

"That horse is more than fifteen hands," said Maisie, using her palms to measure the height of the horse standing before them.

"Only just, love," said Frankie.

"Dad, admit it, you've wanted another horse to look after ever since Chelstone's hunters were sold."

"Mummy, I think Daddy would love this horse," said Anna.

"Why do you say that?"

"His name. It's Theodore."

Maisie sighed. "I don't think your father is so easily swayed by the name of a dead president."

Anna giggled. "Mum, he—"

"Alright, perhaps just a bit. But he will want to know you're safe, that's the main concern."

"Let's get her up on this here Theo, and you can see how she does," said Frankie.

Maisie took a deep breath, closed her eyes and exhaled. "Oh dear, he's 'Theo' already. Alright, just for a few minutes." She looked at the groom standing nearby. "Has he been warmed up?

I'd like to see someone else ride him first. I want to know what he's like from cold, and I don't want Anna to do it."

Maisie, her father and daughter stood alongside the fence to watch the groom put Theodore—who Anna was now calling 'my boy'—through his paces.

"He's nicely warmed up, Mrs. Scott. Very easy-going lad, this one," said the groom as she dismounted. "A true schoolmaster."

Frankie gave his granddaughter a leg up into the saddle and adjusted the stirrups.

"Right, Anna," said Maisie. "Off you go—and only around the outside of that manège."

"Can't I just—?"

"No, just on the flat, walk and trot. No canter. We'll save anything more for when Daddy's here, you know how he hates to miss anything."

Maisie watched as Anna began walking the horse around the outside of the manège.

"She's got a twinkle in her eye," said Maisie, as Anna nudged the horse into a trot. "I hope she doesn't push her luck."

"Love, just concentrate on how she rides, her seat and her hands. She's a good little horsewoman. I know you're anxious—your mother was the same with you when I let you ride old Persephone around the streets after I was home from work."

Maisie felt her father's arm around her shoulders.

"Theodore doesn't look so big when she's on him, does he?" said Maisie.

"She carries herself well," added Frankie.

"Yes, I know that, but—" Maisie put her hands to her mouth as Anna took her prospective new horse from a trot to a canter, and then looked toward jumps set up in the center of the manège.

"I had a feeling she wouldn't be able to resist that jump," said Frankie.

"I can't look," said Maisie, holding her hands over her eyes.

The following morning, Maisie walked a very quiet Anna to the bus stop.

"Was Daddy very annoyed with me when you told him?"

"He wasn't best pleased, Anna." She reached for her daughter's hand. "But to be honest, I think he was just a bit upset at having missed you taking that jump, and he was probably rather scared too."

"I shouldn't have done it, should I?"

"Well, you were asked not to. But the main thing is that your father was able to get through on the telephone and he said he's hoping to fly home soon. He can't wait to see you ride Theo, but remember, buying a horse is a big decision, and big decisions are family decisions. And I doubt anyone is going to rush to buy Theo in the meantime."

"I'm sorry, Mummy. But I knew he wouldn't do anything bad—I could see into Theo's mind, and we both knew we wanted to go over the jump."

"Let's put yesterday behind us, shall we? You've some important tests today, so best to concentrate on those."

"I've done all the work."

Maisie leaned down to kiss Anna, and held on to her for a moment.

"Mum—everyone will laugh at me. You're the only mother who kisses and cuddles when you take me to the bus stop."

Maisie felt her daughter wriggle away from her embrace.

"Give my love to Uncle Robbie." Anna waved as she ran toward her friends. "Bye!"

Maisie sighed. *Mum?* "I'm no longer 'Mummy'—I've become 'Mum,'" she whispered to herself, and was surprised to feel quite bereft as she walked toward Chelstone railway station. Time was passing at a greater speed than she had bargained for—she didn't have to bend down very far to kiss Anna anymore, but instead only had to lean her head forward. The thought of Anna's recent growth spurt led Maisie to segue toward the fate of the four young people lodging with Priscilla. Time was passing for them, too, and she felt it was now imperative to move at speed to secure their safety and their futures—a responsibility she had assumed the minute she refused to reveal their whereabouts to Robert MacFarlane. With any luck, today's confrontation would release her for another step in the direction of their best interests.

"Well, well, well, if the mountain hasn't come to Muhammad, as the saying goes," said MacFarlane, leaning back in his chair when Maisie was shown into his Baker Street office.

Maisie looked around. "Seems you're all moving out of here now—I was surprised not to be sent off to another part of London to find you."

MacFarlane allowed his chair to fall forward. "They've got to put me somewhere before I'm posted off into the sunset with a few bob in the retirement account, haven't they? And as you know, I've still a lot of work to do." He pulled a buff-colored folder from the top of an unsteady pile of papers and nodded toward the chair in front of his desk. "Take a seat and let's have a blether about your antics, shall we?"

"My antics? I was hoping to discuss your capers."

He leaned toward her, folding his arms across the file. "Let's not waste time quipping, Maisie. Neither of us likes messing around, so cards on the table—what do you know?"

Maisie stared out of the window to settle herself for a second, then turned to face MacFarlane.

"Funny, isn't it? This is like so many buildings in London—or I suppose in a number of places around the country," said Maisie. "It seems so benign from the outside, yet until not so long ago, on the inside people were scurrying along corridors and into sound-proof rooms planning death, double-checking security and trying to work out how to win the war, whether their methods were above board, or well below it."

"Brave souls have darkened the doors of these offices."

Maisie shook her head. "As I know only too well—I approved a number of them for service, or did you forget? No, of course you wouldn't forget that I knew two of the women particularly well."

MacFarlane rubbed his forehead. "That was always the hard part, wasn't it? You knew what was being asked of them—and they knew too—but they went over to France, or Denmark, or Belgium or wherever, and they laid down their lives knowing we would have to deny all knowledge of their activities if they were captured. Heaven only knows how I managed to go from being a Scotland Yard detective, to Special Branch, then to the security services and the Special Operations Executive—and now this, doing my bit to mop up the aftermath of a massive bloody mess from here to Nuremberg." He looked down and moved his arms away from the folder, though he brought his attention back to Maisie. "And just to make one aspect of my job even harder, you were avoiding me. I could have done without the trouble, Maisie."

"Robbie, to be honest, I didn't know if I could trust you. I'm a bit more sure that I can now, but I had to keep four young people safe for a while at least."

MacFarlane opened his mouth to speak, but Maisie held up her hand.

"Let me finish, Robbie." She swallowed to ease the dryness in her throat and began again. "We both played a part in sending operatives into the field, and with a full understanding of their possible outcome. Even as we speak, I know there are people here—or wherever they are now situated—who are trying to pin down the whereabouts of missing agents. Or their remains. And now I know the four youngsters were part of what was effectively a resistance line situated across Britain, enlisted from all walks of life and ages—including adolescents—who were trained to undermine the Nazis in the case of an invasion. From what I can ascertain, they conducted themselves honorably and were trained well." She paused, shaking her head. "Were those four young people 'dispensable' because they had no family to speak of? I think perhaps yes, they were considered expendable. And I believe they received instructions to continue being ready for service even after all risk of an invasion had been more or less curtailed and the pressure diminished—and let's admit, it was a relief for us all that Hitler went off to have a go at the Russians instead of trying to cross the English Channel."

"Yes, yes, we know all that, Maisie—but you finish making your points, and then I'll make mine."

"Right you are. They were trained to be observant above all else. To report what they saw and they thought they saw a Nazi-sympathizing member of the aristocracy in his element, and then they thought they saw him killed. So they ran. They ran to someone who they assumed could help them—and he did, which of course undermined you and your fellow people in this . . . this circus, didn't it? Because these local guerrilla groups represent another set of pies you have a finger in, don't they?"

"Excellent work, *Your Ladyship*—go on."

Maisie was quick to nip MacFarlane's goading in the bud. "Robbie, I've seen that look on many men in my time and that comment went beyond your usual cynical banter, so don't even think of trying to belittle me because I'm a woman, or so help me I'll ... I'm not in the mood for it, and I'm trained too, remember? So at this very moment, don't push me. You know only too well that a good number of the missing agents you're now looking for were women, and they came into this building to be interviewed and 'processed' for one of the most dangerous active service jobs." She took a breath, placing her hand against her chest to settle her racing heart. "It's not like you to engage in that sort of repartee, so don't start it now."

"Alright, Maisie, carry on—and sorry for that. You're right, I was out of order. Mind you, I'm enjoying the story."

Maisie felt the red flush of anger that had bloomed across her cheeks begin to subside. The tide was going out on her temper, though she did not care for Robert MacFarlane's use of the word "story." She continued to stare at him, and drew breath before pressing on.

"I'm not going to ask who planned the training of these civilians, though it's probably one of your *M* departments, but not MI5 or even the Secret Intelligence Service. Anyway, the younger civilians in this army were trained, they were allowed to keep their hands in just in case, so to speak, and along the way their loyalty to their superiors was never diminished, and they grew up a bit— so when one of their number witnessed a Nazi get-together, off he went to tell the others. They returned to the house and were just in time to witness the murder of Jonathan Hawkin-Price. They took action and reported what they had seen to the man who was in charge of their training, because they had limited knowledge of others who belonged to the same group—intentional, because if there had indeed been an invasion, the powers that be did not want a captured local operative spilling the beans on a local solicitor, eh? Or even the vicar?"

MacFarlane nodded, his eyes focused on Maisie.

"But I believe that what they saw was a planned assassination by a trained killer who knew they had more to lose than him." She paused, waiting for MacFarlane to interject, but he said nothing, so she took up her account again. "There was an accomplice, and having been to the house and into the town to ask a few questions here and there, I believe the assassin was the chauffeur and the man at his side was the gardener, who also played a part. All very nice and local, like one of those potboilers people took down to the shelters to take their minds off the fact that their homes were being blown apart. And what was their reason for killing Hawkin-Price? I wondered about that, and I think the revelation that their employer was a Nazi weighed heavy on two men who had lost their sons. They had no need to chase after the four witnesses, because due to their contacts—and they were also part of one of these rural resistance groups who made ready to take on the German invaders—they could get the whole thing nice and tidily swept away with a story about suicide. And you helped."

"Any more? Or is that the end of your grand summation of what came to pass?"

Maisie at once felt unsteady, as if someone were moving a carpet under her feet and she might lose her balance. She stared out of the window, again gazing out over the rooftops, for a second remembering Will Beale and his comment that if you looked at the roofline or the trees, you could imagine the streets below had not been blasted apart. Without turning back to MacFarlane, she offered another explanation.

"I confess, Robbie, that it was all too easy to jump to that conclusion, so I am faced with a few varying scenarios. Was Hawkin-Price on our side all the time? Was he a plant? Was his German lady friend for us or against us? And did that man harbor his own bitterness about the terrible state of affairs our country was left in after the last war, so his allegiance turned to the man who was bent upon changing Germany's fortunes?" Again she waited, wondering if MacFarlane would interrupt, but when he made no comment, she picked up the thread again. "I thought he might have been playing both sides, only to face the fate of the double agent, although some of the clever ones made it through quite nicely, didn't they?"

MacFarlane smiled, though it was one of indulgence, not of good humor. "Very good. All sterling thoughts, Maisie—and I would have expected nothing less from you. I like to see a mind whirring around, not accepting the first easy answer to the question."

"I was taught that the power of the question—"

"Yes, yes, I know all that, hen," MacFarlane interrupted. "I know almost every single lesson your Maurice Blanche taught you, because I would lay money on the fact that you've quoted them to me at one time or another. I could write a bloody book about them!"

Maisie stared at MacFarlane, and began to speak in a low, measured tone and with a calm demeanor, all the better to holster any power she had remaining. "What I really want from you is a promise that Mary, Jim, Archie and Grace are protected from any repercussions associated with their wartime activities. I must know they are safe."

"I'm not in the business of taking the lives of children, Maisie. But I had to make sure no one else would—and that I've done.

Suffice it to say, there are people in other departments who have become so used to killing to save others, they would be able to remove the threat of your four kiddies without any trouble at all." MacFarlane sighed. "But I promise you now, they will be safe and will live good long lives, though they must also be reminded of their responsibility to the Official Secrets Act and their country."

Maisie did not respond, and did not look away when MacFarlane stared at her as if to add weight to his words.

"It's my promise, Maisie," said MacFarlane. "And if there's one thing you know about me, I never break a promise."

Maisie waited, watching MacFarlane. "Yes, you're right, Robbie—you've never broken a promise made to me. I will take steps to ensure the youngsters doubly understand the situation and need for secrecy—but I have confidence in them. They have a level of fear that will keep their mouths shut on the subject. And they also have a respect for the work they were engaged in. I think we both know that's something Lord Julian understood, even though he was in far from good health." Maisie reached forward and tapped the folder in front of MacFarlane. "So, are you going to tell the story, or am I going to have to read it?"

MacFarlane stood up, opened a filing cabinet and took out a bottle of single malt whisky and two tot glasses.

"Sun's over the yardarm somewhere in the world."

"That's what my friend Priscilla says—but nothing for me, Robbie."

"It's going on for twelve now, so it's either a drink here or we go down to the pub, and I can't talk freely there, so have a belt with me, for old time's sake. It'll do you more good than that usual tiny cream sherry tipple of yours."

"Do I have to remind you, yet again, about the last time I joined you in a single malt?"

MacFarlane laughed. "I know—I ended up losing you to a Yank."

"Robbie?"

"Nothing—never said a word." He poured two glasses of the smooth, coppery malt whisky and set one in front of Maisie, then lifted the folder and passed it to her. "There, let's sit back, have a sip and both of us take a deep breath while you read this. I'm so worn out, I might even close my eyes for a bit."

—

CHAPTER 12

Maisie closed the folder and placed it on the desk in front of her, then reached for the small glass of malt whisky MacFarlane had poured. He was already on his second glass, and though she was tempted to follow him, she sipped, feeling a welcome sensation that was at once fiery yet soothing. She sipped again and set the glass down.

"Pushes you off kilter, doesn't it, lass? This sort of thing coming to light and it doesn't quite fit an existing template. Or when you know you were right about one thing, but whatever it was you thought you had in your investigative bag of tricks doesn't work very well when you have the whole picture in front of you."

Maisie leaned forward. "I want to be clear, Robbie. Let's take it from the beginning."

"1919."

"Yes. Hawkin-Price was—understandably—devastated by what came to pass during the war. His world had come crashing down. He was the second son of a wealthy family, with all the advantages of money, yet because he was not the heir he had been able to relinquish any familial responsibility, which landed on the shoulders of an older brother."

"That bit's not written in the report."

"It's implied—and I've been trying to get inside his head, what he might have been thinking. Or feeling."

Robbie rolled his eyes and poured himself another measure of the whisky. "Feeling? Here we go—Maisie Dobbs at her sensitive best. And there was me hoping we'd manage to get to the end of this without that word floating around." He held the bottle up as if to query Maisie.

"No more for me. Let's go on." She reached for the folder again. "Hawkin-Price came home from the Western Front with a few war wounds and had to face the fact that his brother was dead, a hero killed in action. Add to that his parents' grief, to say nothing of the responsibilities he was required to assume and with little prior experience—it appears that before the war, Jonathan Hawkin-Price had been something of a dilettante second son." She turned the page. "Yes, he was wounded—some gas damage to his lungs, shrapnel in his legs and perhaps some neurasthenia—so not too terribly, it has to be said, but his whole life had changed. Then the parents died—was it the influenza, by the way?" She turned back to the earlier page. "As I thought, influenza, same as my friend Priscilla's parents. Anyway, as a result of death duties and other financial pressures, Hawkin-Price had to sell off land and start to think about how he could earn a living. Disposing of the land made him pretty angry—he was something of a snob, because he didn't like what he called the 'middle classes' moving in." She looked up at Mac-Farlane. "I mean, poor man, having to live next to a local bank manager."

"Sarcasm, sarcasm, the devil's weapon, Maisie. Must be my presence rubbing off on you."

Maisie conceded a smile. "To continue, I can see he cut back on expenses, staffing and so on, and as time went on, became increasingly annoyed with his government." She looked up. "I heard as much from a local shopkeeper."

"We are aware that he allowed a few of his hard feelings to fly in company, letting everyone know what he thought of the PM or whomever he had in his sights," said MacFarlane.

"He could indeed—and from this report, he became part of a group of very entitled aristocrats who were disenchanted with this country and admiring of Germany—they felt as if they had been the losers, not the victorious. Mind you, there was a lot of trouble in Germany too, as time went on—unemployment as bad as it was here. Hitler made hay with the discontent to press his agenda—that was the key to his power. Then he capitalized on it when he found the ideal scapegoat for all German ills." She shook her head. "Anyway, Hawkin-Price took up with a German princess—I understand there are a lot of them over there."

"Good few here too."

"Be that as it may—she was a Bavarian noblewoman, a widow, and she was a friend of Adolf Hitler. As we know, Hitler liked to forge friendships with the aristocracy on both sides of the English Channel. It was a way of seeking more power by proxy—and he knew his targets very well. The wealthy British with whom Hawkin-Price associated were concerned that the revolution in Russia would extend further, inspiring the working classes at home to rise up, which would threaten their very precious way of life."

"Careful, you sound like you're about to start your own revolution—tricky, considering you were once married to gentry."

Maisie was quick to interrupt. "I'll ignore the implication, Robbie. Let's get on with this clarification, and then I'll leave you to continue drawing a line under these loose ends before you retire."

"Sorry—and yes, you're right—they were rich people afraid of anything that might knock them off their station in life and send them down the road to wait at the bus stop with the ordinary people."

"Right, so they had these get-togethers, parties where they fawned over photos of themselves with the Führer and saluted the Nazi flag, and before the war some of them traveled to Munich or wherever he was in Germany to meet the man himself. But—"

"Yes, the 'but.'"

"It seems from the report that, given his contacts, Hawkin-Price soon discovered some highly questionable, indeed evil, things were going on in Germany—but of course until the war ended, no one knew the true extent of the terror. So he turned and became an agent for the British, time and again coming back with valuable information from his contacts in Germany as well as informing on his aristocratic friends here."

"We now know exactly who they are, to a man and woman."

"But according to this, Hawkin-Price was ashamed," said Maisie, tapping the page. "Deeply, deeply ashamed and full of remorse over his earlier loyalty to Germany. He could not live with himself—to the point where he wanted to end his life."

Maisie paused, reached for her glass and sipped the remaining single malt whisky. "He knew his employees Mr. Chalmers and Mr. King were involved in a local resistance network, and more than anything, he had seen their sons go off to war—they were young men who had grown up on the family estate. He had watched them as children playing in the fields, climbing trees, helping their fathers with their work. King's son polished his motor car every time he wanted to go out." She felt her breath become short as she imagined the scenario described in Mac-Farlane's report. "So he gave two bereaved fathers the task of

THE COMFORT OF GHOSTS

taking his life—an opportunity, if you will. He did not want to live a second longer, so he asked them to shoot him, to have their revenge and be done with it, making it look like suicide. MacFarlane, I . . . I still don't understand—"

"Hawkin-Price told Chalmers and King that he was dying, that he wanted to end it all—and that he was aware they knew of his earlier support of Hitler's Fascism. His desire to be done with life accelerated after news started coming through about the concentration camps, and about the fate of our POWs. And our bloody agents too." MacFarlane shook his head. "Sure you don't want a top-up?"

"If I had any more now, I probably wouldn't stop."

"And who knows what might happen then, eh? I will, if you don't mind."

"Robbie, did you question Chalmers and King after the death of Hawkin-Price was reported?"

"Kirby did it for me. He had an idea something like that would happen—he'd had his eye on Hawkin-Price for quite a while, from long before the man turned." He poured one more glass of whisky for himself and placed the bottle back in the filing cabinet.

"Ah, yes, the mysterious Kirby—mind if I take a detour?"

"Go on."

"I'm amazed our four agents didn't recognize him at some point."

"Don't be, Maisie. You know as well as I do that his office was tucked away and he wasn't exactly known in the town unless someone needed a solicitor, and it's usually only the better-offs who can afford legal assistance. But here's the key—you know how it is when you see someone outside their usual place. Say you always see the woman working behind the counter at the post office and then you're walking along in a different town and she comes toward you—you can't place her straightaway because she's out of her usual context in your life. Those youngsters only ever saw Kirby in uniform and with a completely different guise. They weren't allowed into town much, so even if they saw him, I doubt if they could place him, not with him wearing a suit and with a hat on his noddle. They'd pass him by. Ordinary life can be a perfect disguise."

"True enough, Robbie. But talking about normal life, what will happen to Chalmers and King?"

MacFarlane swirled the liquor around in his glass, staring at the amber liquid before looking up at Maisie. "You know very well that my people stepped in so the death of Hawkin-Price was reported as suicide, because it was in our interests to get the whole thing mopped up as quickly as possible. For his part, before he went to his maker, Hallarden's country squire settled a nice not-so-little retirement trust to look after Chalmers and King, whether the next owner of the house wants to keep them on or not. Kirby wrote up the Hawkin-Price last will and testament according to his wishes, so we know employees will be well supported until the day they die. And if you've heard that the local children's home is likely to purchase the house for the older ones, I would say it's definitely on the cards. It might upset the locals on that avenue though." He sighed. "The middle classes could get uppity when the working classes move in, eh? Mind you, the problem is what to do with your four squatters next."

"Speaking of those 'squatters'—am I correct in thinking that Chalmers was in touch with George, the Comptons' chauffeur, and that's how Lord Julian arranged for them to use the Ebury Place house?"

"Julian was a very important man in Kent, a key link in the

War Office during the Great War. Even in his final weeks, he knew what was going on, so yes, he was fully aware of units ready to be operational across the county in the case of an invasion. And George was involved, so you've no need to talk to him. I've met the man and I know he will be quite happy to leave it all behind and like a lot of others, he won't want to talk about it, and I don't need anything else from him in the way of a statement. Like most of us, he wants nothing more than to put it all in the past. We'll all be happy to leave the war and get on with the peace, such as it is, but it'll be a good long time before it lets go of us, won't it?"

The two old friends ceased to speak for some time. It was Maisie who broke the silence.

"Robbie, it's so hard to reconcile. On one hand, I'm disgusted with these people—the privileged imbeciles who fawned over Hitler, who would do anything to be at a party with him, or to have their photograph taken with that monster. Yet on the other, I'm surprised I feel a little compassion for Hawkin-Price, a man who walked from his study, down his staircase, across his tiled entrance hall and then through the kitchen, knowing that when he opened the door and stepped out, he would be assassinated, and at his own instruction. It seems that once he discovered the depth of the evil unleashed by Adolf Hitler, instead of making excuses—as many had before him—he acted upon what he had learned. But the self-loathing remained to eat away at his soul, and he knew he could not live with himself."

"As it says in the report, he made the identity of every single one of his home grown Fascist friends known to us, and details of how far in with Hitler they were. Needless to say, some we knew and some we didn't. Turns out almost all were followers of that other nasty piece of work, Oswald Mosley—though they call him Tom, don't they? And you know what he's like, because you crossed paths with him some years ago, if my memory serves me well." MacFarlane shrugged. "I'm grateful for Hawkin-Price's service and relieved that he turned to helping his country instead of selling it down the river, but as for feeling sorry for him walking to a death that came quickly? I've neither a shred of sympathy nor an ounce of compassion. After what I witnessed over there when I visited Germany and Poland, at least he didn't stumble starving into a gas chamber and wasn't forced to climb naked into his own grave with a bayonet in his back before being shot. I daresay he'll have all the locals out for his funeral—though being a reported suicide, it won't be a church do and he won't be buried in consecrated ground either. Which is just as well, because no god would have him."

Maisie left Robert MacFarlane's office, but instead of making her way toward Fitzroy Square to see Billy, or to Charing Cross for a train back to Chelstone, she began walking in the direction of Regent's Park. Then she stopped. No, she didn't want to see the park. Instead she wanted to focus on the memory of how it was before the war. Over three hundred enemy explosives had ripped through the park between 1940 and 1945—from incendiary devices and heavy bombs, to the V-1 rockets, weapons designed to undermine the resilience of even the most stoic of souls. A distinct buzzing would herald their arrival in the sky above, followed by silence, the sudden lack of sound when the bomb was about to drop. Maisie remembered people looking up, waiting, trying to work out where the bomb would fall and then running back and forth to escape death as if they were ants caught in fire. The V-2 rockets were faster, made no sound and fell to the ground at three times the speed of sound to kill and maim thousands. Maisie harnessed her thoughts, because in trying to decide whether to walk in Regent's Park, she could see the dead again, bodies torn limb from limb; spirits rising to the heavens while blood seeped into the soil. Thus there was no reason to believe she would find solace in a place she once loved. But she wanted a moment to herself, to consider all she had learned in the meeting with MacFarlane, so she decided to go to her Holland Park flat and just sit for a few moments of quiet before walking along the street to see Priscilla and her four guests. She might even close her eyes for a while, because a deep fatigue seemed to be enveloping her, a feeling she had not experienced since she was brought home from France following her wounding in the Great War.

"We are all on wonderful form," said Priscilla, opening the front door to greet Maisie. "Oh dear, you do look worn out. A nice cup of tea and something inside you will be just the ticket." She took Maisie by the arm and steered her inside. "And do note I did not say 'a nice G and T.'"

"I've already had a drink with Robbie MacFarlane—just a small one though, and it was warranted."

"To do with my four guests?"

"Yes, and that's all I can say, Pris. But they're safe now, so I must consider what to do for them next. I assumed responsibility for them, so it's up to me."

"Let's sit down and I'll ask Mrs. R. to rustle up some tea for us."

Soon Maisie and Priscilla were seated one at each end of the sofa in the sitting room in front of a slow-burning coal fire—coal was rationed, thus only a few embers warmed the room, so the women drew warmth from cups of tea held with both hands.

"I often think we look like a pair of china fire dogs when we're sitting together like this," said Priscilla. "It was the same at Girton, wasn't it? One of us at either end of the sofa in our rooms, putting the world to rights. Little did we know how much right was needed, and within the year."

"I know," said Maisie. She placed her cup and saucer on a side table. "Where are our charges, by the way?"

"The girls are upstairs. Grace most likely has her nose in a book and Mary leafing through copies of *Vogue*—though I now think she wants to be a photographer after reading all about Lee Miller. She's the one who used to be a model, then had a leg up from *Vogue* with her vivid accounts of war and her photographs, so now Mary thinks that line of work is more exciting than stalking back and forth wearing the latest in fashion. She may be right, but I know which one she could land a job in pretty quickly, and it's not messing around with a camera. For their part, the young men have been set to work clearing out the attics in this house. Heaven knows what they will find. Jim told me they had a look round the loft at Ebury Place, but it was full of old furniture and a couple of trunks. Anyway, I've asked that my attic be tidied up, swept and dusted. They don't have to sort out anything—just make sure it looks shipshape and Bristol fashion."

"I think I have a solution for a longer-term place to accommodate them—but I might need your help."

"I think I'd rather like to keep them, because I do quite like them all—and you know me, any chance to be a bossy boots around young people, and I jump at it. Can't do that with my toads anymore, can I? Anyway, what sort of help do you have in mind?"

Maisie regarded her friend, and for a moment felt her fragility. Without doubt Priscilla missed the anchor of motherhood to three sons who were now men. Her husband was attentive and loving, but at the same time he was rooted to a working timetable that contributed to his success as a political writer. She knew she might not have the best solution for Priscilla, but it would give her a purpose for now.

"You remember you told me you kept on the cottage at Chelstone after V-E Day because you loved spending time there?"

Priscilla nodded as she, too, put down her cup and saucer. She picked up a silver cigarette case and lighter. "We were incredibly grateful to you for finding the cottage for us when the bombing became really quite dreadful. We both love it, and Douglas maintains the country atmosphere is good for his work." She took out a cigarette and tapped it on the case before lighting it. "Only three bedrooms though, so it won't fit the four lodgers."

"But Chelstone Manor will."

"What about Lady Rowan?"

"It's a very big house—I think there are about fourteen bedrooms all told. In his will Lord Julian made specific arrangements for the house and immediate grounds—they are to be transferred to the National Trust."

"Clever move, that one."

"It was, but I've already asked Mr. Klein to discuss delaying the transfer to allow us to take in a small number of orphaned refugees from one of the German camps—they're in the Lake District at present, but homes are currently being sought." Maisie reached for her cup of tea.

"Go on, out with it, what's the idea?" said Priscilla, taking a draw from her cigarette, then pressing it into the ashtray. "By the way, I'm making progress in my quest to knock gin on the head. It's a question of keeping on moving. But I can't give up everything at once, though I must confess, smoking doesn't seem to be for me anymore." Priscilla fidgeted, as if not quite sure what to do with her hands. "I just hope that when sugar comes off ration, it won't go straight to my hips. Anyway, go on—what are you thinking, Maisie?"

"Let's transfer your four lodgers to Chelstone. The Canadian officers billeted there have returned home now, and Lady Rowan is moving into the older part of the house, so our youngsters could be accommodated in the Georgian wing. Easy to sort out beds and those rooms are quite large anyway. Then later they will be joined by the other orphans—all young people who must make their way forward, and I think they could help one another."

Priscilla raised an eyebrow. "Ah, yes, and you think I would be a good housemother to 'our four.' Like a no-nonsense patrol leader in the Girl Guides."

"I think you would be excellent at the job."

Maisie watched as Priscilla considered the solution put to her.

"Good thinking on your part, Maisie. I could make sure they continue their education, one way or another. That older lad has quite a technical mind on him—he solved a few problems I've been having with the electricity here. And the younger boy . . ." She laughed. "I'll get him sorted out or he'll end up in a reform home somewhere, though he, too, is quite good with the more mechanical tasks. I think he would do well as an actor too, but that's a tricky path. Douglas has been speaking to a couple of men 'in the know' and apparently even though soldiers are slowly being demobilized, the government is looking at bringing in compulsory peacetime conscription in a few years—calling it 'National Service,' or something like that." She shook her head, as if in disbelief. "So both boys will be called up before they know it and they'll be square-bashing with other unfortunates." She looked down as she wiped a single tear from her cheek with the back of her hand. "If there's one thing I know I can be very good at, Maisie, it's how to make a home for these youngsters, and they deserve to feel the comfort of people who care around them. They are entitled to some tenderness now, and a secure home to bring out the best in every single one of them."

Maisie smiled. "Yes, that's exactly what I was thinking."

"Alright, I'm sold. When do I start?"

"Let me talk to Lady Rowan first—but I think she would like a purpose too, though not in the immediate future."

"By the way—I've had a word with a few people I know in couture, and I've made an appointment to take young Mary to meet one of them. I quickly ran a few of my dresses over to that wonderful seamstress—you know, the one with an atelier behind Harrods. She's altering them to fit, so Mary will look the part when we go. As I said, she'll likely be more interested in what the photographer does, but let's see—the money's attractive and I do believe she will impress people. And if she doesn't, I am sure that girl could talk her way into being a photographer's assistant."

"Good. And what do you think of Grace?"

"Bookish. Can't get her out of Douglas's library, and he said he enjoyed hearing what she's had to say about whatever it is she's reading. Continue her education, that's what I think. In fact, I'd like to see them all catch up."

"That's what I thought. I'll have a word with them, and then I should have it all organized fairly quickly." Maisie looked at her watch. "In fact, I'd like to speak to the four of them together— you can be present; after all, you're going to be keeping an eye on this little pack."

"Priscilla Partridge, the she-wolf!"

"We both know you couldn't be that much of a disciplinarian if you tried!" Maisie became serious. "But there's something I have to ask each of them—something I must collect before I leave—and it's very much in confidence."

Priscilla nodded. "I'll round them up for you."

The four former squatters sat in front of Maisie and Priscilla— the two girls on armchairs and the boys on chairs brought from the dining room. Maisie could not help but smile. It had taken only a day for Priscilla to bring some order, not only to their appearance, but their demeanor. With fresh haircuts, clean clothes and a few good meals inside them, they all seemed to be sitting up a little straighter, with shoulders back and a certain emerging confidence—and without the bluster of fearful adolescents who ached to be more grown up. Looking up at the housekeeper, who entered holding a tray with four mugs of tea and a plate of biscuits, Maisie thought the outwardly stern Mrs. R. might have had a hand in the swift transformation.

Having given her audience a moment to sip their tea and munch on a biscuit, Maisie began.

"First things first—I'm glad to see you all looking so well." She smiled at each one in turn. "Mrs. Partridge tells me you've been very good guests, and I know you've had to endure a difficult time, not least because I had to insist you remain indoors for your own safety."

"Can we go out now, miss?" asked Jim.

"Yes, you can, but Mrs. Partridge has some house rules—and not just for you. When her sons were your age, they had to adhere to the same boundaries. Anyway, before we get to that, let me tell you what we're planning—and it's to give you the very best opportunity to catch up, because you've all been through quite a lot and lost time at school too."

"Are we safe now—will the police or anyone else be coming after us?" asked Mary.

"Sorry, I should have made that clear from the start—yes, you're safe. The situation regarding the event you witnessed has been brought to a satisfactory close, however, there is one thing I must make very, very clear to you." Once more Maisie was struck by their youth, by faces on almost-adults who had borne the weight of childhood wartime responsibility. "You must never, ever speak of what you witnessed to anyone else at any time. If you want to get it out of your system, talk to one another, or talk to me or Mrs. Partridge. The role you were trained for was not a game—it was a very serious plan to undermine the enemy in the event of an invasion."

"But what's going to happen to us?" asked Archie, placing his mug on the side table next to him.

Maisie noticed that the one she had pegged as the Artful Dodger of the quartet was in all likelihood the most vulnerable. Tears filled his eyes, and he looked down at his hands, which he folded in front of his chest as if to prevent anyone seeing the shaking.

"I'm going to look after you, Archie. All of you. And Mrs. Partridge is going to be helping too. We know you each have things you're good at, and we're going to make sure you have the opportunity to get better—for the future. And you'll be moving, but to a lovely house in Kent. In a month or two you'll be meeting some young people there who are about your age, but who have been through much worse than you, and that's an understatement. I've to leave in a minute, but Mrs. Partridge will talk to you about the opportunities we have in mind, and—whether you like it or not—how to make up for some of the schooling you've missed."

"It's alright for Mary, she's going to be a famous model," said Grace.

"And there's plenty of room for you to become a famous something else," said Priscilla.

There was some nudging among the four and a couple of comments back and forth, but Maisie had more to accomplish.

"There's one more thing—and it's a very important one more thing." She sighed, still not quite believing she had to make such a request. "At the end of your training, you were each given a small pill. It was to be kept about your person in case you were taken prisoner by the German army, yet even though the invasion never happened, I know you were never asked to give up the pills. I want you to give me those pills. Now. I cannot leave this house without having destroyed those four pills—and I know what they look like because I've seen them before."

Archie was first to reach into his pocket. He took out a tiny folded piece of paper, and handed it to Maisie. Opening the paper, she nodded. Grace pulled an identical folded paper from her sleeve, and passed it to Maisie, followed by Jim, who leaned down to slip off his shoe to remove the paper and pill.

"Mary?" said Maisie.

"Just a minute." The older girl stood up, walked to the corner with her back to the room and appeared to reach into the front of her dress. She turned and approached Maisie with her hand outstretched. Leaning toward Maisie, she whispered, "It was pinned inside my liberty bodice."

Maisie checked that each wrapper contained an identical pill, and nodded. Moving to the fireplace, she threw the paper wrappers and four cyanide pills onto the glowing embers and watched while small blue flames licked up, destroying the pellets that could have ended four young lives in an instant, and with it all they could have been before they had even had a chance to live.

W ith her charges dismissed—each of them appearing even lighter after relinquishing the pills they had taken care to keep hidden and intact for several years—Priscilla walked with Maisie to the door. Both women were quiet until they reached the threshold.

"We've been through some dreadful things together, haven't we?" said Priscilla.

Maisie looked at her friend, and without thinking rested her hand against the side of her face, covering her scars. Priscilla closed her eyes, and Maisie felt her lean into her palm.

"Does it still hurt, Pris?"

"Sometimes, and I get headaches." She opened her eyes and smiled. "But if I keep occupied, I can get through it, often with the help of an aspirin powder, or a dratted G and T, though I'm doing my best not to think about the latter. And I reprimand myself for letting it darken my day—instead I think of the wounded RAF boys in the burn wards at the hospital in East Grinstead. So many of them are still there, fully members of Mr. McIndoe's Guinea Pig Club. I would never have guessed an esteemed surgeon could be so wonderful."

Maisie removed her hand. "Did he say the pain would subside?"

Priscilla nodded. "In time. I've a check-up just before Christmas—early December. I thought I'd take a well-stocked hamper and something to imbibe, and have a little party with my new young pals, a few of whom are going home." She touched

Maisie on the arm. "Do come with me, Maisie. They're good boys, all of them. Some were only eighteen or nineteen when they were shot down."

"Of course I'll come," said Maisie. She had seen hundreds of facial wounds during the previous war. Priscilla's surgeon, Mr. McIndoe, was a pioneer in facial restoration and skin grafting. His innovative approach included allowing his patients—chiefly young RAF pilots who had suffered burns—to go out into town. For their part, the townsfolk of East Grinstead welcomed their wounded heroes into shops and pubs, and rarely did they have to put down money for a drink. "Those boys are our heroes, Pris— I'll help you give them a party."

Priscilla nodded. "Be grateful for our reasons to celebrate, eh? Right! I'm galvanizing myself for the next thing on my list, and in the meantime, you'd better get on your way. Are you staying at the flat tonight, or going home to Chelstone?"

"Back to Chelstone."

The women embraced, but as Maisie turned to walk down the front steps, she heard Mary calling after her.

"Miss Dobbs, Miss Dobbs. Just a minute. Wait!"

"It's alright, she can hear you, Mary," said Priscilla, putting out her hand to slow Mary's progress. "And please do be careful. The last thing we want is you to fall and end up with a nasty graze on your face, not when you're on the cusp of fame!"

"It's alright, Mrs. P.—I'm quick on my pins."

"What is it, Mary?" asked Maisie, who had walked back to the top of the steps.

Mary put her hand on her chest. "I thought I'd missed you. I should have given you this ages ago, when you first came to the house." She had been keeping one hand behind her back, but now held out a brown paper parcel, tied with red ribbon.

"Is this a gift?"

"Oh no, miss," said Mary. "But I would have bought you one, if I'd had some money. No, this is something I found, and I kept hold of it."

Maisie took the parcel. "What is it? And where did you find it?"

"Upstairs in that big house, the one where we were living when you first came to see us. Ebury Place. Me and Grace were sleeping in one of them rooms—"

"*The* rooms," corrected Priscilla. She looked at Maisie. "Just sorting out the diction."

"We were sleeping in one of *the* rooms," repeated Mary, "where the servants probably slept once. There were two beds in there, so Grace and I made them up with blankets and pillows, but every night when we walked back over the floorboards, there was one that squeaked something rotten."

"Oh dear—I can't begin to suggest different words for that sentence."

Maisie felt color drain from her face as she struggled to retain her composure. "Priscilla, do let her speak. Go on, Mary. I know exactly which room you're talking about."

"Anyway, we got right fed up with it, and one day I thought, I'm going to mend that thing. I had a scout around and found a few tools and a jar of nails in the scullery, so I went and pulled up the floorboard. I thought I could get it up at one end and bash it back down again hard." She grinned. "And I was also hoping to find a bag of diamonds! Didn't find anything valuable, but I found the parcel."

"Did you open it?"

The girl nodded. "Couldn't help myself—but I tied it up again the same way. I know—I shouldn't have been nosy. It's letters, but I didn't read them because it dawned on me that the person what wrote them—" She stole a glance at Priscilla. "Sorry, I mean the person *who* wrote them—well, he might be dead."

"What makes you think that?" said Maisie.

She shrugged. "I suppose because a lot of people died in that war and, well, people die, don't they? I reckon they were sent to a girl who was a servant, living up there in the house."

"I knew all the servants then," said Maisie. "Who were the letters addressed to?"

"Enid someone or other—and they were sent a long time ago. The writing wasn't very good. And what's really funny—not that I'm a detective—but they weren't sent to the house either."

"I don't understand."

"They were all sent 'c/o' a post office. It's in French. Poste Restante—or something like that. Then at the bottom, *To Be Collected*."

Maisie looked at the parcel.

"Go on, you'd better take it, miss. You might be able to find that Enid woman."

Priscilla put her hand on Maisie's shoulder as she grasped the parcel.

"No, I won't be able to find her, Mary."

"Oh, I thought that with you being an investigator, you could—"

Maisie shook her head. "No, no, it's not that." She looked at Mary. "You see, you're right, she's dead. She was killed in an explosion at the Woolwich Arsenal. She worked in munitions, making bombs and there was an . . . an accident, and she was killed." Maisie turned to Priscilla. "I really must go, Pris. And thank you, Mary."

As she ran down the steps, she heard Mary say to Priscilla, "I didn't mean to upset her, Mrs. P. I would have burned them if I'd known. I'm really sorry."

"Not to worry, my dear. I'll speak to her later. Now, come on, let's go and look at some lipstick, and I think you could do with a little rouge."

"I know who those letters were from. Do you think I should have told her?"

"I believe she already knows, Mary."

CHAPTER 13

Maisie walked along the road toward her flat, her mind filled with a voice echoing down the years and an image of Enid when she last saw her at Charing Cross station toward the end of 1914. At the time, Maisie was on her way home from her first term at Girton College, a scholarship girl filled with the bounty of new learning, fresh opportunity, an engaging new friend named Priscilla—and at her first ever party, possibly even a first love—when she spotted Enid, the fellow maid with whom she had shared a bedroom in the servants' quarters at Fifteen Ebury Place. Though there was a distance between them in the bustling station, Maisie could see Enid's hand resting on the arm of an officer in the Royal Flying Corps, a young man in a brand-new uniform who Maisie knew loved gingersnap biscuits. Just a few weeks earlier, Mrs. Crawford, the Comptons' cook, had penned a letter to Maisie with all the news from both Ebury Place and the family's country seat, Chelstone Manor, and among the "this and that" of life below stairs and observations of what was going on "upstairs," she added that Enid had left the Comptons' employ, and was now working in a munitions factory, where the money was, according to Enid, "A lot better than the leftovers we get here."

As Maisie approached the front door of her flat, her shaking hand dropping the keys, she remembered watching the couple at the railway station, and at that very moment knowing they were in love. She had stepped away in the opposite direction so as not to be seen, but as she turned for one last look, Enid met her eyes and raised her chin with a defiant pride. Her red hair was vibrant as ever, yet with livid streaks of glistening yellow due to handling cordite, a poison that discolored the skin, leading to the girls who worked in munitions being nicknamed "canaries." Later, having bid her lover farewell, Enid caught up with Maisie, and it was not long before she confided in Maisie an abiding fear that her beloved would perish, that she would never see him again. Yet as the two women stood to say goodbye, a train pulled into the station with wounded fresh from the Western Front, young men who would be transferred to the line of ambulances waiting outside to take them to hospitals around London. Orderlies were rushing back and forth, bringing stretchers to the train to help the suffering soldiers, many still in shredded uniforms covered in mud and blood. The two women talked a little more, but when Maisie expressed her concern for Enid, her friend's reply came in the form of a challenge, and with her departing comment, she changed Maisie's life.

"You want to worry about something, Maisie? Let me give you a word of advice. You worry about what you can do for these boys . . . you worry about what you can *do*."

Maisie missed her train, so it was late when she arrived back at Chelstone, where her father was the groom in charge of the estate's horses. Frankie Dobbs had news for Maisie when he met her at the station. Enid had been killed in an explosion at the arsenal while working alongside other young women handling volatile high explosives. The tragedy must have happened soon after Enid arrived for her shift. Maisie had taken Enid's parting words to heart, abandoning her studies to become a nurse, to do all she could for the boys. All too soon, she was tending the wounded and dying at a casualty clearing station in France. And the young man Enid was in love with? Viscount James Compton and Maisie were married some two decades later, in the summer of 1934. By September of the following year, Maisie was wearing the black of widowhood, a bereavement compounded by the loss of her child, for the shock of her husband's sudden death, of watching James crash to earth in an experimental aeroplane, led to the stillbirth of an almost full-term baby boy. In an instant, life ceased to have meaning for Maisie.

Yet time had marched on, the passing years bringing her the love of an adopted daughter and a new husband at an age when she thought such sweetness would have passed her by—but still, as she held in her hands the letters James Compton had sent his first love, her world had again tilted on its axis. Every last cell in her being told her she should never unwrap the parcel, never open a letter and never, ever read a line of words from James to Enid. And why was Maisie fearful of the contents? After all, the missives of two young people during late adolescence, the years before they were truly adults, were in all likelihood far from serious and might even verge on comical at times. But Maisie was afraid because she knew their love had been a secret due to their respective stations in life, and such a secret buried for so long could result in something unexpected and unwelcome when exposed to the light.

The telephone was ringing as Maisie entered the flat. Still clutching the parcel, she ran toward the sitting room and reached for the receiver. As she recited her telephone number, two operators exchanged instructions, one establishing that Mrs. Scott was now on the line before adding, "Connecting you now, sir."

"Maisie! I thought I'd try the flat first."

"Mark—oh, Mark, I am so glad to hear your voice."

"Hon—what is it? You're upset—I can hear it in your tone. Is Anna okay?"

"Yes, yes—and I'm sorry. It's been a long day already, and I'm not even near getting on my way back to Chelstone."

"Well, hurry up, because I'll be headed there soon."

"You're here in England? Mark, that's wonderful."

There was a second's silence. "Maisie? What's wrong? Is it your dad? Are you ill?"

"Mark, I am well, truly. I'm just a bit weary—but I'm now so much better knowing you're on British soil. Are you in Southampton?"

"Yep. It's been a long run, via Gander and then Lisbon, as usual, with one diversion to Shannon. If I see the inside of another 'plane, I will just walk off. Anyway, I'm catching a train in about forty-five minutes, so I'll be late home to Chelstone—any chance George could pick me up from the station?"

"I'll do it, Mark—I'll be there."

"Okay, hon. Can't wait to see my girls."

Maisie nodded, holding her hand to her mouth and trying not to give in to tears as she heard the long tone of the disconnected telephone call. At once she began to gather the various items she wanted to take back to Chelstone, pushing them into her old carpet bag. She wavered over the parcel of letters, but pressed it in on top of a pair of shoes and a jacket more suited to the country than the town. She hurried toward the front door, but the telephone began ringing again. Despite not wanting to linger, she knew she had plenty of time to reach Chelstone railway station before Mark's arrival—he would have to change trains at least twice—and if her home telephone were ringing, it might be important. She dropped the carpet bag, rushed back to the sitting room and answered the call.

"Miss—it's me."

"Billy? Are you alright? You don't usually telephone me here."

"Got time for a word, miss? You sound as if you've been dashing around."

Maisie took a deep breath. "I've plenty of time—what's happened? Is it Will?"

"He's been keeping to Dr. Dene's instructions, and I reckon we're on the straight and narrow. But I keep thinking about what your friend Mrs. Partridge said about that dragon, you know, the one that comes up again and again. Anyway, you remember when you sent me off to the country, years ago, when I had them . . . well, the problems with taking stuff I shouldn't and my legs hurting. You sent me down to Chelstone, and it did me the power of good, working on the farm and moving my arms and legs in special ways like that bloke taught me to. It helped me in my head too. I've not forgotten it—I reckon it saved me, gave me something to fall back on."

"I know, Billy—sounds like you think Will could do with a dose of the same."

"It's Doreen who's doing the thinking, to tell you the truth—and she's just given me a piece of her mind, and I don't mind saying, I reckon she might be spot on."

"You're going to have to explain, Billy—I'm not a mind-reader. Not all the time anyway."

There was a pause, and Maisie knew Billy was trying to frame his story.

"Well, we were talking about Will—he was upstairs in bed.

243

Sleeps like the dead, you know, and then he starts screaming in the night. It's like he was a little nipper again, having nightmares, only now he shouts out 'Tenko, Tenko, Tenko!' I go in and sit with him, put my arm around him so he goes to sleep again. Or Doreen goes in. I know there's some who'd say we shouldn't do that with a grown man, that he's just got to knuckle down now he's home, but what can you do? I'm not about to leave him in that state, am I?"

"You're doing everything you can, Billy."

"Anyway, I said to Doreen that Mrs. Partridge called the memories the dragon you have to keep mollified. Those were her words, weren't they?"

"Yes, that's right."

"Doreen looked at me, and I could see she was ready to have a go. 'I've had enough of this dragon lark,' she said. 'That dragon has to be knocked out once and for all, so he never wakes up again. And another thing,' she says, 'I reckon dragons get more dangerous and thrash around when they're getting weaker—so tell that to your Mrs. P. If her dragon is off the leash, it means she's getting better and he knows he's losing his bottle, so don't give him power by talking about him. When the dragon is going down, that's when you have to be made of steel, not straw. Our boy will get back to his old self by looking ahead—by seeing how things could be for him, not down in the cellars of his mind where the dragon lives. And if we put everything we've got into helping him get stronger, he'll be able to do a St. George and put a sword right through the blimmin' thing.'"

Maisie ran the telephone cord through her fingers, a habit when she was engaged in a more serious conversation. "The dragon thrashing around because he's losing power? Hmmm, I think she has a point. Mind you, I don't think Will is quite at that stage—his recovery is still very new—but if you think he would do well in the country, then I will see what I can do to help him navigate the way ahead."

"Thank you, miss. He'll come through it all. I'm sure of that. After all, we love our boy, and like I said, you're not supposed to say that sort of thing about a grown man, but he's our son and he's been to hell. Half of him is still there, and we've got to get him out."

"How about Bobby and Margaret Rose?"

"Bobby? What can I say? Doreen and me, well, we've decided that it's his life. He served his country so he deserves to make up his mind about what he does next and where he goes. As for Margaret Rose—she's a diamond, that girl. Helping out with her brother and determined to be a nurse now. As long as there's no wars for her to be sent off to, I don't mind at all."

"Good," said Maisie. "Look, I must go now, Billy. And . . . and tell Doreen I think she could well be right, about the dragon."

Later, as she made her way out of London and on toward Chelstone, Maisie's thoughts lingered on the fate of the dragon inside her. It was in full flourish, its tail churning back and forth, thrashing up memories of those souls she had gone to war with and the ones who didn't come home. For years she had walked along the street from her garden flat to Priscilla's house, the mansion her friend had purchased from Margaret Lynch, the widowed mother of Dr. Simon Lynch, Maisie's first love. She remembered Simon taking her to meet his parents, and the feeling that his mother and father were tolerating the match because it was wartime, whereas if their son had not been in uniform, they might well have opposed his choice, given that she was the daughter of a different class of people. She and Enid had been in the same boat—not top drawer at all and both in love with what some would have termed "one of their betters"—yet not only had Maisie weathered the prevailing winds against her, but the reading of Maurice Blanche's will following his funeral had made her a wealthy woman, and a woman of means had the power of choice. But even before the legacy that changed her circumstances, Maisie knew that money could never take away the ache of grief.

Another thought crossed her mind, but she pushed it aside, knowing it was the dragon again, tempting her into the depths of dark thinking. It would not have been the first time doubt had hovered in her thoughts like a hornet with a vicious sting—but she wondered if the extent of the inheritance from Maurice rendered her more attractive to James Compton, or to his parents?

Oh what does it matter? thought Maisie, in an attempt to brush off the notion. *James has gone now.* She shook her head, feeling her eyes moisten. *And so has Enid.*

The following morning, with Mark's arm around her shoulders as they walked across fields toward the neighboring stables, their daughter running ahead in anticipation of her father's opinion regarding the purchase of a horse, Maisie felt that all was well—her family were around her, and only that mattered in her world. After visiting the horse, they would stroll home to the Dower House before lunch, and Maisie would continue on to the manor, where she would visit Lady Rowan and coax her into sitting down to share a meal with them. They would celebrate Mark's return together and the possible new member of their animal family.

"I can feel every darn meeting I had last week just slipping away," said Mark as they walked. "I mean, I was only one person on the hinterland of these big shots, but there was a lot of tension in the talks."

"You've a couple of days now before you return to the embassy," said Maisie. "But you don't want to go back, do you?"

"Maisie, like you I went through one war and that was bad enough, even though America was late to the ball. But this war has left misery such as I have never seen before, and my job has taken me into some terrible situations." He shook his head. "I've just spent the past week being a fly on the wall at meetings where my government is being asked to give Britain billions of dollars because it's bankrupt. I've just about had enough." He rubbed his free hand across the back of his neck, as if in an attempt to knead away the tension. "I mean, look at it, across Europe there are orphans everywhere. There are children who have never had any rock-solid stability in their lives and barely clothes on their backs. And there are women picking over bombed-out buildings to find their family treasures—and the gem they are searching for could just be a photograph of someone who died long ago, not something big that can be valued in dollars, pounds, marks, guilders or francs. Anywhere Hitler invaded, people are starving, shell-shocked, and by god I'm a lucky guy to come home to this." He held out his hand in a sweep toward the undulating Wealden countryside. "We've had it bad here in Britain, but at least Hitler never occupied this country—and it's the people who stopped it. They deserve more. Everyone deserves more."

Maisie stopped and turned to her husband. "But what do *you* want to do, Mark?"

"I wanted to come home and be the happy-go-lucky guy for you and Anna." He looked down at his feet, then back to Maisie. "I want us to have a home that's ours, not just yours and I moved in—but *ours*. And it's the right time—Lady Rowan will bounce back, she may be eighty-two now but she's a game old lady, and she deserves to live in the Dower House. Didn't her own mother go on until she was ninety-three? I know how the history works—the Dower House is her proper place now, according to the way things have been done for centuries with her kind of people. Let's build our own house, Maisie. Let's build something together."

Maisie took a deep breath, thinking of the home that Maurice had loved and bequeathed her. But perhaps Mark was right. And she could take the first step, couldn't she?

"Hey, we'd better get going," said Mark. "Look over there—Anna's almost at the stables, and I don't want her to start doing a deal before I get there!"

The deal was indeed done within another hour. Theodore—the bay fifteen hand Cob—would be brought to the stables at Chelstone Manor at some point during the following week. Maisie knew only too well that in time it would be important for a companion for Theo to be found, a prospect that made her smile when she imagined riding out with her daughter.

Frankie Dobbs and Brenda were waiting at the Dower House to hear the news, so while Anna, her father and Frankie went to the manor's stables to make plans for Theo's arrival, Brenda said she wanted to get busy, so she would make some sandwiches for lunch. With her family occupied, Maisie decided to go to the library to catch up with some paperwork before going to see Rowan.

She sat down at the oak desk and pulled the parcel of letters toward her, knowing temptation would get the better of her.

With care she pulled on the ribbon and the bow slipped from the knot. She could see ridges and fading where it had been tied for years, and retied again in a different place after Mary had decided against reading each one of them, which Maisie thought took admirable self-control. She had no doubt that Enid had hidden the letters before leaving her employer—she would not have trusted any hiding place in a dormitory filled with other munitions workers, girls who would have clustered around to read found love letters. She suspected Enid had hidden the letters at Ebury Place with the intention of retrieving them when she returned after the war, even if she remained in situ only for as long as it took to secure another job and a place to live.

As she unfolded the brown paper and lifted the first letter, she was surprised. She had assumed the letters were sent later than the postmark indicated. But these letters were sent in late 1908 and 1909. She closed her eyes and tried to remember what she had been told about James's sojourns in Canada, where he was sent to work for the Compton Corporation, which had valuable interests in timber and mining. As she understood the chain of events, he had been dispatched when Lord Julian decided his son should learn every aspect of the businesses he would one day inherit, and in the process not become the worthless heir to a fortune. She remembered James returning to England at the outset of war, and without delay receiving a commission in the Royal Flying Corps—she assumed his immediate promotion was due to his father's contacts at the War Office.

Tapping her fingers, Maisie retraced her own history at Ebury Place. She was thirteen when she was brought to the house in 1910 to work as the most junior of maids. She had been assigned a bed in the room she would share with Enid on the top floor of the house. Enid was rendered more senior due to Maisie's employment—was she sixteen or seventeen? Maisie couldn't quite remember, and that was the trouble with Enid anyway—you never knew if she was embellishing a story, though to Maisie she always seemed much older and more worldly. To be fair, although they both wanted to "get on" in life, Enid's dreams were different—she wanted to be a lady, to wear the most luxurious silk gowns and be the mistress of a grand house. Indeed, she spent good money purchasing copies of *The Lady*, the journal for women of a certain station. And she practiced her diction, often endeavoring to hide her Cockney accent by adding *h* where it had no place at all. Maisie smiled, recalling the time Enid was talking about Kent, the hop gardens and the "host houses." Without thinking of how it might embarrass Enid, Maisie had commented, "You mean 'oast' house,' Enid. There's no *h* on that word." The memory of Enid's efforts was bittersweet, and her defiance when she said, "We're as good as any of them, you and me, Mais, and posh doesn't make you any better than the next woman."

Flicking through the letters, Maisie noted that Enid had kept them in order of date received, so she took a deep breath and opened the first, catching her breath at a script that was recognizable as that of her late husband—who would have been in his late teen years at the time.

> *My darling Enid,*
>
> *I miss you terribly. My life is so colorless now—no one to make me laugh. There's no one to tell me I'm good as I am, and no lovely girl to dance with when no one's looking. I worry about you—we've really made quite a mess of things, haven't we? But we can start again, and I swear all will be well and we will live happily ever after. How do you feel? I've wondered . . .*

Clutching the fine paper upon which James had penned his love letter, Maisie folded her arms on the desk before her and rested her head. She began to weep, not because she was concerned that James had not loved her—of that she was sure, and it was a mature love, a love that came when neither expected it—but because of what had come to pass between two young people. Had she any need to read further? She believed she knew the rest of the story, that a puppyish longing had been thwarted before such a time as it might have been extinguished by the onward march of years—yet at the same time, she felt the constituent pieces of another mosaic slotting into place to form a different picture. This was an image her heart told her existed; she only had to read on to confirm it. But did she dare?

"Hon—"

Maisie looked up at her husband, standing in the doorway. "Mark, I'm sorry—"

"Brenda's been calling—honey, what is it?" He stepped into the library and knelt alongside her. "What's eating you, Maisie? I don't like to see my wife so sad."

"Just . . . just the past, I suppose." Maisie rested her head on his shoulder.

"You want to run those thoughts straight out of town, Maisie—locking eyes with the demons of the past never did any of us any favors. Only look back when you can laugh about it."

Maisie and her husband stood up at the same time, as Mark reached into his pocket for a handkerchief.

"Here, let me." With a gentle touch, he wiped the tears from her cheeks. "Now, tell me what's going on."

She ran her fingers across the pile of envelopes. "These letters. They're from James to the girl who was a maid at the Ebury Place house when I started work there. She was a few years older than me—and she was killed in 1914. She worked at the Woolwich Arsenal—munitions."

"And I suppose they were young lovers wrapped up in an illicit affair—Romeo and Juliet all over again."

Maisie nodded. "I think any notion that they were like Shakespeare's wronged pair is gilding the lily a bit. James was sent to Canada to learn the family business—and if truth be told, I would imagine it was to get him away from Enid. He must have been about eighteen or nineteen at the time."

"I thought he went later on?"

"That's true. He had a bad time after the first war, a malaise and despondency that went on for a while, so he was dispatched over to Canada again. We got to know one another when he came home to run the Compton Corporation from London. He was much healed by then."

"And he pursued you."

"In a manner of speaking." She smiled. "I suppose I had him running around a bit."

"Poor guy—you did that to me too. So, there's nothing interesting in the letters, other than two kids talking about love while they're still green."

"I expect so."

"Come on—let's go and have some lunch. Rowan's already here—I knew you were busy, so I walked over with Anna. She couldn't wait to tell Grandma Rowan all about Theo. I just hope he doesn't become 'Theo the Terror horse.'"

"Oh don't, Mark. I'll be even more worried—but my father knows a horse and he says he's a gentleman."

"That's three of us in the family then!"

Later, after a simple lunch comprising sandwiches and cups of tea, during which Rowan seemed to be more like her old self, Maisie accompanied her across the lawns at the front of Chelstone Manor house. Maisie thought she could almost see a cloud of melancholy lingering around the older woman's heart, yet during the long lunch, she had made a few jokes and told stories of horses she had owned over the years, thrilling Anna with comments such as "He was a terrible cheat, that horse" or "When my back was turned, he would throw his feed bucket at me if he thought he had been shorted" and "That mare was a sage old bird. The way she would look at me—as if my very presence were a slight on her character."

Now the two women were silent as they walked at a slow pace, Rowan's arm through Maisie's, her other hand clutching a walking stick.

"Old age is a bloody nuisance, if I may say so," said Rowan.

"You may, and I believe you. But you and my father continue to amaze me—Rowan, you still have so much vim and vigor."

"Been bashed around a bit lately, Maisie. I feel bruised everywhere and it all hurts."

"I know—it will take time, but you were sparkling company today. Anna was delighted."

"Anna *is* delightful, my dear. Such balm for an old woman's soul."

As much as she wanted to ask questions about James, instead Maisie decided to broach the subject of even more young people coming to Chelstone Manor, and her idea for their futures. Rowan did not interrupt, as was often her habit—even Lord Julian would often become exasperated when his wife could not wait to add her opinion to a conversation. But as they walked, she listened to Maisie with close attention.

"I think it's a very good idea. Whoever heard of a perfectly good house sitting all but empty while an old woman rattles around in it only to hide when the tourist types come rambling through? Do you think we can get it done? I mean, Julian's bequest was quite specific, though I am sure he would have been all for this idea."

"What you mean is, you would have twisted his arm," said Maisie.

"Same thing." Rowan laughed—the first time since Lord Julian's death that Maisie had heard her throaty chuckle. "One thing about husbands is that they don't know what they want until their wives tell them. Then they swallow it up and spit it out as their idea—and I don't mind, as long as I get my plans on the table and into play. Anyway, what does Mr. Klein say?"

"I had a quick word on the telephone, and he thinks it will work nicely. It's good publicity for the Trust—relinquishing a bequest for a period of time so the young refugees and our own homeless quartet can be set on the right path for the future. He thinks he can press for two years' grace."

"Very good. Plenty of room in the Georgian wing, and I will settle in the older wing. I will have that lovely view of the gardens, and you will still be close, which is excellent, plus I will see much more of your lovely Priscilla. She's such a hoot!"

Maisie laughed. "Oh, she's definitely a hoot by any measure, Rowan—but it will do her good too. She has had some struggles since the first round of operations on the burns, and what with her sons having more or less left home, she's been looking for something to completely engage her, and she is very good with the young."

Rowan was quiet for a few moments, then as they neared the entrance to the manor house, she turned to Maisie. "You know, I always thought I was very good with young people, but I made rather a hash of things with my own son. I've been thinking about it a good deal since Julian died."

"James thought the world of you, Rowan—don't be hard on yourself. I'm sure he was a handful as a boy."

Rowan shook her head. "He may have reignited a love for his mother later, when he was in his thirties, but in his teen years, I didn't do very well and neither did Julian."

"You don't have to look back, Rowan. James was a happy man—we were blissfully content and would have remained so had it not been for the accident. He wasn't even meant to be flying that day, as you know—he stepped in to help out."

"He was a fool."

"Please, Rowan—let's not . . ."

"The trouble is, I don't know what I could have done to make it all much more palatable."

"Make what so much more palatable?"

Rowan shook her head, dismissing her own comment. "You're right—no looking back at the past. It's losing Julian that's done it—bereavement makes you turn your head and look at what might have been, and what you could have done instead. But all in all, even though I admonish myself for sending James off to Canada, it was all for the best." She turned to Maisie and kissed her on the cheek. "Yes, all for the best—and he married you, and your family has become such a gift. You've made up for all that was lost."

Lady Rowan Compton smiled and raised her walking stick when she saw Mrs. Horsley waiting for her. She squeezed Maisie's arm and walked on alone toward the front door of her home, her shoulders square, and with only a swift touch of her cane to the ground. Maisie waited until Mrs. Horsley waved to let her know that Lady Rowan was safe inside. She watched as the door closed, then turned and made her way to the Dower House. Brenda and Frankie had repaired to the drawing room and were napping when she arrived home, while a note was left on the kitchen table to the effect that Mark, Anna and Little Emma had decided to go for a long afternoon walk across the fields before dusk drew down on the remaining daylight. There was little to do, nothing urgent, no telephone calls to disturb her, so Maisie went to the library, where she put a match to the kindling laid ready in the fireplace. As the flame caught the rolled paper and splintered wood, she added a few coals followed by a log. Turning to the desk, she gathered the clutch of letters and sat in front of the fire, ready to confront truths for which she had no evidence, but which—she realized—she had always known in her heart. By the time her husband and daughter returned—and Brenda's voice could be heard in the distance maintaining that she didn't know about anyone else, but she was ready for another nice cup of tea—perhaps all the mosaic pieces would have fallen into place.

CHAPTER 14

My darling Enid,

You have been through so much, though I'm relieved to know satisfactory arrangements were made and you are comfortable. It seems Dr. Blanche found an excellent residence for you at the coast—the sea air will be very good for your health. I'm amazed the other staff at Ebury Place didn't guess what was going on and believed the story that you were going to look after your very ill aunt and would return when she was well enough.

I've written to my parents and asked again if we might be married, but as we are both below the age of consent, my plea has been met with a firm no, and a very clear indication that we would be left penniless. Given the circumstances, it seems the best decision has been made and our child will go to a good home and with any luck will be brought up far away from the life I've known and the life you have endured. I may be too young to assume the role of fatherhood—as my father pointed out among all the other reasons when he lost his temper with me—but I think somewhere in the middle will be good for him, to be brought up not too rich and not too poor. Or her, of course, but I think our child will be a boy . . .

Maisie looked up from the letter and stared into the fire's glowing embers. It was as she had guessed—indeed, as she had intuited in her heart for a long time. There had been a child, born before Maisie came to work at Ebury Place, which, according to dates at the top of the letters, would have been after Enid's return from caring for a fictional aunt who lived by the sea in Brighton. Enid had been delivered of a boy, a child taken from her within weeks of his birth. She had held her son, and then let him go to a "good home" and no more was to be said. By the time James came home from Canada, some five years later, Lord Julian and Lady Rowan had expected all feelings between the pair to have died, suffocated by time and separation—without doubt, the letters had become few and far between following Enid's recovery from childbirth. But having seen the couple together at the railway station, it seemed clear the passing years had inflicted little impact on their love for each other—or had it been reignited after James's return to England?

Maisie stared at the collection of letters. The affair between Enid and James when they were young lovers, both below the age of consent, had resulted in Enid giving birth to James's son. *Our child.*

There was a faint knock at the door, and Mark entered. "I thought you'd be here. Frank and Brenda are having a cup of tea and then I'm going to drive them home—and I have some interesting news for you."

Maisie turned her head, forcing a smile. "Oh, yes, I'll come now," she said, as she stood up and placed the clutch of letters on the desk behind her.

Mark sighed. His tone changed, and he sounded weary. "You've been reading those letters, Maisie. I don't think that's a good idea."

Maisie waved away the comment with a flap of her hand. "Oh, there was nothing really interesting, it was just youthful ramblings." She forced another smile. "What with those young squatters, and now these juvenile missives, I wonder if I shouldn't dread Anna reaching that age."

"I think she's a lot more level-headed, Maisie—and she's got us to fall back on, to provide a solid framework for her to grow. She had a rough start, but a good new beginning—and that's what it's all about, good beginnings somewhere along the line . . . which kind of brings me to my news."

"I'm sorry, my head is full of other things—what's the news then?"

Mark Scott held up a small sheet of paper. "The name of an architect in Tunbridge Wells. I thought we could go see him. We've both got our hands full right now, but maybe sometime before the end of the year. In fact, he and his wife are in the practice together—I thought they might suit us very well."

"Aren't you supposed to have a location in mind before you see an architect? Don't they need a landscape to work with? I think they might require more than just our loose thoughts about a house, and we haven't really talked about it, have we? And I think it's important to have some notion of the views around you."

"Yep, I'm ahead of you there."

"I was afraid you might be—go on."

Mark went on, his commentary becoming more animated as he spoke. "Remember when we were walking back from the riding stables after seeing Theo? We had to take the path onto the road and then loop around to the footpath—well, there's a 'For Sale' sign up at the top of that hill." He used his right hand to add to the description of the meandering route. "I detoured that way this afternoon with Anna and Little Em—I didn't say anything, of course, because I wanted to see what potential it might have before I mentioned it to you. I had a good look, pretending to admire the view and I think it's a candidate for us. It's walking distance from here and the village, and . . . What's wrong?"

"Nothing—just a bit too much at the moment. I've . . . I've some . . . some, well, investigating to do on another . . . another case. Perhaps—"

Maisie felt a tightness across her chest as her words seemed to evaporate into the room. *Some investigating to do.* Dare she? Dare she try to find a man who would be thirty-six years of age now?

"Okay . . . right." Mark faltered, as if he wanted to say more or to ask another question. Instead he ran his fingers through dark hair salted with grey at the temples. "But come with me to see the land tomorrow morning. I could put down the cash right away from my account in London."

"Um, yes, alright—yes, let's look." Maisie smiled. "That's Brenda calling—we'd better get a move on or she will be marching down here with cups of tea, and she's been showing her age lately, becoming a bit wobbly."

Later, after her husband took Frankie and Brenda home to their bungalow in the village, and Anna, jumpy and excited about her new horse, was at last in bed, her beloved dog asleep outside her bedroom door with nose resting on crossed paws, Maisie went again to the library. She now knew the steps that had been taken to ensure Enid had a safe and secret pregnancy, and the care she received when she gave birth to a son. When Lord Julian banished both James and Enid from the house, Lady Rowan had stepped in to enlist the help of the one man she trusted to arrange Enid's confinement and the adoption of her child. Maurice Blanche.

The adoption would have been straightforward, as Maisie knew only too well. It was long known that it was easier to adopt a child than it was to assume responsibility for one of the homeless animals at Battersea Dogs and Cats Home—indeed, there had been a Royal Society for the Prevention of Cruelty to Animals long before there was a similar society to protect children. New adoption laws had been due for debate just as war was declared, and would be up before Parliament soon enough—the fact that they were delayed worked in Maisie's favor when she applied to formally adopt Anna, and again when Mark legally became her father following his marriage to Maisie. In 1909 there would have been few barriers to "ownership" of a new baby. The staff at any institution where the mother gave birth just had to trust the chosen couple were of good character.

Maisie knew where she could begin her investigation—at the clinic founded by Maurice to serve women and children in one of the poorest areas of London. It had been taken over by the local council in 1940 to give immediate first aid and care to civilians wounded during the bombings—but there would still be records held on the premises. At least she hoped they were still available. She gave a sigh of relief. Good—she had a plan, an objective to give her thoughts a framework, a structure to work with, for the letters had caused her to feel ill at ease, akin to how she felt as a girl when her mother died and she heard her father keening the loss downstairs at night, in the belief that his daughter could not hear him weeping. It had been a shock when the solid ground of her childhood gave way to an uneasy sense of unknowing, a point at which she had no trust in the future.

She would not reveal her plan to Mark—not yet anyway. The quest to find James's child would be her secret. She would do it for his memory. After all, though she was not successful, hadn't she done her best to discover the identity of Anna's father, a Maltese merchant sailor, so when the child was older she would know her adoptive mother had made the effort? Yes, she would try, because she now knew the mosaic was not yet complete. There were still pieces to slot into place.

After walking Anna to the bus stop the following morning, Maisie and Mark put on their Wellington boots and tramped across fields of dew-drenched grass to inspect the land Mark had seen for sale. Maisie agreed it was probably a good location for a new house, though of course an application to the council would be required, followed by the wait for approval to build, a solution found to the sewer question—a septic tank would be necessary—and the issue of water and electrical supply. In short, the construction would take years.

"There's always a way of moving things along, Maisie," said Mark. "And look over there—there's a farmhouse, then there's the stables, and they have water and electricity, or at least I think they do."

"The farmhouses around here are still dependent upon oil lamps and log-fired stoves, Mark—and most of them only have an earth closet in the garden and a pump for water outside the back door. That's what the stable has—I saw them pumping water when we went to look at Theo."

"If we get all the latest conveniences, it'll make it easier for them to apply for them too."

"And I just saw a cow jump over the moon," said Maisie, shaking her head. "It's not that simple here, and I am sure there would be similar problems in the more rural parts of America. But, Mark, I've another thought. It might be a good idea to see if any suitable properties have come up for sale in the area, and then perhaps have an architect look at them to see if they can be brought into the twentieth century with all the conveniences."

"Maybe." He looked at his watch. "Hey, you and I should get out of these boots and be running for the train."

"And there's a really important point we must consider," said Maisie, as they turned back toward the Dower House. "We don't know if Rowan wants to live in the Dower House."

"Maisie, the war's over. Let's look forward, together. I'm already at the flat in London that you bought before you met me, and here in Chelstone, while I'm glad we can be around your family and Anna is thriving at a good school, I don't want to just live in another house that was yours before I came into your life. I want us to build our own house, together."

She linked her arm through his. "I know—and I understand. But let's keep our eyes out for other opportunities. You never know what might turn up."

During the latter part of the last century, Maurice had started clinics in two of the most deprived areas of London, Bermondsey and Shoreditch. As Maisie walked along a street filled with rubble and only a couple of back-to-back houses standing, she knew that if he were alive, Maurice would be pained to learn what had happened to his patients who lived on streets that were now tagged for slum clearance. Bold new blocks of flats were planned to house the poor, yet at the same time, solid public buildings ripe for conversion were being ignored, and already the press were commenting that London County Council was doing more damage to the capital than the entire Luftwaffe throughout the extent of the war. As she approached the building that had housed the clinic, her hopes of discovering crucial information regarding Enid's confinement began to evaporate. The clinic was still standing but surrounded by demolition and decay. People were living in the remaining structures, with several families accommodated in one house—as it had been for over a century, since the Industrial Revolution brought so many people from rural Britain into the cities in search of a more abundant life. In those houses, parents and children shared a room, and were glad to have a roof over their heads.

Maisie knocked on the clinic's front door. When there was no answer, she pushed against the handle and gained entry. Beyond a counter at the front, she could hear two women talking in another room, so she stepped around a fallen chair and toward the open door.

"Good morning," she said, as she knocked and entered.

"Oh my goodness," said one woman, her hand to her chest. "You frightened the life out of me."

"I'm sorry, dear, but the clinic's closed now," said the other woman. "We're just clearing up the last few things."

"Closed? But where will people go—especially the women and girls?"

"Not many to go anywhere now, madam. For as long as this building is here, there will be a sign to seek attention at the London Hospital, over in Whitechapel."

Maisie looked around. "I helped here when Dr. Blanche ran it, along with other doctors and nurses."

"Never knew the man, but he was a saint by all accounts. Took care of women no one else wanted to know about," said the first woman.

"Yes, the ones who 'got themselves into trouble.'" The

second woman shook her head. "Makes you laugh when you hear that, doesn't it? 'Got herself into trouble' as if the fella had nothing to do with it. And off he goes and leaves them on their own with a bun in the oven. Thank heavens for the likes of Dr. Blanche, that's what I say. Placed a lot of children, he did. And he helped women who had nowhere but the back streets—they came to him when it all went wrong and it looked like they were bleeding to death."

"He saved lives, that man."

"I knew him very well—and you're right, he saved many lives. But I'm trying to locate his records. I know he always kept very detailed reports on his patients, so I wonder if you know where I might find them?"

"Oh, those old files? Council took them when they put a claim on the clinic after the war started."

"I was informed they'd taken it over, but what did they do with the records?" asked Maisie.

"Burned them in the incinerator," said the first woman. "They didn't have time to do anything else, and what good would it have done? There were women who came in here with all sorts of ailments, and not a few with cancer, or who had black eyes and broken bones from a beating. The records went back years, so the council just got rid of them."

"Oh dear," said Maisie. "I suppose it would have been the same at the clinic over in Bermondsey."

"Just the same—no reason to keep hold of them. The Germans went for the docks and bombed out the working people while they were about it, and now those people want to move on and out, then up into the new flats they're talking about. Mind you, there's already some in the prefabs."

"Yes, so I understand. Anyway, thank you for your help,

ladies." Maisie smiled, adding, "And for everything you've done, working here."

She left the old clinic, her mood low. Now where could she go for information? Perhaps it was time to have a word with Lady Rowan. No, she couldn't do that. Rowan was vulnerable, tired and grieving. But wasn't it only days ago that Rowan revealed what was on her mind? *My children and grandchildren, lost to me.* The comment from a bereaved woman had caught Maisie's attention, though she had attributed it to fatigue, to the weariness of loss pulling her down. Now she knew that she was not mistaken even then—Rowan was grieving not only her two dead children and Maisie's stillborn son, but the child relinquished for adoption.

Maisie set off to return to Chelstone, wondering if this wasn't the perfect time for a word with Rowan about Enid. She would give her a chance to get it all off her chest once and for all. There was another feeling beginning to rise within her, and she knew she would have to temper it in the name of compassion, of understanding. She was becoming angry, not only with the position Enid had been left in—she must have been so scared—but with the distinctions in class that had made her situation so miserable. Maisie was aware that for many of the so-called "upper-class gels" who found themselves in a similar quandary, they might be either sent to a good doctor who would solve the problem, or dispatched to a European spa town for their confinement. Another option was a marriage arranged with haste and the subsequent happy event recorded with an announcement in the *Times* to the effect that the delighted young couple now had a child born *prematurely* on . . .

The woman at the clinic was right—poor girls "got themselves into trouble" and then had to get themselves out of it by any means, and for some, when the chosen means went wrong, Maurice had saved their lives. In that respect it appeared Enid had been one of the more fortunate, after all.

As she walked from Chelstone station with the intention of making her way straight to the manor house to visit Rowan, Maisie held her hand to the belt buckle of her Prince of Wales check jacket, and reminded herself to be calm in the very core of her being. She would confront Rowan, yes, but with a gentle, reassuring hand she would lead her into the past, but not so far as to encounter the dragon. Maisie understood that despite Rowan's jovial mood at lunch the previous day, she was slipping further into the abyss.

The housekeeper showed Maisie into Lord Julian's study where Rowan was seated in one of the leather armchairs alongside the wide box-window with a view across the gardens. She turned her head as Maisie entered, and smiled, her blue eyes clear, though Maisie noticed she had become drawn, her wide cheekbones more prominent. She remembered the younger Lady Rowan Compton, who had discovered her reading in the library in the early hours of the morning. Rowan, as ever quick of thought and tongue, walked with a ramrod-straight back in those days, despite complaining of a hip injury sustained on the hunting field. For the woman who was not only born to the title "Your Ladyship" but was married to a member of the House of Lords, a good political argument was spice for the dish of life. She had been a vocal, stalwart supporter of women's suffrage—and having walked in on Maisie in those early hours when the young maid studied on her own, she had seen a light in her eyes, a curiosity about the world to match her own. Instead of admonishing her newest employee, Rowan enlisted the help of her friend Maurice Blanche—determined that the bright light of wonder would not languish in servitude forever, though the plans set forth by Maurice meant that Maisie had to work harder, with more hours spent studying at night after her below-stairs toil was done.

"Maisie, how lovely of you to come."

"How are you feeling, Rowan?" Maisie kissed Rowan on the forehead before seating herself on the armchair opposite. She pulled the chair a little closer and reached forward to take Rowan's hands in her own. "Being here in his study makes it seem as if he's still with us, doesn't it?"

"I miss him, Maisie." She smiled. "From the moment we met, he was the only man who would have a good argument with me—and he always admitted when he thought I was right, but he pushed me to think all the same."

"I believe you did the same for him too." Maisie squeezed Rowan's hand. "After all, he gave his blessing to your wild plan to help make something of the new under-parlor maid."

Rowan laughed. "And what a very good move that was on my part. I've been able to live vicariously through you, Maisie—and now I have a very spirited granddaughter who reminds me so much of myself when I was that age. All go-go-go!"

Maisie took a deep breath. Was this the right time? She hoped so, and thought it might not become any easier if she waited.

"Rowan, I wanted to talk to you about something that has . . . that has come to light."

"Hmmm, yes, you had that look on your face."

"Look?"

"I've seen it before. It's the 'I'm working on something' look. The 'inquiry' look. How can I help you, Maisie?"

"I want to ask you something about James."

Lady Rowan nodded, bearing an expression Maisie thought

was almost unreadable. She was waiting. *She knows*, thought Maisie.

"It's about James . . . and Enid."

Lady Rowan turned to stare out of the window. "I rather let the cat out of the bag the other day, didn't I?"

"When you mentioned 'grandchildren'?" Maisie shook her head. "I had my suspicions before that, Rowan, though it was a feeling I pushed away for a long time."

"My son adored you, Maisie. Enid was the indulgence of a very, very young man—and if I am to admit it, a very sensitive young man who was sometimes the cause of some exasperation on the part of his father, though later he gave us much to be proud of." She paused, still holding on to Maisie's hands. "I suspect witnessing his sister's death when he was not much older than Anna is now had a more serious effect on him than we might have imagined."

"Perhaps. But here's what's come to light—I'm in possession of letters sent by James to Enid during her . . . her confinement, and—"

"How on earth—"

"James sent them to a post office for collection by Enid, and I believe later they were passed on to her when she was at—well, wherever she was sent to have the baby. When she returned to London, they went back to using the post office."

Rowan was silent, but Maisie wanted to press on.

"Rowan, what happened to the baby—to your grandchild?"

Rowan pulled one hand away and pressed it to her mouth, her eyes blurred by unshed tears.

"I'm sorry—this must be so trying for you," said Maisie. "I should have kept quiet about it. I was wrong to bring it up."

"No, Maisie. I—I think it is time. In fact, well past time for me to talk about it. To air the laundry, if you will."

"Only if you feel up to it, Rowan."

Rowan relinquished Maisie's other hand and reached for a handkerchief in her pocket, dabbing her eyes before continuing to clutch the embroidered linen square.

"I may need your hands again soon, Maisie." She smiled. "Right, I suppose the beginning is as good a place to begin as any. Here we go—and I'm glad I'm in this room. I can speak for both of us, and I do truly feel Julian at my shoulder."

Maisie said nothing, but waited for Rowan to continue.

"I remember suspecting James was rather smitten with Enid. I could see the way he looked at her when he came home from school at the end of term or from a journey somewhere. She would bring tea into the drawing room and he would ogle a bit. Julian had a word with him because it wasn't seemly, and to be honest, I did not want the girl to be under any illusions that such a liaison would ever be met with approval." She sighed. "I know people say times have changed, what with two wars and what we've all gone through, but it was a very different era then—Queen Victoria had not been dead for that long, and people were still covering their table legs for fear of offending visitors. How utterly ridiculous."

"How did the . . . how did the 'liaison' develop?"

"Subterfuge. When two young people set their hats for one another, there is little that can be done to stop them. In short order James announced that Enid was with child and that he wanted to make an honest woman of her. His father hit the roof and said, 'You haven't yet proven yourself to be an honest man, so how do you expect to do that? And what, pray, will you live on, because only one of you knows how to work, and it isn't you!' It was truly dreadful, a horrible scene between father and son. I summoned Maurice and he did his best to pacify them, to settle tempers. The warring subsided for a day or so, and then he came to our rescue with a solution."

"Send James to Canada and Enid to some sort of home to have the baby."

"Julian lost no time in packing James off to Toronto to work in the corporation's offices there—and he also told them he wanted the boy to do some man's work. 'Send him to the mills to get his hands dirty or make him work in the forests,' he instructed. And Maurice sorted out the rest of the problem. A place was found for Enid to spend her confinement, a story was made up for 'downstairs'—thanks to our wonderful butler. You remember Carter—well, he would brook no kitchen gossip, so any out-of-turn speculation regarding Enid's absence was nipped in the bud. And of course a good home was found for the baby. I know she delivered a son and that he was taken from her at two weeks of age. Maurice stipulated the baby should have a period of time at his mother's breast for his future health. Enid returned to Ebury Place—that was *my* stipulation, because I would not see her thrown onto the street—and that was that." Rowan stopped speaking, dabbed her eyes again and stared at Maisie. "Wasn't it?"

Maisie shook her head. "They were seeing one another again just after war was declared in 1914. James had returned from Canada to serve and then Enid was killed just after James joined the Royal Flying Corps. I saw them at Charing Cross station."

"Oh dear." Rowan sighed. "But I suppose it was just a short fling—it wouldn't have lasted. James came home from Canada a different person—more mature, more of a grown man, I suppose. And she was still just a maid."

Maisie felt herself bristle. *Remember she's an old woman. She's not thinking.* She tried to rein in her words.

"Rowan, she was an independent woman, earning a good pay for the day. She was no longer a maid, and knowing Enid, had she lived, she would have made something more of herself and she would have done it without the leg up that I enjoyed. And she gave her life for her country, lest we forget."

"Oh dear, point taken. I'm sorry."

Maisie looked up at the clock on the mantlepiece. "I must run to collect Anna from school presently, but I have one more question. You see, I visited the Shoreditch clinic this morning, but it's being demolished soon, and it appears they destroyed all records when the council took it over before the Blitz. But I've been wondering if, after Enid had delivered the baby, Maurice wrote to you to let you know what further steps he had taken for mother and child."

Rowan's eyes widened. "No, he did not write to us regarding any arrangements made—in fact, he said that although he kept a record of the birth and the adoption, it would not be retained at the clinic. That sort of information would have been far too important to leave there, I mean, we couldn't have any nurses or orderlies looking through the filing cabinets and knowing what had happened to the offspring of Viscount James Compton." She shook her head. "And those were Julian's words, not mine."

"I understand. Rowan, you have been most kind and indulgent. I should go now, but shall I send Anna over to see you? She's still full of the new horse, and I'm afraid I have some work in the library to catch up with."

"Yes, do send her over. She always elevates my spirts—makes me think of the future rather than wallowing in the past. I'll have cook make some ginger biscuits for her." Rowan moved to stand up, reaching toward Maisie for assistance, looking into her eyes.

"Do you think he's happy? The boy—my grandson. Do you think he's having a good life?"

Maisie nodded. "If Maurice arranged it, he would have been very, very well looked after and I believe he would have been set up for the very best future we could imagine."

As Maisie left Lady Rowan in the care of her housekeeper, she was determined to find out one thing above all else. Had James and Enid's son had the very good life they hoped for?

CHAPTER 15

As soon as Maisie collected Anna from school and accompanied her across the lawns to Chelstone Manor to spend some time with Lady Rowan, she rushed home. Throwing her jacket across a chair in the kitchen, she moved into the hallway, but instead of walking on toward the drawing room or library, she opened the door to the cellar.

"Stay!" she instructed Little Emma, who whined and settled at the top of the stairs.

Switching on the light overhead, Maisie made her way down the concrete staircase and looked about her before stepping with care toward the far wall where a number of wooden boxes had been stacked since Maurice had owned the house. A few had been brought up to the library on occasion, when Maisie wanted to dig into records from her years of working with Maurice, but she seldom had cause to delve into documents kept before her tenure as his assistant, and there had never been reason for her to question his work at the clinics during 1908 or 1909.

She lifted one box after another to check the date, then set them aside. At last she found a box marked *Clinic. London. January to June, 1909.* She heaved it aside and set it on the floor. In short order she discovered its mate. *Clinic. London. July to December, 1909.* Again she lifted up the box, putting it on top of the first one selected. She replaced all the other boxes, so they were once more tidy and set against the breadth of the brick wall.

"I've found it, Em. Now to see if what I want is inside," said Maisie, brushing the dust from her hands and clothing, a move that caused her to sneeze several times. She picked up the first box and turned to leave. She would collect the other box later if her initial search proved fruitless.

As she approached the steps, she looked to her right and sighed. Mattresses, pillows and blankets, along with a table and chairs, had been pushed toward the side wall, no longer required because the wartime air raids had ceased; there were no Luftwaffe bombers passing above the house, therefore no reason to shelter below ground. "We're like a little family of troglodytes," Frankie had said once, as ever joking while they rushed down to the shelter, the rumble of enemy aircraft crossing over Kent on their way to rain down death and destruction on civilian London.

"That's a job waiting to be done," said Maisie aloud. "It's about time we moved that lot out of the cellar."

Emma stood up and wagged her tail as Maisie ascended the staircase, stopping only to balance the box on her knee while she turned off the light. She closed the door behind her and continued on to the library, followed by Little Emma. Maisie was grateful for the company; it was a need the dog seemed to understand.

Placing the box on the desk in front of her, Maisie took a pair of scissors and cut into the string alongside a knot that held fast with age and would not give way to a tug. She lifted the lid and took a deep breath. With care, casting her eye over the documents one by one, she began to remove case notes revealing the distress of women to whom Maurice had offered medical care. To open the clinic and keep it running, Maurice had never been shy about accumulating wealthy associations, and then tapping the rich for money. Not one patient in London's deprived areas could afford the treatment, so without compunction Maurice asked for contributions from his friends. Maisie knew that if he had to use guilt or a heart-rending story, he had no doubt that it was the right thing to do—and along the way, he had spent much of his own money together with that accrued from his ad hoc method of raising funds. Given his powers of persuasion, Maurice was able to open another clinic, and did the same in Paris. File after file was testament to the compassion he brought to the people he served. Flipping through the records, Maisie could not help herself reading the first few lines of each case.

Phyllis Bates. Age 42. Toxemia of tenth pregnancy. Three surviving children.

Maisie rubbed her forehead, a habit that seemed to have emerged in the past few years, signaling worry, concern or fear. "Poor woman," she whispered. She knew "toxicity of pregnancy" was a term since superseded when the condition was renamed "pre-eclampsia" and that an American physician had developed a successful treatment protocol some years before the war.

Jane Marks. Age 15. Admitted due to suspected induced miscarriage of unborn child. Severe bleeding. Loss of pregnancy.

Iris Stubbs. Age 10. Attack by male. Patient stated identity unknown but nurse suspects relative. Severe bleeding. Stiches, salt bath and bed rest prescribed.

And so it went on, but with each line read, Maisie became

more dismayed, and stopped reading the reason for a woman's admittance to the clinic. Instead she brought her entire focus to the search for Enid's file. As the knot in her stomach grew, she hurried, putting each record aside as she delved into the box for the next.

"It must be here, it must be here."

At the point where she noticed her anxiety rising—it felt as if the possibility of failure in her quest was bearing down upon her—Emma stood up and bounded from the room when the kitchen door slammed and Anna called out to her.

"Emma—Emma—Emma! Mummy! Mummy! I'm home and Daddy's here—he's early. He knew I'd be with Grandma Rowan, so he came to get me!"

"Just a minute, darling—one minute and I'll be there." Maisie raised her voice. "Go upstairs and change out of your school uniform."

She hurried, moving quickly through the files, some comprising only one or two pages secured by string threaded through a hole punched into the top left-hand corner.

"Maisie, honey, are you—" Mark Scott stood at the door, staring at his wife. "What are you doing? There's paper everywhere. Look—you've just knocked some on the floor. Let me help—" He moved toward the desk.

"No! No, don't touch anything. I might not find it."

"Find what?"

Maisie looked up into her husband's eyes, then away from his inquiring gaze. "This is a collection of patient files, from Maurice's first clinic, in 1909. The notes on Enid must be here somewhere. I know they are and I have to find them."

"Hey, hey, hey—wait a minute." Mark put one hand on her shoulder and moved the other as if to shield the box from further inspection. "What's going on? What are you talking about, 'Notes on Enid'? Come on, Maisie, this isn't like you—you can't do this."

Maisie turned to Mark, lifting his hand away from the box, though she was unable to speak.

"Okay, now I get it—it's to do with those letters, the ones you had no business reading."

She felt her shoulders slump, the task getting the better of her. "Enid and James, they . . . they . . . there was a baby. In 1909."

"I might have guessed." Mark led her to one of the armchairs, and pulled the other alongside. "Here, sit down and tell me."

Maisie began to recount the story she had uncovered from reading the letters James sent to Enid. When she had finished, husband and wife sat in silence for some time until Mark cleared his throat.

"Here's what you have to remember, Maisie—they were a couple of kids and they went too far. They were half-formed themselves. They're not the first to get into this situation, and they won't be the last by a long shot. The Comptons and Maurice did what was right, whether you like how they went about it or not."

"But—"

"I haven't finished, hon." He leaned so their heads were close. "You and I were not so young when we met, fell in love and married. We've both been in love before and for whatever reason, we have both lost that love and maybe had our hearts broken a few times over. We had our eyes wide open from the moment we met. What happened to you in Canada pains me, truly it does, but I'm just glad we didn't let an opportunity to have this marriage go by us because we couldn't stop looking back at the painful times in our lives. So, yes, I can see your curiosity, but not why you'd want to know what happened. It's the past, and it's done." He paused as if to gather his thoughts. "And what I think about that question"—he nodded toward the box of patient records—"is this: if you find notes about Enid and her pregnancy, you can look at the file and you might even discover the child's name. But please do not search for him. If he made it through the war, he's a grown man now, and in all likelihood with a family of his own. His adoptive parents are the only parents he has ever known, and it won't do any good, you looking him up. What are you going to say anyway? 'Hey, you over there, tall blond guy with the blue eyes—I knew your real parents. No, not the people who raised you—they came in off the street to pick up a new baby. Want me to tell you all about the mother who carried you, and the young man who impregnated her?' It's just not fair to him." He shook his head; Maisie felt his exasperation. "Maisie, I know that sounds harsh, but it's what you're looking at doing—without the sugar coating."

Maisie took a few seconds to answer. "Mark, I have to find him. I don't even know what I would do if I located him, but I have to see him, even if it's from afar."

Mark began to speak again, his voice low. "And I guess you've persuaded yourself that you must do that because you want to find out what your son might have looked like. His half-brother."

"You're right—I want to see something of my son. You see, I never saw him." Maisie wiped the back of her hand across her cheeks. "I was sedated, filled up with morphine and barely conscious for days. I was cut open and delivered of a son and even though he was stillborn, I wanted to know what he felt like if I'd had the chance to hold him to me, to wrap him against my body. But they took him away as if he was nothing, just another little scrap to be disposed of. And there's something else."

"I thought there might be."

"Anna. She's an adopted child. She's growing so fast now and I'm scared I might do something wrong, and I thought . . . I thought if I saw him, I'd know if he's had a good life. I would know it could be done. I would feel more confident that someone who's not of the same blood can be a good mother, that I was doing everything right for Anna, setting her off for the very best."

Mark's half-smile was soft, his voice low as if he were anxious to soothe his wife. "You really have gone down the rabbit hole, haven't you? I've known folks who've made a mess of raising their own child, a kid who goes on to have a terrible time, and I've known people who lost their parents in childhood and were given a home by strangers, but it's all worked out for the good. All we can do, Maisie, is our very best for our daughter—it's our job to give her a strong bedrock so she can shape a good life upon it. She's her own individual person, and if we're going to respect her as she grows, it can't be a case of us building it all for her." He looked up at the clock. "And that very special young lady has just come down the stairs with her dog hot on her heels, so let's go and see what we can rustle up for dinner. I think it's a spaghetti night—I'll cook. Okay?"

Maisie held her arms by her sides, her fingers opening and closing, opening and closing. "Yes, you're right. Come on, we should find out what that noise is in the kitchen. I think she's already getting started in there."

"There's one more thing, Maisie—it's not just you taking on responsibility for Anna. There's two of us in this now, especially since I legally became her father. We have her back, don't we? We can send her off into the world with a good head on her shoulders and a nice bank of knowledge, but we will be there if she falls down—and at some point she will because life's not a bed of roses. And Anna has had that lesson once already, even in her short time on this earth."

Maisie allowed herself to be led from the library by her husband, but looked back at the half-emptied box and was sure of one thing. Mark had made a very good argument for stopping the search she had embarked upon, but in every fiber of her being, she knew it wasn't enough. The thought of finding the man her long-dead son might have become was too powerful a challenge for her to ignore, as if someone had thrown down the white glove of duel and said, "I dare you." And she had always liked working in the small hours, when the rest of the house was asleep. Thus it was three o'clock in the morning when Maisie discovered Enid's two-page record containing information on the son she had named James, a baby who a month later was adopted and registered as Robin James Davidson, along with two addresses for Michael Robin Davidson, age forty-five, and his wife, Louisa Jane Davidson, née Edgeley, age thirty-nine. One address was crossed out, superseded by the other, Twenty-one Dagley Road, Bromley, Kent.

Not too far, thought Maisie. *I could drop Anna at the bus stop at half past eight, and be there and back inside three hours.*

"I was wondering, hon, if your folks could come over to stay with Anna for a couple of days this week, you know, before you pick up those kids from Priscilla and bring them down to Chelstone," said Mark, as he sipped coffee while standing in the kitchen the following morning. "You'll have your hands full once they arrive, and it sure would be nice to have some alone time at the flat with my wife."

Maisie turned from the stove where she was stirring porridge for Anna's breakfast. "That's a lovely idea, Mark. I'll have a word with them—they love being here with Anna, and I think they quite miss living with us."

"Good to have the choice though—they were probably relieved to get away from the chaos sometimes, especially when Anna has her buddies over." He rinsed his coffee cup under the tap, leaving it on the draining board. "I'd better be off—the walk to the station is the only exercise I get." Kissing Maisie on the cheek, he reached for his briefcase. "Busy today?"

"Some errands, you know, shopping for a few essentials so we're prepared for the influx of young people." Maisie felt dismay at the ease with which she lied to her husband, but was committed to her plan. "Rowan's getting settled in the old wing of the house, so I want to check on her. Mr. Klein seems to have sorted out all the details with the National Trust and they have been very good about it, so that's all good news."

"Don't wear yourself out." Mark walked to the hallway and called out, "Hey, where's my girl this morning? Gonna say goodbye to your old dad?"

Maisie watched, smiling, as Anna ran into the kitchen, as always followed by her dog. She flung her arms around her father, who looked up at Maisie.

"It's a great life, Maisie—there's plenty of folks who don't have what we have here."

With Mark on his way to the station and Anna ready for school forty-five minutes later, Maisie drove her daughter to the bus stop and waited until she boarded the bus with her friends. She continued waving until the bus rumbled around the corner and was out of sight. Checking her watch, she returned to her motor car for a journey she estimated would take about an hour at most, dependent upon traffic.

Stopping several times to consult her map and twice to ask directions, Maisie slowed the motor car to a crawl as she drove along Dagley Road, a street of three-story Victorian houses with bay windows and paneled front doors embellished with stained glass ornamentation. Most had heavy curtains at the windows, many with lace to deter anyone who would want to peer inside. Only a couple of other vehicles were parked on the street, so it was with some ease that she found number twenty-one and drew the Alvis to a halt on the opposite side of the road. She turned off the engine and took account of the house.

The most obvious point of note was that the property was yet another she had encountered for sale, with a bold sign outside naming the estate agent. She opened the door of the motor car and stepped out, closing it behind her with care—she didn't want to alert neighbors with a slam, though she had already seen a few of the lace curtains twitch as she parked.

The sign bore a bold instruction that all inquiries regarding the house should be directed in the first instance to the estate agent, though a solicitor's name was also listed. Maisie took a notebook and pencil from her shoulder bag and recorded the name and number. The path to the front door was decorated with black and maroon tiles, the latter color reflected in the shade of burgundy chosen for the door. A withered potted plant languished on the vestibule, and the *1* on the door had moved so it was at an angle to the number *2*. Turning, she noticed that the postage-stamp front garden had not been tended for a while, as weeds sprouted from the flower beds and the lawn lacked luster. Stepping back again, she leaned toward the bay window, cupping her hand to see into the front room—it was fortunate that there were no lace curtains—and it appeared some furniture had been left in the house: a couple of chairs, a sideboard, and a table. She sighed.

As Maisie turned to leave, she heard the neighboring front door open. A woman came out wearing a wraparound pinafore over a grey day dress. On her feet she wore tartan woolen slippers with small pom-poms on the front.

"Good morning," said Maisie, smiling at the woman, who had been frowning, but now returned the greeting. "I was looking at the area and saw this house was for sale, so thought I'd stop."

The woman nodded. "I must admit, I heard someone walking along the path and it got me a bit worried—I mean, you never know who might break in these days, what with all the squatting going on."

"True enough," said Maisie. "But I assure you I am not a squatter, just a person interested in the house." She paused, glancing up at the bedroom windows. "It's quite lovely and I have always admired stained glass. And these houses built before the Great War have good-sized rooms, don't they? Usually longer gardens too."

"Oh, the gardens go right back, and everyone keeps theirs tidy. This one was particularly nice, what with Mr. and Mrs. Davidson putting in a lot of perennials and shrubbery." She folded her arms and leaned toward the adjoining wall. "Of course, when their son was a boy, they had a swing and so on, but as soon as he left home, that was it—they put everything into that garden."

"I'm sure it was beautiful," said Maisie. "But what happened to the . . . Davidsons, did you say?"

"Yes. Very good people. Bought the house when young Robin was just a few weeks old—still a babe in arms, he was, when they moved in. Mind you, they were older, you know, for having a new baby. They weren't in the first flush of youth, not like some of them now." She leaned further toward Maisie, lowering her voice. "Girl down the street, young Sheila Slingsby, well, she walked out with one of them American soldiers and got herself into trouble. Seventeen years of age. Her parents said she was sent off to the coast to stay with a relative while she recovered from 'glandular fever'—but we all know where she's gone and why. Couldn't mistake the shape of her, not when everyone else couldn't hold weight on account of rationing."

"Oh dear, poor girl."

The woman shrugged. "They know what they're doing, these silly girls. Got what she deserved, if you ask me. She's spoiled herself for a husband, mark my words—it's not as if any young man worth his salt wants tainted goods, is it?"

"Hmmm," said Maisie. She would have liked to counter the woman's comment, but she needed more information. "I'm interested in the house, but I'm curious about the people who lived there—did Mr. and Mrs. Davidson move to another town?"

"Both dead. Like I said, they were older parents, so young Robin must be . . . let me see . . . yes, about thirty-six now. Very clever young man, that one—went to Cambridge University."

"Cambridge? Well I never," said Maisie. "But so sad that his parents died."

"Mr. Davidson—Michael—he went first. Heart attack, out there in the garden some three years ago. Then Louisa managed to do away with herself rushing down the stairs when she heard one of them blimmin' doodlebugs overhead. I was running in from the garden and heard the scream, so I went in and found her. Terrible way to go."

Maisie put her hand to her chest. "What a tragedy—and dreadful for you too."

"It was instant—neck, you know, broken like that." She

snapped her fingers. "It was Robin I felt sorry for, not being able to come home."

"Was he overseas with the army?"

The neighbor shook her head and again looked both ways. "They didn't say much, the Davidsons, but I reckon he was doing something hush-hush. Saw him after he came back in . . . let me see, it was in the summer, so I reckon about the end of August. It was definitely after V-J Day. I saw him standing outside with Mr. Dunstan, the solicitor. I came out and asked if I could make them a cup of tea, but he just said, 'No, thank you, Mrs. Waters.' And that was that."

"Poor man," said Maisie. "But why do you think he was working on something hush-hush?"

"Clever man like that? Bound to be. His father was a science teacher at the boys' grammar school. Very well liked and highly thought of, you know. Louisa was a librarian before she had the baby. She went back to it part time when Robin started school. Just like his father, he was—very intelligent. They were always together, the three of them, off to the museums or out walking. Happy little family. The boy loved the Science Museum by all accounts, and that's what he was doing at university."

"Science?"

"Physics, I think. Not really sure what it is, but I remember Louisa telling me. Mind you—anything to do with universities and I'm lost." Mrs. Waters nodded toward the house. "Going to see inside, are you?"

"I'll visit the estate agent today, if I can."

"Won't get much joy there—he's referring people to Mr. Dunstan, over at Dunstan, Hallwood and Burns, if they're interested. I haven't seen Robin again since he returned to the house a month or two ago, and that was just the once. That day I saw him, he went in and came out with a single box—probably papers and what have you—and left everything else to be taken by a firm that disposes of household effects. Apparently he asked for the lot to be sent to a warehouse where they help people who've been bombed out, you know, after they've found another place to live."

"How generous." She looked at her watch. "Oh dear, I'd better be off—much to do today. Lovely to talk to you, Mrs. Waters."

Maisie waved and crossed the road to her motor car, aware that Mrs. Waters—who she pegged as the neighborhood fount of all gossip, rather like Miss Rowe at the Hallarden shop—was watching her until her motor car turned the corner. She stopped several streets away and made more notes, then set off for the offices of Messrs. Dunstan, Hallwood and Burns. By the time she arrived at her destination, she had a picture in her mind's eye of Robin James Davidson, a man going on thirty-seven who in all likelihood had been overseas during the war, and who—it seemed—had departed his deceased parents' house with little to remind him of his childhood.

"Here are relevant details regarding the house, though I might add that they could have been furnished by the estate agent, had you stopped there." Edward Dunstan, solicitor to Robin Davidson, pushed a two-page document toward Maisie.

"Yes, I would have gone there first, but the neighbor told me it was best to come straight to you, as the agent was referring any interested parties direct to your office."

"You mean, Mrs. Waters, busybody extraordinaire."

Maisie smiled. "I suppose I do."

The man before her was, she thought, someone Mark might have termed "slick." Though in late middle age, he seemed to be a new breed of lawyer, someone whose suit was pressed, but not so many times that a shine remained along the outer flank of the trouser leg. His shirt was starched, and his tie revealed loyalty to a prestigious school; he wore cuff links at his wrists, and a plain gold pin adorned his tie, which was finished with a perfect Windsor knot.

"You will see the price is both reasonable and reflects the seller's desire for a sale without too much delay." He looked at Maisie and smiled. "I should add that the owner of the house, Mr. Davidson, is married to my niece. As he will shortly be taking up a new position and they are expecting their first child, this is one more element to be brought to a close following the death of his mother. A weight off his shoulders."

"It must have been very difficult for him, given that he was overseas at the time."

Dunstan looked up from the folder before him. "I suppose Waters told you that."

"Yes, she did, but it would have been a safe assumption, given the number of men in our armed services who have been serving overseas and who are now making their way home."

"Yes, yes indeed." He took another sheet of paper from the folder. "Let me just get my secretary to type a few more details for you regarding the right of way at the side of the house. There's an easement at the end of the street providing access to all the gardens via an ancient footpath, and you should have it as it's an important declaration regarding land use."

Dunstan left the office, so Maisie lost no time in leaning forward, turning the folder toward her and lifting page after page until she found the address she had been searching for. Twelve Romney Gardens, Chislehurst. She closed the folder and leaned back in her chair as Dunstan entered the office again.

"Here you are, that's everything. If you are further interested, do go via the agency in the first instance, though I would suggest you do not waste time if you wish to make an offer, as there is much interest in the property."

Maisie came to her feet and extended her hand. "Thank you, Mr. Dunstan. I will discuss this with my husband and we will be in touch with the agent if we wish to take the next step, which would be to view the house."

Leaving the offices of Dunstan, Hallwood and Burns, Maisie felt a frisson of excitement, anticipation and fear in her stomach, as if a snake were uncurling from slumber. Chislehurst was not too far away at all, and she could almost hear a familiar cheeky voice tempting her, "Go on, Mais. Get over there. See what my boy's been doing with himself."

CHAPTER 16

The journey by motor car from Bromley to Chislehurst was indeed more swift than Maisie might have hoped; just over three miles, taking her past the famous Chislehurst caves where some fifteen thousand local people took refuge during the war. The notorious V-1 and V-2 rockets often failed before reaching their London target, instead falling on suburban towns and rural villages in Kent, the widespread explosions decimating whole rows of houses as the bombs fell to earth. But now those caves, man-made from Saxon times for the mining of flint and chalk, had been closed since V-E Day. Maisie wondered if her decision to locate the now grown child of Enid and James was not leading her into her own very dark cavern of misjudgment.

Driving along one of the newer wide boulevards that were a hallmark of the well-to-do "commuter belt" part of town, Maisie located Romney Gardens with ease, and drew up a few houses away from number twelve. She turned off the engine and reached for her scarf. It was one of those days that had started off cold and was becoming more bitter as the hours progressed and she felt the chill—though it was without doubt a feeling compounded by a shiver of anticipation. But what to do next? As Mark had pointed out, she could not walk to the front door and announce herself. She sighed and felt at once overwhelmed. Her husband

was right—she should not have come this far. The past was the
past, wasn't it? And what were those words in the novel Grace
the bookworm had been reading? Yes, *The Great Gatsby*. Maisie
had leafed through a copy and, as was her habit, skipped to the
final paragraphs—she was not sure why she always did this, though
it never spoiled a story for her. The author had written something
that intrigued Maisie, that people were "Borne back ceaselessly
into the past." She gave a half-laugh as she considered the words,
for the truth was that she had not been borne back as if on a slow
rolling wave of nostalgia, but instead had stood at the precipice of
her yesterdays and jumped. Now she had to crawl back out on hands
and knees. *You stupid woman.* She shook her head and reached for
the ignition, again admonishing herself for her decision to come
to Chislehurst. She started the engine, releasing the hand brake to
leave Romney Gardens, never to return. Then she saw him.

She watched as the man—tall, yes, the same height as his
grandfather, perhaps taller than James—pulled up his collar with
one hand and bent down to secure the leash on a young, well-
brushed Golden Retriever. Maisie held her breath. Was this
her chance? "What a lovely dog" she could say, or perhaps "Do
you know the way to . . ." Where? How many times would she
lie about looking at a house for sale? "Chilly this morning, isn't
it?" might sound more authentic. Or, "Oh, you must be the new
people." But were they? She glanced at the house, at the garden
and the man, walking toward her with shoulders hunched against
the cold. He did not wear a hat, and as he came closer, she held
her breath. He had Enid's coppery hair, with sun streaks as if he
had been in a warm climate. Then he stopped.

She watched as the man she knew was without doubt Robin
James Davidson—the son her late husband had sired—stood
quite still. The Retriever wagged its tail and looked up, as if

questioning the decision to halt their foray out of the warm house. The man slipped the glove from his free hand and rubbed his eyes. Knowing what was about to happen, Maisie reached for the door handle as the man fell to his knees and keeled over sideways, the dog now wagging its tail even more, as if the collapse were a game—though the attempt at play became a fierce licking around his owner's face as if to revive him.

It took only seconds for Maisie to leave the motor car, slam the door and run across the street. She knelt down, the dog licking her ears as if she, too, were in on the sport.

"Sir, sir," she said, lifting the man's head. "Sir, it's alright, I'm here, come on, that's it, open your eyes."

The man blinked several times, then began to move.

"I—I don't know what happened," he said, shaking his head.

"Don't do that," said Maisie. "Hold your head still. And don't rush or you'll fall again. Now then, take a deep breath through your nose—the cold will make you cough if you inhale through your mouth."

Brushing away the dog, who was now licking the side of his face, Robin Davidson took a few deep breaths. "I'm feeling better now."

"Right you are. Now then, I'm going to support you, but be careful—and you can lean on me, I can take the weight."

Maisie braced, slipping an arm under his shoulder as he came first to his knees and then to his feet.

"How do you feel?"

"Still a little . . . a little unsteady. I—I really don't know what happened."

"Did you eat this morning?"

He shook his head.

"Last evening?"

"I took a few bites."

"That explains a lot. Come on, I'll help you back to your house." Maisie faltered, knowing she would feign ignorance. "Which one is it?"

"Just along here."

Maisie supported the man as they walked at a slow pace toward the property. The dog ran ahead and waited until the gate was opened and then bounded along the path, barking as he approached the front door.

"He's a happy hound," said Maisie.

"He thinks there will be someone to open the door, but my wife is away visiting her mother."

"Ah, so you've been left alone to cook and thought better of it."

"I can't say I was that hungry."

Davidson opened the front door, which he had left unlocked. He turned to look at Maisie, and it was then that she saw the sadness in his eyes.

"What's wrong?" She rested her hand on his shoulder. "I know that's a very personal question, sir, but—" Should she say more? Would it not be better if she just turned and left the man, having helped him into his house? This was none of her business—but in the moment, she knew the tide of questions would overpower her will. "You are carrying a burden—I can see it in your eyes."

Davidson stared at Maisie. "Who are you? I—I don't know my neighbors because we're new here, and I'm sorry, but . . . I just forget names anyway. Never been able to . . . and I . . . I really must sit down."

"I'll see you to an armchair, come on, point the way."

Holding the man's arm as they walked along the hallway, Maisie kept him steady until he was seated in an armchair in the drawing room. When he was settled, she stepped back and looked around her.

"Sir, this is none of my business, but . . . but this is a very cold house. You should have a fire in the grate. I see you have radiators, so if you are sickening for something, a little more warmth would help."

The man nodded, his eyes staring into the cold fireplace.

"Would you like me to make you a cup of tea?"

He turned his head, his eyes red, moistened with tears. "You're very kind—please, don't bother. I'll sit for a while then—"

"Sir, I can see that all is not well. First of all, I will get you a cup of tea—I can find the kitchen, don't worry. Just sit there. Then we'll talk about getting you warm."

The dog, who had been lying at his master's feet, followed Maisie into the kitchen, whereupon she slumped next to the visitor with an audible sigh.

"So you're down in the dumps too, eh? Let's see what we can do about it." She looked around at the brand-new kitchen, with modern fitted cabinetry and a gas cooker that seemed almost unused. In addition, it appeared a coal-fired stove was the source of power for the radiators, but with fuel rationed, it had been turned off. She filled a kettle, set it on a gas burner and found tea in the pantry. There was milk in a refrigerator, which surprised her as few homes had the appliance—she considered herself fortunate enough to afford one for the flat, even though she was not fond of the constant hum from the compressor.

She found the coal bunker just outside the back door. While the bunker was not full, there was no doubt enough fuel to keep the house warm. She filled a scuttle that had been left next to the door, and brought it in. While making the tea, she considered Robin Davidson; no doubt he was a troubled man, though she knew that while she was still acting within the boundary of neighborly concern, she should see him comfortable then take her leave.

"There you are—there's nothing that cannot be healed by a nice cup of tea," said Maisie, returning to the drawing room. She pulled out a side table and placed the cup of tea next to Davidson. "Now, this won't take me five minutes. I'm very good at lighting fires, so I will just get this one going and then be on my way and out of your hair—thank goodness someone has already laid the paper and kindling."

"You are very kind, Mrs.—"

"Scott. Mrs. Scott." She smiled, then knelt down by the fireplace and set coals on the kindling before taking a match to the paper. "I'll just wash my hands and make sure it's caught and warming you up before I go."

Maisie returned to the kitchen and washed her hands, though as she turned toward the hallway again, she saw a series of notes and cards pinned to a board alongside the door. There were reminders to buy certain groceries and messages to order this or that. The name of the local plumber was on another piece of paper, and then a postcard filled with color, heralding *Greetings from New Mexico*. New Mexico? She had a vague memory of Mark mentioning New Mexico, then stopping when some other topic of conversation came up, but she could not recall the context. Perhaps it was just somewhere he had visited. Giving in to temptation, she unpinned the card and looked at the message, penned in a small hand to account for the limited space.

Hey Buddy. Hope you're feeling better now you're back in England. It's been a long haul, but never forget, you helped bring an end to the war. Good luck teaching the next generation to take over from us. Maybe see you again State-side sometime.

Maisie could not read the name of the friend who sent the card, but as she pinned it on the noticeboard, words echoed in her mind. *You helped us bring an end to the war.* She understood, then, that Robin Davidson was a man of secrets, and in her heart she knew one of them might well be feasting on his soul.

"How are you feeling? Better?" asked Maisie as she returned to the drawing room. She had been followed by the dog, who settled alongside her master once more.

"Yes, thank you, Mrs. Scott—I was taken quite unwell."

He began to move, but Maisie set a hand on his shoulder. "I was a nurse in the first war and again in Spain. I have something all nurses have—the instinct that tells me someone is ailing even before they fall. I was in my motor car and could see you were in some distress."

He nodded, reaching down to stroke the dog's head. "I—I think I'm just tired."

"Do please make sure you eat. If your wife is expecting your first child, she will need you to be hale and hearty."

"Yes, of course."

"I'll see myself out, but do take care."

"Thank you, Mrs. Scott."

Maisie turned to look back as she reached the door leading out to the hallway and watched as James's son stared into the fire. She took a deep breath, then stepped toward him. Reaching into her shoulder bag she took out a calling card.

"Mr. Davidson?"

He looked up at her, almost as if he were seeing her for the first time.

"Mr. Davidson, I know this is going to sound very presumptuous, but it would not be the first time in my life I have done something . . . something my heart has inspired me to do. However, do take this card—it bears my profession and the name by which I do my work. I am a psychologist. I help people who are facing life's most troubling moments. If you feel the desire to discuss your situation, do not hesitate to place a call to my office. Everything I do is in the strictest confidence." She handed him her calling card.

Davidson stared at the card. "It says here you're also an investigator."

Maisie nodded, smiling. "Sometimes the two go together—in fact, more often than not. Do take care."

She turned away, but was startled when he called out.

"Mrs. Scott."

"Yes?"

"How do you know my name? And you know my wife is pregnant."

She shrugged, though fearful of her error. "I—I believe you mentioned it when I brought you in."

He shook his head. "I don't think I did." He sighed and his shoulders slumped again. "But it doesn't matter."

Maisie left the house, feeling foolish. The fact that she had made such an error was testament to the emotional pressure she had brought upon herself. She had revealed prior knowledge of the man's circumstances—a slip she had never made in the course of her work. As she walked across the wide boulevard, she stopped for a moment and stared back at the home of Robin Davidson; at the garden with roses covered in gauze, protection from winter's frost, at the shrubs and flower beds, the wide lawn with a sundial at its center. The son Enid had given birth to now had so much more than his mother might ever have imagined, given her station in life. She would have been so proud, filled with admiration for the man he had become—yet she might also have wondered if the darkness within him was worth whatever sacrifice he had made to reach this pinnacle of success.

Over the next two days, Maisie did her best to put all thoughts of Robin Davidson out of her mind. She orchestrated Lady Rowan's move to the older part of the mansion at the heart of Chelstone Manor, and made final accommodation arrangements for not only the four former squatters, but the eventual arrival of refugees in the new year. Priscilla planned to stay at her nearby cottage to help in situating the young people, and was already discussing entrance requirements with a new technical college in Tonbridge.

"I am a woman with a mission, Maisie," said Priscilla in a telephone call. "I have a purpose and I am at full Partridge speed."

"Good news, Pris, but—"

"And I must tell you the excellent news Mary received today."

Maisie smiled. Her friend was reveling in what Mark termed "Your pal's rocket force."

"Go on, I'm all ears," said Maisie.

"Despite the fact that it took all my powers of persuasion to get Mary to wipe the grimace from her face, she made a very good account of herself with two couturiers. I will add the pout was well disguised by a very wide brimmed hat, and she soon spread a smile when she noted the amount of payment for her trouble—not a bad day's outing for a girl of that age."

"Oh that's good, I wonder—"

"There's more. The photographer—quite well known, you know—suggested she had the 'bone structure' to be on the cover of *Vogue*. He intends to do all he can to ensure she gets there. *Vogue*, Maisie! She has two sittings—well, standings I suppose—lined up and already the telephone has been ringing for her. She may well be back and forth to London a fair bit."

"I think she needs some stability living here at Chelstone, so she can use the train service."

"I don't think she wants to leave her friends, so that will fit in nicely. She's too young to live alone in London anyway. I'll accompany her on a couple more outings, just until I know she can be trusted not to scowl—or put anyone who annoys her into a headlock!"

"Right you are, though—"

"One more thing—and I forgot the most important family news."

"And that is?" encouraged Maisie, knowing any attempt to say more would fail.

"My American future daughter-in-law has received orders and will be 'shipping out'—as she terms it—back to the United States in late January-ish. Tom will be demobilized from the RAF at the end of this year, and they have decided upon two marriage ceremonies, which is wonderful. Her parents—Charles and Pauline, along with Patty's sisters—will be coming over to spend Christmas and New Year with us, and then after Patty is back on home turf, Tom will join her and they'll have another sort of ceremony for all their people over there." Priscilla stopped speaking. Maisie heard the click-click-click of her cigarette lighter. "I'm sure the American affair will be much better catered, and her mother is bringing over a dress because goodness knows, she won't get something that nice in London, but it's very exciting, isn't it?"

"And at least I'll be there to see my godson get married."

"But isn't it wonderful? I mean, I suppose it's the bright side of it all coming full circle, isn't it? Not so dark after all. Simon introduced you to Charles, and then they . . . well, they looked after you, didn't they, when . . . Well, following all that happened to you in Canada. Pauline is a dear, and I must say, I think it won't be so bad, my son living that far away, especially if he gets into this airline business. And who knows, you might even be living there one day!"

Maisie smiled. "I doubt it, Pris—Mark loves it here in England, and there's my father and Brenda, and Lady Rowan to think about."

"Of course—jumping too far ahead as usual. Anyway, must dash. I've to shoot over to Harvey Nichols with Mary. Truly, I feel as if I have a daughter."

With no opportunity to say goodbye, Maisie replaced the receiver, but had only just reached the door when the telephone began ringing again. She lifted the receiver.

"Hallo, miss."

"Billy—how are you? How's Will?"

"Slowly but surely. He hadn't talked much since coming home, but last night his mum went to bed early, so I was in the kitchen, you know, just doing a bit of tidying up—can't leave it all to Doreen, can I?—when he walks in and says, 'Want to go for a walk, Dad?' It was blimmin' freezing out there, but I remembered when I came back from the first war, I walked a lot at night. Couldn't sleep, see, and you know, every now and again I'd pass another bloke in the same boat. I mean, we all knew who we were—soldiers back from over there who kept seeing it all every time we closed our eyes. Anyway, me and Will wrapped up warm and off we went, over toward the park. It's left me tired, no two ways about it, but my boy just opened the flood gates." Maisie heard Billy's throat catch. "I—I don't know how he made it out of there. The things he told me—terrible, terrible things about that place, Changi, and then some of what happened when they were taken to Burma to build that blimmin' Japanese railway."

"How is he today?"

"Still in bed when I left, but Doreen got on the blower to me as soon as I was here in the office. She said he'd gone out for another walk and came home telling her he was starving, so she used the eggs we had left and made him a fry-up. She shouldn't have, what with all that fat, but he kept it down. I know he's got a long way to go, and it's not over by a long chalk, but I think he's on his way out of the tunnel. Slowly but surely, as you said."

"All good news, Billy. Do let Dr. Dene know—he may have some advice for you."

"Will do—but talking about being on the blower, a bloke telephoned about ten minutes ago to speak to you, said he'd like to make an appointment."

Maisie placed her hand against her chest and closed her eyes. *It's him.* She tempered her breathing. "Go on, Billy—I've a pencil and paper. Name and telephone number."

"Mr. Robin Davidson. Seemed a nice bloke. He asked if he should call you Mrs. Scott or Miss Dobbs, so I reckoned he already knew you. I penciled him in and can confirm the appointment, if you like."

The appointment was made for Friday at ten in the morning. Maisie planned to travel to London on Thursday afternoon, spend the night at the flat with Mark and then both would catch the train home to Chelstone on Saturday morning. Priscilla and

Douglas would be accompanying Mary, Jim, Grace and Archie to the manor on Sunday. It was all falling into place—to a point. In proceeding with the appointment to see Robin Davidson, Maisie knew she would in effect be lying to her husband if she did not reveal her plan. And there was something else—Mark had been troubled since returning from Washington. Maisie suspected there was something he wanted to get off his chest—something he wanted his wife to know.

"Your Shepherd's Pie, Maisie—that's what I need. All I can say is, thank heavens for supplies from Chelstone's kitchen garden." Mark Scott took a bite of the food in front of him and reached for his wine glass. He leaned back.

"Not hungry?" asked Maisie. She was used to seeing her husband tuck into every meal with gusto.

"Just worn out, hon. Just really worn out. Too much traveling, too much on my plate—the professional one—and like I said, too many people thinking I have miracle ideas." He took another sip of wine. "And too many changes coming too fast and not the ones I want."

Maisie rested her knife and fork, reaching for Mark's free hand. "What do you mean?"

He shook his head. "Back in Washington, everything's different now. So much has changed since I left—and remember, I'm the guy who always thrived on the next big thing. Send me here, send me there—I was all over the darn globe for the Justice Department. It was exciting—and dangerous at times, as you know only too well. Take Munich."

"Oh, yes, Munich."

"Found my girl there, so I don't mind!" He squeezed her hand.

Maisie smiled. "Even though I put a gun to your neck?"

"Yeah, well, at least you didn't pull the trigger."

They were silent for another moment.

"Tell me more about Washington, Mark."

"For a start the population has doubled since the war began. It's full steam ahead into a new America. They finished the Pentagon, and—"

"The what?"

"Remember, I told you about it? The Pentagon. Big building complex with five sides, full of almost two thousand military. And there are so many working for the government now, all to take us into the rest of this century and onward into the next. There's even a word I've heard so many times now, it's creepy—'superpower.' That's what our world has become. Big guys throwing their weight around—and I'm one of them."

"What do you want to do, Mark? I know it's troubling you."

"Something simpler than being part of what's next. If I was thirty, maybe I'd be jumping in with both feet. But this business with the loan to Britain has worn me thin, and I'm just a small cog in the big wheel of diplomacy. Like I said a few weeks ago—Britain needs that money, and it'll get it, but your people—"

"But Mark—I'm asking what do *you* want?"

"Me? What do I want?" He sighed. "Maisie, I want to finish my work here—I've only a couple more years at the embassy. Back in Washington they like what I do, so my job is settled. After that, I don't know. Maybe spend some time Stateside so Anna can see where her old dad comes from. But more than anything I just want to be happy. Content. The war's over and I don't want any more battles living inside members of my family either." He took a deep breath. "You could say that in all kinds of ways I want to build my own house."

"Then we'll do our best to bring it all to fruition," said Maisie. "We'll make things a bit simpler or we might be able to spend more time in London or go to America over the summer. I want to be here at the Dower House every day when Anna comes home from school, that's a given. But as you often say, we can figure it out."

"We can." He smiled, though Maisie could see it took some effort. "But hey, this dinner is getting cold. Let's eat."

They continued the meal in silence for a while, the only sound coming from a fire crackling in the grate.

"Mark, talking about 'Stateside'—interesting word—I was wondering what sort of significance a place called New Mexico might have had during the war. I think I know, but—"

"What?" Mark pushed his plate away and stared at Maisie.

"I—I just wondered, you know, about a place called New Mexico. I'm not really sure where it is."

"Maisie, forgive me, but—what's going on?"

Maisie rubbed her forehead and reached for her wine glass. "I must tell you about something that's happened. Something I've done. I know you might be . . . might be . . . disappointed, but I—I just had to do it."

"Okay, cards on the table, Maisie." Mark reached for her hand. "And just so you know, you shock me sometimes, my love, but you don't disappoint."

"There's always a first time, Mark."

CHAPTER 17

The following morning, Maisie could not deny the nerves that seemed to have dominion over her stomach as she traveled on the Underground bound for Warren Street station. Having run up the wooden escalator, impatient with its clunkety-clunkety-clunk progress, then through the turnstile, she stopped outside the station and leaned against the wall for a moment. She was afraid. She was concerned she would say the wrong thing, that she could not meet the expectations Robin Davidson might have formed of their meeting. Without doubt, he wanted to be free of whatever ailed his soul—his dragon, as Priscilla would have called it. Then she remembered Billy's recounting of Doreen's lack of patience with any talk of a dragon breathing fire ready to pull her son back into the past. Perhaps that's why they were called dragons, because they dragged prey down by burning and brute strength. She bolstered her resolve. Now was not the time to relinquish power to that other slinking reptile—doubt.

"You alright, Miss Dobbs?"

Maisie turned, smiling when she saw the young man selling newspapers.

"Freddie—sorry, I was miles away." She reached into her shoulder bag for her purse and took out a coin. "I'd better take an *Express* for Mr. Beale." She paid the newspaper vendor. "And how's Mr. Barker? Is his leg still bothering him?"

"I reckon Grandad will go on for a good few years yet, even though he can only hobble about now. He misses selling the papers though—he liked having a chat with everyone who came through on their way to work. But him and Nan are being moved from Camberwell—the council are saying the houses are unsafe now, but none of the houses on their street were bombed out. It's sad—everyone knows everyone else; they've been through the war together and the one before that, and now they'll go to districts where they don't know anyone. Rotten it is, at their age. Grandad reckons it's the bent council, you know, selling out to the building companies."

"He could be right, Freddie. I'd best be on my way now—busy day ahead. Remember me to your Granddad—I miss seeing Jack Barker on this corner."

The boy grinned. "Yeah, but I'm better looking, ain't I?"

Maisie laughed, waved and walked along Warren Street, taking a left turn toward Fitzroy Square and the building that housed the first-floor office she shared with Billy Beale.

"Morning, miss," said Billy, as she entered the office.

"Good morning—and to you, Sandra. Sorry, I didn't realize it was a day for doing the books."

"Hello, miss. I wasn't going to come in, but Martin is in school and Billy telephoned to say the accounts were a bit behind."

"I'm glad to see you." She rubbed her hands together. "It's chilly in here—shall we have the gas fire on for a while? I know we're supposed to be careful, but I've a visitor arriving in a quarter of an hour and I think he's not been well—so let's warm it up for a nice welcome and I'll turn the fire on in my office."

Maisie proceeded to the left, into her personal office where one long table was set perpendicular to her desk. She ignited the gas fire, but kept her coat on, though she removed her scarf and hung it on the hook at the back of the door. Seating herself at her desk, she looked at the table and wondered how many times she and Billy had stood over a long piece of offcut wallpaper to map out the essence of a case, creating a visual story of what might or might not have happened at the scene of a crime, or a dispute or whatever event inspired the men or women who came to her for help. Though not on paper, today she would map the story that was diminishing Robin Davidson from the inside out. She could not rescue him, but she might be able to help him save himself. It was all dependent upon what he was willing to reveal, or whether they would fail in the quest to stop the pain—because without doubt, the man was in pain. And wasn't it so reminiscent of his father's return from France at the end of the last war, the years when James agonized over the death and destruction he had seen while flying over battlefields, and once home became intent upon banishing himself to a retreat for soldiers who could no longer face the world?

Maisie heard a knock at the door and Billy welcome the visitor.

"Miss Dobbs—Mr. Davidson has arrived." Billy stared at her, eyes wide, as he introduced Davidson, who was facing Maisie. In the background, Sandra turned to her with the same questioning stare.

Maisie came to her feet, stepping into the outer office. "Good morning, Mr. Davidson. Lovely to see you again." She introduced Billy and Sandra, held out her hand, indicating the guest should proceed into her private domain, and asked Sandra if she wouldn't mind making tea. "Or would you prefer coffee, Mr. Davidson? We can brew it from ground beans here. It's a legacy from a former teacher, who loved Santos coffee beans in particular."

"Thank you. Coffee. No milk, please," said Davidson, as he clutched his hat with both hands, rolling the brim round and round in his fingers.

"Good, come in and do take a seat. I've pulled up two chairs in front of the fire so it's warmer."

She offered to take his coat, and they exchanged pleasantries until two cups of strong coffee had been set on the table by Sandra, who closed the concertina doors to provide privacy.

"Are you feeling better, Mr. Davidson?"

"Physically, yes a little." He took a sip of coffee and returned the cup to the saucer. "But of course I wouldn't be here if all was well, though I—I must be assured of one thing."

"Go on."

"That anything I reveal in this room has to be in absolute confidence."

Maisie nodded. "You have my word. I promise. And I must also underline that the commitment goes both ways." She smiled. "Of course I could sign a contract to such an effect and you would have my assurance on paper, but I have always thought saying aloud the words 'I promise' confers significant weight upon both parties."

Davidson stared at her. "I think you're right. I promise anything said in this room will remain in confidence."

"Then let's begin. Please—start anywhere and we'll go on from there."

He was silent for a while, staring into the fireplace gas jets. Maisie waited.

"It's all raw energy. The gas. We've taken something natural and done something unnatural with it for our comfort. Coal was meant to stay in the earth, not to be dug up so we can make gas or light a fire with it. And the gasses underground shouldn't be released either—we've done that without thinking of all the poison we've allowed ourselves to breathe in. I believe it will have a consequence, all the taking. Not for you or me, but perhaps for my child."

"That's an interesting perspective." She inclined her head, a gesture indicating openness to whatever might be revealed.

"You know, what I loved about my work—my profession, if you will—was that it went on. I know that's a strange way to put it, but let me explain. I'm a scientist, so when I was in the laboratory, it was rather like being on a sort of journey, as if I were walking along a path where all I had to do was to keep on looking for answers, to continue digging further and deeper." He moved his hand, almost as if he were describing a fish weaving through water. "Theoretical physics is all about trial and error while looking for scientific truths and—I suppose ultimately— how those truths will benefit mankind. You see, I have to keep on asking questions, one after the other—what happens if I blend this with that? What can I do to push through a boundary? How can I take the laws of science, the laws of the universe and bend them to do something different? That's how scientists like me work. We push and push and push to achieve a certain result and we never, ever think about the consequences. Not the real consequences. Because if we did, we might stop, and then who would we be?"

"Hmmm, yes. I can see that—but I think we should spiral into the circle a little more, in a manner of speaking," said Maisie, knowing she had to push Davidson or they would be there for hours discussing the role of scientists in the modern world. "This is the point in my work where *I* begin to set boundaries, and to get to the heart of what ails you. I think it's time to request that you bring these broad observations to a personal level."

"Alright. Yes. Of course. After all, I called because . . . because I cannot live with myself anymore if I don't . . . if I don't get it off my chest."

"Mr. Davidson—Robin, if I may—tell me, what consequence of your work as a scientist resulted in the disturbance at the heart of your collapse on the street?"

He stared at Maisie, the blue eyes so like his father's staring into hers. His answer was blunt. "Along with many others, I killed tens of thousands of innocent people."

Maisie did not look away and kept her voice steady. "Start at the beginning, Robin, then let's walk into the dark part of the story together."

"I am a physicist. I won't complicate this with a few lessons in my field of research, but I work with matter. Matter is all around us and in simple terms my research has been in working toward pinpointing the essence of matter so that it becomes useful. I was recruited by a department called Tube Alloys early in the war. All very innocent sounding, isn't it? It gives the impression that we made something that goes inside an aircraft, a tube for this or that function. Or that we designed the plumbing for buildings, or oil pumps."

"What did you do?"

"Along with other scientists, we were working on a different kind of weapon. Something the world had never seen before. You could say it was a tool we thought could end wars." He paused, reached for his cup and drank the remainder of his now luke-warm coffee. Almost dropping the empty cup onto the china saucer with a clatter, he went on. "We were far ahead of any other country in our research, yet though the government funded our work, the powers that be had scant regard for our discoveries, almost brushed us off as not being important to the war effort.

But we scientists want to get ahead, don't we? We want to beat back the bushes on the path and break through rocks, marching through anything that gets in our way. Through matter. And the reason those at the top paid little attention was because the old men of Britain who waged this war had once been young cavalrymen who first galloped into battle on horses across the African veldt! Top British scientists at our universities—Birmingham, Cambridge, Manchester—were at the front of the pack, then we were getting left behind because people like Churchill couldn't envisage the possibilities, because in the planning for war they could just about fathom what a fighter aircraft could do, let alone cast their eyes forward into the kind of work we were engaged in. But I was thrilled when I was recruited with others from Tube Alloys to go to America as part of an agreement between our countries. I was working on the same things and more, and it was wonderful because our friends across the Atlantic could see the future. They were forging ahead at great speed and they needed our help. They were determined to bring together the finest scientific minds in one place to achieve the ultimate goal, to push through anything that stood between us and the power we were creating. It felt like the pinnacle of my existence, an honor to be among their number—and there were thousands of us."

"You worked on the atom bomb," said Maisie.

Robin Davidson looked up as if her words were an accusation. *Oh how like James you are when your hackles are up*, thought Maisie. *How quick you are to temper when confused by circumstance.*

"Of course—you're an investigator," said Davidson, his frown becoming a humorless smile. "It stands to reason you would put the pieces together."

It was Mark who had helped slot those pieces into place for Maisie. British newspapers had published graphic accounts of the bombing of Hiroshima and Nagasaki, yet the place at the heart of research, where the bomb was developed and tested, was not only a secret, but neither important nor memorable to a population unfamiliar with the geography of the United States—beyond a passing knowledge of famous coastal cities, along with California and Texas, the lands depicted in popular Western pictures shown at the cinema. Yet by the time Maisie left the flat that morning, her husband had furthered her understanding regarding a place called New Mexico and gave a name to the quest to build a nuclear bomb. The Manhattan Project.

Maisie began to intuit the essence of Robin Davidson's confession even before the conversation with Mark. British newspapers from London to Edinburgh put the bombings of two Japanese cities on their front pages, underlining the collaborative work between American, British and Canadian scientists—yet there were words of caution. She had been struck by Wilfred Burchett's account in the *Daily Express*—the Australian Burchett had arrived in Hiroshima soon after the bombings. She put her hand on her heart as she read about the "Atomic Plague" and the terrifying injuries reported. Burchett wrote of witnessing people with even simple wounds that would not heal. He described terrible radiation sickness and uncontrollable bleeding. Many of the survivors would not live for long. Maisie knew it was guilt regarding his association with this outcome that was festering inside the man before her. After all, hadn't Winston Churchill written in the *Daily Mail* that the bombing ". . . should arouse the most solemn reflections in the mind and conscience of every human capable of comprehension"?

"Please go on," said Maisie.

"I—I'm sorry. I'm on edge. I mean, perhaps I wouldn't have felt like this—at least I don't think so—if my parents hadn't died. Then I wouldn't have known and have it all come crashing down."

Maisie felt a sensation akin to a cold arrow of anticipation passing through her heart. "Let's go back to your work in the United States."

"Yes, sorry again. Shouldn't have jumped. I'm restless all the time these days." He rubbed his hands together. "Did you know, Miss Dobbs, that you can rub your hands together furiously, then hold them six inches apart, like this, and it's as if you're holding a ball? Pure energy—and you did it just by rubbing your hands. You can even play with it."

"Robin—"

"But it sort of fits—I was one of those thousands of scientists in a designated location miles from anywhere, and we were, in a manner of speaking, creating a very different kind of energy; one the military played an unconscionable game with. There were those of us who knew, as soon as the test was successful in July, that we had created a terrible beast; that it wasn't yet another bomb they could drop and win a war. This was something that would change the balance of our world forever, and from every perspective. It wasn't simply a bigger, more dangerous weapon to unleash upon an enemy, but no one could see what so many of us could see. And I played a part in building it. It might have been a small part, but that is the legacy I will leave for my son or daughter. That is the heirloom their grandchildren will inherit. I was but a cog in a big wheel creating a monster of unbelievable proportions." Davidson took out a handkerchief and wiped it across his mouth.

Maisie allowed the room to become quiet and Davidson to settle as much as he could before she spoke again.

"What happened after your parents died?" she asked.

He stared at her, then again into the fire. "I came home with my wife—she's British, by the way. Her father was sent out to America with his company just before the war and I met her in New York. Anyway, we came back to England and because my parents had passed away while I was in America and I couldn't get home, I had to sort out their affairs as soon as I arrived back. I was in the attic, going through various papers, and came across a document attesting to my adoption. I had no idea I was effectively a foundling, and the document had only their names as the adoptive parents and nothing else." He pressed his hands together then drew them apart, as if playing with an invisible ball, handling the energy he'd described as if it were something precious, or dangerous if it fell through his fingers. He looked up at Maisie again. "So you see, Miss Dobbs—I do not know who I am. I have played a part in killing all those people—and, I might add, so many more because as sure as eggs is eggs, as time goes on, there will be cancers and heaven knows what sicknesses to take the lives of hundreds of thousands of innocents. Look at what happened to Madame Curie—cancer killed her, and I've had colleagues tell me you cannot touch her papers because they are still riddled with uranium. So, I am a killer who does not know who he is. I could be descended from whole generations of murderers and it was preordained that I would go about the family work, albeit in a different capacity."

Again Maisie had to hold the stare of those bright blue eyes, now filled with tears.

"And I don't know what to do, Miss Dobbs. I mean—why didn't my parents tell me? Why did it have to be a secret? I am so worn out with secrets."

"I have met a good number of killers in the course of my work, and I can assure you I can't recall coming across one who was the victim of a generational sickness leading to another murder." She looked down at her hands, wondering how best to frame her words. "However, regarding the question of your parents' failure to explain the circumstances of your adoption, that is something I believe I might be able to help you with. Let me tell you about someone I loved, during the last war." Maisie recounted her court-ship with Simon, the attack on the casualty clearing station that wounded them both, and the damage to Simon's brain, depriving him of any future thought and action. "You see, I had to endure a long period of recovery myself, so I couldn't see him. Then more time passed and it became easier just to imagine him as he had been before we were both in France, better to leave the truth behind. If I faced him, then I had to accept everything else that happened, and it took me a long time. A very long time. Sometimes too much time passes as we wonder how to approach a sensitive subject, and before long, the perfect moment to do so has passed us by. So I suspect that at first your parents might have been waiting for you to reach an age where you could assimilate such information, but they were perhaps stumped at how to begin the conversation—the revelation, if you will. Then you went off to university. They had set you on the path to your dreams, so how could they at once upend your future by telling you about the adoption? Robin—I have no doubt they loved you too much, and they were in all likelihood very scared of your reaction to what they would reveal."

"I never thought of it like that." He gave a brief smile. "I sup-pose it's rather like forgetting to return a library book, and when you realize how much you owe in fines, it's best to leave it on the shelf and try to ignore the omission."

"In very simple terms, yes, I suppose it is."

More time elapsed as Maisie allowed Davidson to consider her words.

"Robin, tell me, how do you think you might make peace with yourself?"

He shook his head. "I tried to discover the identity of my real parents and just floundered. I think if I knew, I might have the key to finding some sort of calm. And I'm taking up a teaching post at the university in January. I'll be lecturing in physics, so that will be different for me." He gave a laugh that had not a hint of humor to it. "Training the next generation of killers."

"Is that what you want to do—be a teacher?"

He shrugged. "I really don't know. I could get a job anywhere at a university or school, and my father—well, the man I thought was my father—was a very good teacher. I suppose I could slide in a few lessons in ethics, so my charges know they have a responsibility greater than they might ever have imagined. But . . . but more than anything, I want to know who I am."

Maisie stood up and walked to the window, looking down upon a small courtyard where old flowerpots held the remains of blooms long dead, and where once she recognized a wire disguised as a climbing plant and reported the German spy living in the lower flat. He had been put to death in the Tower of London. She shuddered and turned, once again taking her seat opposite Robin Davidson, and pulling the chair closer to her new client.

"When we first met, you noticed that I already knew your name and that your wife was expecting a child. I deflected the observation and denied all knowledge. However, I owe you a profound apology, because you were right. Robin, I made it my business to find you because I know the identity of the woman who gave birth to you and of the man who fathered you. I can reveal that knowledge, if you wish. It's your decision, and might help to bring solace to your soul."

"But—"

"Please—there's more I want to say and it's really crucial you hear this. You must always remember that your parents—the couple who gave you their name, who tended you as a boy and who provided every possible opportunity for you to thrive—loved you very, very much. The fact that they didn't tell you about the adoption might well have been rooted in fear that they would lose you."

Beads of perspiration dotted his brow. "I—I don't know where to start."

"Take your time, I have all the time in the world for you."

"I think I need some fresh air. I—I'll walk around outside then come back."

"Good idea. Take your coat, and don't stay out too long—it's bitterly cold."

"Yes, quite. It is. Thank you."

Robin Davidson came to his feet, reached for his coat and scarf and stepped toward the door, whereupon he turned, face flushed. "Miss Dobbs—what's it to you? How do you know the people who caused me to be born, and why did you want to find me?"

"Because I loved them both, and I wanted only to know that you were happy in this world. That you had a good life. Now I've met you, I promise I will do all I can to make it so. They would want you to be at peace."

"Blimey, miss—who was that bloke? I'm sorry, I had to take a second dekko at his dial, because for all the world he looked like—"

"Billy's right—he gave us quite a shock," added Sandra. "The hair's a bit more reddish, but he looks a lot like Viscount

Compton. We thought he must be a relative—it was probably a shock for you."

"Yes, he is a relative of the family. He's just popped out to get some fresh air and will be back in a minute."

Maisie was aware that Billy was staring at her. "You alright, miss? You seem, well, not like I've seen you for a long time."

"I suppose his looks have rather taken me aback. Anyway, Sandra, do we have enough coffee for another pot?"

"Just about."

"Looks as if he could do with something a bit stronger, if you ask me," said Billy.

"It might come to that—oh, that's the doorbell. Billy, could you go down and let him in? I'll be in my office, you can show him straight through."

"Right you are, miss."

As Robin Davidson entered Maisie's office, Billy nodded toward her and closed the concertina doors.

"Please sit down—would you like another cup of coffee?" said Maisie.

"No thank you. And I must ask, do your staff know why I'm here?"

"First of all, the promise of secrecy extends to both Mr. Beale and our secretary. They do not know why you are here, but if that changes, the information will go no further—beyond anyone you might wish me to discuss it with. Mr. Beale specializes in matters of property security, though he was once my assistant and often works with me on investigative cases. The promise of confidentiality is at the heart of our work."

"I see. Is that how you know my true parents? The investigative work? It crossed my mind as I walked around the square that they might be looking for me."

"I am so sorry, but I must inform you that they are both dead. I can tell you a good deal about them though."

"How did you know them?"

"I was employed at the same house in Belgravia as Enid, your mother. We were below-stairs staff who shared a bed-room together—I was only thirteen when I came to work at the house. I should add that they were very young when you were conceived—Enid was, I think, barely sixteen. James, your father, was the son of our employers, owners of the house. He would have been about eighteen years of age. They were very much in love."

"How did they die? Did they murder one another, or drink poison?" Davidson gave a half-laugh.

Maisie shook her head. "No, it was not that kind of story. Enid was killed at the end of 1914. She was employed at the Woolwich Arsenal and along with other munitions workers lost her life in an explosion. Your father was an accomplished aviator and in 1934 was involved in the development of new fighter air-craft being tested in Canada. The pilot who was supposed to test a certain aeroplane didn't turn up—she had a hangover—so he volunteered, and was killed when the engine failed."

Davidson shook his head. "I suppose my mother and I were in the same line of business, in a manner of speaking. We both knew how to make a bomb. And my father was felled by a young aviatrix who had been out drinking." He stared at Maisie, again holding her gaze. "And how did you know my father?"

"He was my husband."

Maisie did not look away, did not move or fidget to alleviate discomfort. Instead she met Robin Davidson's eyes with her own.

"Oh my god," said Davidson, running his fingers back through his hair. "I think my head is going to burst."

"I saw Enid only hours before she died," said Maisie. "Her death changed my life. I was seventeen and a student at university, but I decided there and then to volunteer for nursing service and lied about my age to be accepted for training. I served at a casualty clearing station in France. And James, well, we fell in love almost twenty years later, when neither of us was in the first flush of youth. I—I saw him die, Robin." Maisie faltered, wondering if she should reveal more. He was bound to ask if there were half-siblings, so perhaps, yes, she should put the question to rest before it was asked. "The shock of witnessing his death resulted in the stillbirth of our son, so you do not have a brother or sister."

"Oh my god," he repeated, leaning back on his chair, and then forward again to look at Maisie. "Do I . . . do I have any relatives at all? Blood relatives?"

"Yes, you do."

"Who?"

"Your father's mother is still alive, but at the moment she is grieving the death of your grandfather."

"What's her name?"

"Rowan. Lady Rowan Compton. Your father was Viscount James Compton, and your grandfather, Lord Julian Compton."

He shook his head. "Descended from the aristocracy. That's a surprise. And it explains a lot—I suppose my mother was the poor little maid eyed up by the young master of the house who impregnated her on a whim, and His Lordship had her sent off to give birth to me so no one was shamed by the indiscretions of the heir."

Maisie shook her head. "I can tell you the circumstances might have seemed like that, but they weren't. In this case, as I said, your parents were in love—yes, they were young, but they held one another in their hearts. Without doubt their respective stations in life resulted in you being adopted, but the man who arranged it ensured that your mother had only the very best of care and that your adoptive parents were chosen with the greatest integrity. Your grandfather elected to do what he believed to be the best for all concerned."

Davidson was quiet for a while, and without asking, leaned forward and turned off the gas fire. Maisie said nothing.

"So, you were a maid, once, along with my mother. How did you do so well? How did you manage to climb up the class chain to marry my father?"

"Fair question, though it's a longer story than you might have time for. You could say that I was adopted too, though I have a loving father of my own, and even though I was given the opportunity of education by people who thought I had a capacity for more advanced intellectual immersion, I still had to work as hard as Enid in the house. The man who arranged Enid's confinement and your adoption also directed my academic progress. I was fortunate to win scholarships, which defrayed most of the costs of my education."

"The luck of the draw, I suppose."

"Enid wasn't interested in the same sort of advancement, but she held no envy toward me. She was my friend."

"What was she like?"

Maisie smiled. "She was very, very witty. She spoke up for what she believed in and she was a no-nonsense young woman. There's an old military term that might describe Enid—she 'didn't take prisoners.' And she would not suffer fools either. Her character was a result of a hard childhood—she was estranged from her people. However, she had a soft side, and I can guarantee she adored you and would have wanted only the best for you, which is why she let you go."

"And my father?"

"Your father was a sensitive man, Robin. He lost a beloved sister when he was only about ten years of age, and I think there was an element of Enid's character that reminded him of her. You see, Enid was fearless, as was his sister. James was also something of a dreamer—that's probably why he was happiest in the clouds. But we married because we loved one another. His death was devastating."

Davidson nodded, staring at his hands. He sighed and looked up at Maisie. "Do I look like them? Do you see anything of them in me, Miss Dobbs?"

"Well, physically, you have your grandfather's height—Lord Julian was just a bit taller than James. Your hair is more like Enid's—James was blond, but she had red hair. You have your father's eyes, and I believe you have his sensitivity."

"Do you think they would like me?"

"Oh, Robin, you were beloved before you were born—they would adore you."

The man was silent for a while. Maisie once more felt a chill creeping into the room, but did not move toward the gas fire.

Davidson looked at his wristwatch and cleared his throat. "I've to meet my wife at the station, so I must be going soon." He stared at his hands, turning them to look at his palms. "Miss Dobbs if . . . if they . . . if James and Enid were to give me advice now, what do you think they would say?"

Maisie exhaled and raised her eyebrows. "That's a very big question you've just put to me, and I'm not sure how you might take the answer."

"Aren't parents supposed to be blunt sometimes?"

"Well, your mother would be, of that I have not a shadow of doubt."

He smiled. "What would she say?"

"Do you really want me to tell you?"

"I do. I came here to get to the bottom of who I am, inside myself, and I think it would help."

"Right, then I will tell you this." Maisie came to her feet. "Imagine a girl about the same height as me. Red hair in curls down beyond her shoulders, with a fiery way of speaking to match—so brace yourself, because she really could let you know what was on her mind." She put her hands on her hips, and leaning forward just a little, she began with just a hint of Enid's Cockney accent. "You've got to get on with it, my boy. Stop feeling sorry for yourself, because what's done is done. You can't change it, so you've got to stiffen your backbone. You've a good job, a very nice roof over your head, and you're well off—so be thankful and instead look around you and see what you can do for people who don't have the same good luck. And buck your ideas up because your wife will be giving birth to my grandchild before you know it, and I don't want him or her to have lessons from their father in being a right misery."

Robin Davidson began to laugh, and Maisie laughed along with him.

"I'm a terrible actress," said Maisie.

"No, no, not at all. Your performance was a good idea—just what I needed. I can imagine her."

"It's far from my usual approach to revealing the truth, but I think Enid was standing by my shoulder, pressing me to do it."

"What about James, what would he have said?"

Maisie took her seat again and drew closer to Robin Davidson.

"I think he would have just listened and he would have encouraged you to follow your heart. And soar. He would tell you to find the limit of your skies and go there. I think he would be in awe of the man you have become."

Maisie watched as Davidson turned his head and closed his eyes, as if trying to imagine his deceased young parents, then looked up and brushed away tears.

"You've been very kind, Miss Dobbs, and helpful—more than I ever imagined," said Davidson. "When I left your office, I thought I should be angry because you had engineered our 'chance' meeting. But with every step as I walked around the square, I found I was just sort of . . . sort of relieved. As if a weight were falling from my shoulders." He glanced at his watch once more. "I must go now. But may we speak again?"

"Of course."

"And your account."

Maisie shook her head. "There is no account, Robin. Nothing at all."

"Do you think Lady Rowan might agree to see me?"

"I think it could be arranged. She's very fragile at the moment, but we are close and I believe meeting you might well be a tonic for her, though I should add that it will also be a shock, even if she's prepared—you see, you are so much like your father."

"I suppose that's why the two people out there couldn't keep their eyes off me—I thought I'd sprouted another head!"

"That's about the measure of it."

As Davidson turned to leave, Maisie stopped him.

"I wonder—would you mind helping me? I have a question to put to you."

"Of course."

"You see, I have a daughter—she's ten now. She's adopted,

though she knows something of her origins because she was brought up by her grandmother until she was four. I suppose I want to make sure she's happy, and—"

"You want to give her a good life."

"Yes, that's right. I married again a few years ago and we dote on her, but I want to know, from your perspective."

Davidson looked down, again rolling the brim of his hat around in hands that seemed so much like his father's.

"Truth, Miss Dobbs. I think truth is the key." He smiled as he looked up. "Even if at some point it means telling her she has to buck her ideas up!"

Without thinking, Maisie held out her arms and embraced Robin Davidson, the man who had given her an image of who her own son might have become.

"And love, Miss Dobbs. Love above all else."

EPILOGUE

The view from the Dower House conservatory opened toward the surrounding gardens, and onward down a slight incline toward the Groom's Cottage, where Frankie Dobbs once lived, having left his job as a costermonger in London to take up the position of looking after Chelstone Manor's horses in 1914, when all the young men who worked on the estate had gone away to war, many to perish on the battlefields of the Somme or Ypres, Delville Wood, Hill 60, Passchendaele or Gallipoli. It was where Frankie tended his rose garden and became a man of the land and not the city, which suited him—and his daughter—very well indeed. Maisie reflected on the passage of time and how one path had led to the next, often by chance and sometimes by intention, though invariably with a few sharp, uncomfortable turns.

The Dower House had been the most beloved part of the generous bequest settled upon Maisie according to the terms of Maurice Blanche's will, along with an expectation that she would make wise decisions, taking every opportunity to be of service given that she had been rendered a woman of some means by the inheritance. Without doubt, over the years she had done her best to adhere to the tenets of Maurice's training, that when a case was drawn to a close, she should tie up all the loose ends threaded through her work. It was a process Maurice had termed "the final accounting" and involved visiting the places and people with whom she had crossed paths along the way as she went about work specific to the assignment. But today was different. Today she felt her spirit had accounted for all that had come to pass in recent weeks. She wanted to feel the comfort of her ghosts, not to stare them in the face as she retraced uneven steps through the chaos of an investigation. Allowing herself the indulgence of rest, she closed her eyes.

An almost elfin giggle brought her back to consciousness, along with a whisper.

"She's awake, Daddy. I saw her eyelids flutter."

"Don't disturb her, half-pint. Your mother's tired—she's been working hard."

"Shall I ask Grandma Brenda to make some tea?"

"That's a good idea, you do that, and I'll sit here."

Maisie felt her husband settle on the other end of the sofa and moved toward him, though she was listless from the afternoon nap.

"Feeling okay, hon? Been a tough week, hasn't it?"

She nodded, half opening her eyes and curling against his body as he put his arms around her.

"I think it's all slotting into place though."

"And you're seeing Lady Rowan this afternoon—to talk to her about Robin?"

"Yes. I'll just have that cup of tea to bolster my resolve and go over there."

"Everything going to plan with Priscilla and those kids? You were on the 'phone with her for a long time this morning."

"Just sorting out a few final details. I think an apprenticeship has been arranged for Jim, the older boy, and another for Archie."

"Who with—a safe-breaker?"

"Might have been a good idea, but no—with an electrical firm. He's light-fingered and liked the idea of working with wires. And Grace is going to school, while Mary—"

Mark laughed. "Graces the cover of a swanky women's journal."

"Very funny. Priscilla predicts she could be very much in demand."

"Especially if someone wants a bodyguard."

"At least we know if a fresh photographer tries to take liberties with her, he'll wish he hadn't overstepped the mark." She sat up and rubbed her eyes. "And Priscilla wants me to go with her when she returns to the Queen Victoria Hospital in East Grinstead. She has an appointment for a final check-up on her skin grafts, and apparently some of 'her boys,' as she now refers to them, are leaving the hospital."

"Mr. McIndoe's Guinea Pig Club?"

Maisie nodded. "Priscilla rather lifted spirits while she was going through the same sort of treatment, though her scars are not as severe as those the airmen have had to endure. And she made the patients laugh, entertained them, so I think Mr. McIndoe and his staff rather encouraged her—with the added bonus that it helped her recover."

"So there's to be a shindig at the hospital?" Mark Scott was thoughtful. "Hey, what if I pick you up afterwards? We can go into Tunbridge Wells on the way home—remember there's the architect I want us to meet."

Maisie stared at her husband, who shrugged.

"It's just a chat, Maisie. Just a step to find out a few things, you know, what's involved in building a house and how long it would take. The builders are all busy at the moment, but in time they'll be out there looking for more work, and who knows? Maybe we'll be ready."

"Yes, of course, you're right—good idea to look at what's involved." She glanced at the clock as Brenda came into the conservatory carrying a tea tray, with Anna in her wake holding a plate of Eccles cakes.

"Mum, Grandma Brenda made your favorite!"

"I'm not even going to ask how you managed to get enough sugar—but I've to be quick as Rowan is expecting me. Don't eat all the cakes while I'm gone!"

Maisie sat in front of the log fire with Rowan, the older woman reaching down to pat her elderly spaniel. "I wish Julian and I had moved into this part of the house lock, stock and barrel. It's so much warmer and with the beams, the heat stays in the room," said Rowan. "But my husband was adamant that the Georgian part was more to his liking."

"The medieval houses were built to be cool in summer and warm in winter," said Maisie. "I'm glad you're settling into this wing."

"I can see right over toward two of the estate farms, and I bet if I squinted, I'd spot Mr. Avis leaving the farmhouse on his way down to the pub!"

"You're in better spirits, Rowan."

"I dreamed of Julian last night. It was as if he were here with me in this room and he gave me a talking to. 'Come on, old girl. I married a fiery woman, not some old bat slouching around in her widow's weeds.' So when Mrs. Horsley came into my bedroom with tea this morning, I said to her, 'I must make a list!' Julian was a great believer in what he called 'the power of a list.' Jot down all the things one wants to accomplish in the course of a day and work your way through them. Even if you are disturbed in the midst of a task, you can go back to the list as if it were a map to get you from A to B. That's the way to get on with life—a list! And when I've mastered the daily agenda, I will add a monthly docket, and then I will look ahead. What do I want to accomplish by the time I'm . . . well, let's say by the time I'm older than I am now!"

Maisie reached for Rowan's hand, as had become her habit in recent weeks. It was the comfort of touch for them both.

"Dear Maisie, do you have good news? Or bad news for which I must brace myself."

"I think it's very good news—but you may well need to brace yourself, Rowan."

"I'm unshockable. My son saw to that!"

Maisie stared at Rowan, and for a second wondered if Enid herself might be in the room, orchestrating the conversation. She had no choice but to get straight to the point.

"Rowan, it is James who is going to shock you again, for I have found his son."

Rowan held her free hand to her mouth and leaned toward Maisie.

"Oh, my darling girl—are you sure? I cannot . . . I don't know what to say."

"Say nothing, Rowan. May I tell you the circumstances, or do you require some time to absorb the news?"

"No—whatever you do, don't leave me. I want to know everything. I want to know all about him. Tell me, Maisie. Tell me about my grandson."

It was late when Maisie walked across the lawns toward the Dower House, and for a moment she stopped to look back at the manor. Truth had at last come to the surface, had eased itself from the boundaries of the past as if it were a splinter rising up through skin. For better or worse, grandmother and grandson would meet soon, and would build whatever connection they chose. It was out of her hands, bar a telephone call here or there, and an introduction. She would look out for Rowan, and indeed James's son, but her work was done.

"Goodness, Priscilla, how on earth did you procure all that fruit? You've outdone yourself."

Priscilla tapped the side of her nose. "Contacts, Maisie. You're not the only one who has a good connection or two."

Maisie looked at her oldest friend, at the long swing coat she wore over a fitted jacket and skirt. As fashionable as ever, she had become adept at disguising the scars along the side of her face and wore a wider brimmed hat to shadow her complexion.

"At least when I see those boys I am not at all worried about this nonsense on my skin." She ran her fingers down the side of her cheekbone. "They're young men, and they want to be out in the world, but it's horribly difficult for them because their faces have changed." She was silent for a moment. "People don't realize how hard it is to lose your face." She shuddered. "Anyway, chin up, self! Tom said he'd meet us there as one or two of his pals are still awaiting more grafts. I think my firstborn cannot wait to get out of uniform—and it's not long now, thank heavens. Ah, here's the train."

Maisie followed Priscilla into a first-class carriage, helping her to push the hamper containing fruit and foodstuffs along with a few bottles of wine onto the rack above.

Priscilla took a seat opposite Maisie and removed her gloves as she stared out of the window. "I don't know about you, but I cannot stand on a station platform or board a train without thinking of all the goodbyes I've witnessed over the past thirty-odd years, from one war to the next—soldiers and sweethearts, their mothers and fathers, the children I watched being evacuated in 1939 and then coming home. So many farewells and not enough hellos at the end of those wars."

"I feel the same, Pris."

"We are the lucky ones, aren't we? We came through the war. And look—all three of my boys are accounted for," continued Priscilla.

"Your 'toads'—my godsons—are all present and correct, so we are indeed lucky, Pris." Maisie stared out of the window as the train rocked from side to side along the route through Kent toward Tunbridge Wells, where they would change trains.

"What's the news on Billy's sons?"

"It looked as if Bobby might follow Tom to America," said Maisie. "Your son wasn't in Billy and Doreen's best books for a while, given his enthusiasm for the whole adventure he's embarking upon and tempting Bobby with his talk of opportunities for aircraft engineers over there. But now it appears Bobby has been offered a position with De Havilland. I suppose if you're in aeronautical engineering, the world is your oyster."

"And Will? He's the one I'd worry about."

"Slow progress. But Billy tells me Will has shown an interest in possibly helping him in the business, but he has another opportunity as well, because there's a small ironmongery not far from their house; they have a sign in the window advertising for staff. And the Groom's Cottage has been empty for a while now, so Billy was wondering if it might do Will some good to have a stint out in the country, perhaps working for Mr. Avis the farmer. One way or another, we will find something to suit Will, a job that will help with his recovery; help bring him back to his old self."

"And you promise me you'll not be swept off across the Atlantic by that husband of yours."

"It's not on my list, Pris."

Having deposited the box of fruit and wine with the sister-in-charge, who raised an eyebrow but then shared a conspiratorial smile, Maisie followed Priscilla along to the ward where young airmen were gathered. All had been wounded by burns to their faces and hands, and all showed evidence of the revered Archibald McIndoe's pioneering reconstructive surgical work. Some were in wheelchairs and others in bed or lounging on armchairs, but with a glass of ale in hand. They cheered when Priscilla walked in, and two came to kiss her on the cheek, after which she embraced every patient, each one an RAF airman who had been rescued from his burning aircraft. Tom had joined his friends before his mother and Maisie arrived. Stepping to one side, Maisie smiled as she watched the teasing, the laughter, the jokes back and forth. Someone set a gramophone on the table, and at that point she took off her gloves and regarded the scars from burns earned when she rescued Priscilla from the bombed building—she knew only too well that she was fortunate in her healing.

Looking up at the gathering, as one song seemed to lead into another, Maisie remembered a moment so long ago, when her first case was approaching its dénouement and she walked among men whose faces had been ravaged by war, stepping forward to place her hand against the heart of a murderer whose mind had been sullied by all that had come to pass in his life. How would they fare, these young men of another conflict—how would they make good lives in a world where people wanted nothing more than to escape their memories of this second world war? She knew, then, that the solution was simple, yet would be filled with both darkness and light along the way—just as it would for Will, just as it would for Robin James Davidson, and all those whose wounds would remain inside, unseen. They had no choice but to step forward into the future, to make the very best of it, with or without help and to the extent that they could.

"Come on, Mrs. P.—start us off singing our favorite song."

"I'll have you know I've no voice, young man," said Priscilla.

"I can vouch for that," called Tom, from the back of the room.

"Make her a gin and tonic, someone!" said another.

"I've given them up!"

"Sing anyway! Give us some Vera, Mrs. P.—she always goes down well."

Priscilla persisted. "I promise, I absolutely cannot hold a tune in the manner of Vera Lynn!"

"Go on, Mum," Tom yelled again. "Belt out the song that got us through the war!"

"Alright, altogether then, come on boys, help me out," said Priscilla. "*We'll meet again . . .*"

Feeling a light touch upon her elbow, Maisie turned as Priscilla's voice was joined by the men who surrounded her, sons all.

"Mark—"

"The motor car's outside. I brought Anna with me, and of course Little Emma had to come, drooling over the back seat."

"I'll just let Priscilla finish this one—she'll be here for another hour or so with the boys, then Tom is taking her home."

"That song again. Come on, let's have a go at hitting the notes, Maisie." Mark smiled, and together they joined in.

Keep smiling through. Just like you always do, 'Til the blue skies chase those dark clouds far away . . .

Mark left at the end of the song, and with the applause dying down, Maisie said her goodbyes and made her way toward the exit. In that moment, she felt lighter, leaving the past behind, as if Fate had asked her to take one final look across the landscape of years, before turning her head toward the future and the building of a new house.

The End

AUTHOR'S NOTE

The Maisie Dobbs series began with a single character who walked into a daydream one morning while I was stuck in commuter traffic. Others joined her in quick succession. The path I created for each of those characters was set against the work of Maisie Dobbs, Psychologist and Investigator, and the events of their day. Those events extended from Maisie's girlhood, when she joins the Compton household, until 1945 and the end of the Second World War. For readers interested in the passage of time and the events reflected in each novel— some apparently small, others momentous on a global scale—an overview of the historical breadth of the series is available here: https://jacquelinewinspear.com/wars-and-moments-in-time.pdf

ACKNOWLEDGEMENTS

I t takes a good number of very talented people to publish a novel, most of whom go unsung as it makes its way from manuscript to the book in a reader's hands. There are so many individuals I could thank for their expertise along the way, but I can only mention a few in these final pages.

Lilly Golden was *The Comfort of Ghosts'* first reader, offering sound editorial advice and demonstrating an ability to identify elements of the story that remained clear in my mind's eye but not in the novel. Thank you, Lilly for your sensitive commentary and wise counsel. At Soho Press, Associate Publisher and Editorial Director Juliet Grames drew my attention to points that needed finessing—Juliet, I am incredibly grateful for your insight and your depth of understanding regarding the emotional impact of writing the closing novel in a series that has defined my life for the past twenty-four years. Managing Editor Rachel Kowal deserves much gratitude for hand-holding this book into production.

Every member of the Soho Press Marketing/PR group led by Vice President/Director of Publicity Paul Oliver is just terrific—thank you all for your hard work.

Soho Press was my first "home" when Maisie Dobbs was published in 2003. The enthusiasm that greeted my return has been an indescribable joy—many, many thanks to Publisher Bronwen Hruska and everyone at Soho. Your commitment to this book has been a gift.

Susie Dunlop and the terrific team at Allison and Busby publishers—standard bearers for the Maisie Dobbs series throughout the UK and Commonwealth—deserve much gratitude for their stellar work and the lovely warm welcome that always awaits me when I come "home" to London.

For their success in bringing the Maisie Dobbs series to a broader world-wide audience, many thanks to Jenny Meyer and Heidi Gall of the Jenny Meyer Agency.

Once again I was stunned by the extraordinary contribution from renowned artist-craftsman Andrew Davidson, who created the perfect image gracing the cover of *The Comfort of Ghosts*. As with previous books in the series, creative maestro Archie Ferguson pulled it all together, and into the mix the added expertise of Soho Press Production and Art Director Janine Agro was a bonus.

Amy Rennert has been my agent and dear friend right from the start, when I submitted an unsolicited manuscript and proposal for a novel called Maisie Dobbs. Thank you, Amy, for the gift of your support, your terrier-like commitment to my work over these many years, and for always encouraging me to follow where my creative spirit might lead me.

On the home front, those dearest to me have been my cheerleaders throughout the "Maisie" years—they know who they are, and they know how much they are cherished and valued beyond measure.